VIABLE THREAT

OUTBREAK TASK FORCE

book one

VIABLE THREAT

OUTBREAK TASK FORCE
book one

JULIE ROWE

Entangled Publishing, LLC
2614 South Timberline Road
Suite 109
Fort Collins, CO 80525
Visit our website at www.entangledpublishing.com.

Select Suspense is an imprint of Entangled Publishing, LLC.

Edited by Robin Haseltine
Cover design by L.J. Anderson
Cover art from iStock

Manufactured in the United States of America

First Edition May 2017

To Koryn, you're all kinds of awesome.

Chapter One

"The only soldier who doesn't carry survival equipment is a dead soldier," Special Forces medic Walter River said to his audience, a room full of men and women in camo. Too full. Fuck the chairs, there wasn't enough floor space left for someone to squat.

The heat inside the room intensified the illusion of claustrophobia and coated his tongue in an acid so corrosive it stabbed at his gag reflex. He fought the pull of his mind as it tried to take him back to another time and place, when heat had rolled across him in waves, and death hung in the air—a moment when his body had known only confused pain, jumbled memory, and bitter betrayal.

Nope, not going back there.

"What do you carry that will keep you alive?" River forced himself to ask his workshop participants.

Several put up their hands and offered the obvious: compass, knife, matches. He was about to ask them to think with their hindbrain, the hypothalamus—also known as the *holy shit I'm going to die* neural structure—when there was a sharp rap on the door. A young soldier saluted and informed him the base commander wanted to see River in his office.

He glanced at his group. "Put together a complete list before I come back."

When River entered Major Ramsey's office, the officer held out the phone without saying a word.

"Hello," River said into the receiver, frowning.

"Sergeant River, my name is Dr. Rodrigues. I'm with the CDC. You were recommended to me by Colonel Maximillian from the Army's Biological Response Team. I need you on the ground at the University Medical Center of El Paso to assist in a medical emergency."

What the fuck did that mean?

He glanced at the base commander. The man thrust his chin at the door, which meant there was only one thing River could say.

"Yes, ma'am."

"Transport is being arranged. I'll meet you outside the emergency entrance." She hung up.

"I'm on loan?" River asked the major.

"Take your weapon." It was an order.

Well, shit. He was back in the game.

River was dropped off at the ER entrance for the medical center fifteen minutes later. He didn't have to wait long for a petite older woman, her gray hair pulled back into a bun, striding toward him. "Sergeant River?"

"River is fine, ma'am. Dr. Rodrigues?"

"Yes. Put this on." She handed him a respirator, the kind people wore in zombie apocalypse movies. Not a good sign.

"Could you wait here for a few minutes?" She sighed, just like his mother would have prior to delivering a lecture on male brains and their lack of common sense. "I have a situation to deal with before I fill you in on everything."

"Sure."

She was gone before he got the word out.

He stood there and took in his surroundings. There were three ambulances in front of the entrance already, and the approaching sound of sirens made it clear there was about to be another one.

Busy place.

Five minutes later, another ambulance showed up. A few minutes after that, yet another rolled in, but there was no one left to receive the patient.

Enough standing around. River abandoned his watch position in favor of wading into the fray.

He stepped up to the rear doors of the newly-arrived ambulance, threw them open, and grabbed hold of the end of the gurney inside. He paused, waiting for the paramedic riding in the back to do his bit, but those seconds were more than enough time for the condition of the interior to register.

Holy *fuck*. The ambulance was splattered with blood, and God only knew what other body fluids. Supplies littered the floor, making it look like a fight had broken out inside the vehicle.

Only there weren't any green rage monsters or kung-fu movie extras to explain the chaos. Just the paramedic and a patient lying unmoving on a gurney.

River waited while the paramedic got to his feet and ensured all the IV lines were untangled before pushing the gurney out. With the majority of his face covered by an air-purifying respirator almost identical to the one River wore, it was hard to tell how the guy felt about the condition of his patient, the situation, or even of his vehicle.

Concern, fear, embarrassment?

Six years in the Special Forces had taught him to compartmentalize emotions and events and his responses to them. The shit going down today had him hanging on to his training by the ends of his fingertips. A cold, painful lump crouched underneath his sternum. Not fear or panic, but close. Alien and unwelcome.

Focus.

River held his end up as the rolling bed cleared the bumper and its retractable legs stretched toward the ground.

The paramedic gave River's Army uniform a measuring glance. "You work here?"

"No, just got here to help about ten minutes ago." River jerked his head in the direction of the emergency entrance to the University Medical Center of El Paso. "There are nurses inside."

"Thanks." The paramedic pushed his patient toward the wide doors.

Behind the guy's ambulance, another rolled in. That would make a total of six since River arrived.

The pit of his gut wound tighter and tighter until he wasn't sure he could even swallow.

He'd seen this movie—one of those medical thrillers where everyone dies—but he never thought he'd be in the middle of one. Again.

Someone called his name.

He looked away from the ambulances to find his new boss of ten minutes waving at him to join her. Next to her stood a man in a dark suit and a respirator of the same type as his own.

Dr. Rodrigues led the way to a spot where they were out of the way but could observe the foot traffic going in and out of the ER doors.

"Ma'am," River said respectfully. "How can I help?" He nodded at the other man.

"This is Agent John Dozer from Homeland Security. He's their lead agent here."

"I'd shake your hand, Sergeant," Dozer said, "but personal contact of any kind is now prohibited." He tilted his head toward the doctor.

So, even Homeland Security had to listen to her. Good to know.

"I asked for you because you've dealt with outbreak conditions before, yes?" she asked River.

"Middle Eastern refugee camp. Last year." Just thinking about it gave him a headache. He'd been shot and kicked in the head by someone he'd trusted. His injuries had cost him more than nearly a day's worth of memories; they'd cost him the unconscious trust a soldier needed to have in his brothers-in-arms. "Some asshole terrorist decided to test his homemade super rabies on several thousand old men, women, and children. A lot of them died."

He studied the doctor, but aside from the deepening of the angry lines bracketing her face, she didn't react. What was he missing?

A glance at the agent provided no more information.

Two more ambulances pulled up, their lights flashing.

A lot of people were getting sick fast. The situation had too much in common with the one he'd been in before, but with one big difference.

This wasn't the Middle East; this was El Paso, Texas, USA.
Shit.

He took another look at the doctor. Despite the particle mask respirator she wore over her face, she looked as if she was ready to strangle someone to death with her bare hands. "You think this is man-made?"

"Man-made," she agreed, nearly biting off the end of the word.

Now he understood why he was here, when he should have been back on base teaching his class on surviving with minimal equipment.

He was going to get to go asshole hunting.

"At least you've some experience with outbreak conditions," she continued. "Most of the law-enforcement people here have never seen anything like it. They may balk at some of the measures that need to be taken."

She didn't sound happy about it. Nope, Dr. Rodrigues appeared to have about as much patience for bullshit as he did. A characteristic he appreciated in a commander, supervisor, or whatever the hell title she wore.

"I'll be vocal with my support of those measures, then. The punishment for ignoring an expert in this sort of thing is usually lethal." He gave her a respectful nod. "Orders?"

"I'm expecting assistance to arrive from the National Guard in a couple of hours, but until they get here, we're stretched thin. Most of my people are either treating the infected, working on identifying the pathogen, or preparing to decontaminate a list of possible infected places. The infection seems heaviest at the university. But, I've sent in an investigator to collect samples at a coffee shop that may be at the center of this outbreak. The earliest infections appear to be concentrated in that location. I'd like you to keep an eye on her and assist, if she needs it."

"At the site?"

"Please. While Dr. Lloyd is an excellent medical investigator, she's at the location alone and isn't familiar working with local law enforcement. I'd like to avoid any conflict."

Conflict associated with scientists usually meant a lack of communication.

"Is she the *absentminded professor* sort or more of a *you're too stupid to understand* type?"

Rodrigues tilted her head to one side, giving his question surprisingly serious consideration. "She's more of a *no patience for idiots* person. She works fine with anyone who behaves like they have half a brain." She sighed. "Unfortunately, there are far too many people in positions of authority who are lucky if they have more than two brain cells to rub together."

River snorted a laugh. "That I can work with."

"I'll get you set up with our Emergency Crisis Communication system, ECC. It's a Bluetooth cell phone on steroids. We have our own mobile satellite uplink and broadcasting tower. Your earpiece also has a camera and a tiny screen. When it's turned on, you can either see who you're talking to or see what they see." She pointed at her ear.

The device looked very much like a Bluetooth cell phone, only slightly larger, with a screen attached to a short arm positioned just outside of the line of sight.

"Cool."

"You'll have to wear a hazmat suit."

"Why?" He pointed at his respirator. "I thought this was good enough."

"Here, it is, but we don't know how the pathogen was initially introduced. I'm inclined to err on the side of safety."

"Yes, ma'am."

"I'll give you a ride," Dozer said. "I've got people headed there, too." He motioned toward a black SUV parked outside the ER entrance.

"Sergeant River?"

He stopped to look back. "Ma'am?"

"Take your rifle."

He'd only ever seen eyes that grim in combat.

• • •

6:03 p.m.

The hole-in-the-wall café in front of microbiologist Ava Lloyd looked so ordinary, except for the overturned chairs, puddles of spilled coffee on the cement, and yellow police and biohazard tape surrounding the outdoor courtyard serving the café.

Safety and biohazard protocols had been followed and security measures taken. It was time to get to work.

Ava let out a deep breath and strode forward to duck under the tape. The hazmat suit she wore made it awkward. The crowd of Emergency Services personnel standing at either end of the courtyard, watching as if it were reality TV, made her feel like a hippopotamus trying to tap dance.

Dancing had never been one of her strengths.

Reading was. She'd read the case file for this incident in under ten minutes, thirty minutes ago, and her breathing still hadn't returned to normal.

The shop had opened at six o'clock, serving early risers both coffee and breakfast on the go. At eleven in the morning, a half dozen people, mostly students from the University of El Paso, had stumbled into the University Medical Center's ER within fifteen minutes of each other, with the same symptoms. High fever, headache, and confusion. Those symptoms grew rapidly worse. Two of the students were dead by two in the afternoon.

In the three hours since the first patient had entered the ER and the first death, another thirty people had either arrived at the UMC's ER on their own or had been transported there by ambulance, all with high fevers and headaches. For some, the confusion became paranoid hallucinations, and they had to be restrained.

The hospital called the Center for Disease Control. The CDC sent an investigative team to determine the cause and epicenter for the outbreak, and patient zero.

Ava was part of a twelve-person team responsible for determining if there was, in fact, an outbreak, what caused it, and a treatment regimen. Within an hour, her team leader, Dr. Rodrigues, had determined there was an outbreak of some kind and called for additional help, but not enough of it had arrived yet.

It wasn't until the three staff members at the café had collapsed, two with blood coming out of their noses and ears, that the team suspected where the outbreak started. The identity of patient zero, the person who'd brought the disease to the coffee shop as a carrier, or as its first victim, was yet to be determined. There were now too many patients to deal with. This was the best place to start investigating.

Ava expected the café to be disorganized and dirty. Yet, if she ignored the overturned chairs and coffee spilled as panic had taken hold of the customers when the police arrived, it appeared clean and orderly.

The bodies of the two dead university students in the hospital morgue begged to differ.

Ava had been tapped for the job of collecting samples from the restaurant, while the rest of the team continued to deal with the hospitalized victims and identifying the pathogen.

The fatality count wasn't going to stay at two for long.

The area was eerily quiet, and combined with the knowledge that every move she made was being monitored by her CDC boss, the local police, the FBI, and Homeland Security, she found herself shaking harder than a leaf on a tree during a hurricane.

Get it together, idiot. You're on camera.

Dr. Rodrigues spoke calmly despite the view she had via the tiny webcam on the Bluetooth receiver hugging Ava's ear. "Ensure you swab all the tables, as well as all the work surfaces inside the café."

"Yes, ma'am," Ava replied as she adjusted the gloves of her hazmat suit one last time.

"A helicopter will be waiting to take your samples when you're done. Until we know what this is and how it's spread, treat this as a level four pathogen. All decontamination procedures must be strictly enforced."

"Yes, ma'am."

Fantastic. The first pathogen she got to investigate as a CDC employee showed Anthrax-level lethality.

No pressure there.

"I'm keeping this call open in case you need support," Dr. Rodrigues added.

"Thank you, ma'am," Ava replied, keeping her tone neutral.

Collecting samples wasn't a technically difficult job—she'd been in weirder places and had sampled odder things—she'd just never done it with so many people watching her and evaluating every move she made.

Ava approached the first table and proceeded to swab its surface, then moved on to the next table and the next, working from the outside of the presumed infection zone inward. She'd collected just over twenty samples and was about to enter the work area of the café, when in the corner of her eye, movement caught her attention.

A young man stumbled and weaved toward the café's order counter. Blond, clean cut, and no older than twenty, he was dressed in jeans and a hoodie and had a backpack hanging heavy on his back. Just like every other student at the university.

How the hell had he gotten past the police? No one should be anywhere near this place without wearing a hazmat suit. It was extremely unsafe.

She walked toward the counter, her mouth open to demand he leave at once, but the dazed, blank look on his face stopped her from saying anything. That, and the beads of sweat clinging to his forehead.

Shit. Could he be another ambulatory victim of the pathogen?

"Are you all right?" she asked him very carefully instead.

He blinked, then finally seemed to focus on her as a trickle of perspiration ran down the side of his face.

The temperature was moderate, certainly not high enough to make anyone sweat.

Oh yeah, he had whatever was killing people. Where the heck had he come from? Had he passed out in some corner or closet and just woken up?

"I'm here to deliver a message to the United States government and its citizens," he intoned, as if he were the voice of doom. He lifted his hand into the air, showing off the cell phone in his hand as if it were a detonator.

Maybe it was. The air in her chest froze solid, then broke up into ragged shards, piercing her insides with every breath.

"Something tells me," Ava said quietly, "his backpack isn't full of textbooks."

"Shit." Dr. Rodrigues's horrified voice whispered into her ear.

"Not helpful," she whispered back.

"Our leaders are corrupt," he continued, weaving on his feet, turning in a circle as if expecting a crowd of people was surrounding him. "Responsible for the deaths of thousands of women and ch...children."

Only the crowd was too far away for making the kind of statement terrorists seemed to want these days. The kind that turned crowds into panicked mobs.

Now what was she supposed to do? Continue taking samples? Something told her he probably wouldn't like it. Terrorists weren't supposed to look like an average American college student.

"No one is here," Ava said as gently as she could, as she dared, "but me."

The young man frowned, glanced around, then asked, "Where did they go?"

She had to work to keep her tone even, when everything inside her wanted to run away screaming. "They, um…left."

"Left?" The young man looked around again. "But I was supposed to deliver a message to the American p…public. Force the military to withdraw troops from…" His voice trailed off.

"Some of them got sick," Ava offered tentatively.

"Oh," the terrorist said, looking at her with a fuzzy sort of pleased expression. "Good. That's what's supposed to happen."

Good?

Was he the delivery system? Patient zero? Had someone gotten him sick, then sent him to a popular coffee shop to infect as many people as he could?

It wasn't something he could have done on his own, could he?

"So far, sweetheart," an unfamiliar masculine voice said into her ear, startling her, "you're doing just fine."

Where had Dr. Rodrigues gone?

"Who is this?" she asked, lowering her voice as quietly as possible so the terrorist-in-training wouldn't overhear.

"He's a security specialist," Dr. Rodrigues said, her voice high with stress. "He's working with us. I've got a situation here at the hospital I have to deal with. Take good care of Dr. Lloyd, Sergeant River."

"I will," he said. There was a click, and then he spoke again. "I'm one of the guys who gets brought into this kind of situation when the shit hits the fan."

There was a lot of background noise, rapid footsteps, people talking. Whoever this Sergeant River was, he was on the move.

A police negotiator, maybe. Whatever his job, his voice was smooth, dark, and deep.

The sort of voice capable of giving you a thrill, even if you never saw its owner. If she had to take orders from someone she didn't know, at least she could enjoy it.

"Keep your volume low and don't get excited," he continued. "Dr. Rodrigues figures your boy has whatever bug all the rest at the hospital have." His tone implied this was a positive thing. She wasn't so sure.

"Is that good news?" she asked.

"Yes," said the terrorist.

Oops, she'd spoken a little too loud.

"He might pass out," Mr. Smooth said. "Which would be the best-case scenario."

The terrorist didn't look any closer to unconsciousness than he had a couple of minutes ago. "So, we wait?" she asked.

"I'm supposed to wait for further instructions," the terrorist answered with a wobbly nod.

"I'm moving into position to help you," Mr. Smooth said. "But, it's going to take a few minutes."

"What does that mean?" She really had to stop thinking of him as Mr. Smooth. She might use the moniker out loud. His name was River, Sergeant River.

Please be police and not military. In her experience, military meant a combative attitude with little regard to safety. Just what she didn't need.

What she did need was a man who lived up to his centered, calm, seductive voice.

"Just keep him busy. Offer him a seat," River suggested. "He sounds confused, so make him feel comfortable. In control."

Well, finally something she knew how to do with her eyes closed and one hand tied behind her back.

"Would you like a cup of coffee?" she asked the terrorist.

"Small nonfat latte with caramel drizzle." He said it absently, by rote. He'd probably ordered the same drink hundreds of times.

"Coming right up," Ava said, trying to ignore her shaking hands as she revved up the espresso machine.

"How much?" he asked.

"On the house," she told him as she worked, only slightly slower thanks to the hazmat suit. "You've ah…earned it today."

"Excellent," River said to her. "Smart girl."

"I'm not a girl," she muttered as she made the drink and passed it across the counter to the terrorist-in-training. She was an experienced doctor, goddamn it.

"What are you wearing?" the young man asked her, his expression clearing. "Are you with the police?"

She froze, her mind unable to come up with a single reasonable thing to say.

"Tell him it's get-your-geek-on day," River suggested.

"It's a costume." Ava pasted a smile onto her face. "Pajama day is next week."

The terrorist frowned, but relaxed a fraction. "Oh." He took a sip of his coffee, and his face lit up. "Good coffee."

"Thanks."

"See if you can get him to sit down," River advised. "Keep him talking."

Maintaining the smile on her face was starting to hurt. "Please, take any seat in the house," she said to the young man. "I'll bring you a…snack."

The terrorist obediently sat on the closest chair.

That was way too easy. She'd met a lot of sick people. Most of them got suspicious and argumentative when faced with a stranger in a hazmat suit, not acquiescent.

"Have you got a plan?" Ava asked the man on the phone as she grabbed a pastry from the display case and walked around the counter to give it to a man who looked like he was still in his teens.

"In motion, sweetheart," River said. "All you need to do

is keep that loony tune distracted."

"Here you are." She handed the terrorist a piece of banana bread. "Oh, would you like butter for that?"

"Yes, please," he answered, his voice so low in volume she almost didn't hear him.

He was starting to sway in his seat.

Come on, dude. Pass out, pass out.

His cell phone rang, startling both of them.

It was the Darth Vader ringtone.

"Seriously?" River said in her ear. "Does he think he's feeling the Force or some shit like that?"

Ava had to bite her lip to keep from snorting. Humor was completely uncalled for, the situation dangerous in a way she'd never experienced before. So, why did she want to laugh so much?

The terrorist answered the phone. "Hi."

He listened for a moment, then nodded, ended the call, and looked into her eyes, regret turning the corners of his lips down.

Nausea doused the urge to laugh and twisted her stomach painfully as he said the last thing she wanted to hear.

"I'm sorry."

Chapter Two

6:21 p.m.

Whoever had designed the hazmat suit either had a hell of a sense of humor, or they hated all their coworkers.

River hit the mute button on his ECC device. As far as he knew, Dr. Rodrigues and Lloyd were the only two people besides him with communication units, but he wasn't 100 percent sure about that, and he didn't want just anyone listening in as he prepared to kill another human being.

He sighted down his scope, settling the crosshairs on the back of the head of the idiot wearing the backpack. The full-body condom wasn't making it easy.

The damn thing was bulky, in the way, and he hated how it dulled his senses, making even simple things like detecting outside vibration or feeling the direction of the wind impossible. Both those things were very necessary to making the shot for a man trying to hit a nut job and missing the woman he had hostage.

"I hope to fuck someone is tracing that phone call," he

said to the general population of law-enforcement types milling around him.

"We are," one of the FBI guys answered. "But it's not as easy to do as the cop shows make it look on TV."

"Don't kill him," the Homeland agent in charge, John Dozer, ordered. "We need to question him."

"You think there's going to be anything left of his brain after the fever he's got?" River asked conversationally. "That's *if* I manage to give him a John Wayne shot?" He shifted his target a little, trying to find a spot on the kid's shoulder or arm that wasn't near any major arteries or veins, but the angle was bad. It didn't matter where he hit the guy. He was probably going to bleed like a stuck pig.

Then River caught a glimpse of Dr. Lloyd's face in his scope.

Her expression morphed in that second from a polite mask to full on horrified.

No soldier ever ignored his gut instinct when it told him to shoot. River didn't intend to start now.

He breathed out and squeezed the trigger.

The terrorist jerked and slumped forward, the cell phone falling out of his hand to clatter on the concrete beneath him.

Dr. Lloyd ducked, but when nothing more happened, she straightened to look around before staring at backpack dude.

"We need to send in medical," Dozer said. He sounded bored.

"I am medical," River told him, pulling himself out of his shooting position.

Cell phones and radios on the various officers and agents around him began to squawk.

"There's been an explosion at Cielo Vista Mall," one of the cops called out to the group.

Before anyone could move, an FBI agent shouted, "A suicide bomber just hit the main gate at Fort Bliss. At least six dead."

"Fuck," Dozer said, not looking a bit bored now.

"I've got this," River told him. "You're going to have your hands full with two secondary locations going up in smoke."

"I'm setting up a command post right here," Dozer said through clenched teeth.

"This area is too exposed and too close to that backpack I'm assuming is full of explosives." River nodded at the man he'd just shot. "Speaking of which, I'm going to need a bomb disposal unit and an ambulance."

Dozer was already on his phone barking orders, but he nodded at River before turning to direct law-enforcement traffic.

River secured his weapon, grabbed the pack next to him, and strode off toward Dr. Lloyd, who looked much too young to be the kind of experienced specialist Dr. Rodrigues had described—a doctor who was trying to stop the terrorist from bleeding to death with nothing more than her hands.

He should be so lucky. If Homeland had its way with the kid, he'd disappear into a very dark, painful hole and never find his way out.

River turned the mute button off on the ECC. "I'm inbound to your location," he told the doctor, then reengaged the mute.

She glanced up and saw him coming. Her gaze took in his hazmat suit, the first-aid kit, and his sniper rifle. It stayed on the rifle. "Did you shoot this man?" she asked. The appalled expression on her face had only gotten more pronounced.

"It was that or let him blow you up, along with this place," River said as he came to a stop next to her. She was small, young, and brown-haired. Reminded him of a sleek little mouse. "I've got pressure bandages for that wound." He stripped the backpack off the guy, picked up the cell phone slash detonator, and deposited both of them cautiously on the concrete in the center of the open-air space. That put it about twenty feet away from Dr. Lloyd and the man she was trying to keep alive. Not nearly far enough away, but better than having it sit right next to them.

River opened his first-aid kit then shifted backpack dude onto the cement. It took a moment to get the pressure bandages secured in place on the terrorist's chest and back, thanks to the hole the bullet drilled through him.

River took out a small portable heart monitor, connected the three leads to the guy's chest, and turned the machine on.

Dr. Lloyd grabbed the stethoscope out of River's pack and listened to the bomber's chest. "You missed his lung," she said, relief clear in her voice. She might look like a mouse, but she sounded like one of those women on a phone sex line. Furry, soft, and sexy.

"Can't get answers from a dead man," River replied.

She tensed up a little, but didn't look away from her patient. "Are you a sniper? With the police?"

"I'm Army Special Forces, which means I can do a lot of things most people don't want the details of." They didn't, not your ordinary civilians, anyway. They'd shit their pants if they knew how many ways he could kill someone.

"Yeah," she muttered in a disapproving tone. "I know all about that."

He snorted. *Right.*

"I investigate infectious diseases," she explained, pinching her lips together. "My mother washes her hands before, during, and after I visit."

The ECC thing in River's ear beeped. He unmuted it, then answered the second call. "River."

"This is Dr. Rodrigues. What's the status of the man you shot?"

"He's unconscious, but alive. He's going to need surgery and a blood transfusion soon, though. And when I say *soon*, I mean right now."

"Arrangements are being made to get an ambulance to you to transfer him to a secure isolation room at the William Beaumont Army Medical Center, but with multiple explosions causing so many injuries and deaths, it's going to take a while."

"He hasn't got a while. If you don't get someone here within the next ten minutes, he's going to bleed to death."

"I can get the transfusion running if they have blood handy," Dr. Lloyd offered tentatively. "It's been a year or two, but I haven't forgotten which end of a needle is sharp and which isn't."

He could, too, but he'd take anything that might create a team vibe between them. "Fucking-A," he said with a grin. "Dr. Rodrigues, can you get someone to deliver a couple of IV sets and three or four units of O negative blood? Dr. Lloyd says she'll push packed cells while we wait for transport."

"Good idea. I'll have someone do that." The call ended.

"I think your boss just hung up on me," River complained.

"Yeah, she does that when things are a little crazy." Dr. Lloyd shrugged. "I'm Ava, by the way. Just Ava."

"Not Dr. Lloyd?" he asked. "Most doctors seem hung up on people calling them doctor."

She looked at him as if he were something on a petri dish. "I spend most of my time inside a lab or dressed like this in some kind of disgusting environment collecting samples. The only time I insist on being called *doctor* is at a staff meeting."

Usually he was pretty good at charming the ladies, but his little mouse wasn't impressed with him one bit. New tactic: find common ground. "How does this rate on your disgusting scale?"

"It doesn't." She rolled her eyes. "I worked for three months in Sierra Leone during the Ebola outbreak. People were dying, lying in pools of their own blood, feces, and urine.

That was if they were in a bed. Lots of them were just left in the street, in the mud, to die."

"That's pretty bad." He had to admit, it was. "The worst thing I've ever seen was in Afghanistan, the aftermath of a family setting off an IED with their ancient truck. All we found were pieces...of them."

"That's...rough," she agreed hesitantly. "I think you win."

"Nah, it's a draw. Invisible things that can kill you are scarier than any gun, knife, or artillery ever invented. Those things are limited by the skill of the person wielding them. Bacteria and viruses, well, no one is in charge of them, and that makes them far more dangerous."

She glanced at him, startled. "Huh, I never thought of it that way."

"Soldiers have a vested interest in anticipating all the ways a body can die. Especially if you want to be alive at the end of your deployment."

She stared at him as if he'd suddenly spoken to her in an unknown language, but quickly turned her attention to the idiot they were trying to save. "Is that what you do? Security and risk assessment?"

"That's part of it. We do a lot of different jobs when we work with other countries and organizations." River paused to do a reading on their terrorist's heart rate.

Way too high. And jumpy.

His ear beeped, and Dr. Rodrigues's voice spoke to him again. "The equipment and units of blood are on their way."

"Understood," River said. "ETA?"

"About ten minutes."

"I'm not sure this guy has got that long."

Rodrigues's voice sharpened. "What's changed?"

"His heart rate is becoming erratic. He's bleeding out fast."

"Homeland Security is screaming at me to make sure he

stays alive and well enough to answer questions."

"Homeland can't always get what they want," River said, without any sympathy. "Besides, we can learn a lot about this guy by studying whatever goodies he has stashed on him and in his backpack."

"I thought it was explosives."

"We're assuming that. No one has had time to look. Even if an explosive is all we find, the materials used to create it can tell us plenty." River pushed the button on the portable heart monitor to get a new pulse, but there wasn't a pulse to get. Only a long, flat line.

"He's in cardiac arrest."

Rodrigues made a frustrated noise, and then her end of the call went dead.

More shit hitting the fan?

Ava muttered, "Crap," under her breath, then began chest compressions.

The heart monitor broke out into beeps, but they were haphazard, erratic, and in no way normal.

"Where's that blood?" Ava demanded.

River looked around, but no one was making any effort to get any closer than the yellow caution tape. There were a lot fewer law-enforcement types around and a lot more civilians, some of them looking none too happy to see a couple of people in hazmat suits busy with a guy on the ground who was leaking out a river of blood.

"I think we're on our own," River said to her. "People are blowing up all kinds of shit all over the place." He glanced at the man he'd shot. "Maybe it's a coincidence, but something tells me whoever sent this kid here doesn't want him to be able to talk."

His mouse jerked her head in one direction to stare at the reduced numbers of cops and agents, and the increasing numbers of civilians, then in another direction and the next, until she'd confirmed his read on the situation.

"Didn't we call for help first?" she demanded. "Shouldn't we get the first ambulance?"

"Call me crazy," River said to her, "but I don't think anyone was all that interested in saving the life of a terrorist over an innocent bystander."

"That is *not* how the health-care system works." She sounded shocked, appalled, even.

"That's how *people* work," he countered. "I doubt there's going to be much sympathy for him."

"What about his family? Friends?"

River shrugged. "Little fish in a big pond." He activated the monitor again, and again got nothing but flatline static. "Shit."

Ava straddled the kid and performed textbook chest compressions, but after a minute, River put a hand on her shoulder and said, "Stop. He's gone."

She snarled at him, actually snarled, and said, "Fuck off."

Well, shit, that was sexy as hell. Which only underscored how fucked in the head he really was.

Chapter Three

6:38 p.m.

Ava's hands itched to smack River. Just one little smack, to release a fraction of the frustration burning a hole in her gut.

No one should be so cavalier about a person dying, no matter what crime they'd committed. Besides, the CDC needed answers this man might be able to provide, like the identification of the pathogen released here, and if it had been altered in some way to make it more virulent and deadly.

As the soldier had said himself, *You can't question a dead man.*

Her arms were starting to ache, but she doggedly kept up with the compressions.

"Dr. Lloyd?" River phrased her name like a question.

She ignored him.

"Ava," he said with more power. "It's been five minutes since his heart stopped beating. He's bled out. Nothing is going to bring him back."

Rage burned hot enough in her blood to singe everything

she touched. She took in a breath to call him a coward, but the sea of red around her finally registered.

The pool of blood beneath the young man had gotten larger. His face had turned stark white and his lips blue.

She stopped the chest compressions. When had she started breathing so hard? She glanced at the concrete again. A bloody lake pooled around her knees, staining her hazmat suit. "I'm just pushing his blood out the bullet wounds, aren't I?"

"Probably," River said in an oddly gentle voice.

"You must think I'm an idiot." Her voice sounded scathing and harsh, even to herself.

"I think you're a good doctor." Still, he used the gentle tone, as if she were a spooked horse.

She snorted. Pity was the last thing she wanted from anyone, let alone this stranger, a man who represented a way of life she'd learned to hate. "Why, because I'm too stubborn to admit I can't help someone?"

"Because you don't give up until all hope is lost." A steel thread of strength and conviction threaded its way through his tone now. "Only then did you stop." It almost sounded like he admired her.

She stared at him, surprise holding her tightly in its grip. Her former fiancé, a soldier who wholeheartedly believed the old adage *might made things right*, had never spoken of her profession with such respect. Old pain snatched the air out of her lungs and squeezed her chest until breathing became something to fear.

Stupid woman.

Adam was gone, killed eighteen months ago in a suicide bombing in Afghanistan where he was training Afghani military and police in counter-terrorism tactics. Adam was gone, along with all her plans for the future. A husband, a family. Gone, because he put the military and his mission at the top of his priority list. Ahead of everything else.

That's what soldiers did. Put the protection of everyone else in front of themselves.

Soldiers…died.

She didn't want to like this one.

Ava shifted off of the body and crab-crawled a couple of feet away. Yes, that's what she needed—distance, emotionally and physically.

"Okay," she said, taking in a deep breath, discovering it hurt less than she thought it might. "Okay. He's dead."

River didn't say anything, only watched her with careful eyes. Adam's gaze had never been careful.

"I'm going to take some samples from him before the ambulance gets here." She glanced at the backpack the soldier had set aside. "What about that thing?"

"We're going to wait for the bomb squad to examine it."

Weird how normal that sentence sounded. As if he were talking about moving a sofa or a refrigerator.

"How long will that take?"

River frowned and looked at the dead body. "Not sure. With all the other attacks going on, it could be a while."

She nodded in what she hoped was a professional manner, then stood, locking her trembling knees when they threatened to collapse, and then went to her collection case. A sterile blood sample wasn't going to be possible, as most of the terrorist-in-training's blood was on the concrete, but she could collect nasal, throat, and other samples.

Her hands shook so badly she dropped the first swab she'd selected.

River wasn't looking at her; he was studying the growing crowd outside the police tape and readying the lethal-looking rifle he carried. He handled the weapon with the same mastery and ease as a violinist might handle a violin.

She ignored her unsteady hands and threw the

contaminated swab away. With the next one, she focused on one task at a time, and the shaking gradually decreased.

"What's your first name?" she asked the soldier as she took a quick temperature reading from the dead man's ear.

"River." He sounded distracted.

"I thought that was your last name."

"It's the only name I answer to." She could hear the hint of a smile in his voice this time.

The temperature that flashed across the tiny digital thermometer's screen made her breathing stall in her chest. "Whoa."

That brought River's head around. "Whoa, what?"

"This guy's temperature is through the roof. 104°F."

"He had it, didn't he, the killer illness?" River asked. "There were thirty plus people in the ER with high fevers when I left an hour ago."

"One of my jobs is to figure out where the outbreak started and who patient zero might be." She angled her head at the dead man. "He's a possible candidate."

"Which pathogen is it? Anthrax?"

"That would fit some of the symptoms, but not all. The consensus was that we might be looking at bacterial or viral meningitis." She looked at the café's order counter. "If someone working there, one of the baristas, was sick with it or carried it, they could infect a lot of people by coughing or sneezing at the wrong time."

"Don't most people get vaccinated for that?"

"*Most* doesn't mean everyone. There are always a few who refuse to vaccinate because they think the vaccine is going to hurt them." She sighed. "Which is stupid, because the only reason vaccines were developed in the first place was to protect us from diseases which cause a high percentage of brain damage, blindness, and death."

"The infection rate seems…high."

"That's the other possible problem. Whatever bug is causing this could have been genetically engineered to be different. More virulent."

"That is not a happy thought."

An understatement. "I didn't think soldiers were allowed happy thoughts."

"Not true. The best soldiers are always thinking happy, even when they know there's a bad guy around the corner, or in this case, on the other side of the yellow tape." The way he said it, as if he were looking at a bad guy right now, snagged her attention.

"What?" Ava glanced at him, but he wasn't looking at her. She turned her head in the same direction as River's and reared back at the number of people staring at the two of them with very unhappy faces.

There were a half dozen uniformed police telling people to back up and leave the area, but few seemed to be following those instructions. As she watched, the swell of voices rose and turned into yelling.

"What's going on?"

"Why are those people dressed like that?"

"Are they terrorists?"

"Ava," River said in an almost-normal tone. The abnormal part was stone, cold serious. "If you have to get any more samples, get them now."

"They wouldn't rush us, would they?" Given the danger it would put them in, it would be a crazy thing to do, but the shouting wasn't calming down.

"A mob doesn't think. They trample." He positioned his rifle so the butt was nestled in the hollow of his shoulder, but kept it pointed toward the ground. "Hurry."

She moved as quickly as she dared. The last thing she wanted was to give the crowd the impression she was in a panic. It could spark a riot.

Her specimen collection case, which looked like a large tackle box, still sat on the counter where she'd left it. She grabbed it and quickly sampled several areas around the order counter, cash register, and pick-up counter.

The crowd was now pushing and shoving each other and the police officers.

"We can't have a stampede. This area, and the body, are likely to be sources of the infection. Anyone who gets too close has a huge risk of becoming contaminated."

River nodded. "Not to mention the danger of explosives. I'm going to make a call."

He did something with his earpiece and spoke softly. After a moment, he nodded at her. "I've asked for a bullhorn. Might as well see if we can talk these people down."

A few seconds later, a policeman set a bullhorn on the ground about ten feet inside the yellow tape, then went back to his position.

"Stay here," River told her, then walked calmly toward the bullhorn.

Alone.

He wasn't...yes, he was. "Wait!" she yelled at him. "It's not safe."

He glanced at her for only a moment, a single moment, but that's all it took for her to see the calm resolution in the set of his jaw, mouth, and eyes. "This is the best option to make our situation safer."

"You don't know that for sure," she called after him, but he ignored her and continued walking.

Toward a horde of people who sounded more and more angry by the second.

Fear gripped her so hard she had to breathe through her mouth to prevent herself from throwing up.

How could he put himself in such a dangerous situation without a shred of hesitation? Nearly a million people in

Texas had a concealed gun license, ergo at least some of those people were armed.

Goddamned soldiers have no sense of self-preservation.

He picked up the bullhorn, faced the crowd, and said, "I'm with the Center for Disease Control. This area is under investigation by the CDC. It is *not* safe. Please clear the area."

The crowd quieted down, a few left, but others shouted questions.

"What's with the plastic suit?"

"How do we know you're not some terrorist?"

"This is a hazmat suit, and I'm in it because there are more than thirty people in the ER who've gotten really sick. Deathly ill. My partner over there and I are trying to discover if this is the source of the disease."

"You mean, you don't know?" someone shouted.

"Does this rifle look like a Magic-8 Ball?" River asked, sounding irritated. "We've got to take samples, then get them to the lab and analyze them, before we know for certain what's going on. In the meantime, all you people are doing is putting yourselves in danger by hanging out here and arguing with the cops."

He paused, then shouted, "Go home."

People looked at each other and began backing away.

It worked. River's plan actually worked.

One of the crowd, a man who'd been asking most of the questions, demanded, "I want to see some identification."

Several people paused to listen.

"Yeah," River said, disgust clear in his voice. "They put pockets in this condom, too. You think they hand these portable goldfish bowls to everyone? Why are you being such a shit disturber?"

"It's my right to ask questions."

"You have a right to be a dick? Really? When did that become law?"

Several people laughed.

Interesting how adversarial that man was behaving.

Ava picked up the small digital camera she kept in her collection kit and discreetly began to take pictures of the crowd.

The man's face turned a deep red. He pointed at River and yelled, "You're part of a government cover-up. This isn't terrorists, this is the military conducting illegal, covert experiments on people."

"A dick, and crazy." River shook his head with mock sympathy. "Dude, you need professional help."

The man bellowed and ran at River, but was stopped by one of the cops, who took the raving lunatic to the ground and handcuffed him.

A few people stayed to watch the arrest, but most of the crowd retreated and left.

"Keep this area clear," River told the police officers. "Possible bomb threat in the backpack, plus the café is hot, in a biological sense. You feel me?"

"Yes, sir," one of them said. "Absolutely." The cop reminded him of a new recruit. Eager to please.

"Don't call me *sir*. That's almost as bad as saluting me." River hesitated, then added, "Call me *sergeant* if you have to call me anything." He turned and seemed surprised to see Ava behind him. "Hey, I didn't hear you come this way."

"Since I was trying to blend in with the concrete, I'll take that as a compliment."

He grinned at her, the sort of grin people on the same team give each other. "Any particular reason for sneaking around?"

"I wanted to take some pictures of the crowd. That guy gave me the heebie-jeebies."

"Yeah, he's a couple of bricks short of a fireplace." River nodded at the café. "Did you get everything you needed?"

"I think so. Let me just pack it up." She returned to her collection kit, made sure she'd gotten all her garbage, and locked the kit.

River stepped behind the order counter. "Place looks pretty clean."

"Looks can be deceiving," she told him, picking up her kit.

A flash blinded her at the same time as a giant hand picked her up and slammed her into the floor.

Chapter Four

6:52 p.m.

River was going to strangle the asshole pounding on his head. And who the hell was screeching at the top of their lungs? It was impossible to determine gender based on the tone, but the sound penetrated his skull faster than a hot blade in butter.

He opened his eyes. Smoke and dust crowded around him in the air like ethereal spirits of the dead.

Nausea churned his gut, and the smell of burnt plastic and flesh filled his nose. Combined with his vicious headache, the whole mess threw him back into a fight he'd lost over a year ago. His mouth, nose, and eyes were full of sand and blood. Pain ricocheted through him like a razor blade in a pinball machine. A razor that was going to slice him to death if he didn't kill the fucker jabbing him with it.

He forced himself to throw off the weight on his back, get to his feet, and attack his assailant, but there wasn't anyone there. Only smoke, rubble, and ghosts.

Reality slammed the last hour's events into his head in a series of flash images, smells, and sounds.

A woman's voice, sexy and arousing.

Squeezing the trigger of his rifle.

The red bloom on the back of his target.

Wide brown eyes, startled and fearful.

His mouse, *Ava*, where was she?

River stood in the middle of a coffee shop, but it looked, sounded, and smelled like a fucking war zone.

The order counter was mostly gone. Wood splinters, chunks of countertop, and shards of glass littered what was the café's work space.

His mouse was somewhere under all that shit.

Adrenaline surged through him, clearing his head.

"Ava," he called as he picked up a large section of the counter and tossed it aside. Why did his voice sound so funny, muffled?

Oh, fuck. The goddamned backpack had exploded.

River dug deeper into the pile of debris and found a hand attached to an arm covered in a thick, flexible plastic. A hazmat suit. "Ava!"

No response.

His stomach dropped into a black hole. *No, no, no.* She was his partner and under his protection. She had to be okay. If she wasn't…

The smell of blood and sand momentarily replaced the scent of burnt wood and plastic.

He was lying on his back on the sand looking at Smoke, one of the toughest sons of bitches in the Special Forces. Blood spatter covered his uniform and face, and he looked pissed the fuck off.

Pain shot through River's head. When he opened his eyes, he was back in El Paso, but he'd gotten a piece of his missing memories back.

Ava.

A little more digging, and he found her back and head.

She was just coming around as he lifted the last of the big stuff off of her.

"What…happened?" she asked, blinking at him like a very young owl. Her pupils reacted normally to the light, and he would have kissed her if they weren't wearing these stupid head-to-toe latex outfits.

"We got blown up." He visually inspected her. "Are you injured?"

She took his hand and got to her feet. "I'm fine…I think." Her gaze examined him, and then she put both hands on his arms. "Where did all this blood from?" She wiped her fingers over a spot on his hazmat suit, inking a trail of blood across the plastic.

He did a quick inspection of himself. "It's not mine." He glanced at the spot where the body of the terrorist-in-training had been. Only a bloody mess of assorted body parts was left. "I think it's the dead man's blood."

The backpack wasn't close enough to the body to do that much damage, but, if he'd been carrying explosives on his body…the damage looked all too accurate.

Ava sucked in a breath, drawing his attention. He watched the color leech from her face. "Check your suit. *Oh my God*, if our suits have been compromised, we could be exposed to… the infection."

Fuck.

"Hold still." River held onto her with both hands on her upper arms and visually inspected her suit. "Turn around." He spun her, ignoring her irritated squawk. "I don't see any holes."

She jerked herself out of his hold. "Now you."

It took her a little bit longer to inspect his suit, and by the time she let go of him, more sirens were audible and growing louder.

"I couldn't find any obvious holes, but that doesn't mean there aren't any." She sucked in a deep breath. "The explosion could have caused any number of micro holes big enough to allow for contaminants to enter our suits."

Not much they could do about that now, and he'd learned a long time ago not to worry about shit he couldn't do dick about. "Well, that sucks."

"Sucks?" she asked, her voice rising and hands clenching into fists. "Are you looking forward to having a fever high enough to cook your brain?"

"Not especially, but then I so seldom use my brain." He gave her his best little boy grin. "Settle down, Mouse. Let's not borrow trouble."

"Mouse?" She pressed her lips together. "Did you just call me a mouse?"

"Small, with silky-brown hair and eyes." He shrugged and glanced at the three emergency vehicles pulling up outside the yellow tape. "Mouse."

She choked. "I'm *not* a rodent."

He had to hide his smile. She was fun to irritate.

One of the vehicles was an ambulance, one a black SUV with no identification, and the third had the CDC logo on the side along with a biohazard sign. It was the size of a small bus. "I like mice," he added. "They're cute."

Ava glared at him, then noticed the emergency vehicles and sighed audibly. "Thank God. The decontamination team is here."

"They're going to clean us up?"

"Yes." The relief in her voice was almost insulting. He was taking good care of her. Neither of them were dead. "Us, and the whole area."

Another vehicle arrived, this one a police vehicle. A guy in a SWAT uniform jumped out and ran over to the CDC bus.

He yelled something, and then four guys from the SUV exited their vehicle to join the conversation. It looked congenial for the first few seconds. Then the SWAT guy started yelling and waving his hands around.

"This party is getting interesting," River said, as the discussion descended into argument.

"Who are those guys?" Ava asked. "There's no time for this. The whole area needs to be decontaminated."

"I think the SWAT guy is here because of the bomb." River nodded at the crater in the concrete. "There could be multiple devices. It's a common tactic with this kind of terrorist attack."

"But—"

"The guys in black are probably from Homeland Security." He crossed his arms over his chest. "They like to think they're in charge of everything. Nobody I recognize, though."

"It doesn't matter what either group wants. Unless they're in a hazmat suit, it would be suicide to come any closer."

"Good point. Let's share that intel." River headed toward the group of men shouting orders at each other.

"Wait," hissed Ava. "What if you're right, and there's another bomb?"

"Then it'll be a short trip." He kept walking, despite her calling his name.

He passed the body and attempted to avoid the majority of the blood coating the cement and the remnants of tables that had survived the blast.

It looked like the entire backpack had been destroyed, but that didn't mean the threat was over.

He kept watch for anyone approaching the area, but the blast and the emergency vehicles seemed to have driven the mob of bystanders off.

The argument between the various law-enforcement officers and the CDC wasn't cooling down a bit. The CDC guy was trying to get anyone to listen to him, but Homeland and SWAT just ignored him.

It was almost enough to make River laugh.

"Hey, Homeland, SWAT," he shouted at the group. "You're seriously underdressed."

The four Homeland agents and the SWAT commander turned to stare at him.

"This is a biological hot zone, fellas," River explained. "You guys come in here with anything less than a hazmat suit on, and you're asking to go home in a body bag."

"Who the fuck are you?" one of the Homeland guys asked.

Weird. Dozer should have alerted any other agents that a Special Forces soldier working for the CDC had shot the kid with the bomb.

"Sergeant River, Army Special Forces on loan to the CDC. Who are you?"

"Tom Geer, Homeland Security. Agent in *charge*."

Interesting. "I thought John Dozer was the agent in charge." River paused a moment to watch Geer's reaction.

The asshole was good at concealing his annoyance, but not quite good enough. The muscles around his mouth tightened enough to betray his irritation.

"He's set up a command post a block south of here," River continued, knowing the smile on his face would piss the other man off even more. "Perhaps you should check in with him."

"It's my job to find out everything possible about the terrorist you just killed." Geer sneered at him. "Since we can't question him, thanks to you, we'll have to settle for the tech over there." He threw a nod toward Ava.

"She's not a tech. She's a doctor with the CDC. I'm sure she'll be happy to talk to you just as soon as she's able."

River turned to the SWAT commander. "Before you do anything, I'd ask for some direction from this gentleman from the CDC, if I were you." River looked at the CDC guy, who stared back at him with his mouth hanging open. "Sir, which protocols do you need us to follow?"

The guy didn't hesitate long. "This is a level four event. Since there is a danger the pathogen could be airborne, hazmat suits are required by all personnel. No one can proceed until we've had a chance to spray disinfectant over the entire area."

"Have you got a suit that will fit over my bomb tech's protective armor?" the SWAT commander asked.

"Do I look like a tailor? Either the suit fits or it doesn't."

"We can't allow anyone in there until we've cleared it for explosives," the SWAT commander said.

"You can't go in there at all without a suit on."

"Where's the bomber?" Geer asked.

"See that red mess?" River pointed it out. "That's what's left of the dude." Despite the urge to annoy the Homeland agent some more, he decided to be more forthcoming. He might need these guys at some point. "He did get a call from someone right before he died and about five minutes before the bomb went off. There are more fish to catch."

"Did he talk to the woman?" Homeland asked, pointing at Ava.

"A little, but with his fever, none of it made sense."

"How do you know that?"

River tapped the device attached to his ear. "We're connected. I heard some of it."

"I want to talk to her," Geer demanded.

"What happened to the samples Dr. Lloyd collected?" the CDC guy asked.

River had no problem figuring out who had the more urgent agenda. "I don't know," he said to CDC guy. "Last time I saw her tackle box, it was sitting on the floor behind the counter. It's probably still there under some debris."

"Can you retrieve it, please? We need to get it to

the identification lab as soon as possible, and we need to decontaminate it first to ensure the exterior of the case is clean."

"Can do. Uh, doc?"

"Yes?"

"Could you do the same for Ava and me? She's concerned there might be holes or tears we can't see in our suits as a result of the explosion."

Geer swore. "This series of attacks is bigger than you and one doctor. We need to find out if there's going to be any more of them."

Footsteps approaching from behind him told River his mouse had taken the initiative. He found himself fighting with the instinct to step in front of her, to protect her from this idiot's one-track mind. There were a lot of moving parts to the situation, and Geer didn't seem to understand just how important the biological hazard was.

"Ask your questions while the CDC performs its decontamination procedures," Ava said, stopping just behind River.

Relief at how accurately she'd interpreted his body language, what he wanted her to do, gave him a boost of energy. He and his mouse were thinking like a team. She was smart, and damn, if that didn't give him a boner.

"We can't interrogate you here, out in the open." Geer clenched his teeth so tightly together he shredded every word that came out of his mouth.

"Interrogate?" River asked, moving to completely block the view the other man had of Ava. "Why would you need to interrogate her? She's on our side."

"He spoke to her and no one else." Disgust and contempt turned Geer's words into targeted weapons. "We want to know why."

"You're seeing conspiracies where there aren't any,

Senator McCarthy," River said with enough sarcasm to melt a hole in the concrete.

"I had no idea I'd be coming here to collect samples until my supervisor ordered me to," Ava said, leaning around River's body to make eye contact with the Homeland agent. "The man had an obvious fever. He was sweating and confused. He thought he was in the middle of a crowd when the only person nearby was me."

"You kept him calm long enough for a sniper to take him out." Geer's tone screamed disbelief. "How did you manage that?"

"Like I said, we're on the same frequency," River said, making a phone out of his hand and fingers. "I told her what to say until I got into position and could take the shot that laid him out. Agent Dozer was standing next to me the whole time. Maybe you should talk to your own people before you make accusations against someone who's actually doing something useful."

Chapter Five

7:12 p.m.

Ava kept her eyes on the four people from the CDC, including the decontamination team leader, Ben White, as they got out of their vehicle wearing hazmat suits and harnesses with dual tanks. Long rubber tubes connected the tanks to spray wands they held ready to use.

The four ignored everyone else, ducked under the yellow tape, and began spraying down River, Ava, and her sample collection kit.

She wasn't sure what the Homeland Security agents wanted to know, especially since she didn't have a whole lot to tell them. "He said something about forcing American troops to withdraw from somewhere." She rotated her arms so the CDC team could spray her properly. "But he was very confused and never finished his…speech."

"Did he say anything else?"

"Someone called him. I don't know what they said, but the terrorist looked at me and apologized."

"Apologized?"

"He said, 'I'm sorry.' A second later, someone shot him."

"That someone would be me," River put in as the team finished spraying his suit. "I saw your reaction to what he said. Whatever you saw on his face scared the shit out of you."

"I don't know what I saw, but whatever the caller ordered him to do, he seemed determined to carry it out."

The Homeland agent glanced around the area, taking in the buildings surrounding the plaza the coffee shop was in. "Someone could have been watching." He looked at his fellow agents. "Have all the buildings with a line of sight to the café and surroundings searched." He turned back to Ava. "I need a description of the bomber. I also need you to sit with a sketch artist. Identifying the bomber is a top priority."

"Any security camera pointed in this direction is going to get you a more accurate picture than a sketch artist could produce," River said. "Dr. Lloyd is an important member of the CDC's investigative team. If you need her for anything else, go through appropriate channels to schedule an interview."

Anger radiating off him, the Homeland agent stared at River. "I don't like your attitude."

"I don't give a shit," River retorted.

The agent took an aggressive step toward River. "Being in the Army isn't going to save you from a lot of very uncomfortable questioning."

"Dude, if you're trying to intimidate me, could you at least look as threatening as my drill sergeant from Basic?"

Homeland's face turned a deep red.

"Dr. Lloyd," Ben said, not bothering to fight a grin. Ava had worked with him twice before, and he treated her like a kid sister, telling her stories of his ten years with the CDC and the hundreds of biological hot spots he'd worked. He could probably decontaminate the area in his sleep. It was Homeland Security's attitude making this interesting for him.

"Dr. Rodrigues needs you and your samples at the hospital now. You, too, Sergeant River."

"Our hazmat suits may be compromised," Ava told him with a glance at her suit.

"You'll be disinfected again, from bare skin out, at the hospital. The helicopter will be landing at the north end of the street in about three minutes." He pointed. "Please make your way there now."

"Homeland has jurisdiction—" the Homeland agent began.

"The Governor of Texas has declared a state of emergency," Ben interrupted. "He's given the CDC the authority to isolate the sick, quarantine the healthy, and investigate the disease. Dr. Rodrigues is in charge. You'll have to speak with her regarding any questions you may have for her or anyone on her staff."

"A state of emergency?" The agent sneered. "For only two deaths?"

"Your information is outdated. Ten people have died in the last hour alone," Ben replied. "We've got over one hundred cases reported now and more pouring in."

An icy rock formed in the pit of her stomach. *"Good God,"* she whispered. "It must be an airborne pathogen."

"That's what we're afraid of. If it is, what we've seen this morning is just the tip of the iceberg."

"Agent—" Ava hesitated. She hadn't heard his name.

"Geer," River supplied.

"Geer." She glanced at River and smiled. "You're correct. Identifying the bomber is crucial. He may have been what we call *patient zero*. We need to know who he is…was. We need to know what his movements were in the last several days. Everything he did, who he was with, who he talked to. *Everything.* I wish I had more information, but he said nothing to me beyond what I've already told you."

"He didn't mention any names?"

"No. As I said, he said he had to wait for instructions, then got that phone call."

"Where's his phone?"

"I left it next to the backpack," River said. "I doubt there's much of it left."

Geer stared at the two of them, frustration a palpable thing on his face and body. "I don't have time for all this shit." He looked at her up and down, as if her hazmat suit was something ridiculous.

A dangerous attitude. For him and anyone he came into contact with. An outbreak like this could rapidly get out of control and spread. Following safety protocols could save your life.

"Make time or get dead," River said with a bluntness that rocked the Homeland agent back on his heels. "This isn't a case of the flu or measles. This shit is *killing* people."

"Measles kill, too," Ava said, wincing when the two men looked at her. "It's a lot deadlier than most people believe." She stared at Geer. What would convince this man the biological threat was as serious and deadly as explosives or bullets?

Geer's contemptuous expression disappeared into a frown as he said in a tone so falsely sweet it could give cavities, "Fine. If the CDC is in charge, it's in charge. We'll see what we can pull off the surveillance footage. Priority one is identifying him, two is determining his movements for the last week. Any other orders, *doctor*?"

Oh, he did not like her at all.

"Do you have River's contact info? We should share information as we receive it."

"I'll get it from Agent Dozer."

"Watch your six," River said to Geer. "EMS is often a high-priority target to these assholes."

"The voice of experience?" Geer asked with a faint sneer.

"Abso-fucking-lutely. This kind of multiple strike is a favorite of today's modern terrorist."

Geer snorted. "As opposed to what, eighties mullet terrorists?"

"And shoulder pads, don't forget the shoulder pads." River gave him a half-salute, then nodded at her. "Let's get to the helicopter."

She grabbed her collection kit and followed him as he damn near ran for the helicopter landing at the other end of the courtyard.

The pilot was dressed in a hazmat suit, as were the two men waving at River and her to hurry. As soon as they were inside and the door to the aircraft was closed, the pilot had them in the air.

One of the men helped her to a seat. The other secured her collection case to an empty seat with the seat harness. Normally, she'd think they were overdoing the safety thing, but given the situation…there was no such thing as overdoing it.

The flight only took a couple of minutes, which was plenty of time to see firsthand just how crazy the situation had become in the hour since she'd been gone to collect samples.

There was an army of ambulances, fire trucks, and police cars at the front of the hospital, all with their lights flashing, but their sirens off. People were milling around, but not as many as all the vehicles warranted. In fact, she could only see seven moving bodies down there.

The lack of noise and imbalance between the number of vehicles and people made the scene below…eerie.

She lost sight of the area as they flew over the top of the building. They didn't land on the helicopter pad; they landed in a back parking lot surrounded by a fence. A lot empty of cars, but full of CDC vehicles, tents, and people in hazmat suits.

Once the helicopter touched down, an entire brigade of people rushed over. Ava hadn't even gotten her harness released before someone had the door open and was reaching in for her sample collection case. It took her a moment to recognize the man as Henry Lee, a tech who was the key person responsible for the hands-on lab work that would identify the pathogen. Once Henry had begun investigating an unknown microorganism, he didn't stop until he had it identified.

"How many samples did you get?" he shouted at her.

"Forty-three," she shouted back. The pilot hadn't turned the engine off, and between that and the noise the rotors made, she could barely hear herself think. "We got blown up, so you're going to need to take samples from us after we've been through decontamination."

He paused to stare at her. "Blown up? When did that happen?"

"About twenty minutes ago, I think." She glanced at River, but he was talking to Dr. Rodrigues, who must have entered from the other side of the aircraft. "It's been a bit chaotic."

Henry nodded. "I'm working in our lab-in-a-box. They set it down on the other side of the parking lot. As soon as you're finished in decontamination, come find me and I'll take some samples from you." He gave her a thumbs-up and trotted off with her collection kit.

Someone on the other side of her shook her arm.

Ava turned to find Dr. Rodrigues examining her with a critical gaze. "Any injuries to report?" she yelled.

"Nothing worth treatment, ma'am. I'd be surprised if I don't have some deep bruising along my right side and back. Did Sergeant River explain about my concern with the integrity of our suits?"

"Yes, there's a decontamination team ready to scrub you head to toe. Report to me after you're done."

"Yes, ma'am."

Dr. Rodrigues ducked away, paused, then came back. "Good job. Sergeant River said you handled yourself well." She left so quickly Ava didn't have time to think of a response. She glanced at River, but he was busy getting out of his harness.

He'd taken the time to compliment her to her boss? Her breath shuttered out of her chest as heat blossomed inside her to spread across her body and up her neck. He kept surprising her. It was confusing.

Focus.

Ava got out of the aircraft and followed another tech from the CDC who led her to a free-standing tent. River was being guided into another tent a few feet away.

Both structures were about twelve feet square with one entry/exit.

Inside, there was a line of three tanks containing different chemicals capable of killing bacteria, viruses, fungi, molds, and spores.

The tech sprayed her down with her suit on first, then had Ava take it off, along with the clothing she wore beneath it. A different woman, one she didn't know, came and took her clothes away without comment.

"Close your eyes and mouth," the tech ordered. "You don't want to get this stuff in them."

Ava complied, and she sprayed her with the first solution, then the second.

"Keep your eyes closed while I scrub you down," she said. "Let me know if any gets into them. We'll need to rinse them properly if that happens."

Ava nodded, and she began scrubbing.

After that, she was sprayed down with a third solution.

Then the tech put a towel in her hand, and Ava could finally wipe her face dry and open her eyes.

"I didn't see any obvious tears or holes in your suit. I also didn't see any evidence of any liquids penetrating the suit."

Ava nearly collapsed with relief.

"I'm going to issue you another suit anyway," the tech continued. "Once you're dressed, Henry wants to see you, then Dr. Rodrigues. After you've seen them and been cleared for work, you can come back here to pick up your new suit."

"Will do. Thanks."

"Be careful. Just before you arrived, I got word that the death toll has grown to fifteen."

Holy shit. "Has the pathogen been identified yet?"

"If it has, no one is saying anything." The tech gave her a wry smile. In other words, they either had no idea what it was, or they knew what it was, but were double-checking the identification to ensure that the first answer they got was the right one.

It had to be something very nasty.

Ava nodded at the other woman, then took the set of scrubs provided, got dressed, and stepped out.

The sun had set while she'd been in the decontamination tent. Portable light towers set up at regular intervals now added a white glow to the fading sunlight.

Two men were talking quietly not far away. One of them had his back to her. He wasn't tall, his body compact, and the scrubs he wore left his muscular arms bare for the most part. He almost seemed to blend into the shadows.

"Sergeant River?" she asked, not completely certain it was him.

He glanced at her over his shoulder. It was quick, no more than a second, but that was plenty of time for her to confirm it was him.

The impact his gaze had on her, now that there weren't

two layers of hazmat suit between them, knocked the wind out of her. His eyes were a warm amber, the bones of his face strong rather than handsome, his black hair trimmed military short. He looked every inch the soldier. Tough. Determined. Deadly. But even the most dangerous men needed help and support sometimes. He'd been assigned to her, which made him her responsibility.

That's all he was, a colleague, a partner, nothing else.

She shivered as a cold ball of ice formed in the bottom of her stomach, telling her it was already too late—he'd saved her life and treated her like an equal partner. For that alone, he'd earned her trust, but he'd gone even further. He'd shown her more respect in the past hour than most men did in a week.

She didn't want him to get under her skin, really didn't.

He turned away to shake the hand of the man talking to him, thanked him, then faced her, giving her a thorough head-to-toe examination. Protective. Proprietary.

He strode toward her, stopping close enough that she had to force herself not to take a step back. "Everything okay?"

In the face of his concern, how could she not care? "Um, yes," she managed to say after taking in a quick, shaky breath. "You?"

"Yeah. They didn't find any holes in my suit."

"Mine was okay, too." She couldn't stop staring at him. He radiated testosterone. How could she have not noticed how seriously freaking *hot* he was?

"So," River drawled after a moment, one corner of his mouth curling up for the briefest of moments. "We need to see that guy, Henry?"

Ava winced. *Get it together, you stupid woman.* "Yes, come on." She led the way to what most people would look at and see as a metal shipping container, the kind used on large ships for items like cars or trucks.

"This is a portable lab?" River asked as they stopped outside a tentlike structure that had been attached to one side of the box. Another smaller tent sat next to it. A glance inside revealed a cot, a case of bottled water, and a few Meals Ready to Eat.

"Yes, fully functional and self-contained." she said, waving at the security camera mounted on one of the support poles of the tent. "Henry, we're here."

"Think of this"—she gestured at the heavy-duty airtight plastic in front of them—"as an air lock."

River stepped back a few paces to examine the entire structure. "A helicopter brings it in?" he asked, pointing at the giant handles on either end of the metal box.

"Yes. It provides its own power through batteries recharged by solar panels, so it can go anywhere."

"An Army doctor I know had something like this, but it was made of canvas and broke down so it fit into duffel bags."

"I know her. I've seen pictures of her tent. It's ingenious." *Wait*, how did he know about it? She watched him sidelong and said tentatively, "I didn't think that tent design had been shared with anyone outside of the Army's Biological Response Team."

"I did some support work for the Bio Response Team last year. Helped set up that tent."

"During the incident when she blew up her lab?"

"Yep, though I didn't witness the explosion."

"Busy shooting bad guys?"

"No, an ex-friend of mine had kicked me in the head. There's forty-seven hours I lost last year the doctors say I'll never get back."

Chapter Six

7:45 p.m.

Ava stared at River with the widest brown eyes he'd ever seen. "Kicked you in the head?"

She had an incredibly expressive face. Every emotion transformed her features into a canvas that spoke with more eloquence than words could ever convey. At the moment, shock and concern dominated. He could watch her for hours and never get bored.

"Yeah, with his combat boots. Asshole. Gave me a hell of a concussion, which turned out to be far worse than the bullet wound he also gave me."

"A *friend* of yours did this?" Her voice rose with enough righteous anger that he almost laughed.

"Ex-friend. He turned mercenary after he left the Army."

"In more ways than one," she muttered.

"Pretty much."

"Any lasting brain damage?" she asked, then paled and sucked in a breath. "I'm sorry." She covered her mouth with both hands. "Oh my God, I'm so sorry. I shouldn't have just blurted the question out like that."

Fuck, she was *cute*.

River laughed and mussed up her hair, mostly because he wanted to see if it felt as silky as it looked. "Don't worry about it, Mouse."

Soft, satiny strands flowed over his fingers in a tactile tease. She stared at him, her cheeks going from pale to red.

He dropped his hand, cleared his throat, and asked, "Henry?"

"Right." She squared her shoulders and led the way, muttering, "Idiot, just keep your mouth shut from now on."

River leaned down to whisper in her ear, "I like your mouth just the way it is."

She whipped around to stare at him, her luscious mouth hanging open. "What?"

"You heard me." After this shit was over, he was going to make a point of spending time with his mouse.

Quality time.

Sexy time.

"Henry?" he asked again, letting his gaze rest on her lips.

She snapped her jaw closed, narrowed her gaze into a glare, then turned on her heel and marched over to the camera again.

She was fun to poke at and tease. All prickly and pretty and ruffled up.

"Henry," Ava shouted at the piece of electronics. "We're here, hurry up." She turned her back on River as if he'd insulted her entire family history.

Adorable.

A minute later, Henry came out, frowning. "Where's the fire?"

River stared at him. He'd seen this guy before. Or his twin.

"An outbreak is worse than a fire," she said tartly. "Haven't you identified the pathogen yet?"

"Sort of." He waved her off her next question. "You know how this works. Dr. Rodrigues will give you the details." He pulled a couple of long, plastic cylindrical tubes out of his pocket. "I need nasal and throat samples."

She opened her mouth.

Henry stuck the swab down her throat, put it back inside its tube, then got a second one and repeated the procedure with her nose.

"Now you," the tech said to River.

He obediently opened his mouth, and watched how Henry moved. Precise and controlled. The edge of a tattoo became visible on his left arm as the man shoved a swab up River's nose.

Bingo.

"Henry Lee?" River asked when the other man had finished. "Special Forces medic?"

Henry froze for a long second, and then his expression turned deadly. "I was discharged ten years ago. You want to tell me how you know that?"

It wasn't a question.

In his shoes, River would probably have a similar reaction.

"I'm good with faces. There are a couple of entertaining stories about you still in circulation. One guy has pictures."

"I know that guy," Henry said with a grin so menacing it would have scared the shit out of a civilian. "He's an asshole."

River returned the smile. "That guy is a general now."

"That just makes him a bigger asshole." Henry's face went blank and so cold it froze River's bone marrow. He'd seen that expression on a few faces before. Most of those men were dead.

Henry pointed at the hospital. "Dr. Rodrigues is waiting for you in the ER. Wear a hazmat suit." He went into his *lab in a box* through the canvas air lock and slammed the door.

Interesting place to find a man who reputedly killed three Taliban fighters in hand-to-hand combat while himself wounded.

River glanced at Ava. She rolled her eyes. "Come on." She headed back to the tents where they'd both been cleaned to within an inch of their lives, her spine as stiff as a steel rod.

"Grumpy much?" he asked.

She didn't even glance at him. "I don't like it when people have secrets."

What planet did she live on? "Sometimes secrets can have you by the balls."

"What?" She shook her head. "No, that's not what I'm talking…" She stopped walking and pinched the bridge of her nose. "He knows what's causing this infection, but didn't share it with us."

"If the information is sensitive or destructive, it needs to be handled or delivered by the correct person, right? He's a tech, right, not a doctor?"

"I understand the reasons why he's not allowed to tell anyone but Dr. Rodrigues. I just don't always agree with it. I'm a doctor, too, and it's not like *I'm* going to panic or blab."

"Someone else might."

"Stop making sense," she growled at him as she resumed her fast, jerky stride toward the tents. "You're pissing me off."

River laughed again.

Adorable.

The techs at the decontamination area were waiting with new hazmat suits. As soon as Ava got into hers, she started for the hospital.

Considering everything they'd learned about the situation so far, River followed without comment.

An outbreak had begun that morning at an outdoor coffee shop near the university. Three bombs had exploded in different locations in and around El Paso, including the nearby military base. The only clue they had regarding who was responsible and why they were doing it was from the ramblings of an ill, young American man. A twenty-year-old willing to blow himself up for some kind of cause.

Now, at eight o'clock, the outbreak had appeared to pick up steam, infecting and killing greater and greater numbers of people.

He didn't blame Dr. Rodrigues one bit for keeping a lid on information.

Noise smacked him across the face as they entered the hospital. The sound of a lot of people talking, yelling, and crying was underscored by the mechanical sounds of heart monitors, intravenous sets, and respirators.

Ten feet inside the doors, patients in gurneys lined the hallway, the trail leading all the way back to the registration/triage desk.

Ava never deviated from her course toward the desk, and River followed in her wake, dodging ambulatory patients, family members, and hospital staff.

Someone grabbed his arm from behind.

For an endless moment, he wasn't in a hospital hallway. He was trudging on sand, the sun burning his eyes, a hot wind scoring his face.

Pain exploding through his head.

Fuck.

He wasn't going dark a second time.

No fucking way.

River spun, twisting out of the hold to find himself face-to-face with a weeping woman. It took more effort than it should have to stand down, to stuff the violence back inside him where it couldn't hurt anyone else.

Her hands clutched at him. "Please, Doctor, help my son. He can't breathe."

Well, shit. "I'm sorry," he said, glancing at the gurney she was trying to tug him toward. "I'm not a doctor." The kid on the gurney was adult tall, but with a teen's underdeveloped musculature. River could hear his panting wheeze from several feet away.

That wasn't good.

"He can't breathe!" she shouted at him, jerking on the plastic of his suit.

Ava appeared next to him, taking the woman's hands in hers. "We've just arrived," she said with calm confidence. "We'll talk to his nurse. The last thing we want to do is the wrong thing."

"Oh…okay," the woman said, letting go of Ava with obvious reluctance. "Please hurry."

"I will." It was nothing less than a vow. She angled her body toward him and said in a voice that carried, "Follow me, Sergeant."

No one else stopped them as they made their way to the triage desk.

Ava leaned down and asked quietly to the nurse, "Dr. Rodrigues?"

"In the back," was the equally quiet reply.

"Who's looking after the teen in the second gurney along the right wall?" Ava asked. "He's in respiratory distress."

The nurse's face reflected unwanted surprise. "We're operating under crisis management protocols." She glanced over her shoulder into the core of the ER. "All patient care plans are on the team care board."

"Thanks." Ava was off like a shot.

A short hallway led them to a bull-pen style setup with a double crescent of desks facing a perimeter of rooms arranged like spokes in a wheel around them. At one end of the desks was a narrow wall covered by a dry erase board. The board had been divided into a table containing patient, diagnosis, and treatment information. A diagram of the ER with room and gurney positions tagged with position codes had been propped up next to the board.

There were a half-dozen people, all in hazmat suits, inside the crescents, fully engaged in their jobs. River recognized Dr. Rodrigues, but not the two men she was speaking with.

No one seemed to have noticed Ava or him arrive.

"Patient G-four is in respiratory distress," Ava said loud enough to catch the attention of several people.

"Dr. Lloyd," Dr. Rodrigues began, speaking to the two men next to her, "collected all the possible location-zero samples. She's a microbiologist and recently came to us from the World Health Organization. She has a knack for untangling outbreak patterns."

"I thought there'd been an explosion at that location," one of the men said. "There were casualties."

"Not precisely," Ava replied. "There was an explosion, but the only death occurred a few minutes before the actual blast." She paused, then asked, "Patient G-four?"

"I've got him," a nurse said, with a grim smile. She rushed out, stethoscope in hand.

"Please give me a few minutes to catch Dr. Lloyd up to speed," Dr. Rodrigues said to the men, then slipped out from behind the desk. She waved at Ava to follow.

River prowled right behind them. No way was he letting his mouse out of his sight in all this chaos.

Rodrigues found an empty consultation room, directed them into it, then closed the door behind herself.

She let out a deep breath. "We're currently at one hundred and thirty infected, that we know of, with eighteen deaths."

That was shitty news.

Ava stood a little straighter. She got down to business, didn't complain, blame, or comment. Fuck, that was hot. "What's the pathogen?"

"Neisseria Meningitidis."

"Why is that a surprise?" Ava asked. "It was at the top of our suspect list when we first got the call."

"This one is different." Rodrigues pressed her lips together until they were a thin white line. "It's resistant."

Ava frowned. "Resistant to what?"

"Everything." She swallowed. "Henry tested it against ceftriaxone, ampicillin, chloramphenicol, and ciprofloxacin. Nothing works."

Holy shit, *none* of the antibiotics worked? Was this some kind of superbug?

"That…" Ava shook her head. "That's not possible."

"We just sent samples off for multilocus sequence typing and serosubtyping an hour ago."

"A new strain?"

"It would have to be to behave like it does. It's killing people in just a few hours, causing high fevers, brain swelling, and respiratory arrest. Sometimes the swelling kills the patient, sometimes the respiratory distress kills them."

"The first case arrived in the ER at eleven this morning," Ava said, staring at nothing. "Six people arrived with the same symptoms within minutes of each other."

River watched her talk and could almost hear the gears turning in her head.

"The first death was at two in the afternoon. The count is now eighteen. Sixteen people in six hours? That's a hell of an escalation."

Wow, she said *hell*. He'd have used stronger language. This situation was rapidly evolving into a catastrophe of monumental proportions against an enemy he couldn't even see, let alone fight.

"That's why the state of emergency was declared. The governor is scared shitless. He didn't even blink before giving the CDC the power to investigate, including directing law enforcement."

"So," River said, thinking out loud. "If things continue to worsen, the CDC can take faster action and issue orders to all those law-enforcement agencies?"

"That, too," Rodrigues said, swallowing as if she'd eaten a mouth full of shit. "But it's not going over well with Homeland Security or an interesting variety of politicians and government officials. I've never seen so many different people try to tie my hands. If the governor hadn't given us the powers he did, I'd be hard-pressed to get anything useful done."

"Got any names?" River asked her.

When she frowned at him, he grinned and said, "I like to keep score."

"Writing something like that down would be stupid," Ava said.

"I've got an eidetic memory," he told her. "I don't need to write it down."

"Useful," she said, as if she admired his talent.

"Yeah, you'd think so, but there are a few drawbacks."

She actually appeared to consider what those drawbacks might be, frowning at him, but shrugged after a moment before turning back to Rodrigues. "How is the infection transmitted?"

"Coughing, we think. It's not airborne for long, but long enough. It's in every mucous sample from every patient we've tested. It's extremely aggressive." Rodrigues paced away, then returned. "I believe its pathogenicity was engineered."

Ava took a step back. "A biological weapon?"

"The extreme rapid onset of symptoms and subsequent death can't be an accident of nature. In a virus, yes, this kind of natural biological leap is possible, but in a bacteria…" Rodrigues shook her head. "Resistance develops over years, not months, and not to every antibiotic we'd normally use to treat it."

"There are a lot of crazies out there who'd love to let

something like this loose on America," River said. "A colonel with the Biological Response Team took out a terrorist last year whose goal was to wipe humanity off the face of the earth. Unfortunately, the nut job shared what he knew about weaponizing viruses and bacteria with at least five men who are still at large."

Ava stared at him as if he were the boogeyman. "I hadn't heard about that."

"That information is confidential," Rodrigues said with a sour expression for him.

River crossed his arms over his chest. "Since you're about to send us on a wild terrorist chase, she should know."

Chapter Seven

8:15 p.m.

Ava stared at River, then at Dr. Rodrigues. Was he right? Were they going to be hunting the person or people behind the outbreak and explosions?

Gathering samples from a deserted location under the watchful eye of several law-enforcement officers was one thing. Seeking out the kind of people who could not only conceive of, but carry out these acts of mass murder...

Her breathing stopped altogether for a moment before stuttering, *painfully*, back to life.

Could anything be *less* safe?

Her boss continued to glare at the soldier for another moment or two, then sighed and met Ava's gaze. "He's right. We have to know if this is a man-made pathogen or not. If it is something someone has created, I can't send just anyone to investigate. I need people who know the science as well as the enforcement."

River leaned toward Ava, his gaze darting right, then left

in an exaggerated motion of his head, and stage whispered, "I'm the muscle, and you're the brains."

Ridiculous and juvenile, but, with his clear declaration of them as a team, she could breathe again without pain.

"Yeah," she whispered back. "I got that, since I'm, you know, the brains."

The corner of River's mouth tilted upward, and then he turned to Dr. Rodrigues. "Do we have an ID for the guy I shot at the coffee shop? He'd be a good place to start."

"Not yet, but I'm expecting that information in the next thirty minutes. Homeland Security was able to get some good pictures of him from the security cameras around the square."

"You talking with Dozer?"

Dr. Rodrigues frowned at River. "Yes."

"Have you talked with an Agent Geer at all?"

"That name isn't familiar."

River grunted, but didn't comment.

"Ma'am," Ava said. "*Neisseria* doesn't require a hazmat suit. Will you be releasing the identity of the pathogen to the press and changing the appropriate safety protocols?"

"Safety, yes, to a certain degree; identification, no," Rodrigues said.

"I don't understand."

"Until we know the true scope of the bacteria's pathogenicity, I'm not releasing anything other than the most basic information. An air respirator with at least a P100 filter should be worn by everyone, and gloves for those who might come into contact with others. Frontline medical staff in hazmat suits." Rodrigues pointed at Ava and River. "You two will wear respirators and gloves, as will anyone assigned to work with you. I saw how that crowd reacted to your suits outside the coffee shop. Public panic is the last thing we need."

"Do you want us to help with triage while we wait for an ID on our dead terrorist?" River asked.

"No. Prepare your equipment and eat while you have a chance." She gave River her complete attention for a moment, taking a step toward him and angling her body so her back shut Ava out. "You are to be armed at all times unless and until I say otherwise. You don't let Dr. Lloyd out of your sight. Her safety is your responsibility."

Ava managed not to snort at that. Fat chance she had of remaining safe in his company. Their investigation was inherently unsafe, which was almost as dangerous as her attraction to him.

"Yes, ma'am," he drawled.

"I'll contact you the moment I have that identification." It was clearly a dismissal.

"Yes, ma'am," Ava said, then turned and left the building by the same route they'd come in. They passed the teenager who'd been in respiratory distress, and his mother. His body was covered in a soiled sheet, and his mother was weeping uncontrollably on the floor next to the gurney.

Her heart went out to the other woman, but she couldn't let her emotions hijack rational thought. Things were going to get worse before they got better.

River and she returned to the decontamination area and removed their hazmat suits. They were given respirators that conformed to the face for a good seal and had orange filters on either side of the mask, safety glasses, and surgical gloves.

When Ava asked for spare respirators and gloves, Sarah only gave her a couple sets.

"Until more supplies arrive, we have to ration."

"Where can we eat?" Ava asked.

"There's a clean room set up across the parking lot for staff to eat and sleep."

"Thanks." Ava led the way.

"Clean room?" River asked. "Portable?"

"It looks like a giant marshmallow. Air coming in or going

out is filtered through HEPA filters. Don't be surprised if your ears pop once we get inside."

They walked around a couple of tents set up over crates of water and Meals Ready to Eat to find the air-filled construction.

"An air lock?" River sounded surprised.

"Yeah. The CDC doesn't joke around."

They entered the air lock through a door that zippered open and shut. As they walked the short distance to the inner door, the air pressure became uncomfortable enough that she pinched her nose closed with the fingers of one hand and blew until her ears popped.

River did the same.

Inside the second door, the room was deserted, with only a few picnic-style tables and a half-dozen cots set up with blankets. To one side of the entrance was a stack of water bottles and MREs.

Ava grabbed one of each and sat at one of the tables.

River sat across from her, a crooked smile on his face. It suited him, gave him a rakish air that had her pulse speeding up. "You and I are partners."

She knew that. "So?"

He leaned forward and asked, "How can I help you do what you need to do?"

What?

Ava had to force her jaw to close. He'd been ordered to work and support her, but this kind of open-ended question with no conditions—she hadn't seen it coming.

She scrambled to regain her composure. "My job is to locate the source of the infection as well as track and record the spread of the infection." She shrugged. "It would help if you kept people out of my way and encouraged them to evacuate if the risk of infection is high."

"Clear away obstacles, crowd control, and bodyguard."

He nodded and leaned even closer. "Here's what I need to do all that." He paused.

She sat forward.

All trace of mirth left his face. "If I tell you to get down, run, or stop, don't think, don't ask questions, just do it."

What? "Do you believe I'm a target? Or is anyone dressed like me a target?"

"Both. Neither. I'm not assuming anything but the worst-case scenario."

"What's the worst-case scenario?"

His face hardened into concrete. "More bombs, bugs, and bodies."

She waited for more, then realized his gaze had gone fuzzy, as if he were thinking hard and only seeing with his mind's eye. His expression changed from one second to the next. Pain, anger, disgust, contempt, and more pain. His muscles stood out, as if he'd locked himself in place, but that control was costing him.

Whatever he had in his head was horrible.

What could be worse than what they'd seen already today?

He had an eidetic memory, he'd said. She supposed it might be a sort of torture to not forget. It would take a very strong-willed person to compartmentalize the horror, to put it in a box and close the lid on it. She'd seen horrible things, but he had, too. War amplified horror.

There was more to admire about this man than just his sexy voice and exterior.

"Okay," she said, opening her MRE. "I can follow your orders, if you can follow mine."

His gaze refocused on her face. "Then we're in business." He held out his hand.

She put hers in it and they shook, once, twice.

"We're going to be so awesome as partners, you're never

going to want me to leave," he said with a smug grin.

She yanked her hand away. "It doesn't matter how great we work together, that's all we're doing. Work. So, don't get all territorial."

"It doesn't have to be just work, you know."

Did he really want her, or was this a case of being the only woman around? "You call me a mouse, but I'm really just a lab rat."

His grin disappeared. "That's not a nice way to talk about yourself."

"Look, I've tried the romance with a soldier thing. It didn't end well."

River stared at her, his gaze searching hers for longer than she was comfortable. "He was an idiot. I am not one."

Wow, she was going to have to pull out the big guns. Regret softened her voice more than she wanted, but it had to be said. "He was my fiancé, and he died in the line of duty."

River's stare froze. "Fuck." He paused, his hands closing into fists. "Fuckity fuck fuck."

She allowed her eyebrows to rise, but kept her response contained to that.

"How long ago?" he asked after several seconds.

"About a year."

He bared his teeth and leaned toward her again. "Allow me to repeat myself. I'm not him."

Oh, River.

"He was Special Forces, too."

River exploded to his feet, jolting and freezing her in place. He paced back and forth in front of the table like a man who didn't know what to do with himself.

He stopped suddenly to pin her in place with a gaze so full of rage and despair it was a wonder that he didn't explode. "He made you feel like a lab rat?"

"No, not really. He just…" How could she explain it?

"We'd been together for a long time. Our relationship was comfortable and safe. Only, it turned out that it wasn't safe at all." She swallowed down the grief and the guilt that always seemed to accompany it. "When he died…" She snorted a derisive laugh and looked at her hands. They were clenched together, her knuckles white.

He sat again and covered her hands with his. "Look at me."

If he'd ordered or demanded, she'd have had an excuse to fight him, but his request was softly spoken, a request wrapped up in a plea.

She met his gaze, and what she saw there jolted her again. So much pain and regret, as if he knew exactly how she felt. Felt it, too.

"I won't make promises I can't keep," he said, his tone turning his statement into a vow. "I don't know what's going to happen in the next hour, let alone the next few days, but I can promise this."

Her breathing came to an abrupt halt as she waited for him to finish.

"I think you're the sexiest thing I've ever seen, and the smartest person I've met in a long time."

Her jaw dropped open.

"I won't lie to you or fudge the truth for your own good. I'm asking you to keep an open mind, Ava. That's all."

The heat from his hands swept up her arms and through her with strength that made her face warm and her mouth say something completely different than what her brain was telling her to say. "I'll think about it."

His smile started in his eyes and slowly moved across his face. "I can live with that."

Finally, her brain kicked in. "I'll think about it *when* this is over and *if* we're both in the same part of the country. That's a big *if*," she cautioned.

"Trust me."

Oddly enough, she did. And if that wasn't the most dangerous thought she'd had in a long time, she didn't know herself at all.

Ava tugged at her hands and busied herself with her MRE. While she waited for it to heat, she pulled out her cell phone from one of the side pockets on the right leg of her pants.

"Why is your phone in a sandwich bag?" River asked.

"To keep it from being contaminated," she answered, without looking up.

"Huh. Smart." She glanced at him, to see him smiling at her. "Got another bag I could have?"

She reached into the same pocket, pulled out another bag, and handed it to him, then went back to looking at the pictures she'd taken with her phone. The crowd River had spoken to had been aggressive and ready to rush the police. Why?

She got a good picture of the man who'd argued with River, his mouth open and finger pointed right at her new partner like he'd done something horrendous. Given the situation, that much anger seemed out of place.

She turned the phone toward River. "Remember this guy?"

He grunted. "How could I forget that dick?" River frowned as he began eating his food. "Way too eager to start shit."

"It felt, to me, like he *wanted* to attack you. He was so… angry." She'd been afraid that anger would set off a stampede. River had stood there alone, confronting all that rage with nothing but a half-dozen police officers, a few traffic pylons, and yellow caution tape to keep the mob from trampling him.

Idiot.

"Too angry." River chewed with the thoroughness of a

man deep in thought. "Could you send me a copy of that picture? I'd like to see if he's on anyone's radar."

"What's your phone number?"

He gave it to her, and she sent him the photo.

"You took a huge risk when you confronted that crowd," she told him, her tone as even as she could make it. He'd scared her. *Badly*. But, she didn't want him to know just how shaken she'd been when he'd strode away from her. It was irrational, the depth of her fear. It resided in the deepest part of her soul. A dark, cold pit inside her she hadn't been consciously aware of until that moment. "Things could have easily gotten out of hand. You put the safety of those police officers and yourself in jeopardy."

His eyebrows rose as she spoke.

So much for keeping it professional.

Damn it, she *sucked* at this.

He didn't say anything for a few seconds. Then, while he ate, his head tilted to one side.

"I think part of the problem is that you and I got assigned to work together without so much as a hello. Which means neither of us knows much about the other."

"Does that mean you know how to handle a crowd?" She tried not to sound too skeptical, but she didn't think she succeeded.

He nodded. "I've performed in training roles for foreign military and police forces. I've taught everything from guerrilla warfare to crowd control." He gave her a nod. "I had a pretty good idea of what would work to get them to disperse, but I should have told you what I was going to do before I did it."

Ava blinked. Was he apologizing to her?

"I won't make that mistake again." He met her gaze with a steady regard that was in no way apologetic.

She dropped her gaze first. "Thank you," she muttered, right before shoveling a fork full of food in her mouth.

Though he wasn't smiling, she had the distinct impression he was laughing at her.

Jerk.

"So, you said you worked in Africa during the Ebola outbreak."

Was there a question in there somewhere? She glanced at him and found a smile on his face. The kind a parent wears when their kid just got 98 percent on a math test.

"Where else have you worked?" Even his voice sounded happy.

What the hell was he up to?

"I worked for three years for the World Health Organization, first tracking the annual influenza infection patterns and the bird flu across Asia. Then, investigating recurrent cholera outbreaks in Tanzania and the Middle East. I also investigated the stubborn repeated occurrence of Middle East Respiratory Syndrome Coronavirus (MERS-CoV) in South Korea and Saudi Arabia."

"What was your biggest takeaway from those jobs?"

He made it sound like her job was of the fast-food variety, when it was actually the most exclusive restaurant in town.

"Travel," she answered, "has a huge impact on infectious diseases. The world population is so mobile one aid worker can carry the flu and infect other people in a different country within hours."

"How can that be mitigated?"

Two questions, and he'd already asked more about her job than Adam ever had.

Adam hadn't wanted to know all of the details and dangers of her job. He recognized her work was valuable and a service to not only the United States, but the world, and had supported her 100 percent. Still, he hadn't learned more about what she did than that.

He'd been caught up in his own training and missions, too

busy to ask more than surface questions.

River was deep-sea diving in comparison.

So far, he was doing it alone. Nope, for safety's sake, one should always have a diving buddy.

"Tell me more about your training," she said. "Aside from crowd control, what do you learn?"

He thought for a moment, then shrugged. "I speak five languages. I'm a medic, which means I'm closer to a physician's assistant than an emergency medical technician. I've also been trained in dentistry and veterinary medicine. I've twice had to vaccinate the entire population of a village for diseases that are almost nonexistent here. There's a lot more to it. It takes longer to train a Special Forces medic than a fighter pilot."

"Five languages?"

"Can't get along with people if you can't communicate with them."

Get along with people? "You're in the military. Isn't that a contradiction in terms?"

"Not if you want to win."

"A war of words?" she asked, trying to understand.

"When you fight a war in another country, the only way to win in the long run is to communicate with, and educate, the locals. Empower the good guys so they can deal with the bad guys on their own."

"How do you know who's a good guy and who's a bad guy?"

"Lots and lots of talking." He pursed his lips in a rueful gesture. "But, sometimes the good guys are really the least bad of the bad guys."

"Sounds like a dangerous job with no guarantee of success, and the price for getting it wrong is death."

River snorted. "You've just described every armed conflict since the beginning of time."

Was he really that blasé about it? "How can you live with that kind of risk hanging over your head like a…a guillotine?"

"It's no different than the danger you face when you're in the middle of an infectious disease outbreak," he replied with a shrug. "You gather all the information there is, you use your understanding of the situation and its dangers, then you formulate a plan to deal with it."

She must not have looked convinced, because he continued with, "Crossing a busy street at rush hour is dangerous, too, but pedestrians do it all the time, every day, despite the possibility of getting hit by a car."

"Cars and armed men shooting at you are not on the same level of dangerous."

"How we manage risk is the same."

His mind was made up, but then so was hers. "So, what do you do with people like that idiot Homeland agent? He wasn't listening to you or me, and it's not like you can shoot him."

River laughed, an open, unfettered sound that relaxed a restless, anxious part of her she'd been unable to ease since Adam died. Until now.

The absence of strain unbalanced her. Panic of a different sort teased her senses, and she found herself hyperventilating to keep it at bay.

On her second heavy breath, he stilled, his gaze taking in *everything*.

She had about a third of a second before he called her on it. Before he asked questions she didn't want to answer.

"Sergeant River."

Ava jerked her head around at the not-quite-masculine shout.

A tall, broad-shouldered man in a rumpled suit strode toward them.

"Agent Dozer, Homeland Security," River said as he got

to his feet. "This is Dr. Lloyd, from the CDC."

"Doctor," Dozer nodded at her before addressing River again. "I have some new information."

He took the spot next to River and leaned in, speaking to both of them. "The name of the kid River shot is Roger Squires. He's the oldest son of John Squires, who owns Gold Inn, an international hotel chain. Roger was a student at the U of El Paso, majoring in political science. He was in his fourth year, held a 3.9 grade point average, and from what I've gathered so far, seemed like a completely normal, intelligent American twenty-two-year-old."

"Have you spoken to his family?" Ava asked.

"No. There was no answer when I tried to reach his parents. We have agents on their way to his parents' home and his dorm room at the university."

"Have both locations been cleared by CDC personnel?" River asked.

Dozer frowned. "No."

"Call them off," River ordered.

Dozer's eyebrows went up.

Was he high enough in the Homeland food chain not to have many people telling him no?

"River is right," Ava told the agent. "Until they've been cleared by CDC personnel, both locations could be biologically hot."

Dozer looked at her for one second, then pulled out his cell phone, hit a button, and relayed her instructions. He ended the call, then gave them both a fierce smile. "I don't think we're going to find anything at his parents' house."

"His dorm has two things that make it more likely to contain useful information," River said.

"What's that?" Ava asked.

River held up a finger. "Roommates." He held up a second finger. "Questionable cleaning habits."

"Thank you for volunteering." Dozer grinned, punching in a number on his phone and tapping the speaker icon.

Dr. Rodrigues's voice called out a hello.

Dozer explained what he wanted River and Ava to do.

"We've done a level one background check on the first hundred people to report sick at the hospital," Rodrigues told them. "Half of them live in the same dorm building or within a quarter mile of it on the university's campus."

"Well, shit," River said, giving her a half-smile. "The kids on a campus like that are too fucking mobile."

"This is going to make containing this bug a lot harder," Dozer said.

"It's possible the coffee shop wasn't ground zero for the infection," Rodrigues said tentatively. "Investigate Roger Squires's dorm. Dr. Lloyd, take whatever equipment you need. Sergeant River, her safety is your number-one priority. Your second priority is to assist in the investigation using whatever tools you deem necessary."

Agent Dozer's choke was in no way quiet.

"Does that include my M24?" River asked with far too much glee.

"I assume that's your rifle?"

"Yes, ma'am."

"Yes. Agent Dozer, please coordinate with law enforcement and assign an appropriate escort for Dr. Lloyd and Sergeant River."

"Yes, ma'am," he replied.

"Good. I expect updates no less than every fifteen minutes."

"Very good, ma'am."

"Make sure your people follow orders, Agent Dozer. Their lives, and the lives of thousands of Americans, depend on it. I know some of your agents don't think the CDC is the appropriate agency to be in charge of this disaster, but if this infection gets away from us, the death toll could be astronomical." Rodrigues ended the call.

"Is that true?" River asked Ava.

"If the sick aren't isolated from the healthy, or if someone exposed carries the pathogen to another location, it could spread. From the pattern of infection and death we've already seen, it would be devastating."

"As bad as Ebola?" he asked.

"Oh no," she said as she thought back to the chaos of the emergency room. It was a scene she'd witnessed hundreds of times when she was in Sierra Leone during the Ebola outbreak. Though she didn't like making predictions about how virulent a pathogen was, she wasn't about to hold back the truth from her new partner. "Much, much worse."

Chapter Eight

8:55 p.m.

"*Fuck.*"

She had to agree with River's assessment. "That's about the size of it."

"And it's resistant to the antibiotics used to treat it, right?"

"Yep."

River swore a long, unbroken sentence. "What's our plan?"

"You two get yourselves sorted out," Dozer told them. "Meet me in ten minutes by the decontamination tents so I can assign you some people to assist."

"Will do," River said.

Ava waited until Dozer was gone before answering River's question. "Contact Ben White. He's the decontamination team leader. If the dorm is location zero and not the coffee shop, we're going to need him." She got to her feet and deposited the remains of her MRE and water bottle in the appropriate trash containers.

River was right behind her. "I left my M24 with Bill. I need to pick it up."

"You left your weapon with a man you just met?"

"I left my weapon secured in a lockbox with a professional of the CDC."

"Really?" She pointed at herself. "Member of the geek brigade here. You didn't sound all that happy to leave it with him, to rely on one of us for...what did you call it?" She arched a brow. "Oh yeah, help with your weapon."

He grinned at her. "There's help, and there's *help*."

"From Bill?"

"I'm working with him on this mission. That makes him a brother."

She couldn't stop a snort from escaping. "I'm working with you, too. Does that make me your sister?"

His response was immediate. "Fuck, *no*."

"What am I, then?"

"My mouse." His voice was low and rough, and it sent a heated arrow through her.

Allowing him to use a pet name for her was a bad idea, no matter how much parts of her liked it. "I am not your *rodent*."

"But you are mine."

What did he just say? "Excuse me?"

He met her gaze squarely. "My partner. My responsibility."

It sounded reasonable, sort of, but there was a thread of heated steel in his tone that said his commitment to keeping her safe went further than it should. "Have you always been this territorial?"

The look on his face was one she hadn't seen in almost two years. Raw, heated, and focused solely on her. "Nope."

He wanted her?

No, it had to be her own feelings of attraction toward him reflecting back at her. Anything else was crazy. She wasn't pretty or witty or a girl who knew how to flirt, not even with

Adam.

She and Adam had dated since their last year in high school. They'd been lab partners in chemistry class, and that relationship carried on after school. She went to university, got her medical degree, then specialized in microbiology. Adam had gone into the military, and though they didn't see a lot of each other due to his frequent deployments, their relationship had been comfortable.

Easy.

This partnership with River felt…different.

More.

He'd made a point of putting her in charge, not something Adam had ever done. How long could it last?

"Men are confusing," she muttered to herself.

River laughed and nudged her shoulder with his own. "And women aren't?"

She rolled her eyes. "You are a twelve-year-old."

"Guilty."

She stopped to face him. She couldn't afford to have him question her authority once they picked up their escort. "You'll back up my orders to our law-enforcement partners, won't you?"

His brows rose, the smile slid off his face, and then he nodded slowly. "Whatever you need, Mouse."

The sincerity on his face melted the uncomfortable ball of ice in her chest. "Okay."

She started walking again. They were rapidly approaching the CDC's decontamination area in the parking lot. There was just one more thing she needed to say before anyone else was around.

"If you must call me Mouse," she said quietly, "please don't do it where other people can hear."

"Giving a fellow soldier a nickname is a sign of trust," he replied just as quietly. "A sign to everyone else that we're a team."

"Well, my mental nickname for you is Mr. Smooth, but I doubt you want the Homeland agents calling you that."

"Mr. Smooth?" he asked in a very quiet voice.

Her stomach dove into her shoes. Shit. How stupid was that? She could see it on his face. Surprise. Comprehension. Speculation.

Me and my big mouth.

"Could you just forget you heard me say that? Please."

"That kind of…confession gives a man a lot to think about," he said, his voice a heated whisper. "Don't think I'll be able to forget."

She glanced at him and had no problem recognizing the wicked desire on his face. A ball of ice formed in the place where her stomach used to be. "I…I just screwed up big time, didn't I?"

He froze, then frowned. "What?"

She threw her hands up in the air. "The way you looked at me just now, like I'm some bimbo throwing herself at you for…for meaningless sex."

"Huh?" He stared at her with his mouth open.

"How could you not lose respect for me? I objectified you the moment I met you." She swallowed hard. *Pull yourself together, you twit.* "I'm sorry."

"Sorry?" he asked, his frown that of a man who'd completely lost the thread of a conversation. "For what?"

"Haven't you been listening to me?"

"Sort of," he answered without hesitation. "I'm still stuck on the *sex* you mentioned."

Yep, she'd destroyed all hope of working with River as two equal professionals. God *damn* it.

She'd lost her mind as well as her judgment. She'd really thought River was a good guy. A dependable guy. A *safe* guy. "I'll tell Dr. Rodrigues to assign someone else to ride herd on me."

"What?" He pulled her to a stop and leaned down into her personal space bubble. "Like hell you will. *I've* got your back."

"But, you just admitted to being distracted by sex."

"I can compartmentalize."

He was too close, too intense. She stepped back and crossed her arms over her chest. "You don't respect me anymore."

He followed. "How the fuck did you arrive at that conclusion? I respect you more than anyone else here." He gestured toward his own chest with one thumb. "*I've* seen you in action."

"But you just said—"

"I was surprised. A man doesn't hear every day a woman he thinks is hotter than hell say she thinks the same about him. Maybe not more than once in a lifetime."

"Oh." But did he respect her? "So, you'll follow my orders?"

"Yes, ma'am."

"You won't try to…" How to ask if he could put the attraction stuff aside? She wasn't ready for this. Might not ever be ready to have any kind of relationship with another soldier. A man who would always put someone else's safety above his own.

The lust faded completely from his face, replaced by a lopsided smile. "I'll be whatever you need me to be."

The sincerity in his voice soothed frayed nerves. She studied him. There was an openness to his face and posture that told her he was telling the truth.

"Okay." She let out a breath. "Okay. Right now, I need you to be a soldier. We're fighting a war most people can't even imagine, let alone see. We don't even know who our enemy is."

He stepped back, nodded decisively, and said in a firm voice, "Yes, ma'am."

She could do this. "Get your fancy rifle. I'm going to call Ben White."

River saluted, then trotted off while she made the call.

"Looks like our escort is here," River said as he returned with his rifle a few minutes later. "You've got this, Mouse. Remember, you're giving orders, not suggestions. They're here to help you, not the other way around."

"Okay." She strode toward the gathering group of men, River keeping pace with her on her right.

A dozen men were gathered outside vehicles ranging from the black SUVs Homeland's agents seemed to drive to marked police cars. One face in particular stood out from the rest.

Agent Geer watched Ava and River approach with a contemptuous twist to his mouth. "Don't tell me you two are running this operation."

Chapter Nine

9:07 p.m.

"It sure as hell isn't you," River snarled at the asshole. The last thing Ava needed was this kind of pushback.

"Agent Geer," she said, her tone colder than the North Pole in midwinter, "I see you still haven't learned how to get along with people."

Nice shot, Mouse. River had to work to keep from laughing at Geer's scowl.

She looked the other men in the group. "Who else is here from Homeland Security?"

Geer's face didn't change as he gestured at three men dressed in similar dark suits to his own to his left as he introduced them.

"Gentlemen," Ava said. She looked at the eight uniformed policemen. "Officers, my name is Dr. Ava Lloyd. I'm with the CDC. It's my job to track down the source of the infection and ensure that it's eradicated or under the control of the CDC."

Geer shifted on his feet and said something under his

breath.

"You have something to add, Agent Geer?"

"Under the control of the CDC?" he asked. "Homeland Security *will* have some say in that."

River had to force himself to keep from reacting. Couldn't he punch the guy just a couple of times? That wasn't asking for much, was it?

"Homeland Security is not equipped or authorized to contain, investigate, or store biological samples," Ava told him. "Homeland Security may receive reports, analyses, and recommendations from the CDC regarding the pathogen responsible for this outbreak, but a say?" She shook her head. "No."

Geer opened his mouth, probably to argue, but Ava spoke first.

"Agent Geer, a moment of your time, please." She gestured a little ways from the group and waited until he started walking before following him.

He didn't go very far. Well within earshot of the group.

Jackass.

"Do you know our orders? What we're supposed to do?" Ava asked him.

"We're going to Roger Squires's dorm to search for evidence in the terrorist bombings today. There may be evidence of this pathogen you're looking for there as well."

"Is that...*all* the information you were given?"

"There's been little time for an in-depth debrief," he said with a sneer. "But I don't expect you to understand that."

That was it. *Enough.*

River stepped forward, got in the other man's face. "Speak to her again with anything less than respect, and you and I are going to have words."

Geer flashed his teeth, not backing down an inch. "Threatening a Homeland Security agent is extremely stupid."

"Hindering an investigation during a state of emergency with assholery behavior is a whole lot more stupid." River pointed at Ava. "*She* is in charge, not you. *She* knows what to do so we don't get infected and die, not you. Shut the fuck up and do your job, or get the fuck out of the way."

"Sergeant River," Ava said, her tone a warning.

He waited a second, then took a step back.

"River is correct, Agent Geer. More than half of the infected have come from that dorm or the area immediately around it. There's no question that we'll find the pathogen there." She had Geer's attention now. "Either drop the macho bullshit, or leave."

Geer's face became a mask of rage.

"Think," Ava said, before Geer could speak. "I'm a subject specialist, not law enforcement. My job isn't to arrest the persons responsible. It's to find them and stop them from releasing more of the pathogen. Arresting them is *your* job."

Geer's face slowly dissolved into a frown as he stared at her. Then he looked at River, the question he wasn't asking clear.

"I'm with her. Security, risk assessment, weapon, whatever she needs. Also, not arresting people."

Geer studied both of them for a few more seconds, then relaxed his body posture. "Microbiologist, correct?" he asked Ava.

"Yes, we're dealing with bacteria, not a virus."

"Anthrax?"

"No. Nothing with spores."

"Is there a reason you're not saying what the pathogen is?"

"Dr. Rodrigues wants to be certain of the identification." She paused, then took a couple steps back to include the rest of the Homeland agents and police officers in the conversation. "We're treating this bug as if it is highly contagious. Respirators, gloves, and safety glasses must be worn by everyone."

She had all their attention now.

"When we get to the building, Sergeant River, myself, and two of you will go inside to uh…" She glanced at River. She needed the right police vocabulary to explain.

"Clear the building," he supplied.

"Thank you," she said to him. "A CDC decontamination team will meet us there. Any questions?"

"So," one of the uniformed cops said. "The respirator is enough protection from the infection?"

"Yes." She looked into the faces of the men, searching for more questions. All River saw was a determination to get the job done.

"Let's get everyone outfitted." She turned and led the entire group back to Sarah and Bill's area.

River sidled close as Geer approached Ava and said, "Officer Palmer and I are volunteering to go in with you."

"Palmer?" she asked.

A uniformed cop came forward. He started to extend his hand, thought better of it, and pulled it up into a salute instead. "Ma'am."

"Where have I seen you before?" she asked him.

River took another look at the guy. "You were one of the officers on crowd control outside the coffee shop, right?"

"Yes, sir," Palmer replied. "Saw you two in action and volunteered to help." He bounced on his feet like an enthusiastic puppy.

"Officer Palmer," Ava began. "We're investigating the disease, not the terrorists, or whoever is detonating bombs. If you're looking for *action*, helping the bomb squad or the SWAT team might be better choices."

"Thank you, ma'am, but I know how dangerous an outbreak can be. My grandmother died last year of pneumonia along with five other people in her retirement home." He squared his shoulders. "This is my town. I'm not going to let some criminal mastermind go on a killing spree, no matter what weapon he uses."

Ava glanced at River.

He gave her a short nod.

"Okay, you're on the entry team." She turned to call out to Bill. "Can you get these two ready right away?"

"Sure." He waved at Geer and Palmer. "This way."

Sarah handed out respirators, safety glasses, and gloves to the rest of the contingent.

"Are you sure these are going to be good enough to keep us from getting sick?" one cop asked, holding up his respirator.

"As long as you're not swimming in it, they're perfectly adequate protection against most bacteria." She walked over to the officer and took his mask from him. "You do need to make sure it fits snugly to your face." She put it on him, then checked the fit. She wasn't satisfied and carefully bent the edges of the respirator to conform to the guy's nose. "Also be sure to pull on the plastic ties so it's nice and tight." Again, she demonstrated, using the officer as her mannequin.

As soon as everyone was ready, they got into vehicles and left. The four of them got into a CDC van, while the Homeland agents took their SUV and the cops buddied up in twos in police cars.

Ava grabbed a backpack-style first-aid kit in the van, checked its contents, then did the same for her fancy tackle box.

The men watched her with curious eyes.

"I'm not sure what we're going to find," she told them when she was finished, maybe two or three minutes from their destination. "There may be casualties."

"You mean, dead bodies?" Palmer asked from the driver's seat.

"Yes. A lot of people become confused, even hallucinate,

due to a high fever, so they may not be entirely rational."

"So," Geer drawled. "Dead *and* crazy people."

Ava shrugged. "The situation requires extra vigilance and possibly a strong stomach."

"You deal with many situations like this?" Geer asked in a tone that wasn't quite disbelief.

The son of a bitch needed another attitude adjustment. Soon.

"I spent several months in Sierra Leone during the Ebola outbreak. I was also in Syria briefly before the WHO pulled out of the country."

Palmer let out a low whistle. "Dangerous work."

"I'm a firm believer in plan for the worst, hope for the best. Proper preparation and attention to safety protocols can mitigate a lot of the danger."

"We're here," River announced as Palmer pulled up outside a large apartment-style building. The rest of their escort joined them on the sidewalk.

The few students walking in the area came to a stop to stare at their group.

"The four of us," Ava said, gesturing at their entry team. "Will go inside to evaluate the situation. The rest of you, stay here to wait for the CDC decontamination team to arrive. Don't allow anyone to enter the building." She stopped to bite her bottom lip. "Split up and cover all the exits. Make sure anyone who comes out is detained until we can clear them medically. They don't get a choice."

"Yes, ma'am." A couple of the cops said without hesitation.

"Officer Palmer and Agent Geer will keep in contact with you using your radios, so keep the channel clear."

There were nods all around.

She turned, putting her back to River to made eye contact with Geer and Palmer. "Let's go."

She trusted him at her back. A statement of trust that

settled old hurts he hadn't realized were still bruised, but behind her wasn't where he should be. He needed to be in front going into that building. Assessing the danger was his job.

He slipped past her a few feet from the door. "Palmer," he ordered. "Take the rear. Geer, watch for passive threats. I'm on the live ones."

"Passive?" Geer asked.

"Explosives, shit that's out of place."

Geer grunted, but it didn't sound like an argument, so River went ahead and opened the door.

No one was visible.

"Squires's dorm room is 307," Ava said.

"Good enough." River brought his rifle butt into the hollow of his shoulder. He cradled it in his hands, ready to pull the trigger, but kept it pointed at the floor.

For now.

He led the way to the second floor without running into anyone and carried on to the third.

"This place is too quiet," Palmer said from his position at the rear of their party.

River didn't much like it, either.

They arrived at the correct door. River stepped to one side so Ava could knock.

No answer.

She knocked again, louder.

The bark of a cough reached them through the door of the apartment, followed by the rattle of the lock.

The door opened, and a young man stared at them, his eyes bloodshot. "Yeah?" He blinked, then slowly turned his head to look at all of them. "Cool outfits."

"El Paso police," Palmer said.

"If you're looking for the source of the weed smell, it's not us, Officer," the kid said, with a slightly fuzzy smile.

"Roger Squires live here?" River asked.

"Yeah." The kid finally seemed to see River's M24, and his eyes got wide. "Whoa, dude."

"We need to see his room," Ava said, stepping forward.

The kid didn't move. "You need a warrant for that."

River shifted to draw the kid's attention to him. "Roger is dead, kid. We don't need a warrant."

The kid sucked in a breath and asked, "How did he die?"

"It's better if you don't know." If the roomie didn't get out of the way, River was going to make him move.

"How are you feeling?" Ava asked.

"Not so good," the kid said. He started coughing, a bubbling wet sound that left bloodstains on his lips and the shirtsleeve he used to wipe his mouth.

"I'm a doctor," Ava said. She turned to Geer. "Contact our people outside, and let them know we've got at least one person with symptoms here who needs to be taken to hospital. If the CDC team has arrived, send two of them in."

Geer nodded without hesitation and immediately got out his hand-held radio and began talking.

River took a step forward, and the kid fell back, turning to lead them inside the apartment. He sat down on a battered sofa, and Ava pulled out a stethoscope from her pack. She placed the speaker end on the kid's chest, the earpieces dangling uselessly. It was a digital device, the heart rate displayed on a tiny screen.

She pulled out a digital thermometer as well and took the boy's temperature.

"105," she reported calmly. "Do you have a headache?"

"How'd you know?" he asked, frowning a little. "My neck hurts, too."

The somber expression on her face told River this kid had it.

"Which room is Roger's?" she asked.

He pointed. "He's not there, but his roommate, Daniel, is."

There were two closed doors down a short hallway, one on the right, one on the left.

"A bedroom, and what else?" River asked.

"Their bathroom," the kid said. "But it's not working. Roger said the shitter was backed up or something, and it smells like something died in there. It's the door on the left."

River walked down the short hall, but stopped before he opened the bedroom door to examine it for anything that shouldn't be there. The doorframe and knob looked untampered with.

He opened the door with one hand, keeping his rifle steady with the other. Ava peeked over his shoulder.

Someone lay sprawled across one of the beds. River walked forward, rifle ready, but the kid's sightless eyes told him he wouldn't need it.

He glanced at Ava and shook his head.

Fuck.

"At least one casualty," Ava reported to the entire apartment, her voice inflectionless.

Chapter Ten

10:10 p.m.

Ava guessed that the boy on the bed had been dead for several hours at least, his extremities cool to the touch.

The second bed in the room was empty and unmade. Roger's? Other than the body, nothing seemed out of place. The contents of the room were exactly what you'd expect in a student's dorm room. Two twin beds, two desks with a chair each, and two chests of drawers. A few dirty items of clothing were strewn on the floor with no more or less than the normal indifference two young men might display.

It only made the death of the room's occupant seem that much sadder.

Outside the bedroom, the apartment's live occupant was having a meltdown.

"Dead?" he demanded of someone, his voice cracking. "What do you mean, he's dead?"

"Sir." Palmer's voice was an order. "Sit down. A medical team is on its way. You need to remain calm until they get here."

"I'm going to die, too, aren't I?" the kid wailed as he started to cry. "We're all going to die!"

Ava put the commotion out of her mind and searched the room slowly, looking for anything obvious that might explain the boy's death. Nothing. Until she saw one of those warm-it-up-in-the-microwave heating pads around his neck.

Damn.

River was looking in the closet and under the bed. He glanced at her and shook his head. "Nothing."

She left the bedroom and looked in the kitchen. Dirty dishes in the sink. An open half-loaf of bread on the counter along with a dirty butter knife and an open jar of peanut butter.

There was nothing in the space that said *terrorist, radical,* or *disenfranchised.*

Agent Geer stood in the open area between the kitchen and the first bedroom. He could see the feet of the dead boy from where he was standing, but he'd turned away. "Any evidence of what happened here?" he asked her.

"If it weren't for the heating pad around his neck, I'd say I'd have to wait for the autopsy."

"Sore neck," Geer said with a tight, angry mouth.

"Yes." Another death to add to the total.

"Everything clear?" River asked Geer. "Any weapons or explosives?"

"Not so far," he replied as he walked into the bedroom.

The bathroom door was closed. Ava walked over and tested the knob. Locked. A knock didn't result in a response.

"Hello?" she said with more than enough volume for someone to hear through the door. She knocked again, but still no response.

River approached and pulled out a slim tool from his tool kit that looked like something a dentist would use, only the last inch of the tip was perfectly straight. He thrust the tool into the narrow hole of the bathroom doorknob, and with one twist of his wrist, had the door open.

There was no movement or noise from inside the bathroom.

She went to slip past him, her hand seeking out the light switch.

He shifted his weight to block her way. "Wait. Let me clear the room."

She backed up, and he gave the door a nudge with one foot.

It opened slowly.

The bathroom was dark, and she couldn't see anything besides linoleum. River stepped into the room and then right back out again.

The smell hit her, one she recognized from her medical school days—decomposition.

"Can you grab my flashlight out of my backpack?" he asked her, both hands on his rifle in such a way that it told her he wasn't going to let go. "It's in the outside pocket on the right side."

She got it and shined it into the room.

A shelving unit stood in the bathtub, covered in glass and plastic containers in a menagerie of sizes. Fluid dripped from somewhere on the shelves onto the bottom of the tub in a steady two-second count.

"Biohazardous?" River asked.

"I can't see any labels, so I have no idea." It would be safer to assume the worst, however.

She shined the light toward the sink and counter, passing over the toilet, but paused at a long lump huddled on the floor between the toilet and the counter.

"What?" she began, then caught her breath as the shape resolved into that of a body. It might have taken longer to identify the lump if it weren't for the flip-flops sticking out from a pair of pajama pants.

She moved the light upward to the counter. A row of metal objects reflected the light dimly. No, they weren't in a row; they were arranged in a pyramid.

"Out," River said in a soft, dangerous voice.

"What?" Identifying the substances on the shelving unit was going to be a priority. Examining the dead body, not far behind. Their respirators were perfectly adequate to protect them from any biological substances.

"Back away slowly," he ordered, his tone no louder than before. He shifted and pushed her backward as he retreated out of the room.

There was too much to do, and she didn't want to go. "Why?"

His head angled toward the counter. "Those are grenades."

She looked at the pile of roundish objects. They didn't look like much. Like someone stacked them there without really thinking about it. "But, they're just sitting there."

"No, they're not," he hissed. *"Out."*

She backed up another foot. "How do you know they're grenades?" She glanced at the collection of containers on the shelving unit. There were microbiology culture petri dishes behind some of the bottles and several smaller bottles containing no more than a few cc's of a cloudy fluid. "They could be anything, and I see—"

"Those are M67 fragmentation grenades," he interrupted, his voice much louder now.

Everyone turned to stare at him for one brief moment, and then there was an explosion of swear words and movement as Palmer grabbed the sick student and hustled him toward the exit.

River pushed her completely out of the bathroom, then grabbed her by the arm and also marched her toward the apartment's door. "They have a range of about fifty feet. Which means we have to evacuate the entire building."

"Are you sure?" Geer asked sharply.

"There's a half-dozen of the fucking things," River answered. "At least one on the bottom has no pin."

"Anything else?" Geer asked the question as if the situation were all their fault. "How certain are you about these grenades?"

"100 percent," River said, with more than a hint of growl to his voice. "Thanks to Uncle Sam, I can ID pretty much any explosive or firearm there is. I've also spent a fair amount of time in the sandbox, where IEDs were on every other road we drove, so I'm pretty good at picking those out, too."

Geer didn't back down. "They could be a decoy, a ruse to slow us down."

"None of us are equipped to investigate if it is."

"But…" Geer began, taking a step toward the bathroom.

River made a frustrated noise at the back of his throat. "You want to play hide-and-seek in a bathroom full of fragmentation grenades, a corpse, and Dr. Frankenstein's shooter bar, go right ahead. Just wait a minute so the rest of us have time to leave." He shook his head. "It wasn't nice knowing you."

Geer's face got so red Ava was afraid he'd have a stroke.

She cleared her throat. "Sergeant River, perhaps now is not the time to piss off one of our team members."

"You mean, right before he blows up the whole building?" River snorted. "Oops."

Geer didn't say anything, but he didn't need to. His expression promised unhappy things in the near future. Still, he followed them, reluctance a noticeable hesitation in every step.

"The only team that guy is on is his own," River muttered as he shoved her out the apartment door behind Palmer and the sick kid. They half-walked half-ran down the hall and stairs to the main floor.

As they moved, River shouted at Palmer. "Radio that multiple unstable explosive devices have been found in the building. A full evacuation of this dorm and the surrounding buildings needs to happen *now*."

"Remember your hazard equipment," Ava interjected.

After Palmer relayed all that, River continued with, "There's a strong possibility of biological contamination inside one of the units. Any responders must be wearing CDC-approved safety gear." He paused for a brief but silent moment. "Just in case you're not clear, Ava *is* the CDC."

Palmer relayed that, too. There were about two seconds of silence, and then a cacophony of voices shouted questions.

They reached the main floor hallway with way too many people yelling over Palmer's radio.

She tried to make sense of the questions, demands, and outright yelling, but it was impossible.

A step behind her, glass shattered.

She jerked around just as the fire alarm began to blare.

"Fastest way to get everyone out," River told her with a shrug.

He was probably right.

They went out the door, and their investigative team surrounded them.

"What happened?"

"What did you find?"

"Evidence of the infection," she told them, raising her voice so everyone could hear her. As she finished speaking, two large vans with CDC markings pulled up.

"The CDC decontamination team has arrived. That means all of you"—Ava pointed at the police and Homeland agents around her—"need to concentrate on rounding up everyone coming out of this building. They're going to need to be isolated until we know if they're infected or not."

"Did you find any evidence of Roger Squires being involved in the terrorist attacks?" One of the Homeland agents asked. Toland?

"Not specifically. We found two dead," she told him. "I won't speculate on cause of death."

"We also found a bunch of unstable fragmentation grenades," River added, because they needed to know exactly what that threat was, too.

"Unstable?" Toland asked. "What does that mean?"

"They're rigged to explode, if moved."

Toland looked past them. "Where's Geer?"

Ava looked around for him, but no Geer.

"He was with us when I pulled the fire alarm," River said, looking around also. "Son of a *bitch*."

"He went back?" Ava asked, unable to imagine a reason for him to do that.

River stared at her for a moment, then he stepped up to Toland with a steely-eyed glare. "Do you guys have more than one agenda with this case?"

"Like what?" Toland answered, matching River's scowl with one of his own. "What possible agenda could we have besides the containment of this disease and the terrorist threat?"

"Oh my God," Ava said, staring at the Homeland agent. "The only person who answers a yes or no question with another question is a guilty person. You answered with *two* questions."

"Where did you hear that? Dr. Phil?"

"Fucking *spooks*," River growled. "Always think you know more than everybody else. This is no time to play politics or whatever game you've stuck your dicks into. We've got dead bodies, sick college students, and enough explosives to blow this entire building into tiny, tiny bits. If Geer isn't very careful, he could get himself, and a lot of other people, killed."

"I don't know what you're talking about," Toland proclaimed. "And we don't have time to argue about it. We have to get this building cleared."

River looked ready to strangle the man. Ava wanted to help, but he was right about not having time for this argument now.

But she wasn't going to let anyone she didn't trust get more than peripherally involved in the situation.

"Ben, over here," she called when she saw him approaching with three other members of the decontamination team. "Can you go inside and escort people out? There are explosives, and it's biologically hot."

"Another hot zone?" Ben shook his head. "We'd better not have too many more of these. We're getting stretched pretty thin."

"I know, but this one is serious. There are two fatalities inside, and they both appear suspicious."

Toland stepped up to Ben and gestured at his safety gear. "I need to be one of the people that goes in."

"Sorry, son," Ben said, despite the fact that Toland looked a solid ten years older than him. "She's the one giving the orders, not you." He included Ava in his reply. "They've started triaging people in a tent outside the ER entrance to the hospital. There's a line." He gave Ava a nod. "We'll clear as many people as we can, but we might need help getting into any locked apartments."

"I can get you in," River said. He turned to Palmer, who still had a hold of Roger's roommate. "Why don't you let Agent Toland ask some questions of Mr. Squires's roommate here?" River gave the agent a tight-lipped smile. "I'm sure a live witness might have a great deal of information of use to Homeland Security."

Toland pointed at the kid. "He's Roger Squires's roommate?"

"Yep, we also found two bodies in that apartment. You might want to ask him about those, too?"

"Our conversation isn't over," Toland said to Ava and River.

"What is it with everyone threatening me today?" she asked River in a tired voice. "You'd think once was enough."

"Any idiot can go through life without making enemies." River said cheerfully. "Congratulations. It takes character and intelligence to make people want to kill you."

Chapter Eleven

10:20 p.m.

What the fuck was going on with Homeland Security?

River didn't know what they were thinking, but they weren't acting in the best interests of any of the other agencies and people working the terrorist attacks and outbreak. Were they playing some game of their own?

Assholes.

They were putting a whole lot of other people—first responders, law enforcement, and civilians—in danger with their stupidity. He was going to get to the bottom of it. Just as soon as he got his hands on Geer.

The fucking fucker.

There was a stream of college kids coming out of the dorm now. Most of them looked confused, irritated, or bored. They lost those expressions as soon as they saw the cops, suits, and CDC people wearing respirators.

The CDC had set up a couple of portable light towers, throwing shadows across the ground and all those faces. Their eyes appeared shrunken and black, as if they were all already dead.

Ava began directing everyone, getting two of the cops to sort the kids into healthy looking and not so healthy. She kept glancing at him with an expectant expression, probably waiting for him to head back inside with the decontamination team to assist in evacuating the building. She probably thought she was going back in there with them. She was the lead doctor slash investigator, after all.

There was just one problem with that.

He had no intention of letting his mouse go back in.

The grenades in that bathroom were dangerous. He hadn't been exaggerating. One of them had to stay in a safe zone in case the damn things exploded.

Of the two of them, *he* was the most expendable.

She was going to be pissed if she figured it out, but he'd rather that than injured or dead.

The stream of students coming out of the building began to die down, and River caught Ben White's gaze with his own and gestured with his rifle to go in.

Ben headed for the door accompanied by another CDC guy.

"Palmer," River called out. "Go with them." He pointed at Ben.

"Roger that," Palmer said.

River turned to look at Ava, who was watching him with a frown on her face.

"Aren't we going in to clear the building and search for Geer? I thought time was—"

"We will," he interrupted. "But getting all the civilians out, the sick to the hospital, the rest to where ever you need them to go, is the priority. We've got to get all these people at least a block away without turning the move into a stampede." River shrugged. "If Geer does something stupid and blows himself up before we can get him out, I'm okay with that."

Ava let out a sigh. "He's on our side. Remember?"

River huffed. "For a good guy, he sure is an asshole." He glanced around. Things were still too chaotic. "Time to start the roundup." He'd managed to beg a radio off one of the cops, attaching it to Ava's belt so she wouldn't lose it.

"Okay, everyone," Ava said over the radio. "We need to move these people a block away. Homeland Agents, you're in charge of the healthy group. Take two of the El Paso police officers to help you. The rest of the police, please come see me for your assignments. Agent Toland has custody of our witness, and Sergeant River—"

"Will bring up the rear, corral latecomers, and shoo everyone else away," he interrupted.

She didn't look unhappy at his interruption, just added, "That's it. Let's go."

River waited until most of the students were moving, albeit slowly, before lagging behind and slipping back inside the building.

He found Palmer, Ben, and the other CDC guy knocking on doors and left them to it.

He approached Squires's apartment the same way he would have approached any hostile location, moving steadily forward with intense caution and awareness of his surroundings. Aside from the fire alarm blaring, the hallway was void of any sound, movement, or people.

The door to the apartment was locked.

Son of a bitch. Geer was in there. No one else would have locked it.

River pulled his lock picking tools out of the side of his pack and went to work. At least all the noise from the alarm would cover any sounds he might be making. The door open, he put his lock picks away and grabbed his weapon.

Cautiously, he stopped just inside the doorway to see if he

could detect Geer's location.

A shadow moved down the hall toward the bathroom with the corpse, telling River where he was.

Fucked, that's where. The asshole was currently in *fucking fuckville*, but moving quickly into s*tupidfuckerton*.

River walked toward the bathroom on soft, silent feet, his rifle snug to the hollow of his shoulder, the business end leveled heart-high on a man Geer's height.

As he crossed the last few feet toward his destination, Geer's back was clearly visible through the doorway. He examined the selves in the tub, picking up and putting down one container after another.

River glanced at the grenades on the counter on the opposite side of the small room.

They hadn't moved. Yet.

Geer put a container down and picked another one up, lifting it so he could see the bottom.

"Put that shit down before you kill yourself with it," River said in a calm, even tone.

The agent froze, then glanced over his shoulder. "I'm under orders to collect evidence." He didn't put the container down.

"Of what? Reckless disregard for human life? Bingo. You won that contest already."

"My orders come from a higher source than you," Geer said from between clenched teeth. Sweat gathered into beads at his hairline, then ran down from his temples.

"What a coincidence. So do mine." River completely ran out of patience for the moron. "Put it down and back out of the room. *Now*."

"Damn it, I have orders to find the source of the infection."

"Every person working this disaster has the same orders, asshole. What makes you so special?"

"You don't understand." Geer blew out a noisy breath

and blinked. "I can't believe I'm saying this, but get that microbiologist up here. I can't figure out what's what."

The dude was fucking nuts.

"Geer, five feet behind you are enough explosives to turn you and anyone in that room with you into nothing more than pink mist. There's no way she's coming up here until those grenades are rendered safe."

"We don't have time for safe," Geer bellowed, going from rational to insane in about two seconds flat. His hands shook so hard River could see them vibrating. "Thousands of lives are at stake." He looked prepared to do just about anything. A level of willingness to do a job that could get him and other people killed. And he hadn't hesitated to do it.

Geer's behavior suddenly made horrible sense.

"What the fuck haven't you told the CDC?" River asked softly, watching the other man intently. Was he wobbling on his feet? "Someone gave you additional orders. *Different* orders? What are they?"

The agent shook his head, but not in negation, more like he was trying to shake something loose from his own head. "We got a tip about this attack. We just didn't know when."

"You knew who, though?" Geer never once showed surprise. That had bothered him earlier, but now it made sense. "You *knew* about Roger Squires?"

Geer gave a wheezy sort of laugh and tried to wipe his face with one hand, but his hand was inside a glove, and his face was behind the respirator. "We thought we had him contained. He was leading us to his recruiter, but instead, this outbreak happened. Then the explosions. We realized we'd lost control of the asset." He looked at his hand like he'd never seen it before.

"Asset? You considered an American college student recruited by God-knows-what terrorist group an *asset*?" Of all the stupid-ass things to do. "This is why no one likes working with you guys," River said, not bothering to hide his disgust. "You're a bunch of arrogant fuckers."

Geer's expression hardened, and he turned back to the shelving unit.

"What else did you find?" River asked. When Geer glanced at him with a frown, he added, "You've been up here a while. What else did you find?"

"Nothing."

"You expect me to believe you? Not happening. *What else*?"

When Geer didn't respond, River decided it was time to go fishing.

"You were looking for a paper trail. Something to lead back to whoever this kid was working with, right? Did you find it?"

Geer just stared at him, blinking owlishly.

River snorted. "You didn't. That's why you're in such a panic and so willing to blow yourself up." River thrust his chin at the assorted scientist equipment and solutions in the bathroom. "You're not going to find the answer just sitting on a piece of paper, waiting for you to pick it up. Dr. Lloyd and the rest of the CDC people are the only ones who can figure out what this shit is." He tightened his mouth and gestured with his rifle. "Time to get out, Agent Geer. Now."

Geer didn't move for a long couple of seconds, but finally, he came out of the bathroom and walked past River. "You're making a big mistake."

"Yeah, yeah, that's what all the assholes say. Let's go before those grenades go off and I have to share my ride to the pearly gates with you."

"I'm not the only asshole around," Geer muttered thickly.

They got out of the apartment and down the hall without incident, but on the first flight of stairs heading down, Geer stumbled and had to catch himself on the handrail to avoid falling. His arm shook like he'd overdosed on coffee and hadn't slept in days.

"You okay?" River asked

Geer didn't respond. He walked a couple more steps, turned the corner, and paused at the top of the next flight of stairs. Slowly, he leaned forward, then began to fall.

River reached out with a hand to catch him, but he misjudged how fast Geer was going down and missed.

The Homeland Security agent dropped like a sack of heavy artillery and mostly rolled down the stairs. He landed at the bottom of the flight on his back, his arms and legs spread out so haphazardly River knew the other man was unconscious.

Just what he didn't need. Dead weight.

Was the agent actually dead?

River leaned down and noted the other man's chest rising. Okay, so he was alive. Great. River grabbed one arm and hoisted Geer over his shoulder in a fireman's carry.

At the bottom of the stairs, he ran into a couple of students who looked at him as if he were the boogeyman, then ran the whole way down the stairs ahead of him.

River made it to the bottom floor and managed to get out the side entrance without dropping his cargo.

The lawn where all the students had been gathering was empty now, with a couple of police cars parked in front. River followed the noise of people up the street and realized Ava had moved everyone a block away. He was halfway there when a guy in a CDC hazmat suit ran toward him with a rolling gurney. One of Ben White's guys.

"What happened?"

"He passed out and fell down the stairs," River said. "He was shaky before that and looked like he might be running a fever."

"I'm marking him as showing symptoms," the guy said,

taking a marker out of his tool bag and writing exactly that on the respirator on Geer's face. He put the marker away, then grabbed the gurney and was about to go back into the fray of first responders, police, and hysterical students.

"Wait," River said. He opened Geer's tool bag and pulled out a small, tattered notebook and two cell phones. One of the phones looked like new, the other had a cracked screen and a few dings and nicks in the casing. He put the new one back, then shoved the beat-up phone and the notebook into his own tool bag. "Okay, you're good to go."

The CDC guy pushed the gurney to a waiting ambulance, conferred with a couple of hazmat-suited paramedics, then loaded him into the vehicle.

River caught sight of Agent Toland and the other two Homeland agents arguing with someone, punctuating whatever they were saying with sharp, forceful gestures. One of them shifted and took a half-step to one side.

They were arguing with his mouse.

She spotted him through the same narrow gap between the men shouting at her and he saw her lips form the word, "You!"

Shit, his radio was still off.

He winced, mouthed, "Sorry." And turned the sound back up on his Bluetooth.

"—the hell have you been?" Ava shouted in his ear.

The other men on the same channel winced. She could sure yell when she wanted to.

He sucked in a breath to answer, but she wasn't done.

"You could have been killed! What if those grenades had gone off?"

"The building had to be cleared," he managed to say when she stopped yelling long enough to take a breath.

"Ben and Palmer were doing that," she snarled as she pushed her way past the agents to stand in front of him with her hands on her hips. "Another person going in there was monumentally…" She paused, looking him up and down before finishing with, "*Stupid*."

"I call bullshit on that," he said, crossing his arms over his chest. "If I hadn't gone in and gotten Agent Geer, he'd have died in there."

That got Toland's attention. "What do you mean, you got Geer out? Where is he?"

"In one of the ambulances." River turned and pointed it out.

All three Homeland agents moved toward it at a run.

"You," Ava said, as if she were crushing glass with her teeth, "took an unacceptable risk."

Some risks were necessary. "Define 'unacceptable?'"

Her mouth opened just as a wave of light, heat, noise, and vibration smacked into him from behind.

Chapter Twelve

11:16 p.m.

Behind River, light bloomed, followed almost simultaneously by heat and an invisible kick, knocking Ava backward off her feet. Airborne and out of control, fear had enough time to yank out the bottom of her stomach before she hit the ground.

Something grabbed her, so she landed only partially on the unforgiving pavement, her left elbow and hip cushioned on the resilient elastic of muscle and man.

River.

He simply didn't know when to quit, did he?

The heat wave continued to roll over them, the force of the blast tossing smaller objects like paper and soda cans through the air.

River covered her body with his, tucked her head into his chest, and held it there protectively.

She wanted to punch him for taking all the risks and wiggled to get free. He released her far too slowly.

"Are you okay?" he asked as he finally allowed her to

inch out from the shelter of his body.

"I'm fine." She had to work to unclench her teeth. "For someone who's been blown up twice today." She got to her feet and brushed herself off.

His gaze searching, he took a step toward her, his hands reaching for her.

She waved him off. "No, no, I'm fine. You, however…" She looked him over. He'd taken the brunt of the blast for her. "Are you injured?"

"I don't think so." He spun around and showed her his backside. "Anything?"

"No, you appear to be completely intact." She looked past him at the obliterated building. A ring of fires burned in a wide circle around what used to be the home of over fifty people.

The total devastation sent a shiver over her. River had been right about how large a blast those grenades would cause.

"That," she said, her voice rising, "is how I define 'unacceptable.'" She smacked him on the side of his head. "If you'd taken just a minute or two longer, you'd have been in there."

He stared at the remains of the building.

The roof was completely gone, most of the walls, too. All that was left were bits of the steel rebar used in the support beams and framing. "That explosion was way more powerful than it should have been."

His observation stopped her from ranting further. "What do you mean?"

"I only saw six grenades. Even if they all went off at the same time, they wouldn't have been able to cause an explosion *that* big. Destroy the apartment they were in and maybe the ones surrounding it, but not the whole building."

"Are you suggesting something else caused the

explosion?"

"Or added to its power."

"Like gas? I didn't smell any, did you?"

"No."

"What does that leave us with?"

"Deliberate sabotage with either additional explosives or some other flammable something extra."

Someone planned this? "Why would anyone want to blow up a dorm?"

"I can think of two reasons." He turned to regard her. Gone was the joker, the good old boy who didn't take anything too seriously. In his place stood a confident, experienced soldier capable of doing whatever it took to reach his mission goals.

Lord help anyone who got in his way.

"What two reasons?"

"The main reason terrorists attack—to inspire fear and panic. Secondly, to destroy evidence of whatever they're doing and who might be involved."

She glanced at the burning debris. "I'd say they accomplished all of that."

"Maybe not." His eyes narrowed in a way that changed his face from dangerous to outright scary.

"You found something?" she asked, lowering her voice.

"I found Geer," he corrected. "Before I handed him over to medical, I may have helped myself to a couple of items from his tool bag. Things I think he found in Squires's apartment."

"Things Homeland Security is looking for?"

"Probably, but I'm not feeling the need to share at the moment. I'm not sure their goals are the same as ours. They seem pretty tight-lipped about too many things, and they're more uncooperative than usual."

"That's an understatement," Ava agreed without reservation. Geer and then Toland had both become pretty big pains in the ass very quickly.

The wailing of fire trucks and police vehicles blared, getting closer and closer.

"Oh no." She sighed. "What are the chances all these people have the proper infection control gear on?"

"Not a fucking chance in hell."

She glanced around, looking for the law-enforcement members of her team. "We don't have enough people to keep all these students separated from the incoming personnel and the sick ones from everyone else."

"I'll see if I can talk to the fire captain," River said in a tone that made it a suggestion rather than an order. "You worry about the students and the sick. Broadcast what you want everyone to do. Make your orders simple, and solve one problem at a time. In a situation this fluid, it's a bad idea to try to assume how things are going to go."

She nodded. "Be ready to zig, not zag."

His grin bolstered her flagging confidence. "Exactly."

"Okay," she said, not entirely sure she was, in fact, okay. "Let's go."

She didn't see him again for thirty-five minutes.

During that time, Ava managed to get all the students sorted out into three separate camps.

One, the obviously sick. Thirteen men and women sent to the hospital in a transit bus commandeered for that purpose.

Two, the largest group, forty-seven people with direct contact with the sick, but showing no symptoms. They were in the process of being sent to one of the university's gymnasiums, where they would stay under observation for the next twenty-four hours. Minimum.

Three people under suspicion of being involved in the terror plot. They were rushed off by two of the Homeland Security agents. Ava didn't get their names, but she did take a couple of pictures of the group with her phone.

River kept most of the newly-arrived fire and police

personnel from coming into contact with any of the students. The firefighters working to put out the fire put on their sealed facemasks and breathed oxygen from tanks. Had River suggested that?

The biggest nuisance now was the media, TV crews, journalists, and photographers. They started showing up only minutes behind the fire trucks, getting in the way, asking everyone questions, and trying to physically investigate what remained of the dorm.

Ava hadn't spoken with any of them yet, but she'd seen River and a couple of their policemen herding them away. Somewhat forcibly, with his rifle held in such a way that no one could mistake his willingness to use it.

With the last of the students getting on to the bus, she'd better check in with River. Before he shot someone.

She found him with a man wearing a respirator— Homeland Security Agent Dozer. The two were talking quietly about twenty feet away from them, but keeping an eye on the gathered media people.

She approached River, the clipboard she had been using to keep track of people in her hands. She needed to find someone with a complete list of who lived in the building that no longer existed.

He caught sight of her and waved her over. "Agent Dozer has information for us."

The bald man resembled a rough-cut granite boulder and looked just as friendly.

"Agent Dozer," Ava said.

"Doctor." The agent nodded respectfully to her. His voice was deep, but had a sharpness to it that told her something was wrong.

"Dozer was just telling me that he's unaware of any orders Geer had specific to searching Roger Squires's apartment," River said quietly. "Geer, Toland, and the other two guys were supposed to look for any terrorist connections, but only if it was deemed safe by the CDC to do so."

"Unaware?" Ava asked. "Could he have gotten orders you weren't aware of?"

The agent shrugged. "Geer has political connections here in Texas. It's possible someone called in a favor." He said it like it happened often and wasn't a concern, as if it were nothing more than a simple annoyance.

"A *favor*?" Ava asked, enraged at the stupidity of it. She wanted to kick someone, punch and scream and shout, but she could do nothing with more than a half-dozen TV reporters watching. Even at a distance, body language spoke volumes.

So did shouting profanities at the top of her voice.

No. No shouting profanities while the media was watching. She could wait until later and attempt to calm down. Then she would tear a strip off several people.

She pasted a smile on her face and said in a suitably professional tone, "Does that burning building behind you look like something that should have resulted from a mere favor? This situation isn't a simple biology experiment gone wrong or the result of a couple of students attempting to make rocket fuel in their room. None of this was an *accident*."

Dozer tilted his head to one side and bowed slightly to her. "I agree. Unfortunately, we can't ask Geer what he was doing. He hasn't regained consciousness. He's at the hospital now, but with the number of sick continuing to rise, every hospital in the city is damn near overrun. We don't have the people to station someone at his bedside waiting for him to wake up."

"What about the other agents he was with?" River asked. "Toland has been a pain in the ass, too."

"He claims he was just following Geer's orders. Geer was senior. He told him the CDC was trying to cover up the real cause of the outbreak and blame it on a bunch of stupid, but innocent, students."

"But we didn't even know about the student connection until Roger Squires showed up at the coffee shop this afternoon."

"Yeah," Dozer said, with a weak smile. "I didn't believe that story, either."

She glanced at the smoldering building. "And now we'll never know Roger Squires's role in all of this."

"His roommate might have information that can tell us quite a bit," Dozer said. "I'm going to interview him now."

"Please let me or Sergeant River know if you find out anything useful."

"Will do." He left them.

River glanced around. With the students gone, some of the emergency crews were leaving. Firefighters were still soaking down the remains of the building, but the fires were out.

"I have something to show you, but not here," River told her softly. "We need a place to examine what I found and talk in private."

"I also need to talk to Dr. Rodrigues and deliver the samples I took." Ava's shoulders slumped. "She isn't going to be happy with me. This"—she gestured at the smoking ruins—"was not what she wanted me to accomplish." She'd be lucky if she didn't lose her job.

"We learned quite a bit before it blew up," he said. "We now know that Squires was more than peripherally involved in today's attacks, but finding grenades and a mad scientist's beaker collection in there wasn't something anyone saw coming. I think your boss is going to be fine with the headway we've made on the investigative side."

"My job was to track down the source of the outbreak. I have some samples, sure, but I doubt it's going to be enough. Our only suspect is dead, and there's probably not enough left of the corpses we found in the apartment to figure out their identities."

"Listen, Squires and probably a few others were up to their eyeballs in antiestablishment, antigovernment, anti-America shit. We're lucky we didn't find a lot more dead bodies." He looked around, then added, "Let's see who's left of our team."

Ava sent out a text message to everyone and got four responses from the El Paso police.

"If you need a local for anything, a ride to a location, *anything*," Officer Palmer said, "call me."

"Thank you." It was refreshing to have someone eager to help rather than getting in the way. "Do you mind if I mention your offer of assistance to Homeland Security and the FBI? They may need the same kind of help."

"Absolutely." He saluted both of them, then went to his own vehicle and drove away.

"Good man there," River said. "Didn't panic, didn't need orders to get the roommate out of the apartment. As soon as he heard the word *grenade*, he hustled the kid out of there."

"I wish we had ten more of him."

Ava and River took their CDC van back to the hospital. He drove while she texted and tried to call Dr. Rodrigues, but she got no response.

When they arrived back at the decontamination area at the hospital, it was to see several military vehicles and camouflaged soldiers wearing respirators and gloves along with their weapons.

"The National Guard?" Ava asked.

"No," River said. "These are all medical. They're from Fort Bliss."

"Oh. Dr. Rodrigues probably asked for more help."

"That's not good news, is it?"

"No, not really."

He parked, and they made their way into the decontamination area.

Henry must have been on the lookout for them, because he met her outside the decontamination tent and took her samples. "You can tell me more about these when you're done here," he said, patting the sample case.

"Do you know where Rodrigues is?" Ava asked.

"Giving a press conference," he answered, walking backward away from her, "but she should be finished soon. She wants to talk to you. You're supposed to meet her at my home away from home." Henry stopped walking for a moment. "Is it true you blew up an entire building?"

Ava rolled her eyes and glanced at River. "I told you she wasn't going to be happy about that."

Chapter Thirteen

12:45 a.m., March 28th

"You didn't blow anything up," River told Ava. "In fact, the situation could have been much worse if we hadn't gotten most of the residents out of the building. Remember that." He nodded at Henry. "See you in a few."

Henry saluted, then hurried off with Ava's sample container held firmly in both hands.

When River glanced at Ava again, he didn't like the deep furrows on her forehead. "What's up, doc?"

She didn't even smile. "I'm tired, hungry, and frustrated, because it doesn't feel like we're getting anywhere." Her hands tightened into fists. "It seems like we're eight steps behind the bad guys and losing ground."

"It's not as terrible as all that. We've got a trail to follow, and it's going to lead us where we need to go. The worst thing you can do at this stage is get impatient." He thumbed over his shoulder at the male decontamination tent. "Is that where I'm going?"

"Yes, standard procedure." She led the way.

Despite washing their hands in three different kinds of solutions, they kept their respirators on.

After they were finished, they walked to Henry's mobile lab-in-a-box, but neither Henry nor Rodrigues was visible.

Ava sighed, then sat down on the pavement and leaned against the metal outer wall of the lab. "I could sleep right here," she muttered, closing her eyes.

"Yeah?"

"Yeah. I learned to take catnaps whenever I had a chance when I was working the Ebola outbreak. I thought residency was hard." She cracked her eyes open and shook her head. "There were a couple of weeks during the outbreak where there was a gap in having enough healthcare workers. Many of the ones who'd worked through the initial few weeks had died, and no new people were arriving to take their places."

She sighed, stopped talking, and closed her eyes again.

He could imagine her working for days without much sleep or food. She was one of those people who didn't give up when the situation got difficult. She'd have found a way to get around it. That was seriously *hot*.

"Quit flirting with me, Mouse."

She cracked one eye open to glare at him. "What?"

"Catnapping is a skill all elite soldiers learn. We might have to be awake for days at a time. Short power naps are the only way to function when shit's going down." He winked at her. "You just proved you're a badass mentally, as well as cuter than fuck."

She snorted and closed her eyes again. "No one in this outfit is cute."

"Are you kidding me? You're totally banging."

She cracked that eyelid open again. "You must have a respirator fetish," she said in the same get-real tone, but the corners of her eyes wrinkled in a smile; he'd gotten the response he wanted. Just enough silliness to lighten her mood, without making it awkward. Because after all this was over, his mouse was going to find herself in a very personal, private, intimate mousetrap with him.

A half-dozen individuals came toward them from the direction of the hospital. Half of them were in hazmat suits, and the other three were wearing respirators. One of those was Dr. Rodrigues.

"Incoming," he said to Ava as he got to his feet.

She pushed herself up to stand next to him.

"Dr. Lloyd, Sergeant River," Dr. Rodrigues began before she'd even come to a stop. "This is Fort Bliss Base Commander Major Ramsey, FEMA Assistant Director Sanderson, Homeland Security Supervisory Special Agent Marble. We need your debrief regarding the university dorm explosion. We've gotten some details from some of the Homeland Security agents that accompanied you, but, quite frankly…" She stopped to take in a breath. "I'm not sure I can believe their report."

"Who gave you the report, Agent Dozer or Agent Toland?" River asked

"Toland," one of the men wearing a respirator said.

"I'm afraid Agents Geer and Toland had different priorities than Dr. Lloyd and myself." River paused for a moment to let that sink in. "Instead of complying with Dr. Lloyd's orders to leave the building once we discovered two corpses and six live and primed to go off fragmentation grenades, Agent Geer remained to search it. He declined to share with us what he was searching for, but he did say he had orders." River put air quotes around the word orders. He looked at Marble, dressed in a hazmat suit so clean it had to have just come out of a box. "What orders do your people have here, sir?"

"They're to find the terrorist cell and assist the CDC."

"They sure have a funny way of going about all that," River said.

The Homeland agent's face didn't change or move one iota when he said, "Agent Toland reported that you and Dr. Lloyd ignored his concerns and suggestions as well as opportunities to gather evidence."

River opened his mouth to refute that crap when Ava stepped on his foot and moved to stand a step in front of him.

"With all due respect, Agent Marble, Agents Geer's and Toland's demands to investigate the dorm and identify and arrest suspects before the building had been properly cleared put many people at risk. I explained the protocol, but the moment those orders became inconvenient, they ignored them."

"We are in the midst of an ongoing terrorist attack on United States home soil," Marble countered with a cold, self-righteous tilt to his mouth. "Ending this attack must be everyone's top priority. In order to apprehend the people responsible for that explosion, the one at Fort Bliss and other places today, some law-enforcement individuals may be required to take additional risks. My people are prepared and willing to do that. Are you willing to give your life in service to your country?"

Dr. Rodrigues stared at the agent as if he'd punched her in the stomach.

Ava stood a little taller, and River took a half-step closer to her. A silent way to say he had her back.

"I am, and I do it every day," she said, her voice steady. "But I don't think you realize the true scope of the risks I'm talking about."

"Please," Marble said, his cold smile turning lethal. "Educate me."

River had to work to keep his face immobile, when he really, really wanted to smirk at the other man. His mouse was about to school Homeland Security.

"Even in the face of an armed man, a law-enforcement professional might take risks to draw the shooter out so someone else could attack from a different direction." She paused. "Would you agree with that?"

"Yes."

She tilted her head to one side. "But that assumes you know who your enemy is, where he is, and what weapons he might have. Biological terrorism doesn't work that way. You could be carrying the pathogen right now in your nasal passages. One sneeze could infect several other people, because all they have to do to be hit by the weapon is stand within five feet of you and breathe."

Listening to her lecturing the asshole made River hard. He had it bad.

Ava's voice turned stern. "You and your people are unqualified to make a risk assessment in this kind of battle, Agent Marble. In Agent Geer's rush to find evidence, he may very well have infected himself and contaminated his clothing with the pathogen. Anyone else touching his suit could infect themselves if they so much as rub their eyes before washing their hands."

"She's correct," Dr. Rodrigues put in. "The hardest part of controlling any outbreak of any infectious disease is compliance with isolation and prevention procedures. Because people can't see the danger, they seem to unconsciously assume one of two things: that everyone is infected, or no one."

Marble's lips twisted as if he were eating something distasteful.

Ava looked at Dr. Rodrigues. "Thirteen of the students living in that dorm are showing symptoms. The rest have been sent to the location you set up for asymptomatic isolation until they can be cleared."

Fort Bliss Commander Major Ramsey took a short step toward them, his gaze on River. "Tell me about the grenades."

"Military issue. Six of them. They'd been piled in a pyramid, with one or more of the pins gone from the three on the bottom." The major had maintained a calm expression until River mentioned the placement of the grenades, and then he winced.

"Why is that important?" Ava asked.

"Military training," River muttered.

"How could they have gotten get them?" Dr. Rodrigues asked.

"Black market. Arms dealing," Major Ramsey said.

"Grenades weren't the only things we found," Ava said to her boss. "There was also a large number of unmarked substances in the same room as the grenades. Some of them appeared to be cultures, but I wasn't able to get any samples of them before we discovered the grenades and evacuated."

"Did you get samples from other areas close by?"

"Yes, ma'am, but not as many as I would have liked."

"That will have to do."

"Dr. Rodrigues," River said. "I'd like permission to continue investigating the Roger Squires connection to the attacks."

"His family and home have been cleared by the CDC and Homeland. Nothing was found."

"I'd like to widen the search to his friends and acquaintances, fellow students, and teachers at the university."

"Background checks have been done on all of his known associates," Agent Marble said. "We haven't had the manpower available to investigate in person yet."

"That young man looked me in the eyes, no farther away from me than you are now," Ava told the agent, her voice rising. "And threatened harm if the United States government didn't do what he wanted. He had a *bomb* in his backpack and another one strapped to his body. He was willing to kill himself for whatever cause he was involved with." She swallowed. "Something, or someone, convinced him that his own country was so awful he felt he had to give his life to make a point. That something or someone is still out there. I'd like to stop them."

"We've seen student radicalization in other countries," River said. "Just not too often here in the USA."

"I'm well aware of the possibility, Sergeant," Marble said. He turned to look at Dr. Rodrigues. "I asked for the same investigation an hour ago, but was denied."

Did every smug asshole work for Homeland Security?

"We didn't have the information an hour ago that we have now," Dr. Rodrigues said with a lift of her chin that said she didn't care if Homeland was unhappy. "Now that Dr. Lloyd and Sergeant River are available, they can take on that task."

"I'd like to talk to Squires's roommate," River said.

"He's being questioned now," Marble said.

River shrugged. "Not by me or Dr. Lloyd."

"He wasn't making a whole lot of sense when I left." Marble sighed. "He appeared to see things in the room that weren't there."

"Shit."

"Where is he now?" Ava asked. "I'd like to examine him and take some samples."

"We talked to him in one of the family conference rooms near the ER. A nurse brought in a cot for him to lie on. We stationed a police officer outside his room." Marble didn't seem too pleased to be leading their merry band, but he would look like a dick if he said no. The whole group went back into the hospital.

"Have you released the pathogen to the public yet?" Ava asked.

"Yes. *Neisseria Meningitidis*." Dr. Rodrigues said. We've

confirmed it's a new strain and it's resistant to every antibiotic we've got. It seems to prefer brain tissue most of the time, but if it does get a foothold in the lungs, it's proving to be deadly there, too."

"Any idea why this one seems so easy to transmit?"

"Not yet. It's going to take more time before we have the genetic details."

A few steps ahead of them, Marble paused to open a door. He went inside.

River followed him in, Ava right behind him.

There was no one else in the room.

No one at all.

Chapter Fourteen

1:10 a.m.

Ava stood in the doorway of the small room, staring at the empty cot. "Where is he?"

No one had an answer for her.

"Fuck," River spat. "Where's your guy?" he asked Marble. "The one who's supposed to be questioning the kid?"

"I don't know." Marble's cheekbones were slashed with red. "But I'm going to find out." He charged out of the room, punching in a number on his cell phone as he went.

"Ethan Harris is likely infected," Dr. Rodrigues said. "He's supposed to stay in isolation. If he goes anywhere outside the hospital, he could easily infect anyone he comes in contact with. We *need* to find him."

Energy drained out of Ava, leaving her exhausted and shaky. "I don't even know where to start looking."

River cleared his throat. "I may be able to help with that." He opened the tool pouch attached to his belt, then strode over to the small coffee table and laid a cell phone and a notebook on it. "These came from Roger Squires's dorm room. Agent Geer had them on him when he collapsed."

"He gave them to you?" Ava asked. She couldn't see him cooperating that way.

"Not exactly."

"You took them from Geer without his knowledge?" Dr. Rodrigues asked.

"He wasn't awake for me to ask him," River said, his tone unapologetic. "I did ask if he found anything before he collapsed. He said he hadn't."

"He lied." What was wrong with these people? How was she supposed to work with people who refused to understand how dangerous the situation was?

"Whatever is in these was worth him risking a lot of lives," River said. "Including his own."

"You waited until Marble left before mentioning these. Do you have a reason for that?" Dr. Rodrigues asked.

"I don't think most of the Homeland Security agents involved in this disaster are playing with the same rule book as the CDC," he answered. "Out of all the agents I've met since I arrived, only one has shown any respect for your authority and orders—Agent Dozer."

Dr. Rodrigues gave River a sharp look. "I've worked with him before, so perhaps he has a better understanding of what we do." She muttered something else under her breath Ava didn't catch, then ordered, "Give me the phone."

River handed it to her, then handed the notebook to Ava. Now he had a smile that was all *I'm sorry* and *it was for your own good.*

She took it without comment, because if she said anything, it was going to be angry and unprofessional.

She scanned the notebook. The first few pages had lecture notes in a political science class focusing on international politics. About a dozen pages in, the notes became less organized and interspersed with rhetoric slogans denouncing American interference in other countries. Class notes ended at page twenty-five. From there on, the writing in the notebook was disjointed and displayed the angry rhetoric usually seen and heard from terrorists outside of the United States.

All that was, at this point, almost expected. What she didn't expect to see were the chemical formulae and biological observations normally seen in a microbiology lab written in the margins and in the middle of unrelated sentences.

"Ma'am," Ava said, turning the notebook toward Dr. Rodrigues and showing her a page.

"The notes indicate an experiment designed to create a drug-resistant strain to the antibiotics we'd normally use to treat a patient with bacterial meningitis."

"Fuck me," River breathed.

"Language," Dr. Rodrigues warned, without looking up.

Ava turned the page and gasped.

Both River and her boss looked at her.

"What?" Dr. Rodrigues asked sharply.

"They also tried mixing methicillin-resistant *Staphylococcus Aureus* with meningitis bacteria in order to create a new resistant strain." She searched the notebook for more, but found no mention of the results from either experiment. "There's nothing here about results." Ava flipped through the pages in hopes that she missed it the first time.

"If whoever did this was successful," Dr. Rodrigues said in a tight tone, "we could be looking at an untreatable meningococcal disease outbreak capable of killing thousands of people."

"We need to find the source," River said. "We need to find their lab."

"You need to find them. Period," Dr. Rodrigues said. She handed River the phone. "There are a number of texts between Ethan Harris, Roger Squires, and what looks like

several other students. I can't make sense of half of it. Text speak is not one of my skills." She looked ready to pronounce on a dead body. "Do whatever is necessary, but find them."

"Yes, ma'am," she and River said at the same time.

"I'll talk to Agent Dozer and fill him in on that you two are trying to hunt down Ethan Harris," Dr. Rodrigues said. "As for the rest of them…what you share is at your discretion."

"Yes, ma'am," Ava said.

Rodrigues frowned. "Find a quiet spot and decode that notebook and phone. Eat, while you're at it."

"Yeah, it's going to take me a few minutes to untangle all these messages and decipher this book," River said with a wince.

Ava led the way out of the hospital and back into the area the CDC had commandeered. Despite the late hour, there were lots of people around. Hospital staff, CDC personnel, police, EMS, and the National Guard. It took them a few minutes to wash, remove their respirators, and change into clean scrubs before they could go into the clean tent.

Food consisted of more MREs. Ava had eaten a lot of them in Africa during the Ebola crisis. The one she grabbed ended up being spaghetti and meatballs. Not her favorite, but not bad, either.

"I can't believe we got blown up again," she muttered. Her bruises had bruises, making her whole body one big ache. The moment of the explosion lighting up the night sky behind River would forever be imprinted on her retinas. For a moment, one terrifying second, she'd thought they were all dead. The pain of landing hard had almost been welcome, because it proved they were still alive.

"This kind of terrorism is ruthless," River said, his voice matter-of-fact as he ate. "These terrorists want to hurt as many innocent people as possible. Incite as much fear as possible." He leaned forward, ducking his head to meet her gaze. He gave her an it'll-be-okay-princess smile. "Don't let that fear influence you too much."

That grin made her want to punch him. "Are you sure you're not underestimating the danger? You went back into that building without telling me." She shoved a forkful of food into her mouth to give herself a chance to think before she said something she might regret. "You promised to talk to me, to share your ideas and plans with me." A promise he'd broken. She sucked in a breath and ground out, "*Remember?*"

He pinned her in place with a gaze sharp enough to flay muscle from bone.

And said nothing.

"Sorry," she mumbled after several seconds, her face heating until it was uncomfortable. "Didn't mean to yell. I just…you scared me."

His stare didn't lighten at all. "You've got to trust me to do my job. It's not always possible for me to consult you on every decision."

"I'm not your mother," she snapped. "I don't expect you to ask permission to pee. I do expect you to tell me when you're about to do something that might *kill* you."

He raised an eyebrow. "Are we back to traffic and risk assessment?"

She shoved her MRE to one side and planted both palms on the table so she could get right in his face and snarl at him. "I turned around, and you were *gone*."

He sat back, a grin flirting with his lips, his posture relaxed. "I knew you'd argue with me about going, and I didn't have time to convince you it was the right thing to do."

"No," she said, forcing herself to sit down, to not reach out with her bare hands to strangle him. "You assumed I would argue and took it upon yourself to decide to go in there, leaving me to look like a fool every time someone asked me where you'd gone."

He frowned. "Who…?" His lips twisted, and he said something under his breath. "Fucking Homeland agents."

"Yes, them. Thank you for cementing their opinion of me as a minor inconvenience. I'll be lucky if I can order someone to get me a cup of coffee."

That surprised a bark of laughter out of him, but his humor didn't last. Maybe there was something hopeless in the expression on her face or in the bleak tone of her voice that even she could hear. Whatever the reason, he mumbled, "*Fuck*." And rubbed a hand over his face. "I'm sorry," he said, reaching out to offer his hand, palm up, on the table. "I'm sorry, Mouse. Can we agree to trust each other?"

She stared at his hand. He had no idea how hard this was for her.

She blew out a breath, then met his gaze. "You think a handshake is going to change how you do things when the situation goes sideways? When you make another one of your executive decisions?"

"It will, if we agree not to make a decision that will get either of us killed."

"What if we can't talk?"

"That's where the trust part comes in." He wiggled his fingers.

Could she trust him? He'd backed her up with all of the Homeland agents. Despite his flirting, he treated her like a professional when anyone else was around.

She slowly put hers in his.

His hold was gentle, but firm. "My job is to support you. I can't do that if you don't trust me. I know it's hard, but if I disappear, it's because I've identified a danger, and I have an opportunity to remove that danger. I'm not going to do anything just to piss you off. Unlike several of our Homeland agent friends, I don't have another agenda. My only concern is making it safe for *you* to do your job."

She looked away. He made it sound so rational, so easy to let him put himself in harm's way, when all she wanted to do was…what? Keep him safe? No one in this entire city was safe. Her head might understand that, but her gut was tight with terror and something more she didn't want to think too closely about. "What if I need you…for something, and you're not around because you've gone off on a one-man mission?"

He ducked his head until he caught her gaze. "I can't promise shit won't go down, but I do promise to be available for anything you need from me, if at all possible." He grinned at her, a boyish, teasing smile. "And I am available for *anything* you need from me."

It was a lot harder to pretend his words didn't affect her than it should have been. She rolled her eyes and pulled her hand out of his grasp. "Stop it."

He chuckled and picked up the cell phone again.

A distant roar, followed by repeated pops, jerked Ava's head up. Explosions. Gunfire.

"Oh no," Ava whispered. She glanced at River, but aside from stiffness in his shoulders, he seemed engrossed in reading text messages. "Will this change anything for us?"

"Not really." He did look up then, his gaze on her face. "I've seen this kind of tactic used before."

"Tactic?"

"Continually hammer a dug-in or fortified enemy with multiple attacks at random locations. This creates an environment of confusion and pulls your enemy's focus away from what's really important."

"Blowing up another building is just a distraction?"

"There's likely more than one reason to do it, but distraction would be at the top of the list. Their goal is probably to pull resources away from dealing with the outbreak and the sites that have already been bombed."

Ava couldn't imagine the mindset it would take to

conceive of such a ruthless strategy.

River didn't sound surprised or even concerned. Like this kind of *tactic* was to be expected. How many times had he faced this scenario in order for him to recognize it with no dismay? How burned out, how tired, how emotionally battered did a man have to get to live in that kind of hell inside his head? Her whole body ached at the thought, at the realization.

River had been that beaten and damaged. And yet, he still managed to tease her every chance he got.

A squawk of amplified white noise crested over the area, then a firm male voice said, "Please remain where you are. If you try to leave hospital property, you will be detained. Water and food will be distributed by members of the National Guard."

The message repeated.

Activity outside the clean tent had River pocketing the cell phone and standing up. A moment later, Agent Dozer walked in.

"What's going on?" Ava asked him.

Dozer held up his hand, continuing toward them as he talked. "A bomb went off outside the mayor's office. Ten dead, others injured. We're locking everyone down until a sweep of public buildings can be done. We're hanging onto control of the population by a thread as it is."

"What can we do to help?" River asked.

Ava couldn't stop from glancing at him. He said *we*.

"Stay here and out of trouble, until told differently."

Now wait just a minute, they could help. "But—" she began.

"You're not the only people with orders to rest. We need you ready to investigate the pathogen," Dozer said before she could finish. "Stay out of trouble," he said, stressing each word. "Until I or Dr. Rodrigues says otherwise." He glanced around, his gaze pausing on the cots. "Get some sleep. You might not have a chance to get any later." He turned to go, then paused and tossed one more sentence over his shoulder. "And stay together. I don't want to have to hunt to find you." He was gone.

So, now they were stuck here, ineffective and impotent.

"What time is it?" she asked.

"Almost two o'clock," River answered, after looking at his watch. "A good time to crash."

Only a half-dozen cots. That wasn't going to be enough. There would be others arriving soon, looking for a place to rest.

"It's about to get busy in here." River's voice sounded about as excited about the incoming crowd as someone suffering from agoraphobia.

"Let's go see Henry. He might have room for another couple of cots in the tent next to his lab."

She led the way out of the clean room as a line of CDC people came in. Yup, way too many people in that small space.

Henry was working in his lab, but said they were welcome to use his cot. Then he informed them that there weren't any more to be had. The hospital had taken the majority of them to accommodate the increasing number of patients, family, and staff working the emergency.

His single cot sat inside a small tent set up next to the lab-in-a-box. It was probably meant to sleep three or four people, so the cot looked forlorn at the rear of the structure.

"I'll sleep on the ground," River said, lying down in front of the cot as if it were a foregone conclusion. He closed his eyes, his body as stiff as a board.

Ava frowned. Something wasn't right with her partner. "Are you okay?"

He snorted. "Fine. Get some sleep, Ava, while you can."

He didn't sound okay. He sounded tense, stressed, and a

second away from exploding, not sleeping.

Her sense of wrongness only grew, but she didn't have a specific complaint, just a feeling.

She got on the cot, drew the thin blanket over herself, and closed her eyes.

For a while, she floated, not quite asleep, not really awake, until something woke her completely. According to her watch, only an hour had passed. What woke her?

She glanced at River and realized after a second that he was tense. Too tense to be asleep.

"Hey," she whispered. "What's wrong?"

He sighed, opened his eyes, and looked at her. "I'm..." He hesitated so long she wasn't sure he was going to finish. Finally, he said, "I can't sleep. Shit is keeping me up."

"Mental shit?"

"Yeah."

That she understood. So, what would make him feel better?

She glanced at him again, his face in shadow. Something told her he didn't share this kind of thing lightly.

When was the last time he'd hugged anyone? Lowered his guard and relaxed with someone he trusted? He claimed to trust her. Maybe it was time she called him on it.

"Get in." She heard herself say it, but couldn't quite believe it had come out of her mouth. What did she think she was doing? She couldn't fix him. She couldn't even fix herself.

"What?" He sounded even more incredulous.

"Don't argue with me..." He should, he *really* should. "Just get in." She lifted the edge of the blanket. This was a bad idea. Unfortunately, it was the only one she had.

After a couple of seconds, he rolled to his feet and slid under the blanket and onto the cot. Now they were pressed together, chest to chest.

"This is a bad idea," he said, his voice almost subvocal.

She almost laughed at his verbal repetition of her thoughts.

"Shut up." She wiggled a little, until she could get one arm around his waist, then buried her nose in the crook of his shoulder. "Go to sleep."

The last thing she remembered was his sigh ruffling her hair.

Why was it so hot?

Ava tried to push the blanket off, but it was too heavy. It was also warm and smelled like... She opened her eyes to find herself on her back, River covering her with his body. He had one leg between hers and one arm under her head. The other was draped over her waist, but his hand... A breath stuttered out of her. His hand was curved around her breast. He wasn't doing anything, it was just resting there, but it was distracting. Arousing.

No wonder she was hot.

Desire moved through her body, waking parts of her that had been asleep for a long time. She was tired, so tired of being alone. She'd missed this, the feeling of strong arms around her.

She hadn't felt this way since...stop it. *Live in the moment. Be in the moment.*

The last two times Adam had come home on leave, he'd been the same as ever, but she'd still felt alone, disconnected from him. When she'd tried to find out what was wrong, he'd shook his head and told her all he needed was her love and support.

She'd given him that, but had felt even more alone.

Her body softened around the thigh between hers, pressed against her sex. She wanted to rub herself all over him, have his hands all over her. It had been so long since she felt anything but grief and hurt. River made her feel cherished.

She *wanted*.

He mumbled something and shifted, coming over her a little more, his hand shaping her breast. It felt so good she arched her back, shoving her breast into his hold as the long, hot, and hard length of him pressed into her belly.

Pleasure rushed through her arteries like champagne bubbles.

She'd lost Adam to a dangerous situation he thought he had under control. Control on the battlefield was a mirage. A fact he knew, but had forgotten. At least, that's what she thought had happened, why he'd put himself into the danger that killed him.

River was proving to be…not different, but he was willing to talk about how he made decisions, negotiate how he made them in the future. She hadn't expected it when she found out he was in the military.

He made her feel like an equal partner.

She hadn't expected that, either.

His body threw off a lot of heat. He surrounded her, the hard planes of him, his scent, and she wanted more, wanted to forget the pain of the past year and the shock of getting nearly blown up twice. She wanted to feel pleasure again.

His erection was impressive. She rolled her hips, stroked him with her body and was rewarded with his hand massaging her breast a little.

Her breath caught at the surge of pleasure his touch set off, then stalled as guilt stabbed her with an icy pick.

What did she think she was doing? This was sexual assault. He wasn't awake to give consent.

Hovering between her conscience and desire, the decision to pull away disappeared as he moved. He ground his hips against hers, then moaned, and his mouth was on hers, his tongue licking and stroking. The thigh between hers rose and rubbed against her, short-circuiting her brain.

Wait. What was she going to ask him? Something important?

She pulled her mouth away from his. "River?"

He kissed his way down her neck. "Yeah?"

Okay, he seemed awake. Now what? Should she just come right out and ask him to give her an orgasm?

He paused. Everything paused. "You want to stop?"

She had to stop herself from yelling *no*. "I want...I haven't..."

"You *want*?" he whispered right into her ear.

Lungs working so hard and fast, talking for her was difficult. "Yes."

His voice was a velvet purr. "What do you want?"

The question made her squirm uncomfortably. "I..."

He flicked a finger over one nipple.

Lightning shot through her. She clutched at him, unable to think, let alone voice her desire.

"Do you want to come?" he asked in her ear.

"Yes." She wasn't going to do this alone. "And you."

His mouth crashed onto hers, kissing her with a lust she could taste.

"Soft, silky mouse," he whispered as he pet her, ran a hand through her hair.

"How are we...how do we...?"

Lips teased her ear, caressed sensitive skin. "Baby, we're going to do this with clothes on. Mostly."

She swallowed. How did she get herself into this situation? "Yes. Good." And quiet. Quiet was good, too.

His mouth took hers in a kiss so carnal she felt like she'd been dropped off a cliff. Her stomach went weightless, her skin hypersensitive to every touch of his hands, his mouth, his breath.

"You're fucking gorgeous," he muttered as he teased her nipples with one hand while she arched her pelvis up to meet his erection. He rocked against her, making them both moan softly.

They kissed for long, lush seconds while he played with her body.

She stroked him with her hands, searching out all the places that made him shudder and touch her with growing desperation.

"I want to taste," he growled, as he suddenly reared back so he could shove her shirt up.

She helped as much as she could, but the cot and his weight made things difficult. After a few seconds, he got it up and pulled the cups of her bra down. He stared at her for a long second, then dove down to suckle hard at one nipple, then the other.

The pleasure swamped her, sucked her under, and gave her something she hadn't felt since Adam—passion, and a palpable connection to someone whose sole focus was on her. It was *alive* in her.

Thank *God* she'd gotten herself into this situation.

Ava sent one hand down River's body until she could cup and stroke his erection through his clothes.

"This is quite the handful," she breathed into his ear.

"Fuck," he groaned as she gave him a squeeze. He shuddered, and his hands moved to focus on her breasts and between her legs. His fingers rubbed her clit through her pants and teased the opening to her body. She began to move, her hips riding his fingers and thigh hard.

"That's it, Mouse, take it," he whispered hoarsely in her ear. "Give it to me."

"It?" She couldn't keep up, her brain too focused on what he was doing to her, with her, for her.

"Your pleasure, sweetheart. Pleasure."

Her hand was still around his erection, only he'd short-circuited her brain to the extent that she'd stopped stroking him. She wanted him with her all the way.

"And I," she told him, her voice husky as her hand shaped and caressed him, "want yours."

With a low groan, he took her mouth, his kiss a wild thing as his hands drove her to the edge. A nip to her bottom lip sent her over.

He caught her cry with his lips, then groaned and thrust into her hold with several short digs that culminated with him stiffening in her arms. Several seconds later, he sank down on top of her, his arms going around her. He nuzzled her neck and gave her lazy, long kisses.

"Feel better?" she asked.

"The best." His voice, a deep rumble in her ear, made her wish they were in a room with a door that locked. "You?"

"Yes." It was true. She did feel better.

"Good. Sleep," he ordered.

She yawned. "Okay."

Chapter Fifteen

6:23 a.m.

"Dr. Lloyd?"

The man sounded close. Familiar. Not a threat. She rolled over, giving whoever it was bothering her her back.

"Ava!"

Wow, someone was grumpy.

Ava opened her eyes and looked over her shoulder to find Henry standing next to the cot, glaring at her.

She frowned back. "What?"

"Dr. Rodrigues has lifted the travel restrictions for EMS, CDC, police, and military. It's time for you to get back to work and my turn to get a little sleep."

Sleep? Memory of what she and River had done together rushed through her mind, scalding her with sensuous heat.

Ohmigod. They'd gotten each other off like two randy teenagers sneaking in some nooky. It should never have happened. She should be sorry and embarrassed. Instead, she felt…rested.

"Where's River?" she asked as she untangled herself from the blanket and clambered out of the cot.

"Bathroom."

"That sounds like a good idea."

Henry lay down on his back and threw an arm over his eyes. "At least you two weren't noisy."

Ava stared at him. *His security cameras.*

Heat crawled up her neck and face, but she pretended she hadn't heard and walked away. His chuckle was soft enough to only follow her for a few feet.

The bathroom was a wash truck used for widespread emergencies. It had bathrooms equipped with running hot water and showers. She cleaned herself up, then went in search of River. She found him in the clean tent, eating and reading on the phone he'd stolen off Geer.

She grabbed an MRE and sat down across from him, determined to lock their make-out session in a box in the back of her head. It would distract, disarm, and derail her thinking otherwise. Professional, calm, and intelligent—that was her mantra for today.

"Anything probative?" she asked, nodding at the phone.

He gave her a hot look, making her breath catch. So much for locking the damn box. His words, however, were all business. "It's full of exactly the kind of stuff you'd expect in a college student's phone. Text messages to friends, and he's busy on social media, posting lots of pictures, but oddly, nothing at all for the last three days."

"Nothing?" That wasn't good.

"No pics, texts, or anything else outgoing. It's like he shut his phone off or stopped talking to the whole world."

"That is a little weird. Could he have a second phone?"

"Maybe. That would explain the lack of action on this one."

She watched him scroll through the text history on the

phone rapidly, and then he went back to read some more thoroughly. Those hands had been so tender yet strong on her.

Get your head in the game.

She cleaned up their food containers.

He glanced up when she returned to their small table. "I think I know where we need to look."

"Okay," she said, taking note of movement in the doorway. Walking into the structure were Toland and the two Homeland Security agents he'd been with earlier.

"Homeland is here," she said quietly.

River put the phone away in a pocket, as if it were his own. "Let me do most of the talking."

He must have a plan. At least this time he told her before he did something…creative.

The Homeland agents stopped a few feet away from the table, looking unhappy and angry.

"How's Geer?" River asked. "We haven't heard anything."

"Dead," Toland said.

Oh no. Finding out why the man had acted as he had was now going to be a lot harder.

"Fuck," River said, and it sounded like he meant it.

"I'm sorry for your loss," Ava added. "Did he regain consciousness at all?"

"No." Toland stared at River. The agent looked like he was barely holding his composure together. "Did he talk to you before he collapsed?"

"We mostly argued about his being there. He was in the apartment bathroom, looking at some test tubes and vials of…something. Nothing was labeled, and he seemed really worked up about it. I asked him if he'd found any evidence or explanation for the bathroom science experiment, but he said he hadn't. He thought there was something important about all that goop, but the grenades were in the same room. I finally convinced him to leave, but he didn't get far before he passed out." River shrugged and glanced at Toland's wingmen. "Did you get any information from that roommate of Roger Squires? Is he still in the wind?"

Toland relaxed slightly. "We haven't found him yet. The little shit gave a convincing *I don't know nothing about nothing* act, but he did let slip that there were several other students who seemed to spend a lot of time in that bathroom."

"Could he have been lying?" Ava asked.

"Anything's possible." He looked at them pointedly. "Are you still investigating?"

"Yeah, despite getting raked over the coals for blowing up a building," River said wryly. "The roommate's name is Ethan Harris. He's the only lead we've got, so we're going to start at his home here in El Paso. It turns out his father is Senator Mark Harris."

"I've met him," Toland said, his shoulders relaxing even further. "Not the easiest guy to talk to."

"Yeah? Do you know him well enough that he'd cooperate with you? Quickly?" River asked. "Time is not our friend."

"I think we could handle that," Toland said with an almost smile. "What are you and Dr. Lloyd going to do in the meantime?"

She didn't like the suspicion in his voice. Was Toland trying to protect someone? "I thought we'd head to the university, go through his locker, maybe talk to a couple of his professors. See if anyone has noticed a change in young Mr. Harris's behavior, find out who he hung out with." River made eye contact with all three agents. "Contact us if you find out anything. We'll do the same."

"Of course," Toland said in a slightly offended tone. The three agents grabbed some MREs and settled in to eat.

"Respirators or hazmat suits?" River asked her.

She shook her head. "Respirators."

River sighed. "Thank God. I'm not a fan of hazmat suits. I

was beginning to understand what a goldfish feels like."

She tried to hide her smile as she asked, "Getting dishpan hands?"

He chuckled. "Yeah, that's next."

They left the clean tent, picked up their respirators, safety glasses, and gloves. River checked his weapons while Ava restocked her sample case. She added a few field tests for controlled substances as well. If they were investigating students, she wanted to be able to rule out narcotics like cocaine, meth, and ecstasy.

They took one of the CDC vans, one of the smaller ones, and River drove toward the university.

"Now that we're alone," Ava began, "are we really going to the university?"

"Yeah, but not to talk to any professors."

When he didn't say anything more, she sighed and said, "Okay, I'll bite. Why are we going there?"

He grinned and glanced at her. "If you were trying to create a superbug and you wanted to hide what you were doing, where would you do it?"

The bottom fell out of Ava's stomach, exited the vehicle, and bounced down the road. "In plain sight," she breathed. "I'd hide it in a microbiology lab."

"That's what I'm thinking, too," he said. "So, how would you hide it in a lab frequented by a lot of people? That's the part I don't have figured out."

"Educational labs keep known bacteria alive in cultures so they can use them whenever they want for teaching purposes," she told him, excited by the prospect of making real progress. "If there's someone doing graduate work, they might be using specific bacteria to test a theory." Excitement quickened her rate of speech. "Those samples would be labeled so no one else would accidently use them."

"Could they test their superbug without attracting

attention?"

"Sure. That's what happens at university labs. Students and researchers manipulate bacteria, test new antibiotics, create new technology, whatever applies to their field of study."

"So, no one would notice? No one checks?"

"If a graduate student is involved, their mentor should notice, be following the research, results, offering advice…" Her voice trailed off. "But Roger Squires wasn't a grad student."

"Could he have done it alone?"

"No, I don't think so. Manipulating bacteria to achieve a new strain would take a great deal of knowledge and time. Dangerous organisms are controlled by the CDC. We'd know if someone was using a resistant strain in any research."

"Has anyone checked?"

"One of the first things Dr. Rodrigues did after we got here."

"So, we're looking for someone who could provide the right kind of instructions and a place to conduct the appropriate work. A professor or a *mentor*," River said with a ring of finality that was scary cold.

"Did you see any mention of a mentor on the phone?"

"No, but if this is a terrorist cell, they'd be careful to appear as friends or fellow students."

"How many people are we talking about?"

"Probably eight or nine, including Roger Squires."

"That many?"

"That's typical for a terrorist cell. Usually no more than ten people. After that, it's harder to control."

"Who's in control?"

River snorted. "That's the sixty-four-billion-dollar question, isn't it?"

Chapter Sixteen

7:28 a.m.

A couple of police cars blocked the main road onto the university grounds. The cops who came up to the van's window were wearing white disposable masks. River had to consciously relax his shoulders. What they were doing now, hunting terrorists, was fucking dangerous. He didn't want his worry for Ava triggering interest from outsiders. If he didn't need her expertise, he'd make sure she stayed at the hospital wearing a hazmat suit.

"Sir," one of the officers said. "The university is closed. They're sending everyone home—staff, students, everyone."

"We're with the CDC." Something River shouldn't have to say, given how well marked the vehicle was.

"I'm not authorized to allow anyone onto campus," the cop said.

In other words, he didn't want to be responsible for anything that might happen if he let them in.

River gave the other man an agreeable nod. "I get it, but

we're not exactly civilians, Officer. We're supposed to collect samples from the building that blew up as well as high traffic areas around the main buildings. That's it."

The cop glanced inside the van, but there wasn't much to see. Ava's collection kit was visible, but his rifle was out of sight, hidden under a couple of boxes of masks and gloves.

"Okay, just a moment." He walked away, shouting at the other police officer to move his car.

River drove by them, giving them a wave and a nod.

"That was impressively vague," Ava said as they drove down the empty road. The other side of the road, the one leading out of the campus, was clogged with vehicles.

"It should keep them from wondering why we're going where we're going."

"Do you even know where the lab is?"

"Sure I do." He tapped his temple. "It's all right here."

"How reassuring," she said drily.

He couldn't help the chuckle that escaped him at her tone. She was tough. She'd been held hostage by a fevered crazy man and blown up twice in less than twenty-four hours, but retained the ability to joke about the shitty situation they were in.

He'd served with soldiers from all branches of the military—strong, capable, disciplined—but to be an elite warrior took something else not everyone had. She knew who she was, and like every good Green Beret, Army Ranger, or Navy SEAL he'd ever met, she put other people first. The team first. The safety of innocent lives first.

That need to serve and protect was an endless well of strength no workout could build. Sometimes you could train it into people, but for the best of the best, it was part of them from the beginning.

"You remind me of one of my trainers."

"Oh?" She raised a brow. "A trainer of what?"

"Hand-to-hand combat. Most guys took one look at her and proceeded to stick both their feet in their mouths. She's only about five feet tall, but shit, on the first day we trained with her, she put every guy down hard in less than thirty seconds. Even the guys who thought their black belt in karate meant something."

"*I* remind you of this person?" She sounded astonished.

"Yeah," he said. "You're tough, too. You give a shit without the bullshit."

Both her eyes were wide. "That's...that's quite the compliment." Her voice had a vulnerable quality to it. He'd surprised her, in a good way. "I'm not always tough, though." She paused, then continued. "I've had my share of breakdowns where I cried until I looked like someone had beaten me."

"Did you leave? Stop whatever you were doing?"

"No." She sounded insulted. "I blew my nose and went back to work."

"Exactly. That's what a tough person does. Accepts the shitty shit, vents, then finishes the job."

"Oh." She turned her head to stare at the road, but that one little word told him she was vaguely disappointed.

He didn't want her feeling like she was lacking in any way. So he added, "It's also seriously *hot*."

Her head jerked in his direction. "What?"

"Sexy." He grinned. "A woman who knows who she is, confident and smart..." He glanced at her. A blush had turned her face red. He wanted to touch her, feel the heat infusing her skin. "Later, I'm going to kiss you a hell of a lot."

She glared at him. "You're assuming there's going to be a later."

"Seriously hot," he repeated in husky voice. "Our *nap* wasn't nearly enough."

"But...I..." She closed her mouth, breathed deeply a couple of times, and tried again. "I'm dressed like an extra in a zombie movie. How can you even think about…that?"

"Mouse," River drawled his name for her. "You've been spending time with the wrong men."

"And you're the right one?"

"Yep."

"Now you're just being ridiculous. What we did…earlier, was blow off steam."

He didn't like the sound of that. "I'm keeping things light so I don't scare you off, but I'm serious."

"I'm a geek, and I'm the only woman around."

"That's an insult to both of us."

She sighed. "You're right, I'm sorry, I just…I lost my fiancé a year ago, and I'm still finding it hard to move on, I guess. Part of me is scared to move on."

Well, *shit*. "I'm sorry. Was it…bad?"

"Is any death easy?" She hesitated, glanced at him, then continued. "He was a soldier. He was training soldiers in the Afghan Army. There was an accident, friendly fire, I was told."

"I heard about an incident like that." The soldier who died hadn't been anyone he knew directly, but a couple of guys on that same training mission had said the victim of the friendly fire had a habit of jumping with both feet into a situation, when he should have done more planning.

Her fears about safety and assessing risks accurately made a lot more sense.

"Damn, that's a shitty way to die," River said to her as gently as he could.

"He used to say that my worrying about him unnecessary stress. He knew what he was doing, and he trusted the people he served with. I should have trusted him more—" That last word was cut off abruptly as she audibly sucked in a breath.

Shit, she was trying not to cry.

"A deployment can be harder for the people who love us

back home than it is for the soldier themselves. We're usually kept pretty busy, but our family members have plenty of time to worry and imagine all the things that can go wrong." All he could see in her eyes were tears threatening to fall.

"Yeah." It was barely a whisper. "And when it does all go wrong, we have to no way to cope and no one to blame."

"It's nice to have a faceless enemy to hang all the shit on. No one has to think too hard about that. Don't have to rationalize death when we can blame it on an extremist. It gets harder when the cause is avoidable or accidental." He glanced at her again, but she was studying her gloved hands. "The sad truth is, most of the time death makes no sense. We're all going to get there. All we can do is our best until our time is up."

Something suspiciously close to a sob came out of her. "Is this your version of *suck it up, princess*?"

"I don't know. Is it helping?" Because if it wasn't, he was the biggest asshole ever.

She snorted a laugh, which sounded weird with her respirator on, then she shook her head and muttered, "Men." She looked away, but her left hand touched his shoulder, squeezed once, and then it fell away.

A spot in the center of his chest that had been wound so tight it made breathing difficult let go, allowing his chest rise and fall with air for the first time in what felt like hours. He hadn't hurt her, maybe even had helped her.

He wanted to do it again. Wanted her to reach out and touch him because he was just as hurt as she. Not for the same reasons, but the result left him in a similar place.

A couple of minutes later, River pulled up and parked outside a nondescript brick building.

"Is this it?" Ava asked.

"It should be."

There were no people in sight.

They got out of the van, Ava grabbing her specimen collection kit at the same time as he snagged his rifle.

"Let's hope no one sees us," she said.

River led the way to the entrance. "I believe in the CYA combat strategy."

"CYA?"

"Cover your ass."

She groaned. "That's not a combat strategy, that's a life strategy." Then she called Dr. Rodrigues, telling her that they were checking out the microbiology lab at the university as a precaution. She listened to for a moment, then said, "Interesting. We'll let you know if we find anything." She listened again. "No ma'am, Sergeant River is armed."

She ended the call.

"They got more information on Ethan Harris about five minutes ago. He's listed as taking two first-year microbiology classes. One last semester and one this semester."

"So everyone knows?"

"Yep. I suspect Homeland Security is going to be joining us shortly."

"Well, let's see what we can see before they get here."

He led the way inside, looking for anything that might be out of place. The bastards had blown up a college kid and coffee shop, a mall, the main gate at a military base, a dorm, and city hall. He wouldn't be surprised to find anywhere they might have worked or hidden stuff to also have IEDs.

There was a room map of the building near the stairs. A number of labs were listed, as well as lecture rooms and a few instructor offices.

"Any clue on that phone about which lab to start with?" Ava asked him.

He shook his head. "The building should be empty. Why don't we nose around and see if anyone is still here?"

"The straightforward approach is nice, for a change." She

gestured for him to lead the way.

"When have we not been straightforward?"

"How about the first time I heard your voice telling me how to keep a terrorist with a high fever calm?"

"There was nothing overly sneaky about that."

"Okay, how about you stealing that phone and notebook from Geer?"

"He stole it in the first place."

"Or us not telling Homeland about this little trip."

He frowned at her. "Whose side are you on?"

"Just keeping it honest."

They reached the second floor, which was where all the labs were housed. They began opening doors, or trying to. Everything was locked.

River muttered about paranoia in academia as he picked the lock of the first door they tried.

The lab inside was dark, and the only things alive were the bacterial cultures Ava found in incubators. They were labeled with the names of bacteria.

Ava went through them all.

"These are all commonly found bacteria from the human body. No pathogens here."

"Next lab."

River picked three more locks before they found a lab containing pathogens that made Ava's mouth tighten in disapproval.

"They should have better signage regarding the danger of these organisms," she said as she looked around the room.

"What are they?"

"Clostridia bacteria. Some of them are very pathogenic. They cause things like gas, gangrene, tetanus, and botulism."

"Why are you surprised to find them?"

"They're anaerobes. They don't survive in the presence of oxygen, but they do form spores, and that's what makes them dangerous."

"Spores? Like Anthrax?"

"Close. These need to be handled with more care and more protective equipment than I'm seeing in here."

"Could one of these bacteria cause the disease that's killing people?"

"No. Meningitis is quite different."

"Then we need to carry on."

She nodded, and they moved on to the next lab.

River crouched in front of the doorknob, his lock picks out when she tapped him on the shoulder and pointed at the bottom of the door. Light.

None of the other labs had lights left on.

They looked at each other, then he rose from his crouch and waved at her to follow him.

They stopped some distance down the hall.

"Maybe we should call for…" She took a second to find the correct word. "Backup."

"Like who? Homeland?" he asked her as he stroked his rifle. "They're on their way. Do you want to wait for them?"

"Not really."

"Then why consider calling them?"

She gestured at him, then herself. "There's just the two of us."

River smiled. She had no idea how deadly he could be. "Two is all we need."

"But—" she sputtered. "Really?"

"Yeah."

"What do they teach you in Special Forces school?"

"I already told you that."

"You told me about your medical and language training."

"We're military first. I know how to kill in more ways than most people can count."

She stared at him, her eyes wide, and didn't seem to

breathe for a couple of moments. "What if…" She paused, and he let her gather her thoughts. Her face was pale, and there were dark circles under her eyes.

He'd frightened her.

Idiot.

"Roger Squires's apartment had grenades in it." Her voice grew more confident as she spoke. "What if this lab has its own booby trap?"

Her question indicated he hadn't completely fucked up. These terrorists had shown no hesitation in using explosives so far, and it might make her feel better if he took a little extra time.

"I know we have to find the source of the pathogen, but we need to be safe about it."

There was that word again. Safe. Nothing about this situation was safe, but, maybe he could compromise. River reached into the tool kit attached to his waist, took out a dentist's mirror, and showed it to her.

"Let's have a look, shall we?"

Damn, if her eyes didn't light up at the sight of the tiny tool. There was no reason for his cock to sit up and take notice, but it did. Stupid thing.

Fuck, he had it bad.

He kept his rifle out of the way with his left hand as he got down on the floor in front of the lit-up lab and eased the mirrored end under the door. There were about two inches of space to work with, more than enough.

What the mirror allowed him to see had him freezing in place.

The doorknob had a wire attached to it.

He followed the wire and found its end tied to the pin of a grenade that lay against the wall next to the door. The moment anyone opened that door, they would pull the pin out and blow themselves to hell.

"*Fuck.*"

How the hell had anyone managed to set up that booby trap and still leave the room?

Were there other hazards?

He let the mirror show him more of the room.

"Fuck, as in *what a fucking mess*, or fuck, as in an *IED*?" Ava asked.

How could she ask that question like it was an intellectual query and not the fucking disaster their situation was? Again.

"IED," he replied shortly, then just to be sure she understood him completely, he added, "When I catch the fucking fuckers, they're going to be fucked."

She opened her mouth, then closed it.

That was probably the smart thing to do.

He turned the mirror to see more of the left side of the room and found a body. "Someone's in there, lying on the floor. Want to bet they're dead?"

"Not really. I believe you. What else can you see?"

He angled the mirror so he could scan the wall farthest away from them. A large grocery-store style refrigerator took up most of the space. It looked mostly empty. "There are petri dishes and other lab equipment on the floor. Looks like they cleared out a bunch of stuff, and neatness didn't count."

"Can you get us inside safely?"

"Not with the equipment I have on me."

It was going to take time to get the right equipment, and even then, this wasn't a military mission with his team in a foreign country. He was going to have to follow law-enforcement procedures, bring in someone from the bomb squad.

It could take hours.

Hours they didn't have.

Chapter Seventeen

8:12 a.m.

Ava's hands shook, she was so angry.

She was tired of arriving too late.

Tired of finding victims.

Tired of explosive devices stopping her from doing her job.

She pulled out her cell phone and called Dr. Rodrigues. She was so angry it took two tries to enter the correct numbers.

"It's me," she said, knowing she sounded like she wanted to kill someone. "I need a list of everyone who used the lab in room number 217 in the biology building at the college."

"You found something?" her boss asked, sounding exhausted.

"Another dead body and another grenade. If we open this door, we blow ourselves up. However, given the use of the grenade, there may be important evidence in there."

"Let's try to avoid another explosion, shall we? I'll make some calls and get back to you."

Something in Dr. Rodrigues's voice caught Ava's attention, and she tapped the speakerphone tab so River could hear. "What happened?"

"The college was cooperating completely with us until about fifteen minutes ago. Now I've got lawyers trying to put limits on our powers of investigation in court, and the college won't give us any more information until the judge makes a ruling."

"Can they do that in a state of emergency?"

"They're arguing the state of emergency is unwarranted."

"Unwarranted?" Shock turned her voice shrill. Ava couldn't believe it. "How many people have to die before it's warranted?" She wanted to hit something.

"You got lists of Roger Squires's classes and those of his roommates' classes, too, right?" River asked, joining in on the conversation.

"Yes, that came in before this latest brouhaha."

"Compare those lists with anyone in a position of authority at the college. Maybe someone's kid got mixed up in this, and Mom and Dad are trying to do damage control. This place needs to be off limits to everyone until we can get in there and figure out what happened," River said.

"Homeland sent agents. They should be there any time. They'll assist you in securing the room."

"Understood." He looked unhappy, but resigned. "And if this lead doesn't pan out?"

"Sergeant River, I'd like you to take a look at the bombing sites at the mall and at the army base. Dr. Lloyd, I'd like some samples from both sites as well. Is there evidence of the same types of explosives being used? Could the grenades you keep finding come from the base?"

The stairwell door at the opposite end of the hall opened, and three homeland agents came through it. Toland, and another two they'd already met.

"What did you find?" Toland asked, once they were close enough to talk without shouting.

"One lab has lights on. I gave the room a visual check before opening the door and discovered it was booby-trapped with a grenade." River held out the dental mirror.

Toland took the tool and laid it down flat on the floor in front of the door. He took his time, using the mirror to check as much of the room as River did. He got to his feet and held the mirror out to River. "The wires and grenade seem like a rudimentary mechanical trap to me. I can't say I've seen anything close enough like it to suspect a specific terrorist group."

"It sort of reminded me of the kind of trap used to catch rabbits or small game," River said, nodding.

"How did they get out?" Ava asked. The question had been bugging her since River described the tripwire tied to the doorknob.

"We need some better optical equipment and a bomb tech," River suggested. "I think the only trap is the trip wire, but I'm not willing to risk anyone's life on it."

"The FBI has the kind of equipment we need." Toland pulled out his cell phone. "Their bomb experts might be the best people to call in."

"Do you think this is it?" Ava asked River quietly. "Have we found the source?"

"Maybe the place the bug was manufactured, but there's got to be more people involved in this. Someone called Roger Squires at the coffee shop. The explosions at the mall and the gate at Fort Bliss were caused by suicide bombers, who almost always have a handler. Someone to choose the target, provide the explosives, and keep the bombers focused on their targets."

"An iceberg," Ava whispered. "What we've seen so far is just the tip of the iceberg. Most of it is below the waterline, out of sight."

"Yeah."

"Whatever is in that lab might help reveal who else is involved."

"Maybe." He sounded uncertain. "What I don't like is how easy it was to get here. Too easy. No hocus pocus, just a straight line from A to B. It was a straight line to the dorm and another straight line to this lab. Evidence left where it could be found with names and locations. I think we're being led around by the nose."

"What do you suggest we do? Ignore the lab?"

"No. If we can disarm the trap and get in there safely, I'm sure there will be plenty of intel in there. I'm just thinking that whoever is behind all this left lots of low-hanging fruit to distract and delay us."

"Okay. So, we need two teams? One to investigate here and another to push forward, past the low-hanging fruit?"

River nodded. "Time to check in with Dr. Rodrigues and fill her in on what we've found and what we think needs to happen." He glanced down the hall at Toland and the other two agents.

Ava backed up several steps and called Dr. Rodrigues. "River is…suspicious."

"This is a complicated situation," the other woman said slowly. "One that's rapidly getting worse. The death toll is now at sixty-three, with another two hundred and fifteen showing symptoms. We need to know who created this strain and how they did it to have any hope of understanding this bug quickly."

Ava understood her boss's priorities, but if River was right, they needed to figure out what the real endgame was.

She glanced at the knot of men quietly discussing how best to get inside the lab. Three of them in their dark suits, wearing respirators. River wore his respirator and scrubs with his body armor on overtop and his rifle cradled in his arms, but that wasn't what set him apart.

He was of average height, but in every other way, he was exceptional. Observant, intelligent, motivated, and yes, decisive. Even wearing safety gear covering more than half of his face, he was easily the most attractive man she'd met in a very long time.

Despite his tendency to irritate and flat-out make her angry, she respected him. He offered his trust first. His respect, and then he'd offered her pleasure before taking his own.

Yes, she did trust him.

How, in the few hours since they met, had *that* happened?

Allowing herself the luxury of depending on another person was not an easy thing for her, and yet she'd done it. She hadn't even hesitated.

The room spun, and she bent over to combat the disorientation.

Suck it up.

"I don't disagree," she said to the other woman. "I'm concerned at the length of time it would take to create this strain. Months. It would take someone in authority and probably a lot of money to make it happen."

"Information," Dr. Rodrigues said. "We need more. If you come across a lead you think deserves investigating, do it. Don't wait for permission from me."

"What about the college's court challenge?"

"A booby-trapped door, a grenade, and a dead body will be more than enough evidence to kick that crap out of court."

Ava ended the call, then took in deep breaths until the dizziness passed. She walked back to the knot of men clustered around the lab door, with no good news to share.

A door at the opposite end of the hall opened. El Paso police officer Palmer and several men wearing FBI-marked gear along with respirators strode toward them. The FBI agents nodded at Ava and River, then went around them to approach the booby-trapped door and the Homeland agents who waited next to it.

"How are things in the city?" Ava asked Palmer. "Are people complying with the quarantine?"

"Most are. There are always a few idiots who think it's a license to go shopping with a crowbar instead of cash." His tone was dry, and Ava found herself liking the man.

"We appreciate your help," River told him. He approached the group of men.

"How are you doing, ma'am?" Palmer asked. "Get any sleep?"

The question jerked her head around. Had there been a hint of innuendo in his voice? His expression didn't show it, a combination of earnest innocence.

"Yes, thank you."

His gaze turned concerned. "Ma'am, can I give you my personal cell phone number? Just in case you have any questions about the city or need a fast ride somewhere?"

A local source of information might be very helpful. "Thank you, that's a good idea." She dug out her phone and handed it to him so he could enter his number.

"How long have you lived in El Paso?"

"All my life," he said with pride as he handed her phone back.

The huddle of men broke up, drawing her attention.

River walked back to her. "They're going to cut the wire connecting the grenade to the door." He said it like he was asking her for permission. This was his forte, not hers.

"Okay."

"They'd like us to leave the building."

"Why?"

"Mostly because we've been blown up twice already."

Really? "FBI Bomb techs are superstitious?"

He gave her a lopsided smile. "No one would ever admit it." He tilted his head toward Palmer. "We're not the only ones they want out. Homeland and Palmer have to leave, too."

Toland and his two buddies surprised her when they walked to the exit as River was speaking and left first. Palmer followed with Ava and River right behind, all six of them thumping down the stairs from the third floor and outside. They walked across the street, then turned to watch the building.

"The trip wire was quite simple in its construction," Toland added. "The lead tech has twenty years in, and has seen—"

A punch of sound, light, and vibration knocked them all off their feet as a fireball erupted out of the side of the building.

On the second floor.

Chapter Eighteen

8:47 a.m.

Pain rushed through River's head. He had to get up off the sand, had to stop the man who'd betrayed him. But it wasn't sand in his nose, it was dust, and cement under his hands.

El Paso, Texas, not the Middle East.

River picked himself up, his weapon in his hands, to scan the area, looking for follow-up threats. A tirade ran through his head. *Fucking cocksuckers. Goddamned fucking cocksuckers.*

Must have been a second booby trap or IED the FBI hadn't seen and set off. Three more men dead, and a room full of evidence and answers *gone*.

A moan and movement from Ava had River crouching over her, one hand on her shoulder keeping her in place so he could check for injuries.

She stared at him with wide, shocked eyes.

"Are you hurt?" he demanded, the anger roiling in his blood making it hard to speak. He didn't want to talk; he wanted to beat the shit out of something. Someone.

"I...what..." She blinked a few times, then glanced past him at the building they'd just left. "Again?"

"Again," he answercd in a growl. "Three fucking times we've been blown up." He grabbed her other shoulder and gave her a little shake and put his face a couple of inches from hers, his respirator bumping hers. "Are. You. Okay?"

"I think so," she answered absently, her gaze a little unfocused. "Oh my God, the FBI agents, they're..."

"Dead," Toland said, his tone flat. He stood, staring at the flames and smoke.

"I'm done," River told him, striding over to snarl and shove his respirator into the other man's face. "*Done.* You feel me?"

Toland glanced at him, his eyebrows crowding low. "What?"

"Done playing nice. I don't know what the fuck you're trying to do or who you're protecting, but get in my way, and I will make your entire world hurt."

Toland stared at him for a moment, glanced at the burning building, then said, "If anyone gets in your way, I'll hand you the gun myself."

Son of a bitch. "Talk."

"Senator Mark Harris called in a favor."

"Harris?" Ava asked. "As in Ethan Harris?"

"Yeah, his father."

There was a special place in hell for elitist assholes. "What did he tell you?"

"That it was all a misunderstanding. Ethan was in the wrong place at the wrong time, the bad fortune of having the wrong roommate."

"When did he feed you this bullshit?" River asked.

"Shortly after we identified Roger Squires."

"Jesus Christ, you've known this for hours?"

Next to him, Ava began speaking rapidly, "Yes, ma'am.

River, me, and the three Homeland agents are all right. The FBI agents…were still inside when the explosion occurred."

She listened for a moment, then said gently, "Ma'am, I'm sorry, the entire side of the building is gone."

The silence following her statement weighed heavily with too many souls taken too early.

"Tell her we're heading back to the hospital," River said, tired, so fucking tired of the stupidity that seemed to be a disease as deadly as the one they fought. "We need to have a chat with Agents Marble and Dozer as well as Fort Bliss's Major Ramsey."

Ava repeated that, then ended the call.

Palmer stepped closer, blood dripping down the side of his head. "What can I do to help?"

"You need to have the cut on your head looked at," Ava told him.

"It's fine."

"It's bleeding all over the place." She pointed at his shoulder, glistening with wet blood.

"You're coming with Ava and me," River ordered. He turned to Toland. "You're going to stay here and direct the first responders. We're going to have a chat with your supervisory agent, Dr. Rodrigues, and the base commander. You'd better hope you assholes haven't fucked up this disaster any worse than you already have."

"Yeah," Toland breathed out. "Go."

River grabbed Ava's arm and herded her toward the CDC van. Palmer climbed into the back.

He drove with controlled violence, his hands clenched so hard on the steering wheel he wondered if it would snap in half.

How could anyone be so selfish or stupid that they would try to misdirect the investigation? Yet, Senator Mark Harris had done exactly that.

If Ethan Harris was part of this series of attacks, and his father knew it, the man had just made himself an accessory after the fact in every single death that had occurred today. If he didn't know, if Ethan lied to his father, it still didn't justify asking investigators to ignore his son's involvement.

Wouldn't a politician want to be as transparent as possible in an incident as large as the one El Paso was currently experiencing? Wouldn't he want to be seen as impartial and fair?

"I don't understand," Ava said, still sounding disoriented. "The senator's actions make no sense to me. How does the senator asking Homeland to protect his son, even though his son may know who else was in contact with Roger Squires and his backpack of death, benefit him? He's obstructing justice."

"He probably thinks he's got the right lawyer to beat that kind of charge."

Behind them, Palmer snorted. "There's always someone who thinks the rules don't apply to them."

"Stupid," Ava muttered.

"Stupid kills," River replied.

They arrived at the hospital, but were redirected by military personnel not to the area the CDC were set up, but to what looked like the receiving bay for supplies, food, and equipment. Another armed soldier had them park the CDC van next to two others.

"Dr. Rodrigues said they had a mob try to rush the decontamination area about ten minutes ago. We're to use the staff entrance on that side of the building."

River parked, then shut the van's engine off and got out. Agent Dozer waited for them at the door. That he was wearing a hazmat suit wasn't a surprise, but the blood splattered over enough of the outside of it to make it…remarkable.

Dozer let them in.

"Interesting couple of hours?" River asked, eyeing the

blood.

"Almost got too interesting," he replied. "Could have used you behind your rifle to thin out the really desperate ones. Approximately fifty people broke through the barriers around the decontamination area." Dozer sounded tired. "As near as we can figure, there was a rumor we have a cure, a one-shot treatment or something."

"Casualties?" River asked.

"Three injured when they fell and were trampled by the people behind them. A couple of shots in the air brought things to a halt, but those were some angry folks."

"So a mob of people rushed the CDC? Like we had a giant sign pointing to some conveniently ready injection needles they could just take? That's ridiculous." She stared at Dozer, her gaze tracking the blood on his suit. "This isn't gonorrhea. If we had something, we'd be giving it to people."

"Who started the stampede?" River asked.

"Good question, with no good answers." Dozer looked at them. "Come on. Rodrigues has news."

He, Ava, and Palmer followed Dozer as he led them to a bank of elevators. They went up a couple of floors and got off on main.

The doors opened to chaos.

People were crowded into the entire space near the elevators and down the hallway in both directions. As soon as the doors opened, and they could be seen in their respirators, several of people began yelling.

"My wife can't breathe."

"My son has a fever, and he won't wake up."

"Where's the medicine?"

"Homeland Security," Dozer yelled, holding up his badge.

The people closest to him moved back a few steps, and Dozer wasted no time taking advantage of the space and stepped out of the elevator.

River followed. His rifle held in both hands seemed to give plenty of reason for the crowd to get out of the way. Holding her sample case in front of her, Ava stuck close to him.

They entered the ER bull pen. It was full of hospital and military medical staff. Most of them were on the move, but a few were lying on narrow cots set against the walls, asleep.

He hoped they were asleep.

Dozer led the way to Rodrigues, who was speaking to a half-dozen people in hazmat suits.

A nurse grabbed Palmer by the arm and made him sit on the floor. A military medic sewed up the cut on Palmer's head. The cop gave him a thumbs-up, and River nodded in response.

"The public needs to isolate themselves," Rodrigues was saying. "If they're sick, they need to stay at home, call in to the CDC hotline, and wait for a medical team to pick them up. If they're not sick, they need to stay home and away from public places where they might come into contact with someone who is sick."

The six people all had their phones or tablets shoved in her face. Recording. They were reporters.

"Meningococcal disease is highly contagious," Rodrigues continued. "Avoid person-to-person contact. If you're not sick, stay away from hospitals and medical clinics or anywhere people are congregating. These orders are in effect for at least the next forty-eight hours. We will continue to update the media every six hours, unless there's a change. Thank you."

The reporters left with almost laughable haste.

Because no one was laughing.

Rodrigues waved at Dozer, Ava, and River.

River got down to business. "It was a trap, set deliberately in advance to kill anyone investigating Roger Squires and Ethan Harris. The size of the explosion suggests…" If his team commander were asking, he wouldn't hesitate to state his opinion, but Rodrigues wasn't military.

"Suggests what?" she asked.

"Permission to speak freely?"

"That would be refreshing," she said, in a tone devoid of emotion.

"I think you've got a fox in the henhouse."

Dozer laughed, probably more than Rodrigues liked, based on the severe frown she leveled at the Homeland agent.

"I take it you agree with him?" she asked the agent.

"Yeah," Dozer said, the smile dying on his face. "We might have more than one."

"*Domestic* terrorism?" she asked.

"I've always appreciated your ability to boil things down to the simplest denominator," Dozer said. "And I think you're right. Someone called in a favor before we got here. Ethan Harris was supposed to be off-limits."

"Someone should have told Ethan Harris about that," Ava said.

"Well, he's not off-limits," Rodrigues said flatly. "I don't care if you have to send in the Marines. Find him."

"Yes, ma'am." River saluted.

"Is there any progress on treatment?" Ava asked.

"We won't know until tomorrow morning. Henry is testing several antibiotics in combination. Samples of the bacteria have also gone back to the CDC in Atlanta for more testing." She sighed, and River realized that she wasn't as angry as he thought.

She was fucking tired.

"Ma'am," Ava began hesitantly. "When was the last time you took a break?"

"I don't remember." Rodrigues waved off both of them. "It's not important. Forget about investigating the other bombing sites for now. You two need to speak with Ethan

Harris's father. Ethan is likely infected, and that makes him dangerous all by itself. We also need to know why he ran, and if he has any information about this series of attacks."

"You have doubts about his involvement?" River asked.

"I'd like proof of his involvement."

"He's in it up to his neck, at least peripherally, but given the amount of shit that is following him around, no, I have no doubts."

"I agree," Dozer said. "Three explosions, you're out."

"The court challenge?"

"I got a call from the lawyers ten minutes ago. The case was tossed out. The other side is filing new challenges, but I don't think they'll be any more likely to succeed than the first one."

"Do we have any law-enforcement support?" River asked.

"Unfortunately, you two are on your own."

"The senator probably won't even open his door to us," Ava said. "We're dressed like we work in the morgue, and we don't have any official identification the senator is going to accept."

Rodrigues considered them for a moment. "What if I sent a couple of soldiers in uniform with you?"

He'd take a meter maid. "That'll work."

"I'll call Major Ramsey and have him assign a couple of steady guys to act as your credentials." She gave them a grim expression, already punching in a number on her cell phone. "One of you needs a working ECC device. Stay in touch."

She turned to wave closer several medical staff waiting a few feet away as she spoke into her phone.

Multitasking this clusterfuck had to be a bitch.

"You want to come with?" River asked Dozer.

"Can't." He nodded at Rodrigues. "I'm her *credentials*."

There was something in Dozer's gaze that told River the

other man wasn't there just to back up her orders.

"Stay here while I organize that escort and get you a new Bluetooth." Dozer strode away and into a storage closet on the other side of the bull pen.

"I can drive," Palmer said, on his feet again.

River glanced at the medic, who nodded.

"Okay, you're on the team," River told Palmer. "Take a minute to wipe some of the blood off. The last thing we need is some civilian taking one look at you and deciding this is the zombie apocalypse."

Palmer glanced at himself and grunted. "I keep a spare shirt in my car. Give me five minutes to clean up and change."

At River's nod, the cop jogged out of the room.

"How are you doing, Mouse?" River asked, keeping his voice low and his attention on Dozer.

"I'm…okay." She sounded hesitant.

"Okay?" he asked. "*Okay* is for people who don't know what the fuck is going on around them. You are *not* one of those people."

She looked at him, frowning. "I'm tired of getting blown up, and that's not a phrase I ever expected to say." She glared at the world in general. "I want to hit someone," she said, her voice rising. "And I'm a doctor."

Chapter Nineteen

9:32 a.m.

Ava wanted to do more than hit the people behind all this death and destruction. She'd like to kick and stomp on them, too.

"I don't blame you," River said, his voice too agreeable. "I'd like to get in a few punches myself."

"Stop being so nice," she hissed at him. She wasn't a child to be placated with a few *yes dear, you're absolutely right dear* phrases.

River took a step closer, invading her personal space. "I don't do nice."

She held her ground, sick to death of the whole situation. "What do you do?"

She couldn't see his mouth, thanks to the respirator, but his eyes told her he was grinning. His gaze slid down her face to focus on her lips.

Really?

She rolled her eyes. "Forget I asked."

"No changes." His voice rumbled through her, ensuring she'd never forget. "No take backs."

She took a step away as Dozer came back. He handed River a new ECC device. "Your escort is waiting for you in the decontamination area."

"I thought it was overrun," River said.

"The area by the mobile lab wasn't."

River nodded at the agent. "As soon as Palmer gets back, we're on our way." He glanced at Rodrigues. "Stay close to her," he said to Dozer. "The terrorists may figure out she's the one calling the shots, not the governor or FEMA."

"That occurred to me, too." Dozer's smile was so vicious Ava found herself backing away a couple of steps.

"She said she worked with you before," River said. "When was that?"

Dozer's face hardened. "SARs outbreak in 2003."

River had seen Dozer's expression on other men. Men who'd survived monsters and death. "Watch your six," River told him.

"You, too." Dozer nodded at her. "Doctor."

"Agent."

Dozer walked over to stand behind Dr. Rodrigues.

"Something happened to him," Ava whispered.

"Something bad," River agreed.

"Sorry it took so long," Palmer said, approaching them. He'd changed his shirt and washed the blood off his exposed skin.

"I'll take point. Palmer, you've got the rear."

"Yes, sir."

River glanced at her. "Let's go."

"Yes, dear," she said in a nasal whine that had both men looking at her like she'd lost her mind.

River shook his head. "Let's see if we can check in with Henry." He led the way out of the ER via the staff exit.

The mess outside had all of them slowing down.

Yellow caution tape lay torn and limp on the ground, hugging cement curbs and broken safety barriers. Those barriers, made of wood and plastic, had been snapped into chunks and broken apart.

A lone shoe and a black handbag had been shoved against the side of the building, blood splattered here and there on the pavement.

Ava shook her head. "It looks like the ring at a pay-per-view wrestling tournament."

"I'll have to take you to a live match some time," River said, looking around.

"No thanks. I prefer to leave my work at work."

"I can appreciate that. What do you do for fun?"

"Sudoku."

He snorted and leaned down to whisper. "You are a prickly one, Mouse."

"Keep calling me a rodent, and you're going to find out how prickly."

"I don't know, that sounds like it could be fun."

Damned if she didn't agree.

Off to the left was a line of CDC vehicles parked bumper to headlights. A narrow gap between two vans was guarded by two soldiers in Army uniforms carrying rifles and wearing respirators.

Henry's lab sat on the other side.

They approached the two soldiers. Ava held out her CDC ID badge. River and Palmer gave their names.

"You're on the list," one of the soldiers said after he consulted his tablet.

On the other side was another sort of chaos, one composed of a brigade or two of soldiers guarding the perimeter. Or was it a unit? She'd have to ask River what the different groups of soldiers were called.

Inside the boundaries was another tent set up with food and drink, a first-aid station—about ten times too small—and an area covered by another larger tent where people were sleeping.

They headed for Henry's lab and were met by Major Ramsey and two armed soldiers.

"Privates Hall and Castillo," Ramsey said. "If you get them dirty, clean them before you return them." He walked away.

"Sir, ma'am," one of the soldiers said. "Your orders?"

"We're going to interview a senator," she told them. "He isn't going to be happy about it."

"Yes, ma'am," Hall said.

"Do you talk?" River asked the other man.

Castillo finally opened his mouth. "Only when I've got something to say, Sergeant."

"Good enough."

"We've got a military vehicle standing by."

River gave Palmer the address of the senator's home, and they headed out.

The home they ended up at was only about ten minutes away and in an affluent part of the city. There probably wasn't a house on the block worth less than a million and a half. The senator's home was the largest Ava could see, and it had a gate across the driveway.

It was closed and had a no trespassing sign on it.

They parked outside the gate and tried to push it open. Locked.

"Got a crowbar in that machine?" River asked the soldiers.

Castillo nodded and got something out of the rear cargo area. The crowbar he handed River was black and looked like it had been used a few times.

It didn't take River two minutes to force the gate open.

They all got back into the Hummer painted in desert camo and drove up to the front door.

"Stay here," River said to Palmer. "Everyone else with me." He hopped down and knocked on the door.

A scratchy-sounding man's voice came from an intercom box next to the door. "You're trespassing. The police are on their way."

"Mark Harris, this is the CDC," River said. "We need to speak to you, sir. It's a matter of some urgency."

"I've already spoken with Homeland Security."

"Yes, we're aware. However, there have been a few developments. We have several follow-up questions."

There was no response.

River knocked again. And again.

"The police are on their way," the voice said again. "I will have you prosecuted to the fullest extent of the law."

"Actually, sir," River said, his voice warm with apology, "the CDC will have *you* prosecuted to the fullest extent of the law."

"Stay right there," the voice said.

"Like we were going to go anywhere," Ava muttered. She gave River a narrow-eyed look. "Why are you being so nice to him?"

"I wouldn't call it nice," River said in a wry tone. "More of a here's something sticky-sweet so you'll walk into my trap."

"You are a very strange man," she said, shaking her head.

"I blame it on the head injury."

The door opened. A silver-haired man with broad shoulders and a square jaw stood in the doorway. "Explain," he barked.

River held up his CDC ID badge. "Senator Mark Harris?"

The man in the doorway stepped back and tried to close the door.

River stuck his foot in the doorjamb, then put his shoulder

to the door and shoved it open. "I'll take that as a yes."

Ava followed, with the two soldiers right behind her.

"Get out," Harris ordered. "Stacy, call the police!"

"You said you already called them." River shook a finger at the senator. "You lied, didn't you?"

Mark Harris ground his teeth together. "I will end your career."

"Really?" River asked, stepping into the senator's personal space. "I've already survived three explosions today, so you're welcome to take your best shot." It was a threat.

This was getting them nowhere. "Where is your son, Senator?" Ava asked.

"None of your damned business."

"It's very much our business." She sighed. "He ran away from Homeland Security."

The senator's face didn't change. So, not a surprise then.

"He was in protective custody."

That got a snort out of him.

"He was showing symptoms of an illness that's killed sixty-three people so far *today*." She searched his face for any sign that he might understand just how much danger his son was in.

Nothing.

"Mr. Harris, your son's roommate, Roger, had the same symptoms before he died. His other two roommates were found dead in their apartment. An apartment with a bathroom full of chemicals and bacterial cultures."

"Don't forget the half-dozen fragmentation grenades," River added. "We have a lot of unanswered questions, and Ethan is the only person who can answer them."

"You don't know what was in that bathroom, because, oh yes, it exploded. All you have is guesswork and assumptions based on too little information." The senator drew himself up and pronounced like a preacher on Sunday, "I won't let you accuse my son of anything just because he's convenient. These terrorist attacks have nothing to do with him."

"Sir, we need to talk to him so we can rule him out as a suspect. By accident, he may have overheard or seen details that could save lives and prevent any other attacks."

"You have no proof he's involved any more than any other college student."

"One," River held up a finger. "His roommate had a backpack full of explosives, which were detonated in a public place. Two" — another finger went up — "his apartment contained several military-grade explosive devices, two dead bodies, and a bathroom full of science equipment. Three" — a third finger went up — "we attempted to search the college biology lab he used as part of a course he was taking. The door was booby trapped. The room exploded, killing three FBI's bomb squad agents and taking out the entire second floor of the building." River dropped his hand. "Three strikes, Mr. Harris."

Mark Harris frowned at them. "What biology course? He wasn't taking any classes like that."

"It's in his student profile."

"How did you get that?" Harris asked, his face turning ruddy. "The college challenged your right to that information in court."

"Sir, given the speed at which the infection is spreading, and killing, the court convened an hour ago. The case was thrown out, and the CDC's authority in this state of emergency was upheld."

Harris staggered back a step, his jaw slack. "No. My lawyer would have informed me."

"I suspect he will soon. But it means that if you lie to us or hinder our investigation, you will be charged with obstruction of justice." Ava took a step toward him. "Please, if Ethan has the illness, and I think that likely, he needs immediate advanced medical care. He won't survive on his own."

The senator drove his hands through his hair, clutching at the short strands like he wanted to rip them out. "He's not responsible for it. He couldn't be."

"Where is he?" Ava asked.

"Not here," Harris answered, all of the fight gone out of him. "He said he was in trouble early yesterday, but it was a misunderstanding, and he could handle it himself. He didn't want us to get involved."

"But you asked someone," River said. "A friend, in Homeland Security, to look the other way?"

"Geer is a family friend. He wanted to help."

"Geer is dead." River dropped that bomb without any warning.

Harris jerked back like he'd been punched. "What?"

"A few hours ago. He collapsed in the college dorm where your son lived. I barely got him out before the explosion, but he died shortly after."

"Oh my God."

"He was showing symptoms of the illness."

Harris stared at River like a man who'd just discovered that he'd lost everything.

"Where did Ethan go?" Ava asked.

Mark Harris's voice shook. "He said he had proof the police would want to see and friends who could help him."

"Which friends? What proof?"

"I don't know!" Harris's eyes were bloodshot and full of tears. "He said he would call."

"How did he get to these friends? Does he have a car?"

"He took mine."

"GPS?"

"Yes, it's got it."

River pulled out his cell and punched in a number. "Dozer? I need to find a car registered to Senator Mark

Harris."

Ava watched the senator's face, noting his shaking hands and the sweat beading on his forehead. "Sir, were you in close contact with Ethan today?"

"He's my son."

She'd take that as a yes. "May I check your temperature?"

He nodded, and she pulled out the packet of disposable temperature patches and put one on his forehead. It displayed the indicator for a severely high fever.

"Sir, you need to go to the hospital."

Chapter Twenty

10:03 a.m.

River heard the word *hospital* and stopped pacing to look at the senator. Sweaty, flushed face, glassy eyes, and emotional.

"Does Ethan have a phone with him?"

"He left it in his room," Mark Harris said. "He said he didn't want the police to be able to find him until he was ready."

"And that didn't make you nervous, him talking about hiding from the police?"

"At the time, it seemed more reasonable."

"How about now?" River snarled. "Still reasonable?" When the senator just looked at him blankly, River shook his head. "Where's his room?"

"Up the stairs, second door on the left." Harris's shoulders drooped, and a sob shook him. "I'm sorry. He's my son."

River didn't answer his plea for forgiveness. Neither did Ava.

He nodded at Castillo to stay with Ava, then went up

the stairs to Ethan's room. It had all the normal things a college student would have: bed, chest of drawers, desk with a laptop computer on it, and dirty clothes on the floor. The housekeeper hadn't had time to clean up after him. Good. He'd bag up the clothes and give them to the FBI for their forensic techs to look at.

He opened the laptop and stared for a moment at the prompt for a password. He tried a few of the most popular ones with no result, then tried a few that might be on a home-grown terrorist's mind. He hit pay dirt with *jihad*.

The computer was virtually blank. No files, documents, or spreadsheets. His internet search history was empty, and he had no email.

The shithead had erased everything.

But maybe not good enough. The FBI's tech guys might be able to resurrect it.

A cell phone sat on the desk next to the laptop. It looked blank, too, as if it had been reset to factory settings.

He'd take both devices with him.

A look around the rest of the room didn't reveal anything new about the kid or what he might be involved in. It was all so ordinary and average, but it was also all so superficial, as if he were a character in a movie and this was nothing more than a set. Hadn't his father noticed any changes in his son's behavior? Or was he just too wrapped up in his own little list of issues, grievances, and events to pay attention?

He picked up the electronics and dirty clothes, then left the kid's room. Nothing left there but broken promises and discarded dreams.

As he went down the stairs, his ECC device beeped.

"River."

"The GPS on that car isn't functioning."

"Thanks." *Fuck*.

He raised his voice. "We're heading back to the hospital."

Mark Harris grabbed Ava's arm and pulled her to a stop. "Please, help my son. I can't believe he'd willingly do anything to hurt anyone."

"You think he's been coerced?"

"It's the only thing that makes sense."

"Ava," River said. "We've got to go."

They got into their vehicle, the sound of sirens everywhere in the city, and filled Palmer in as he turned the Hummer around and drove back the way they came.

"Do you think we'll find Ethan Harris in time?" Ava asked.

"In time for what?"

"To stop whatever is supposed to happen next."

"I don't know," River answered her. They'd been five steps behind the orchestrator of all this evil all day. "I'm not even sure we'll find him alive."

"That's what I'm afraid of, too."

"What are the chances he's the brains behind all this shit?" Palmer asked.

"Nah, it's not him," River said. "How this kind of terrorist cell works is pretty consistent. A slightly older student plants a few seeds, talks about how government is too big and wants too much control over people's lives and money. Then a teacher comes in, someone not too old or too young, to explain how the world really works and that America is actually the school-yard bully. The leader is the one who sells you bad weed and watered-down alcohol, then beats you up just to feel like he's in control of something."

They weren't more than two minutes from the hospital now.

"Ethan Harris isn't in charge, he's cannon fodder. Disposable. But he might know enough for us to figure out who the leader is."

"If he's like Roger Squires, he'll be prepared to die for his cause," Ava said. "That makes him dangerous."

"Makes him a weapon. Something none of us should forget." River glanced at Ava and at the soldiers in the backseats to include them in the warning.

Ava met his gaze and nodded.

Palmer slowed the vehicle to a stop behind a line of cars and trucks. None of them were moving.

"I'll check the situation," Hall said as he hopped out and jogged down the side of the road and out of sight.

A minute later, he came back and went to River's side of the van. He rolled the window down.

"Traffic is backed up a couple of blocks, and it doesn't look like it's going to get unblocked for a while."

"Shit," River glanced at Ava, then said, "Okay, let's park here and walk in."

They all got out of the vehicle and strode at a not-quite jog toward the center of the chaos. River took the point position, with Ava and Palmer right behind. Hall and Castillo brought up the rear. People gave them a wide berth as they moved.

The guard herded them through a smaller checkpoint and had them wait for Dozer to meet them.

"Any leads besides the GPS?" Dozer asked.

"We've got Harris's laptop and clothing," River said, handing them over. "I'm hoping he didn't manage to delete anything permanently. The clothing might be able to tell us where he's been."

The agent took the bag of stuff with the air of a man who had a lot on his mind. "Is the senator sick?" The question was directed at Ava.

"I think so. He's showing most of the symptoms."

"Damn." For a moment, Dozer stared at the ground, then he glanced at the two soldiers. "You gentlemen should report back to your command."

"Yes, sir," they said in unison. They gave River a respectful nod, and another to Ava, then left.

"Sergeant River," Palmer said, rubbing his head with one hand. "I'm sorry, but I think the adrenaline wore off. My head…"

"Get yourself checked out," Ava told him. "You might have a concussion after all."

"Yes, ma'am. I'm sorry," the police officer said with a wince.

"We've got a triage station for personnel working the emergency setup over by the decontamination area," Dozer told him. "They'll get you sorted out."

"Thank you, sir." Palmer headed out after giving them all a wave.

Dozer regarded River and Ava for a long moment, then said, "Until we get a fresh lead, we're at a standstill with the investigation. I'd like the two of you available to head out on a moment's notice. Eat, and get some sleep. You might get half an hour or several hours, but take the downtime while you can." He turned and went back into the hospital.

"Let's hit decontamination," River said, nudging her in that direction.

"I'm not all that hungry," Ava protested.

"Eat anyway."

They got cleaned up, grabbed a couple of MREs and water, then ate as quickly as possible. The clean room was full of people, some eating, others sleeping on the cots that filled every available space.

River didn't have to say anything to Ava—she followed him out of the clean room and over to Henry's corner of the area. She knocked and asked if they could use his tent to rest in again.

His answer was to come out to talk to them. The guy looked as if someone had gutted him.

"What happened?" Ava demanded. "Another explosion?

What?"

"The number of deaths have really jumped." Henry told them. "Campus security did a sweep of all their buildings. They found a lot of bodies in several dorms. The death toll is now approximately three hundred and forty-two dead and seven hundred sick."

"Approximately?" How could there be an approximate number? Either a person was dead or not.

Ava gasped and covered her mouth, her hands shaking.

"There are so many people coming in now that it's difficult to get a firm count." Lee's laugh was devoid of humor. "They've run out of space in the morgue."

River wanted to let loose a few colorful words, too, but Ava's cool pallor and distress told him he needed to keep that shit in his mouth. "We're on standby until further notice."

"Right," Lee said, looking around. "What the hell, use my tent. It's where Rodrigues will look for you first anyway."

"Thank you, Henry." Ava's voice was a little wobbly, and that was enough to cripple River where he stood.

She went into the tent, and he followed.

"Is there anything worse than this?" Her voice was barely audible.

Finally, he had an answer for a question. "A complete and utter clusterfuck."

"Yes. Okay." She nodded. "That. So, how do we deal with a clusterfuck?"

He snorted. "You just do."

"I thought you guys always had a plan."

"The situation is too fluid for any plan to last longer than the next new piece of information or event."

"So, no plan?"

"You plan for the worst." He smiled at her. "Good thing we're dressed for it."

Ava sighed. "Do you ever *not* have a comeback?"

"Sure. That would have been the last time I got shot."

She rolled her eyes. "You guys are such a pain in the ass when you're like this."

"Like what?"

"Making jokes about everything."

"Hey, it's the only way to stay sane in my line of work."

"Eh," she said, her voice squeaky. "I'm not convinced."

"Don't hospital staff make jokes sometimes?" River asked. "Maybe even when it's not politically correct?"

"Yeah, but we tend not to do it when we can be overheard by nonhospital staff, 'cause we don't like to get, you know, *sued.*"

"At least no one is shooting at you."

"Depends on how you define shooting."

"Rifle, pistol, bullets. How do you define it?"

"Syringes, needles, medication."

River snorted, old disappointment in the belief that medicine could cure all a person's ills a grinding ache in his gut. "Yeah, all you need to solve a problem is the right magic potion."

"Bullets are a better way?" she asked, the challenge in her tone sharp enough to put a metallic taste in his mouth. "How many problems can you solve with violence?"

She couldn't be that naive. "Sometimes force can only be met with force."

"That's not problem solving, that's war."

"What do you think we're in the middle of? A picnic? A party?" He glanced at her, noting her crossed arms and furrowed forehead. "Terrorism has been a part of every war since the beginning."

"So has using bacteria and viruses as weapons," she retorted. "People have been dipping arrowheads into feces in a deliberate attempt to infect their targets with lethal pathogens for thousands of years. In the fourteenth century, the Tartars threw plague-infected corpses into the city of Kaffa to cause an epidemic. The Russians did the same thing to Reval, Estonia, in 1710. Weapons that can only be combated by your so-called magic potions."

"It's an underhanded way to fight a war."

"Is there a good way?" She shook her head. "These people aren't going to follow the Geneva Convention or any other rules of engagement. They want to win, even if they have to kill everyone on both sides to do it."

"It's fucking crazy."

"Yes." She sat on the cot and leaned toward him. "So, how does a crazy person think if they're trying to kill everyone?"

Unfortunately, he knew the answer to that. "They use a bigger bomb."

"What kind of bomb?"

"Why settle for just one?" He shrugged. "If it were me, I'd get as many bangs in for my buck as possible."

Ava gasped, as if he'd stabbed her in the chest with a red-hot blade. "The more the merrier, huh?" she asked, sour disillusionment twisting her words. "Kill as many people as you can. That's the goal?"

River stared at her for what felt like a long time. It was probably only a few seconds, yet it seemed like forever, before he said, "No. Fear is the goal. Killing in large numbers is part of how they drive the fear."

"Why use an infectious disease as a weapon? Wouldn't blowing things up be enough?"

"An outbreak and explosives have two things in common," River said softly. "Shock and awe. They're loud, large, and flashy. One is quick, the other slower, leaving no place safe."

She stared at him. "That's just…evil."

"And they aren't done yet."

"So, more explosions?"

"Likely." He nodded. "It'll be something visible and

shocking."

"Okay," she said, sounding like she was choking on the word. "I'm scared now."

He glanced at her. "No, you're not really scared yet."

"How do you know? We've known each other all of what?" She looked at her watch. "Not even twenty-four hours."

"Have you ever been certain you were about to die? Absolutely sure?"

She blinked. "No."

"Then you haven't been scared enough."

She wet her lips. "So, scare me." It was a challenge and a dare.

He moved to stand in front of her, then crouched down so he could easily run the back of his fingers down her face. "Scaring you is the last thing I want to do."

The things he wanted to do to her, with her, required time, privacy, and a large bed. He tried to imagine how long it would take to work her out of his system and…couldn't. She delighted him in every way from her soft skin, deep eyes, and sharp intelligence to her stubborn strength of will. She was his match.

Fear rolled over him in a dark, icy tide. Violence was his business, and it followed him with the mercilessness of a shadow, tainting everything he touched and every thought in his head.

He didn't deserve her, not with the ghosts of his fragmented memories haunting him, ambushing him. He was damaged. Wounded in mind and body.

But, some of his missing memories had surfaced. He'd finally let go and trusted someone—*her*—in a way he hadn't been able to since he'd been kicked in the head. His memories were coming *back*.

Could he have more than just a day-to-day existence?

What if he left the Army? It had crossed his mind more than once, but with nowhere to go, it had just been a passing thought. What if he looked for work in...Atlanta...where the CDC was headquartered?

She covered his hand with hers, keeping it trapped against her soft skin. "Every time I think I understand you," she whispered, "you go and say something that confuses the heck out of me."

He shrugged, enjoying the feel of her under his hand in a way that satisfied something ravenous deep at his core. "I'm a simple soldier."

She tilted her head to one side. "No," she said slowly. "No, you're not." She leaned forward and kissed him.

Chapter Twenty-One

11:22 a.m.

River froze under her lips.

Surprise.

She'd certainly surprised herself. There'd been no internal dialogue or decision-making process, just a bone-deep, *heart-deep* need for his touch she refused to deny herself. Not if things were as dangerous as River claimed they were.

And they were. So many sick. So many dead. With no end in sight.

She wanted him, wanted the pleasure, the care she knew he would give her, even if was just for an hour. It would hurt to see him walk away when all this was over, if they both survived, but it was a risk she was willing to take.

He still hadn't moved, and she almost smiled at the idea of seducing him. She'd never seduced anyone before. How hard could it be?

She ran her tongue across his bottom lip, and he detonated, his hands yanking her off the cot and onto his lap.

Not hard at all.

Her knees landed on either side of him, proving to her that some parts of him were very hard indeed.

He took her mouth and plundered it with an urgency that made her crazy in return. She wanted him inside her, not his fingers, his cock. She rocked against him and bit his bottom lip at the same time.

He growled low, almost silently, but the vibration went all the way through her, as he shoved his hand down the back of her pants. His long fingers caressed and teased her, making her squirm and moan.

"Shh," he whispered in her ear. "There are people all around us, and those little sounds you're making are *killing* me."

She nipped his earlobe, then sucked on it, and he jerked beneath her, his breathing becoming choppy. His fingers were busy coaxing cream from her body, but she wanted more than that.

Ava jerked herself away, checked the tent's closure. Zipped up tight. Giving River a grin, she tore off her clothes, all of them.

His mouth fell open as he took her in. She didn't give him time to protest or try to talk her into putting some of her clothes back on. She went to her knees in front of him and attacked his pants.

"Ava," he breathed, his hands coming up to cup her breasts, tease her nipples. "Fuck me, you're *gorgeous*."

"Yes, please," she told him in a voice so soft she was almost mouthing the words. She tried to undo the button on his pants, but he brushed her hands away and undid them himself.

He shoved his pants and briefs down his legs until they were just above his knees. "One of us needs to be able to react quickly if someone comes," he said in that soundless whisper.

He yanked a condom out of a small pocket in his pants and rolled it on.

Ava didn't comment; she was too busy staring. She hadn't been with anyone since Adam, and River's cock was every bit as large as she'd thought it was when she'd stroked him to orgasm.

His hands pulled her toward him, breaking her concentration, and she reached for him. When her hand wrapped around him, he hissed soundlessly.

She straddled him again, kissing him as she guided him with one hand. He entered her, slowly, carefully, at first, but his thrusts gathered momentum, and soon he was all the way in. He hit places inside her that made her want to moan and cry. Bending her backward so he could take one of her nipples into his mouth, he sucked hard while he loved her.

Her climax seemed to come out of nowhere, detonating a chain reaction of pleasure that had her biting down on the heel of her hand to keep from screaming. River increased his pace, taking her harder until his own orgasm shuddered through him.

For a few moments, they rested together, their arms around each other, and it was so easy, so comforting, she wanted to stay that way for the rest of her life.

Voices outside the tent, none too close but audible nonetheless, tore her out of her fantasy and dropped her back into cold, cruel reality.

River gave her one last, lingering kiss, then lifted her off him. While she dressed, he got the condom off and added it to a small bag of garbage near the tent's door.

Putting on her clothes felt awkward, and her body shivered in the chill air. What had she just done?

River came up behind her and wrapped his arms around her. "Hey, you okay?"

"Yes, just…wow, that was so inappropriate. Anyone could

have walked in on us."

His body shook. He was laughing.

"It's not funny." She elbowed him.

He kept grinning. "Sweetheart, you didn't give me any options. You had your clothes off so fast, I haven't recovered yet." He kissed her neck. "I probably never will."

"You could have...protested."

"Not a chance. You're a fucking bombshell." He kissed her again. "Come on, let's get some rest."

He nudged her toward the cot, and she lay down while River stretched out on the mat Henry had lent him the last time they rested here.

River hadn't slept well then.

"Are you okay down there?" she asked, peeking over the side of the cot.

His eyes were closed, but he smiled. "Yeah, you have well and truly tamed my ghosts for today."

Ava rolled onto her back. What did that mean?

The next thing she knew, someone was calling her name.

Ava sat up in a rush and stared at the man poking his head into the tent. Agent Dozer.

"You awake?" he asked.

"Yeah, yeah," River said, also sitting up. His position on the floor put his head just above her waist. He glanced at her. "We're up."

"We've caught a break," Dozer said with a satisfied grin. "Police patrol spotted the senator's car at a motel." Dozer pulled his head out of the tent.

River stood, already wearing his boots. She had to put hers on.

"You okay?" he asked her.

"Yeah. How long did we sleep?"

He checked his watch. "Only about thirty minutes."

"Huh. I feel oddly refreshed."

River's grin was massive.

She shook a finger at him and mouthed, "Don't you dare take credit."

He just kept smiling.

Dozer was waiting for them with Private Castillo about ten feet away from the tent.

"The police said there was no activity at the motel," Dozer told them. He nodded at Castillo. "He's all I can spare right now."

"No problem," River replied. "We'll check this out and let you know what we find."

Ava watched their faces as they talked and wondered at the calm she saw. "You think he's dead, don't you?"

"Only if he's lucky," River muttered.

Dozer didn't respond, just glanced at her before saying to River, "Keep in touch."

"Our vehicle is this way," Castillo said, starting out at a fast walk. Ava grabbed the equipment she needed to take samples, if there were any to take. River had his rifle, a handgun, and at least two knives she could see. Castillo was armed with another rifle, not quite as fancy as River's.

They donned respirators, gloves, and safety glasses, then left the clean area for wherever their vehicle was waiting. Castillo already had the address, so he drove.

No one said anything on the drive to the motel. It was all Ava could do to keep herself calm. She would be cautious and careful. Everything else was out of her hands. Breathing in and out in a slow, even pattern finally helped to loosen the fist around her throat.

The motel wasn't a very inviting-looking place. 1970s-era design with an interior courtyard badly in need of fresh paint and new concrete.

Castillo drove in at a crawl and parked a few spaces down from the only luxury vehicle in sight. There were a few other cars in the lot, but they were old, battered, and dirty. If the kid was trying to hide, he wasn't doing a very good job of it. His dad's shiny car stood out like a diamond in a coal pile. "Do you think he parked in front of his motel room?"

"Is anyone that stupid?" River asked.

"Well," Ava tilted her head to one side. "If he's sick, he might be. Confusion is one of the symptoms."

River shot a hard glance at her, then resumed his visual inspection of the motel's courtyard. "Yeah, he was definitely off in la-la-land." He craned his head around to look at Castillo. "How far are we from the Fort Bliss main gate?"

"About ten minutes."

"Do me a favor," River said. "Go see if anyone is working the desk. Find out if the driver of the car that's worth more money than this entire motel is checked in and into which room."

"Will do." Castillo hopped out and trotted to the manager's office.

The small amount of calm she'd managed to acquire drained away. If Harris was dead, their investigation was also dead. They needed him alive and able to answer questions.

A couple of minutes later, Castillo slid back into the car. "He's in room 124."

Before she or River could respond, Ava's cell phone beeped. River put his hand to his ECC Bluetooth as well.

Dr. Rodrigues said, "Three grade schools have been hit with explosions."

Children? The terrorists targeted *children*? "Oh my God," Ava whispered.

"Luckily, no one was inside. One of the television stations received a bomb threat about twenty minutes ago, which included a line reading, *The attacks and disease will continue until all American troops are withdrawn from Syria and Afghanistan. No one is safe.* As a result, the state of emergency has been expanded to include the entire El Paso County. I've also put the entire county under quarantine. All public buildings and services have been closed."

Tired. She sounded so tired.

"Find the source, the terrorists…whoever is doing all this, and stop them. By any means necessary."

"Ma'am?" Ava's stomach twisted tight so fast, nausea hit with dizzying effect.

"Public safety is at risk, and if things continue to escalate, the outbreak could spread exponentially. This strain of Neisseria seems to survive longer on surfaces, and its contagiousness tells me it's being spread through casual mucosal contact."

"Understood," River said, his voice calm and cold. "We're at the motel now. We'll contact you if we find Ethan Harris or anything connected to the attacks."

"Good." There was a click, and Ava realized their boss had just armed their most lethal weapon, a man who carried something far more dangerous than a rifle.

Fury. Until now, the rules of engagement on home soil had been very restrictive. Dr. Rodrigues had just given River permission to ignore many of those restrictions. He had a target now—eliminate those responsible for the chaos.

Heaven help them.

River looked at her, no hint of indecision in him. "Castillo and I are going to start with the room we think he's in. You're going to stay here."

"What do you mean, *start*?"

"Break down the door and hope he's there."

At least he didn't say *shoot first and ask questions later*. She'd take that as a good sign.

"Okay. Just…be careful. I refuse to deal with any more explosions today."

He blew out a breath, which made him sound like a

masked evil Jedi with his respirator on. "Our track record on that isn't so good." He gave her puppy-dog eyes. "I don't know if I can promise that."

She rolled her eyes. Nope, not backing down on this. "Trying counts."

River glanced at Castillo. "You ready?"

"Give the go, Sergeant."

River opened his door and crouched on the pavement next to the van. He repositioned his rifle, then said, "Go."

Both men were gone with a speed and silence that left her gaping. They crouched on either side of the room's door. River nodded once, then Castillo kicked it in. River dove inside, as if he'd been shot out of a cannon.

She found herself holding her breath as she waited to hear gunshots, but no sound emerged from the dark doorway.

Ten heartbeats later, River stepped out and waved at her to come in. Though he wore his respirator, she could read frustration and disappointment in his posture, back rigid and straight.

So, no good news, but no explosions. She'd take that result.

She exited the van and approached him. "What did you find?"

His answer was short. "More questions."

The room was dark, the curtains pulled shut, and cold. Had someone turned up the air conditioning? There was an overturned chair and lamp on the floor. The bed was a mess, and on it Ethan Harris lay on his back, unmoving. There was no missing the bullet hole in the center of his forehead.

She approached with caution and examined the dead man visually.

The signs of meningococcal disease were evident in the frothy blood at the corner of his mouth and in his nose. His damp hair. An autopsy would have to be done to be sure.

River searched the room, but there wasn't much to find.

Not even a cell phone.

"Was Harris part of the attacks or just the wrong guy in the wrong place?" Ava asked River as she took a sample of blood from Harris's nose with one of the collection swabs she carried in her belt tool kit.

"There's absolutely nothing here besides the body." River did not look happy about that.

"And his father's vehicle," Ava reminded him.

An odd noise caught her attention—a deep-throated boom that was as much a vibration as sound.

River made a call to Dozer with his ECC device. "Dozer said a suicide bomber just drove a vehicle overland through two barbed wire fences into the base. He got within fifty feet of a barrack before his car blew up."

"Oh my God."

"Any causalities?" Castillo asked.

"Seven."

"Fuck," the soldier hissed.

Ava stared at Harris's dead face and had to restrain the urge to kick him. He was already dead. He wasn't the one she wanted to hurt anyway. The one she wanted to hurt was still out there, sending college students to their deaths. "I hate these people," she snarled.

"Get in line," River told her in a growl. "Got enough samples? We need to move."

"Yes." She dusted off her hands. "Yes, I'm done."

River strode over to the open doorway and looked out.

The sound of vehicles entering the courtyard had her taking a half-step back. Several vehicles.

"Who?" She glanced at him, but River was moving.

He closed the door, locked it, turned, then said in a calm voice, "Go out the window facing the alley. Go. *Now.*"

Castillo ran to the window and shoved the curtain aside. The sliding glass pane refused to move, despite the soldier's repeated attempts to force it open.

Ava gaped at him. What was going on?

Someone knocked on the motel room door.

River grabbed her by the arm and shoved her toward Castillo. The soldier put his elbow through the glass, knocked most of the loose shards away, and clambered out the window. River motioned her to follow Castillo out, but just as she prepared to hoist herself onto the sill, a rapid rattle of shots ripped the air, and into Castillo. He fell to the ground.

Her muscles froze her in place. Not even her diaphragm moved, holding her witness to the growing blood pool beneath the soldier. She'd seen death in many of its guises, but this one told her a story she'd never fully heard before. She and River were next. No way forward or back, no escape.

A bellow broke through the ice as a hand reached around her from behind, flattened against her collarbone and pushed her backward into the room and onto the floor. River took her place at the window, looking for the shooter.

Bullets punched their way through the walls of the motel to finally stop in the interior wall adjacent to the window, narrowly missing River.

He sighted down his rifle and returned fire.

The motel room's door exploded inward, raining splinters all over Ava. She threw an arm over her face to protect her eyes, but the shards of wood still stung her exposed skin like a nest of angry hornets.

Men surged through the door.

River turned and fired at them. The first three were dead before they hit the floor. One landed only a few feet from her. He was young, blond, and wore the same jeans and casual button-up shirt any college student might wear. The expression of shock on his face slowly smoothed out, leaving him as blank as an untouched canvas.

"Get up," River yelled at her, jerking his head toward the

window. "Go, go, go!"

Castillo had gotten shot going out that window.

Lying on the floor wasn't an option, either. She rolled and got to her hands and knees. That's when more men came through the door.

More jeans.

More screams.

More blood soaking into the worn carpet.

She stayed down, still, watching the point-blank shooting with horror's hands wrapped around her neck, choking the ability to breathe out of her.

River was a silent menace behind and to her left. There was no sound or movement other than the weapon he used with complete competence. The young men trying to rush into the motel room were full of rash energy, yelling words and phrases in another language as they died. All with the same intonation as if they'd learned it by rote.

The fight went on for what seemed like months, but was probably only a few seconds. Two men crowded the motel doorway, firing at River. The man on the right went down to one knee, and someone behind him fired into the space he vacated. River jerked and grunted. His rifle slipped, his right arm hanging oddly limp.

The man on his knee collapsed, but the one next to him advanced, followed by two more, who pointed their weapons at River's head.

"Drop your gun," one of the young men ordered in a tone so close to a whine that it grated on her nerves.

Someone stopped in front of her, wearing black military-style boots. She glanced up into the muzzle of a rifle.

"Drop your weapon," Boots said, his voice controlled, certain. There was nothing rote in his body language or tone.

River stood completely unmoving for one long second, then he said in a tired-sounding voice, "Okay." He breathed deeply, and when she turned her head to look at him, lines of pain bracketed his eyes. "I can't untangle myself from the weapon, though. My right arm isn't working so good."

He'd been shot? She sucked in a breath, the first in a long while, and pushed up from her position on the floor, but the man in front of her put the gun to her forehead. "Down."

The muzzle of the weapon was surprisingly hot.

"She's not armed," River said, pain a living thing she could hear in his voice. "She's a doctor."

Boots didn't move. "Take his weapon and his mask," he said to someone.

Ava watched out of the corner of her eye as the whiner roughly took River's rifle from him, ripped the respirator off his face and the ECC Bluetooth out of his ear. He ground the communication device into the carpet with his heel.

"You son of a bitch," Whiner said, coughing. "You're gonna die, but it's gonna be slow."

"Yeah?" River said in a tone that didn't seem too concerned. "I'm not the only one, asshole."

Whiner shoved his gun into River's face. "What did you say, you fucking murderer?" He pushed the muzzle of his gun against River's forehead. "Huh? You threatening me?"

Boots stepped away from her, grabbed Whiner by the arm, and pulled him back. "Don't let him anger you. He's hoping you'll kill him quickly."

"Not a chance," Whiner said, coughing some more. "I'm in control."

He was sweating, and his cough sounded productive.

"I highly doubt that," Ava said.

"Shut up, bitch," Whiner moved toward her, but Boots backhanded her before the kid could take more than a step.

"Woman, you will keep your mouth shut."

She landed on her side, facing one of the dead men. The world narrowed into a long, hollow tunnel, turning everyone into shadows and speech into intelligible echoes.

How long before she joined the bodies on the floor?

Something tugged at her face, and she remembered to breathe. Her vision returned as someone reached over, pulled her respirator off, and threw it in the corner. River was shoved down next to her a moment later by Boots, who then began issuing orders as if he were some sort of evil mastermind.

Whiner stood over them, his smile enough to turn her stomach.

"Keep grinning, moron," River said to him. "Maybe you'll die happy." He chuckled, but it sounded forced.

The kid, enough lingering baby fat on his face and arms to put him at eighteen or nineteen years old, sneered. "You're the one who's going to die."

"I've been hunted by men who actually know how to point a rifle, and dude, that isn't you."

The kid looked River over. "You're a soldier. Were you over there? The Middle East, murdering the poor farmers who can't put enough food on the table to feed their families because our government is too fucking greedy to help?"

He sounded like a brainwashed cultist.

"Nope. I was over there," River said, "trying to save those farmers from asshole drug lords who think Americans are stupid." He gasped with theatrical flair and widened his eyes. "Hey, that's you."

"That's it," Whiner said. "You're dead."

Chapter Twenty-Two

11:11 a.m.

River ignored everything but the moron in front of him who held his handgun like a gangster, almost sideways. It would be a miracle if he didn't shoot himself or one of his own buddies by accident.

He wanted their attention on him, not on his mouse, who lay not two feet behind him on the bloody carpet.

"What's the cause, *Kemosabe*?" River asked Moron. "What fabulous line of bullshit did they feed you to turn you into a traitor?"

"*Kemosabe*? Don't fucking insult Native Americans by using—"

"I *am* Native American," River interrupted. "So fuck you and the ugly horse you rode in on."

The tall terrorist wearing combat boots, who looked a few years older than Moron, pulled at the idiot's arm. "Enough. Back up."

"He killed six of our people," Moron said, his jaw clenched

so tight it looked as if he'd had his mouth wired shut.

Too bad it wasn't.

"Our men were prepared to die," Tall said. "Don't cheapen their sacrifice by giving this ignorant fool more of your attention than he deserves." Tall smiled, one comrade to another, as if they were in charge of everything.

River started to laugh. More of a chuckle, really, but it gathered energy and momentum as seconds went by.

Tall and Moron started at him, the disgust on their faces so strong it made him laugh harder.

Tall shifted, disgust devolving into the kind of fury precluding a serious ass kicking.

River tensed his abdominal muscles, anticipating those boots impacting his gut with everything the kid could put behind it.

"Why do you want us alive?"

Ava's question froze Tall in place. His muscles slowly relaxed as the question seemed to circle the room, refocusing Tall, Moron, and the two other gunmen who'd come in behind them on her.

Fuck.

Tall stared over River's shoulder at his mouse for two long seconds, and then he glanced at River and stepped back.

"Load the woman in the van. Tie him up and leave him here."

The men moved to follow orders.

"If you need my cooperation in any way, you won't leave him here to die slowly of blood loss," Ava said.

"Ava, *don't*," River hissed at her.

Tall didn't even look at him. He smiled at Ava, and it was ugly. "You'll cooperate, or we'll do things so horrible to you, you couldn't imagine them."

Shit. She wasn't going to let that go.

"What do you see when you look at me?" she asked him.

"A young woman sheltered by the easy life in the United States? Someone who's never known a moment of hardship, thirst, hunger, or pain?"

"That's what you *are*," Tall said, showing her his teeth.

Ah fuck, here it comes.

"I have treated people in war zones and in quarantine. I have faced men with guns and witnessed torture. I have gone without food or sleep for days. *You* don't scare me. So, if you want my cooperation, you'll allow me to stop his bleeding. Otherwise…"

She'd thrown down a gauntlet. What the fuck would these little boys, who thought they were men, going to do about it?

Tall pointed his rifle at River's head, then said to her, "You have one minute."

Ava was up and forcing him onto his back a second later, muttering, "Where is it? Where is *it*?"

"Right armpit." River studied her face. There was blood splattered across the skin of her chin, and from just below her eyes all the way up into her hair.

"Any chest pain?" she asked as she dug her fingers into his body armor, trying to get it out of the way. "Difficulty breathing?"

Was she kidding?

"This doesn't feel any better or worse than the last time."

She hummed under her breath just as her fingers hit something that made his shoulder radiate pain. He jerked under her hands, but managed to keep quiet.

She lifted the edge of his armor, then hooked her fingers into his shirt and tore it. "Good, it hit high and missed your lungs. Bad, it may have cracked your scapula." She opened one of her leg pockets and pulled out a triangular bandage, the kind medics use to make a sling, and stuffed it under his armor.

"What does that mean?" he managed to croak, despite

the pain all her digging around the pressure bandage caused. He knew what it meant, but he wanted his audience to think he was unable to deal with his wound.

She put her hand on his neck and looked at her watch. "No shooting rifles for a while."

"Woo," he said, his voice artificially high. "A vacation."

She crossed her eyes at him.

What the fuck?

Before he could ask out loud, she said, "Your pulse is… okay, but you've lost a lot of blood. Do *not* try to use your right arm or shoulder, or you could puncture a lung or an artery. Make sure you seek medical care as soon as possible." She crossed her eyes again.

The hospital was tapped out, and she knew it. Was she trying to tell him something with the crossed eye bit?

"This isn't a trip to the hospital," Moron said to her as he grabbed her by the hair and hauled her to her feet. "Your minute is up."

Ava looked at the moron and said, "I promise to do what I'm told." Then she looked at River and crossed her eyes a third time.

Geez, she was trying to tell him everything she said was opposite of what she meant. What had she said to him?

No shooting rifles.

Don't use your right arm.

Seek medical care.

The bullet obviously didn't do much damage. It just hurt. Wuss.

"Can I shoot him anyway?" Moron asked Tall.

"No, we need him to give the cops a message." Tall crouched down next to him and casually put the muzzle of his weapon on his shoulder. And pushed.

River didn't bother trying to hide any pain, but he didn't want to overdo it, either, so he settled for wincing and grunting.

Tall leaned in and said softly, "Tell the police, the FBI, and Homeland Security that our reign of terror isn't over just yet. We might hang around El Paso, or we might move on to another city." Tall shrugged. "But we're *not* done."

"What, no manifesto?" River asked, letting his voice come out hoarse. "No demands?"

Tall patted him on the cheek. "Maybe next time." He stood, walked three steps away, then turned and shot River point-blank in the chest three times.

Son of a bitch, those hurt.

Ava screamed and tried to get away from Moron, who jerked her back, then had to chase her after she twisted out of his hold. She only got a couple steps away before he grabbed her around the waist and carried her, kicking and screaming, out the motel room door. His boss and the other two stooges followed.

Tall knew River was wearing armor, knew the bullets wouldn't likely penetrate to do any real damage. He was just fucking with Ava's head and making River hurt because it was fun for him.

Asshole.

When he caught the guy, he was going to rip him a new one. And he was going to catch him. Tall had made a huge mistake.

He'd left River alive.

As soon as their vehicle was gone, River levered himself off the floor and went out the window. Castillo was still lying in the alley, his weapon on the ground beside him. River picked up the rifle.

He dug out his cell phone and called Dozer.

"Dozer here," said the agent.

"We just got jumped by our terrorists. I've been shot. It's not too bad, but Dr. Lloyd has been taken. Can you track her cell phone?"

"Only if she keeps it on and it doesn't get thrown out or destroyed. Hang on."

River could hear Dozer talking to someone, asking for a trace on Dr. Lloyd's crisis phone.

"Okay, she's still online. She's moving, heading back in this direction."

"She's in a van with at least four other people. They're armed, and they *think* they know what they're doing."

"Are you telling me we're dealing with more college-student terrorists?" Dozer did not sound impressed.

"Yeah. If they don't manage to kill themselves first, we're going to have to put up with a bunch of kids who think they know something about warfare, complete with bad movie lines."

"Is it too late to quit my job?"

That made River laugh. "Sorry, man. Until this emergency is over, Rodrigues is the only person who can help you with that."

"I'm doomed."

"At least no one has shot you yet."

Dozer didn't respond immediately, and River waited, hoping for an update on Ava's location. "Okay, it looks like they're headed for the university."

There were manned road blocks between the motel and the university. "If they get stopped by anyone, they're going to shoot."

"Give me a minute to clear the path." Dozer was gone.

River waited, using the time to check his shoulder. It hurt like a son of a bitch, but there wasn't as much blood as he expected. Maybe his body armor had caught part of the bullet and it just went through the meaty part of his under arm. He checked Castillo's rifle, then went back inside the room to wait.

He fucking hated waiting. Every second that went by

meant another second his mouse was with those assholes. They'd threatened to hurt her, and they would if they decided that would get them something they wanted. Or if she pissed them off too much. His mouse was too smart for her own good and too quick to share her insights, no matter how inflammatory, with everyone.

If they touched her, he'd rip them apart with just his hands.

Dozer came back on without warning. "She's stationary at the university. The chemistry and computer science building."

"They went back to the university? You're sure?"

"Yeah. Where were you hit?"

"A through and through near my armpit. It's messy, but shouldn't slow me down."

"What do you need?" Dozer's voice was calm.

"Seeing as how the hospital is at full capacity, I'm not looking for an ambulance right now. What I could really use is wheels and maybe a little backup."

"You might as well ask for the fucking moon. The roads are jammed a mile in every direction around the hospital. You heard Rodrigues has imposed a twenty-four-hour ban on all travel and public gatherings in the entire county? Anyone caught outside without a respirator and fucking Green Lantern ring will be put in lockup."

It was the right thing to do, but it was going to make his job a lot harder. "Great. Now I have to hide from the good guys and the bad."

"River, you *are* a Green Lantern ring."

"Did you just call me *special*?"

Dozer laughed. "Yeah, with a goddamn superhero cape." The laugh died. "Listen, give me a couple minutes to see if I can arrange transport for you to the university campus."

"You do that. I'm going to see if I can plug this hole in my arm a little better." He began removing his body armor. He had to take off his shirt to see the wound clearly and realized it could have been a lot worse.

The bullet had drilled a hole through his triceps, but missed hitting the brachial artery. He was able to wrap the bandage around it and secure it tightly. It hurt, but he welcomed the pain. He'd learned a long time ago to use it to stay focused. Once he got his body armor on, it supported the wound fairly well.

After he had himself put together, he called Dozer again. "Got anything for me?"

"Yeah, but it's a little unconventional."

"Dude, I'd take a mule."

Dozer chuckled, but it sounded tired. "You'll be okay with this, then. I'm sending a transit bus."

That wasn't far from a mule. "What's the punch line?"

"The driver is a retired drill sergeant."

Seriously? "El Paso public transit hires drill sergeants?"

"They couldn't keep anyone on a couple of the college's routes. Rowdy riders. No one gives the drill sergeant any shit."

"I fucking believe it. What's his ETA?"

"About ten minutes."

"What does he know?"

"You're Special Forces, you've been shot, and you're going after the assholes responsible for the terrorist attacks."

Jesus.

"Is he armed?"

"He's got a license to carry, so I assume so."

"I actually feel sorry for the assholes. A drill sergeant on the warpath is about the worse thing I can think of to sic on them."

"I kind of wish I could watch."

"I'll make sure my report is detailed."

"I look forward to hearing about it when this shit is over. The travel ban is going to keep me on my toes, so if you call and I don't answer right away, keep calling." He paused for a moment, then said, "Good luck."

"You, too," River replied. He picked up Castillo's weapon and walked toward the entrance to the courtyard.

To wait for his bus.

If things weren't so fucked up, he'd laugh.

The bus pulled up next to him a few minutes later, and the door opened to reveal a grizzled gray-haired man with a regulation buzz cut, a respirator, and the eyes of a madman on vacation.

"Well now, are you my special snowflake?" the driver asked, his voice roughened by either too many cigarettes or too much yelling. Probably both.

Drill sergeants always ask trick questions.

"Yes, Drill Sergeant," River replied, as if he were still in basic training. "Permission to board the bus, Drill Sergeant?"

The old geezer laughed. "Get the fuck on, Snowflake, and point me in the direction of the sonofabitches who need their asses kicked."

River boarded, and the driver shut the door.

He held out a hand. "And call me DS. I'm retired."

They shook. "River."

"Nah," DS said. "I'm going to call you Snowflake, unless there's trouble. *Then* I'll call you River." He put the bus in gear. "Where are we going?"

"The chemistry and computer science building at the university."

The evil eyes were back. "Buckle up, Snowflake."

Chapter Twenty-Three

11:33 a.m.

Anger was too tame a name for what coursed through Ava's body like a molten river, scorching everything it touched.

Rage was a little better.

Murderous. That sounded right.

She doubted she looked homicidal at the moment. Not after screaming, crying, kicking, and blubbering all over the college kid trying to hang onto her. All of them could see the result of tears and snot running unchecked down her face. She hoped she looked hysterical.

She hoped they thought she was terrified of them.

She was terrified, but of the Neisseria they no doubt carried, not of them specifically. These boys, *children*, were rejoicing in their triumph of winning a battle against two armed soldiers. Premature celebration.

Had they forgotten the six dead of their own they left behind?

There were only four of them left.

Were four all there really was? The van they were in had no backseats in it. Someone was driving, another person riding shotgun, and two in the back with her. If she got loose, there would be one fewer. She had plans for the asshole who'd shot River. Plans that involved her hands wrapped around his throat. Plans that ended with only one of them still breathing.

He had a smug expression on his face whenever he glanced back at her. The prick. Just because a girl has an ugly cry doesn't mean she isn't busy plotting to kill you. In fact, if you're the cause of the ugly cry, she probably *is* plotting to kill you.

The driver was arguing with Boots, telling him they should hide and not go back to the university, while Boots insisted that since the CDC had already been to the university, they weren't likely to go back.

Had someone made a law about that when she wasn't paying attention?

Nope.

They'd blown up a lab along with three FBI agents/bomb techs. There was going to be CDC, FBI, and Homeland Security all over that building just as soon as the demands of the outbreak allowed for an investigation.

"What do we need her for anyway?" the driver asked.

"She is going to be part of our next message to the government."

"Yeah, but what do we need her cooperation for? I mean, you gave her time to help that fucking soldier."

Boots's chuckle had a nasty edge. Malicious in a way that made her stomach twist and dive straight into the ground.

"I wanted to see if she cared about him, so when I shot him, again, she'd understand how fucking hopeless it would be to try to stop us." He turned to look at her and said, "And now you know."

She wiped her face against her shoulder, then said, "I

know what you're doing and what you are." She glanced at the other men. "Do they?"

"We're all part of a movement," Boots said proudly. "A rebellion against the greedy, cruel actions of the American government and military. They're the ones who started the war on terror, invading countries like it's their right. Killing civilians and freedom fighters indiscriminately. Peaceful protests have done nothing. Less than nothing. It's past time to wake the American public up."

"By killing large numbers of your fellow citizens?" she demanded. "That makes sense to you? *Really*?"

"Sometimes it takes a very hard shock to wake people up to the truth."

"The truth is," she said very softly now, so softly every man but the driver leaned closer to her, "that you're a spoiled sociopath who's managed to convince enough disenfranchised, impressionable young people that somewhere in all your rhetoric, you're *right*." By the time she got to the last word, she was yelling.

Big mistake.

Their faces, which had been tense with worry, now settled...hardened.

"You're gonna *die*, lady," Boots said to her with a slick smile. "That's the only truth you should care about."

She opened her mouth to allow her anger and frustration to mock him, then thought better of it. She had to find a way to stop these foolish boys from doing any more damage. Getting shot before she figured out how wouldn't help her. Of course, they might just want to shoot her in front of an audience. Video it live on the internet with the location of their choice as the backdrop.

"What about all the children who are dying, who are going to die because of the disease you've set loose?" she asked, letting go of the plug on her emotions, so fresh that tears streamed down her face. "They're innocent."

"No one is innocent." Boots laughed, a cynical, sneer of a sound. "They'll grow up to be as selfish and greedy as everyone else. Now, they won't."

One of the young men with her in the back sucked in a breath.

"Genocide isn't the answer," she said between sobs. "Education is. Stage an intervention. Show them what they should be doing. You d-don't have to kill people."

"Like I said before, peaceful protests went nowhere."

"Ch-change is hard, and it doesn't happen fast with a country as large and spread out as ours is."

"Shut the fuck up."

"You have to keep…keep trying. You need the majority of the population behind you to make the changes you seem to want. Killing them isn't going to give you that."

He pointed the rifle at her head. "If you don't shut up, I'm going to shoot you right now."

She stopped talking, but she wasn't quiet. She let herself cry and sob until Boots yelled at the two men in the back. "Shut her up!"

Ava waited for one of them to hit her, or for some other aggressive act to occur.

The guy to her left held out a tissue.

She stared at it without really understanding what it was or why he would give it to her. Offering your hostage a tissue couldn't be part of the terrorist handbook, could it? He waved it at her when she didn't take it right away. "Don't make this harder on yourself than it has to be," he said softly.

As she wiped her face, the guy behind her said, "My little sister is only five. The only thing she's guilty of is eating too much candy at Halloween."

"So, what?" Boots asked. "You want to switch sides?" He pointed his weapon at the younger man. "Too late for that."

"I'm not bailing on our mission. I just don't think little kids are guilty of all the shit their parents do. Get them into a family that has the right values and teaches those values, and they'll be great citizens of the world."

Boots grunted and lowered his rifle. "Interesting. I never thought of that." He appeared to consider the idea. "Take the kids and adopt them out," he muttered under his breath.

She hadn't thought these idiots could get any more reprehensible. Wrong. *Worse*, there was nothing she could do about it.

The van slowed. In the distance, flashing emergency lights caught everyone's attention.

"Whoa," the driver said. "There's cops ahead."

"Try another road."

"Which one?" The driver's voice shook. He was beginning to panic.

"Just turn right here, and we'll figure it out."

All four men craned their heads around to check for pursuit, but the roads were eerily empty and silent. The driver pulled over to the curb and parked.

Ava considered an escape attempt while they were stationary, but just as she made the decision to try it, Boots shifted his attention to her.

"Don't even think it, lady."

That drew the others' attention.

A cruel grin spread slowly across Boots's face. When he dropped his gaze to stare at her breasts, she held her breath and waited to see what he would do next. Or not do. As one second flowed into two, then three, her imagination gave her more and more unwanted possibilities, twisting her stomach until it was so painful she could barely breathe. Boots believed in his cause wholeheartedly. The others were followers, not happy about killing little kids, but they would follow his orders. If she pushed now, tried to talk sense into the followers, she'd only succeed in getting shot. Or raped.

The guy behind her spoke up. "According to my phone, there's a route delivery trucks are supposed to take into the college."

"That sounds good," Boots said, finally looking away from her.

The boy with the phone gave the driver the first set of directions, and he pulled away from the curb.

"Hey, how come it's so quiet?" the other kid in the back with her asked. "No cars, no one walking, everything looks closed."

Boots turned and looked at her.

She couldn't see how the truth could help them. "I think there's a travel ban. Possibly a quarantine." The depth of hate in his face constricted her throat, and she had to clear it in order to keep talking. "To try to keep the outbreak from spreading."

"We're gonna get pulled over," the driver whined.

The kid beside her joined him in complaint-land. "They're not going to arrest us, not after we killed all those people at the mall and the Army base. They'll just fucking shoot us."

"If you don't stop bitching," Boots said, "*I'll* fucking shoot you." He chewed on his bottom lip for a moment. "No one is chasing us now, so we'll keep going." He turned to the driver. "Follow the speed limit."

"Okay, okay," the driver said, but his tone told her he was close to panic. He probably didn't know what to do, so he'd grab onto anything that sounded reasonable.

"Relax, guys," Boots said in a tone that dripped confidence. "Our encore performance is going to send a message no one in Texas is ever going to forget."

"Is it going to work, Sam?" the kid beside her asked. "Will it make the government withdraw troops from—"

"Shut up," Boots said. "Not in front of *her*."

So, his name was Sam.

"Who's she going to tell?" the guy behind her asked. "It's not like there's anyone around." He gestured at the empty streets and deserted sidewalks.

"I'm not taking any chances. She works for the CDC, probably one of those lab rats who creates superbugs."

She opened her mouth to deny it, but Boots sent her a look so filled with venom she choked on her own words.

"She's smart." Boots sneered at her. "Aren't you, lab rat?"

Oh no, the only person who got to call her a rodent of any sort was River.

"Call me a rat again," she said to Boots, uncaring of the bullet he could put in her head if he chose to, "and I'll rip your balls off."

His eyebrows went up while the two young men in the back with her leaned away.

It was the driver who spoke. "You do know we have the guns, right, lady?"

"Listen, assholes," she told them, suddenly tired of it all. "You can take your self-absorbed, whiney, *hey, let's save the world by killing everyone* bullshit and shove it. I thought the bureaucracy in Africa was ass-backwards, but you guys take the cake."

"Africa?" the driver asked.

"Yes, the Ebola crisis, remember that?"

"Yeah."

"I was there for four months, trying to save lives. What were you doing? Oh yes, planning to release your own plague on Texas and a few bombs, too. Was achieving your goals of world peace taking so long that you decided to just kill everyone instead?"

No one said anything, not even Boots.

"Have any of you even spent time out of North America on a humanitarian mission?"

No answer.

"I'll bet you've never even gone camping without all the equipment known to man in your backpacks. You don't know a damn thing about what people need or want. All you're doing is trying to get an adrenaline rush by being rebels. Well, congratulations, you've achieved it. You've managed to kill several hundred completely innocent people, people who have nothing to do with the establishment you seem angry with. Just what have you accomplished today? Other than proving you're lazy."

"You're thinking much too small," Boots told her in a cold tone. "And peace isn't what we're after. We're the instrument of change. Our government doesn't govern anymore. They argue, yell, and piss each other off. No one negotiates, no one compromises, they don't even talk to each other."

"Selfish bastards," said the guy behind her.

"Useless, greedy, and ignorant—that's our government," the kid next to her said.

"The only way to rejuvenate a great society like the United States is to put it under stress. *Force* the public and government to do something." Sam smiled. "History is full of examples of civilizations that rose and fell in this way."

"Like the Roman Empire," one of the boys with her in the back said.

"The French Revolution wiped out an absolute monarchy," the other added.

History was never meant to be viewed through lenses of only black and white. "You think inciting another revolution is going to change our culture for the better?"

"Yes."

"But at what cost? Are you prepared to sacrifice not only yourselves, but your families as well?" She turned to look at the guy behind her. "Your sister?"

"Collateral damage," Boots said. "History will remember

us as freedom fighters. The instigators of change, and the events here in El Paso as the first of many that will usher in a new and better America."

She looked around her. Aside from the driver, who was watching the road, they all wore the same expression of blind devotion and utter belief.

There would be no convincing them to stop whatever they planned to do next. These young men had been turned into living weapons.

Chapter Twenty-Four

11:46 a.m.

River never imagined he'd be trying to storm a university to save a woman who meant more to him than any woman should after knowing her less than a day.

A woman he desperately wanted to kiss and caress without the possibility of anyone interrupting them. A circumstance he was determined to fix the first chance he got. He wanted to stroke and pet his mouse until she was as desperate for him as he was for her. Alone. Naked. No rushing.

And, *fuck me*, he was doing it during an outbreak with a retired drill sergeant watching his back.

Fucking spoiled, stupid, rich kids. Someone had gotten to them, convinced them the best thing to do with their lives was to make a big statement by blowing themselves up. When he caught that guy, there was going to be blood. Lots of it.

DS pulled over to a curb, turned on his hazard lights, then turned and gave River another one of those evaluative once-overs only a drill sergeant could deliver, and said, "How much shit are we dealing with?"

"A whole pile of steaming shit," River replied. "We've got an outbreak of deadly meningitis. Probably more than three hundred dead by now. Once you get it, it kills you fast. On top of that, we've got a bunch of college kids running around with military-grade weapons blowing shit up, thinking all of this is going to save the world."

"Jesus Christ on a pogo stick," DS muttered under his breath.

"One of them shot me three times in the chest, knowing I wore body armor, just to make the woman he kidnapped panic."

"Why didn't the puke just kill you?"

"I think he wanted me to hurt, and not just from the bullet bruises. The woman he took is…valuable."

"You say that like she's the love of your life, Snowflake. Got a crush?"

There was no use hiding it. DS needed to know he'd do some serious shit to get her away from those assholes. "What can I say, DS? Smart women do it for me."

"Christ, save me from lovebirds," the older man muttered. "So, you're ready to go over the wall for this woman?"

"Over the wall and into Wonderland, DS."

The drill sergeant looked him over with a gaze that missed nothing. "You already took a bullet today, son."

"I'm Navajo. We eat bullets for breakfast."

The laugh that came out of the retired drill sergeant's mouth was malicious. "Got a plan, or are we going to make it up as we go along?"

"A bit of both. I figure we use your God-given talent to create a distraction so I can go in and get my girl."

"A distraction." The DS said it like most people would say *leprosy*.

"They've got the same FN SCAR rifles like mine, and

grenades. I'd prefer you keep them so confused about which way was up so they don't know where to point or throw any of it." River glanced at the building. What were they doing in there with Ava right now? Nope, couldn't think like that. "You got a weapon besides your voice, DS?"

The old man reached down and picked up an old fashioned lunch box. Inside were a Beretta and three clips. "You're not the only one who likes to eat bullets."

River smiled. "Are we related, because that's badass!"

DS smacked his cheek a couple of times. "If you want to be a drill sergeant when you grow up, Snowflake, you gotta get *mean*."

River pulled out his phone and consulted the floor plan for the building.

"Problem number one," River began. "We don't know their exact location. Problem number two, we don't know how many people we're dealing with or how they're armed besides rifles. Problem number three, we don't know what they plan to do, so if it's to go out in a big bang, well…we could go *poof* along with them."

"Son," DS said with a huge sigh and a shake of his head. "You've gotta stop hanging out with pansy-ass doctors. *Poof?*"

River grinned and shrugged. "Let's do a little recon and find out where they are. Then we can move on to distract and destroy."

"Now you're speaking my language."

The drill sergeant shut down the bus, and they tried the front door. Locked. So were the rest of the entrances, but none of the doors or windows had been damaged.

"Someone let them in," DS said. "Or one of those little assholes has a key."

River returned to one of the single side-door entrances and pulled his lock picks out of a pocket in his pants. "So do I."

DS snorted and watched as River picked the lock, which only took five or six seconds. They slipped inside and quietly shut the door. The stairwell they were in was empty and closed off from the rest of the building by another door. River listened for several seconds, and after hearing nothing, eased it open a tiny sliver.

No sound. No movement.

They slipped inside, closing the door soundlessly.

Listened.

Footsteps, very faintly, came from the left. Voices, two of them, followed right after. Growing louder.

"Sentries," River said in a whisper that didn't carry. "Two of them."

"Hide in the stairwell," DS said.

River nodded, and they eased back into the stairwell. River allowed the door to close, but kept the latch depressed so there'd be no noise when he opened it after the sentries passed.

Two men walked past, talking about how they were going to take out as many fascist government fuckers as they could.

The smile on the drill sergeant's face turned merciless.

Oh, this was going to be fun to watch.

River lifted his right hand with three fingers up. He lowered them in sequence.

They went through the door like a pair of Doberman Pinchers at full speed, silent and with weapons out.

River rammed the butt of his rifle into the back of the man on the right's head, knocking him out.

DS jumped the other one at the same time, his arm across the tough guy's throat while poking the shit out of his kidney with the muzzle of his Berretta. "Make a sound, maggot," he promised the guy in a harsh whisper, "and I'll shove my 9mm so far up your ass you'll be shooting bullets out of your mouth."

The guy stopped struggling.

"Hand your weapon, very nicely, to my friend here."

The kid complied without a peep, though his hands shook like they were his own personal earthquake.

"How many of you are there?" DS asked.

"There's eight others…in the big chem lab," the kid said, his voice sounding like it came through a telephone wire.

"What's in the chemistry lab besides people?"

When he didn't answer, DS tightened his grip, cutting off the kid's air.

"A…"—he coughed as DS loosened his hold—"a… bomb." Something about how he said it pinged River's *oh shit* meter.

"How big?" River asked.

"I dunno. Real big." He grunted.

Yeah, that headlock had to hurt.

"Describe it," he ordered the kid.

"I only saw the crate it's in. It's nailed shut."

"Did anyone tell you how far away you have to be, to be out of the blast zone?"

The kid stopped breathing, staring at River with a new terror that hadn't been on his face the moment before. "No. No one said anything about blast zones."

Fuck, there were eight people, plus Ava, who were going to die.

"Did you sign up to be a suicide bomber?"

"No." The kid's laugh was waterlogged. "Are you kidding?"

River could see the gears inside the kid's head turning. He suddenly grabbed DS's arms, not pulling at them, not trying to get away, holding onto them like a lifeline. When he spoke again, his voice broke. "I don't want to die."

He and the kid stared at each other for a couple of long seconds.

"Kid, I don't think you're supposed to get out of this building alive," River told him as gently as he could. He appeared completely spooked.

"I…I really don't want to die."

Jesus, now he was crying.

"Neither do we," DS said into the kid's ear. "You going to squawk if I give you a little more air?"

"No, s…sir."

DS relaxed his hold, but didn't release the kid. "Don't call me *sir*."

"Did you see a woman in that room?" River asked.

"Yeah, Sam brought her. He said she's part of a secret government plan to bring over Ebola and use it as a weapon on American citizens. You know her?"

"She *fought* Ebola. She's one of the good guys. Who's this Sam guy?"

"He's in command."

"What's he look like?"

"Tall, scary. He's working on his PhD."

River glanced at DS. "Sam is the guy who shot me. Sam is really starting to piss me off."

"Shooting you didn't do the trick?" DS shook his head.

"Shit, you gotta get her out of there, man," the kid said quickly. "I think Sam was going to shoot her, video it, and load it onto every social media website there is."

"And after that?"

"He…" The kid swallowed hard. "He never said. Not one thing, and the dude follows his schedule closer than a nun on spring break."

"That don't sound too good," DS said with a snort.

"No, it doesn't."

"What are you going to do with me?" the kid asked, looking from one to the other.

"That depends," River said. "On whether you can keep

your mouth shut."

"Sir, I won't say a thing until you tell me to. Just please don't leave me tied up inside this building."

"How do you feel about transit buses?" DS asked him.

"Right now," the kid said, his voice breaking on a sob, "I'd take a riding lawnmower to get out of here."

No one said anything for a few moments.

"It's your call, Snowflake," DS said.

"Let's stick him and his buddy on the bus."

It took them a couple of precious minutes to get Mr. Helpful and his unconscious friend trussed up and tied down to the seats inside the bus.

"How much time do you think we have?" DS asked as they headed back inside.

"Almost none at all."

River pulled the building schematic off the internet and studied the layout for a few seconds.

The lab was an interior room with no direct access to the outside, not even windows. Which made it easier to defend from an outside force, and harder to escape from.

"We need to draw some of them out."

DS grinned. "Leave that up to me."

"Don't get yourself killed. I'm supposed to return you to the City of El Paso relatively undamaged."

"Just you be sure to let me know when you've got her out of there, so I can hightail it out before this Sam character blows us all to shit."

"Don't worry, you'll know."

The shit-eating grin on River's face must have communicated an entire novel of how he'd know, because DS raised one somewhat surprised eyebrow. "They told me you were a medic."

"Yeah," River said, his grin only getting bigger. "But I'm special, remember?"

He left the drill sergeant laughing his ass off, then circled around to the opposite side of the building, picked another lock, and went inside. He didn't have to worry about more sentries wandering around the building. The drill sergeant was making his presence known without the use, or need, of a PA system.

"Jesus H. Christ, this building was supposed to be evacuated hours ago," the old man bellowed. "What the flying fuck are you bunch of little pukes doing in here?"

Holy shit, that man could yell.

There was a crash and rattle as several metal objects hit the floor, and a rush of indistinct panicked voices, before one rose above the others.

"Get lost, old man, before we shoot your fucking mouth off."

Someone laughed. That wasn't going to last.

"Son," DS began in a patient tone. "If I were your old man, I'd have you over my knee so I could beat your ass until you looked like a baboon."

A stunned silence followed.

"It's just a goddamned garbage man," someone said. "Shoot him."

There was a series of gunshots and a scream, then DS called out, "I never said I was the fucking janitor."

River used the cover of noise and movement to get closer to the room where the college kids were clustered.

A few more shots. "I'm your worst goddamned nightmare, maggots. I'm your personal drill sergeant. Get your ears wet boys, 'cause I'm going to fuck the shit you have for brains right out of your heads."

"Holy shit, I know that guy," someone said in a surprised tone. "He drives a city transit bus."

"He's not a cop or with the Army?"

"No, man, he's retired. He was some kind of drill sergeant."

"What the fuck is he doing in here?"

"You think the world doesn't know you're here, fuckers?" DS's voice echoed through the hallways. "Bus drivers are a gossipy bunch, and we see everything."

"So, why is it just you, old man?" That was Tall's voice. It matched perfectly to the voice of the asshole who'd shot River three times just for fun.

"I took little fuckers like you and turned them into men for over thirty-five years," DS said, with a dark chuckle. "I don't need anyone else to help."

"You bit off way more than you can chew," Tall shot back. "We're armed and don't take orders from no government pussy."

"So far, all you've done is piss on the situation, boy. It takes a hero to shit on the ceiling." The DS laughed again, and it sent a shiver up River's spine. That old man had evil down to an art form. "That's all that's going to be left of you by the time I'm done. Shit. On. The. Ceiling."

River almost started laughing himself, but worry for Ava was building. He hadn't heard her voice yet, and that wasn't like her.

Had they gagged her?

Had they hurt her or killed her already?

Chapter Twenty-Five

12:21 p.m.

Ava shook with the desire to punch the idiot standing in front of her with a gun pointed at her head. He was another college student who looked like he'd been on a weekend bender. He hadn't shaved in a few days, and he needed a haircut and a shower.

He smirked at what the man shouting at the group of student terrorists said. Something about all of them being nothing but shit. Shit on the ceiling.

She didn't think it was particularly funny, since the man yelling was probably right. They were going to end up as nothing more than shit on the ceiling. She sat on a crate holding a large explosive device. Boots had taken gleeful pleasure in showing it to her as soon as they walked into the room where all of his stupid buddies were waiting. Then he'd told her she was going to be famous.

For getting shot, then blown up.

They were going to video it all, stream it live over the

internet on every social media venue there was.

And they would get what they wanted. They knew what the government and military were doing. What the police, FBI, Homeland Security, and even the CDC were doing. The American government would cow to their demands, pull their military out of places it didn't belong.

They were going to change the world.

They were so dumb.

"Noah, Ryan," Boots said. "Kill him."

"The old guy?" one of the two men asked. Ava wasn't sure which was Noah and which was Ryan.

"No, the ventriloquist using him as a dummy," Boots said with a sneer. "Of course the old guy."

The two students glanced at each other, shrugged, and went to the door. The one in front looked outside, in both directions, then proceeded out with the second man right behind him.

For about ten seconds, there was only silence.

A soft groan floated down the hallway and into the room, followed by an aborted yell. No shots fired. Silence for another three seconds.

"Report," Boots shouted.

"Your little boys are too busy relearning how to breathe, puke." There was a note of sarcastic glee in that old voice that made Ava want to grin. She managed to keep it to herself. Just barely. "Maybe you should send three next time, eh?"

The remaining people in the room, six, including Boots, murmured, shuffled their feet, and backed away from the door.

Boots spun to glare at everyone in the room, but when his gaze met hers, he stopped.

Ava could see her own death in that gaze. If she said something, he'd kill her. If she said nothing, he'd kill her anyway.

Fuck it.

Today was a write off anyway.

She sighed and said in a bored tone, "So much for your revolution."

Boots exploded into movement, striding up to her and putting the muzzle of his gun against her chest.

"Go ahead," she said, in that same even voice. "Kill me. It's not like you haven't promised to kill me already." She leaned into his weapon. "Like you plan on killing every person in this room."

Now the stares of his little soldiers became alarmed.

"Sam?" one of them asked.

"She's a puppet of the government and full of shit."

She studied Boots's profile, noting the sweat beading on his face. "Did you infect them all, too?"

His head jerked in her direction.

"When did you infect them?" she asked. "It's an incredibly fast killer in some people. Slower in others." She looked at a couple of the other student terrorists. "Do they even know?"

Boots flashed his teeth at her and raised his weapon. "Time to die, bitch."

"You first, asshole." The words were formed by a voice that had a wealth of experience in it. And it sounded like the man who spoke them was in the room.

By the time Boots and his friends got to the door, that man, and his insulting cackle, were down the hall, around the corner, and out of reach of the bullets they sent after him. Sam kept going, and two of his buddies followed, yelling obscenities as they ran and fired.

Ava hoped off the crate, but the remaining terrorists turned their weapons on her. She made herself stop, raise her hands, and meet the gaze of the young people staring at her. "I don't want to die. Do you?"

"Don't move," one young man said to her.

"On your knees, bitch," yelled another.

Gunshots echoed through the building, sounding close and far away at the same time. Was she hearing things?

The terrorists inside the room with her jumped. A couple of them ran to the door to peer out of it. The last one yelled at them to get out of the line of fire, that they were being attacked by the Army. Maybe they should blow the bomb up?

That was talk she didn't want to hear.

"You sure do panic easily," Ava said into the chaos. "Is that all it takes to rattle you? A retired drill sergeant?"

One of the young men pointed his rifle at her. "Shut up!"

"Help me," someone yelled from outside the door.

There was a flurry of movement, and someone came in with Boots draped over his shoulder. Blood covered Boots's left arm, and his rifle hung forgotten and dangling from his right shoulder. His people fluttered around him, squawking, reminding her of a flock of frightened chickens.

"Where is the other guy who went with you?" Ava asked.

Boots ignored her, but one of the guys who'd stayed behind glanced out the doorway. "Jose. What happened to him?"

"That old geezer killed him," Boots said, wincing as the guy helping him lowered him to the floor.

"He's dead?" the same kid asked.

"Yes, Dan," Boots yelled. "He's dead. That fucking ancient piece of shit shot Jose in the head."

Dan looked as if he was going to cry.

"Your little friend isn't dead." The time-roughened voice bounced off the walls of the hallway and into the room, giving it an oddly discordant quality.

"I saw you shoot him in the head," Boots yelled back.

"You're blind as well as stupid, puke. One of your shots punched a hole in the wall, and a piece of drywall cut his head. I only shot him in the leg a little."

Ava had to smother a laugh. A little?

"You're not going to stop us, old man," Boots yelled. "We're doing what's best for the American people, saving them from the brutal excesses of a government who doesn't care about anything but money and power."

The old guy's laugh sounded delighted. "I'd try to understand your point of view, puke, but I don't think I could get my head that far up my ass."

Ava winced and muttered, "Burn."

Boots's face went scarlet with rage. "I'm going to kill you, you crazy old man."

"With your aim?" The old man's guffaw was loud and insulting. "Come and get me, puke, and don't send someone else to do your dirty work."

"You can't go, Sam," one of the guys hissed in a higher voice than Ava expected.

She took a closer look and realized this guy was a girl. Short hair with an athletic build, she stared at Boots as if he were some kind of celebrity.

"You're injured, and we need you to…" She glanced at Ava before continuing in a softer voice, "keep to the schedule."

Schedule? How much more mayhem did they have planned? Was there more than the bomb in the crate behind her?

Come to think of it, why would they want to blow up a bomb in a deserted lab in an empty building on the university campus?

"I'll go," said the guy who'd brought Boots back. "I'm not scared of an old man."

"For the love of fuck," the old man yelled. "What in fuck-fuck land are you fuckers doing? Isn't anyone interested in getting their balls handed to them in a tuna can? I'm getting *bored*."

"I'm going," the kid said, taking a couple of steps toward.

"Brian." Boots stopped him with one word. "Go around. Shoot him in the back."

Ava swallowed a bitter mouthful of disgust. She couldn't let this stand.

"Jess," Sam said to the girl. "If that bitch tries to say anything, shoot her."

Jess marched over and pointed an overly large handgun in Ava's face.

She didn't know what kind of gun it was, but watching Jess's hand shake from holding it up told her it was way too much gun for the stupid twit.

"Get the first-aid kit," Sam moaned to no one in particular. "Someone needs to patch me up."

"She's a doctor, right?" Dan asked, pointing at Ava.

"I don't want that Ebola-infested bitch anywhere near me."

Ava rolled her eyes. What a crybaby.

"Dan," Jess said. "Watch her while I take care of Sam."

Dan took a couple of steps toward her and pointed his gun at her.

Ava didn't bother watching him back. It was more interesting to watch Jess inexpertly try to bandage up the bleeding entry and exit wounds on Boots's left arm. It was bleeding enough that he was going to have issues with blood loss soon. All Jess did was wrap a bandage around his arm, which wasn't going to do much over the long-term.

She shook her head at the job the girl was doing and gave Dan a slanted look that communicated quite clearly what she thought of it.

Dan took another couple of steps closer so he could see what Ava saw. A large pool of blood on the floor.

"Fuck." He met Ava's gaze. "What's she doing wrong?"

Ava tilted her head to one side. "I can talk now?"

"Yes!"

Ava turned her attention to Boots and Jess. "Given the amount of blood he's losing, an artery must have been nicked or cut. You need to pack both the entry and exit wound with gauze, or he'll just keep bleeding until he passes out. Eventually, he'll lose enough blood to die."

"Why should we trust you?" Jess snarled.

"I'm a doctor." She shrugged. "Trust me or not, it's up to you."

"You're one of those doctors who came back infected with Ebola."

"I *fought* Ebola for three months, but I never became infected. I've dedicated my life to saving lives. Unlike you, I have no other agenda than that, so you can believe me or not, I don't care."

"Why would you do that?" Dan asked.

"Do what?"

"Go to Africa. Risk getting sick."

She stared at him and wondered if he'd ever taken a trip to anywhere that wasn't sanitized and groomed. "Because it was the right thing to do."

Jess stared at her with narrowed eyes for another moment, then began unwrapping the bandage around Boots's arm. She packed gauze into the entry and exit wound and re-bandaged it.

Ava gave her a slow clap. "Congratulations on learning something useful."

Boots stared at her with glittering eyes. "Shoot her."

"What?" Dan frowned at his leader. "Why? She just saved your life."

"She's mocking us," Boots said, his teeth clenched so tightly they shredded his words. "I'm sick of it."

"You're feverish, hurting, and probably quite dizzy," Ava said. "You probably think you're having a bad day, right?" She glanced around the room at the other student terrorists.

"I've been blown up three times already. And your fearless leader is about to blow me up again, probably along with all of you, just to prove a point." She looked at Boots and gave him a tight smile. "By the way, what is the point? I don't think anyone has ever actually communicated that."

"Our demands are clear. We want the United States and allied military out of the Middle East."

"Why haven't you told the media? Or put that on social media?" She waved her hand at the world outside the door. "Because no one knows what this is all about. All the public knows is that some terrorists have released a biological weapon and blown up some people at the mall."

"We're not terrorists," Jess shouted. "We're freedom fighters."

Ava snorted and crossed her arms over her chest. "America thinks you're terrorists."

No one said anything for two long seconds.

"What the fuck is taking Brian so long?" Boots asked.

"You told him to go around," Dan pointed out. "He's probably being careful."

The old man's cackle bounced off the walls. "Hey, puke, thanks for sending the snack. He wasn't much of a meal, though. I'm still waiting for you to man up and come get me yourself. Your friends are getting lonely."

"Shut up," Jess yelled. "I'm going to kill you, you crazy old man!" She stomped toward the door.

Dan grabbed her and forced her away.

"What fresh fuckery is this?" the old man asked. "You got a pussy doing your dirty work for you now, puke?"

Ava winced. That was going to set off an explosion bigger than the bomb she was leaning against.

Yep, Jess's face turned a mottled red. She screeched and jabbed her elbow into Dan's stomach. The kid let go of her, coughed and bent over, clutching his midriff.

Jess ran out of the room as Boots bellowed at her to come back.

If there weren't the very real danger of dying, she'd be entertained by all of this.

She'd settle for smacking all of them until they saw reason, but that wasn't likely to happen. The bomb inside the crate she leaned against was going to rip her and everyone here apart.

Multiple shots rang out, serenaded by Jess's screaming obscenities.

"Go after her," Boots ordered Dan. "You," he said to Brian. "Stay with me."

Dan picked himself up and shuffled toward the doorway.

All the lights went out.

A cell phone went off. The Darth Vader ringtone.

The room went silent.

"Someone help me get the phone out of my pocket," Boots said in a pain-tightened voice.

"Oh no," Ava breathed out. "Not again."

Chapter Twenty-Six

12:32 p.m.

River ran harder than he'd ever run before.

The hallway was marginally lit by red emergency lights, separated by too much space to provide sufficient light for any emergency evacuation. He was counting on the college-age terrorists finding the sudden loss of power disorienting, because the time to wait, to distract, was over.

He'd heard the phone ring.

Someone else, someone *not here*, was pulling the strings of these poor, stupid kids who thought they were fighting the good fight.

The bomb in the lab was going to go off. Either one of students would detonate it, or it would be remotely detonated, just like the bombs at the coffee shop earlier this morning.

He had to get Ava out of there.

The DS had done more than his job distracting and harassing the students. He'd also captured half of the remaining kids. River had frog-marched them out to the bus and tied them up with the first two. No time left to draw out the rest. He just hoped he'd get Ava, himself, and the DS out before it went off.

Someone was yelling worse than a drunk sailor on leave inside the lab, screaming for help getting his cell phone out of his pocket. There was a man–size shadow in the doorway to the lab. Not Ava; she was too small.

River deliberately plowed into the person in the doorway, knocking them back hard enough that they crashed into someone else inside the room. The two bodies hit the floor in a tangled, furious mess.

"What the…?" someone barked, just as the phone went off again.

"River!" Ava darted toward him from the rear of the room.

He grabbed her hand and towed her out of the room. "It's go time, DS," he shouted, as they ran.

A couple of shots followed them, showering them with drywall, but that only gave him more reason to run faster.

They rounded a corner and another, then hit the exit door to the stairwell that he and the DS had come in. River had Ava outside two seconds later.

She slowed, probably thinking they were safe. He didn't agree and pulled her toward the street.

"River," she gasped. "Slow down. I need to…catch my… breath."

"We need to get to the bus."

"Bus? What bus?"

He tugged her around the building, until the vehicle came into view.

"A transit bus?" She sounded confused. "What…?"

"It's a long story."

They reached the vehicle, and he went on first, just in case any of their captives had gotten loose. Nope, they were all tied up nice and tight, just as he left them. They were rather vocal about not liking the situation, however. He ignored them.

River sat in the driver's seat and reached for the keys, but they were gone. Damn it, the DS had them.

A man hurtled through the darkness toward the bus. Compact with a buzz cut of gray hair that reflected the moonlight.

"Make a hole," he barked as he reached the door.

The old man got on board so fast Ava almost tripped over her own feet to make room for him.

"Get outta my chair, Snowflake."

River vacated it as fast as he could. "I think we should be as far away from here as possible, DS."

"Yes," Ava said. "The bomb is a lot bigger than the one that blew up outside the coffee shop. Sam showed it to me. It's in a big crate."

"What did it look like?" River asked as the DS started the bus's engine and got them rolling down the street.

"Oh, um, I don't really know. It was covered in black plastic." The bus picked up speed as Ava spoke.

"You're all going to die," someone shouted from farther inside the bus.

"Shut the fuck up, Jose," someone else yelled. "*I* don't want to die."

"Shut your pie holes, all of you," DS yelled. "If I have to come back there, you'll all wish your mother had swallowed."

The shouting ceased.

Ava glanced at the various students he'd tied to seats. "How many people are here?" she asked.

"We grabbed every terrorist-in-training we could and tied them up in here."

"And our driver?"

"Sergeant Ken Sturgis retired. Homeland Security asked me to help out Snowflake here." He chuckled. "Never thought

I'd be going into a combat situation while working for the El Paso transit authority."

A flash, followed by a boom, shattered the windows in the bus and pushed the vehicle up and sideways. It knocked River and Ava off their feet. The entire bus shuttered and rocked as if it were caught in a tornado.

Their captive passengers shouted in alarm.

River managed to grab Ava and protect her with his body, but they still got tossed around.

A few seconds later, the bus came to rest. He got to his feet, Ava rolling to her knees next to him, and looked out what used to be a window. Behind them, the building that had once housed the chemistry lab was gone. Parts of the neighboring buildings were gone, too.

"Holy shit." He hadn't realized he'd spoken until he heard the words coming out of his own mouth.

"River," DS said, his powerful voice oddly gentle. "You'd better check your girl. She's bleeding."

River jerked his attention from the devastation outside to Ava as she wavered on her hands and knees. River knelt next to her, putting one hand around her waist so he could offer his body as support for hers. He pulled out a flashlight and shined it over her, looking for injuries.

She had blood coating the right side of her neck, shoulder, and arm. It glistened in the light, twisting his stomach with something he was not going to admit was panic.

"Where are you hurt?" he asked, trying to see if there were any other obvious injuries, though he wasn't entirely sure where the blood on her right side was coming from. "Ava?"

"I don't...know." Her voice came out breathy and uncertain. "What happened?"

"We got blown up."

"Again?" She looked so confused.

"Yeah." He wasn't taking very good care of her. He was

going to get fired. Fucking fired.

Hell, he'd fire himself as soon as this shit was over. She was a doctor, for fuck's sake. Neither trained nor prepared to deal with explosions, bullets, or any of the violence attached to him.

He was the biggest danger to her health and safety.

She blinked a couple of times, but the confusion didn't leave her face. Fuck, did she have a concussion?

"DS, I need you."

The old man appeared at his shoulder a couple of seconds later.

"Hold this so I can see what I'm doing," River instructed, handing the flashlight to the other man.

DS took it, and the beam of light followed River's hands as he skimmed them over her body, looking for all the injuries she might have suffered. He found the source of the blood—several cuts on the right side of her neck, probably from shards of safety glass when the bus windows shattered. More nicks in her shirt along her back revealed smaller cuts, but nothing that needed more than simple bandages. There was a solid bump, along with a deep cut just below her right ear. Much deeper or lower, and it could have nicked her jugular. She'd have bled out too quickly for anything to save her.

She needed stitches, but the hospital wasn't a safe place anymore. It was overrun with infected and dying people, and she wasn't wearing a respirator. Hadn't been for the last hour.

"I need a first-aid kit," River said to the DS. "A good one."

One of the kids groaned. "I think my arm is broken."

"You dumb shits are lucky to be alive," DS snarled at them. "If we hadn't brought you with us, you'd be dead back there. Be happy all you have is a broken arm." He turned to River. "I've got a small one, but she looks like she needs more than that."

River considered his options, which, admittedly, were

limited. The medical center was a no-go, due to the outbreak and its extensive overcrowding. Fort Bliss Army base was locked up so tight a piece of paper couldn't get through. What was left?

All the college students sniffled and moaned in pain. The one who'd complained about his arm whined, "Come on, man. This really hurts."

River raised an eyebrow and asked the DS, "Ever robbed a pharmacy before?"

"Nope, but something tells me I'm about to."

"I'd better clear it first." River said, pulling out his cell phone.

Smashed and unresponsive.

"Shit." He looked at DS. "Have you got a cell phone?"

"Sure." The old man reached into a pocket and pulled it out.

River punched in Dozer's cell phone number and waited for the agent to answer.

"Dozer."

"It's River. I need—"

"Did you rescue Dr. Lloyd?" the other man interrupted.

"Yeah, I've got her, but—"

"You know anything about a big explosion at the university?"

"Yeah," River said cautiously.

The pause that followed felt oppressive. "Again?" Dozer asked, his tone part disbelief and part irritation.

"Yeah, well, what can I say? People either love me or hate me. These guys..." He sighed. "They really hate me."

"Any casualties?"

"Yeah, at least three, maybe four...of the terrorists. We've got another four live ones with us on the bus, too."

"Is that the entire cell?" Hope turned his voice almost excited.

"Nope, Darth Vader is still out there pushing all the buttons."

"Darth Vader?"

"The bastard uses the Darth Vader ringtone when he calls his minions."

Another pause. "What do you need?"

"Permission to rob a pharmacy or doctor's office."

Another pause. "Say again."

"Ava got pretty beat up, lots of cuts and abrasions. She also has an egg-size lump on her head. I need to check her out, but I don't think bringing her there is good idea."

A string of expletives rushed out of the phone, making River wince.

"No. Things aren't out of control here, but we've got every bureaucrat who thinks he's in charge of picking other people's noses trying to tell Rodrigues what to do. That's on top of standing room only in the triage tent we set up outside the ER. We've set up more tents to accommodate the sick. We had a couple hundred cots delivered three hours ago, and they're all full."

"So, about that pharmacy?"

"Yeah, do what you need to do. Just leave a note or something."

River would have laughed if the situation weren't so fucked up. "Will do. I'll contact you when I have something to report." River hung up. He looked at the DS. "Do you know a good place to rob?"

DS snorted as he handed River a small first-aid kit. "Let's see if I can get this rig to run before we begin our life of crime."

The bus's engine turned over with a high-pitched whine that died down after a few seconds. The DS got it back on the road and pointed the vehicle toward the city. River swept the closest seat free of glass and debris, then picked Ava up and deposited her on it. She gasped and grabbed his shoulders, but didn't complain.

"I'm going to clean up your neck first and see if I can do something about that cut, okay?"

"Okay," she said, her voice barely audible over the unhappy engine.

"Feel any new injuries?" he asked, concerned there was more he hadn't found when he ran his hands over her.

"Don't think so. My head hurts a lot."

"I think you've got a concussion."

She gave him a one-sided smile. "I figured that out."

He opened the kit and used a couple of alcohol swabs to clean her neck. The cut was still bleeding, but not dangerously so. There were some butterfly bandages in the kit, so he used them to close the cut, then didn't hold back on the gauze when he bandaged it up. She never made a sound.

"How's that?" he asked, her ear only a few inches away.

"It's…better." It came out as a whisper. She turned to look at him, her eyes wide, and cupped his cheek, respirator and all, with one hand. "You've got cuts, too."

He couldn't move, wouldn't look away. She held him in place with nothing more than the soft touch of her hand and a gaze that seemed to see all the way down to the bottom of his soul.

He'd do anything to have her look at him like that for the rest of his life.

"I'm fine," he whispered back, unwilling to break the bubble of intimacy around them.

She laughed, and it wiped out any pain he might have been feeling for seconds that seemed like forever. "You're a tough guy, Mr. Smooth, but even soldiers need help once in a while."

If it meant her hands on him, he'd gladly lose his tough-guy image for good. "You have my permission to heal any part of me you want."

The joy left her face, like water running down a hill. "I've been exposed to several people who have the Neisseria. These cuts are probably the least of my problems."

"Don't go there," he told her, bending even closer, maintaining eye contact with her. He wanted to kiss her, but if he took his respirator off, she'd probably give him shit for the rest of his life. "You sound more lucid now."

"The dizziness isn't as bad, and I don't think I'm going to puke onto your boots anymore."

"That's a good sign."

"Whoopee." Her laugh contained no humor, and her eyes glistened with unshed tears. "I'm sorry."

"For what? You haven't done anything wrong."

She tilted her head to one side. "Given my current condition, I think there's room for improvement."

"Don't you give up on me," he ordered. "You don't know if you're infected or not."

"I'm trying to be realistic. You know, avoiding the whole false hope thing."

"I was an ass when I said that."

One corner of her mouth curved up. "Only then?"

He couldn't help chuckling. "Shit disturber." He let his gaze roam her body again, cataloguing all the injuries he could see.

She had a number of other cuts and abrasions that needed to be cleaned and either stitched or held together with butterfly bandages, but he'd already used up the DS's meager supply. River stood and looked over the four young men he had tied to various metal parts of the bus. They all needed first aid, too.

"There's a doctor's office and pharmacy coming up, Snowflake," DS said over his shoulder.

"I lost my lock picks," River told him. "Do you have any?"

"Sure," DS said, with a wicked grin. "But I call mine a

crowbar."

"Got two of 'em?"

"Always carry a spare, son," DS said as he pulled their unhappy vehicle up to the curb. "You never know when you're going to need it." He put the machine in park, turned off the engine, and opened the door. "After you."

Chapter Twenty-Seven

12:57 p.m.

The pain in Ava's head throbbed along with her heartbeat, radiating up from the base of her skull. While the immediate urge to vomit had passed, nausea still had a strangle-hold on her stomach. At least the dizziness had disappeared, though she was afraid to move too quickly in case it came back. Blown up again.

She was sick and tired of it. Of the futility of all of it. If Boots weren't already dead, she'd kill him herself.

The expression in River's eyes, concern, care, and the gentle way he handled her, made her *want* to live, *want* to be strong, for him. Though, his coming to her rescue wasn't the smartest or safest thing to do.

So many risks. He'd ignored them all, and, with only a retired drill sergeant turned bus driver, had engaged three times as many armed idiots in an urban skirmish with the slim hope of getting her out alive. It made her want to rant at his foolishness and accuse him of breaking his word to her, all while hugging him close. The absurdity of the past twenty-four hours had gone beyond crazy and into unbelievable.

Who had this much hate inside them? Who could plan the deaths of so many people in such rational detail? There had to be a motivation behind it all. Was it revenge, or were they dealing something colder—a psychopath testing the limits of their intellect against law enforcement's capability? They'd have to be charming and persuasive, inspiring and able to instill loyalty within a tight-knit group. Like the leader of a cult.

"Hey, Doctor," one of the students called out. "Can you help me? I think my arm is broken."

Good. Maybe he'd think twice before joining the next irrational cause.

"What do you expect me to do about it?" she asked instead.

"Well, you're a doctor, so…"

"I'm a doctor who has a concussion, thanks to you and your stupid friends. All I'll be able to do is throw up on you."

"Oh. Could you untie me, then? It *really* hurts."

"What part of *throw up* didn't you understand?" As if she'd let any of them loose to carry on with their crusade.

"Shut up," one of the others ordered. "If she lets you go, I'll kick your ass anyway. You're going down."

"What the fuck is your problem?" Broken Arm asked. "You're as much a part of this as the rest of us. Remember how excited you were when you thought you'd get to blow up soldiers?"

"I didn't know Sam was planning on killing all of us, too, asshole. I thought we were just trying to force the government to do the right thing. I never signed up to kill myself." His voice rose to a whine that stabbed her temples. "It was all supposed to be a secret. Not a fucking slaughter."

"What are you talking about?"

"My dad sent me a text. My mom and sister are sick, thanks to the disease that was just supposed to make people sit up and take notice of our cause." He sneered. "*Our cause.* What a joke. On us."

"They're sick?"

"Yes, like *on death's door* sick." He started to cry. "And I helped do it to them."

"God, you're such a wuss," one of the others said. "We all knew going in that what we were doing was going to hurt people. What the fuck did you think was going to happen when we were making those IEDs?"

"I thought we'd be fighting cops and soldiers, not attacking little kids," Whiner shouted as he thrashed around in an attempt to get free.

"You're an idiot," Broken Arm said in a cold voice.

"You're all idiots," Ava said to them. "Every last one of you, to think you could control a biological weapon like the bacteria you morons weaponized."

"It was supposed to wipe out Fort Bliss," Whiner said.

What? "Say that again?"

"Shut the fuck up."

"Fuck you, asshole," Whiner shouted back. He turned and met Ava's gaze. "Getting loose in the city and on campus was an accident."

"An accident?" If she wasn't afraid of making her head hurt worse, she'd get up and throttle all of them. "What about your merry band of rebels? Was it part of the plan for all of you to die either in one of the explosions or of the bacteria you created?"

"It wasn't part of any plan I knew of," the kid explained.

No one said anything for a couple of seconds.

Then Broken Arm sighed. "Only a couple of us volunteered to do the suicide bombing thing. Sam said it wasn't a sure thing, anyway."

"So, the fact you're all infected and showing symptoms is also an accident?"

"We are?" he asked. "But…"

"Whether you knew it or not, you're all suicide bombers."

No one said anything for a long time.

And River thought she was naive. Black and white, she'd once thought that way, but somewhere between the flu and Ebola, her view of the world had gained an infinite, unknown number of colors.

River and Sergeant Sturgis came back on board the bus, carrying a couple of bags each full of stuff. River strode over and dumped the contents of his two bags onto the seat next to her. He opened up gauze, alcohol, and several butterfly bandages and began cleaning the cuts and bandaging them with narrow eyes and lines of strain between his brows.

"Are you angry with me?" she asked in a low voice so no one would overhear.

"What?" He blinked and stared at her. "No, I just…" He took in a deep breath and let it out slowly. "I'm having to work really hard to resist the desire to kill the fuckers we managed to save."

She couldn't miss the fact that he never once glanced at said fuckers. "Some of them were misled. They didn't realize that their leader was going to sacrifice them all for the cause."

He snorted. "That doesn't make me feel all that charitable toward them. They knew what they were doing was illegal, immoral, and idiotic. They just wanted to feel the thrill of killing someone without the punishment that goes along with it."

River closed another long cut with butterfly bandages, his touch gentle and soothing.

"Okay, I have to agree with that, but they're still just flunkies. We haven't found their leader."

"Sam was our leader," Broken Arm said. "He's dead."

"Small brains, big ears," River muttered. He raised his voice and said, "There was another person who is at least partly responsible for the planning of your homicidal insurrection."

"No, there isn't. Everyone was at the chem lab, or dead."

River shook his head again. "Nope, there's someone else. Someone who had the Darth Vader ringtone on Sam's phone."

All four of the students had confused expressions on their faces.

"There wasn't anyone else," Broken Arm insisted. "Honest."

"Like any of you maggots can be trusted," Sturgis said. He turned to River with the scariest eyes she'd ever seen. "I bet I can make one of them talk."

"As much as they deserve it, I don't think we're allowed to torture them." River did sound somewhat disappointed.

"So, call Homeland Security," Sturgis suggested. "They torture people all the time."

One of the boys started to cry again.

"Or, let me call the base. I know a couple of guys who could make all four of them disappear."

That brought a question to Ava's lips. "I've been wondering. Their plan was to set off explosions on the base and release their pet bacteria on the soldiers stationed there." She had everyone's attention now. "How were they going to get into the base? I mean, it's not like they could just walk in. They'd have to scale patrolled fences, then pass for soldiers until they planted and detonated their explosives."

"They couldn't," Sturgis said. "Security's too tight." He glanced at the boys. "How were you going to do it?"

"I don't know," Broken Arm said. "Sam said it was all taken care of, though. Someone on the inside was going to let us in."

"In a vehicle?" River asked.

"I don't know. Sam didn't say."

"Any of the rest of you know?"

They shook their heads.

"Someone on the inside…" River muttered.

"A traitor?" Sturgis shook his head. "That ain't good."

"The base commander is already infected," River said. "That's going to cause some confusion."

"So, is that the point?" Ava asked. "All we've heard is that they want the military to leave the Middle East, but there were no specifics."

"What are you getting at?" River asked her.

"I'm wondering if this terrorist cell made up of American college students was created for the sole purpose of adding to the confusion. Keep everyone trying to combat the outbreak and find the perpetrators of the explosions off balanced and confused."

"You're saying that whoever recruited the first one—this Sam—never told him what the real plan was?"

"Maybe he did," Ava said, shaking her head. "Sam seemed awfully cagey about what was going to happen next. Kept talking about the big bomb going off and how big of an impact that was going to have."

"I never signed up to die like that," Whiner said.

"Me neither," said another.

"Cowards," Broken Arm said again.

"So, we haven't met the architect of all this horror," River said.

"I don't know about that, Snowflake," Sturgis said. "Assholes who think they're entitled to kill anyone they want generally can't stay away from the scene of the crime. They want to see the dead, take satisfaction in seeing all the pain their weapons cause."

Ava stared at Sturgis, with her mouth hanging open. River, however, didn't look surprised at all.

"Yeah, they do."

"How do you know that?" Ava asked the retired soldier.

"I knew a drill sergeant a few years ago who took too much pleasure in beating the crap out of recruits. Our job is to toughen them up, get them in shape, and establish a sense of community. That guy, he loved hurting the weaker ones, but he was real careful to keep it just on this side of the line." The tone of his voice at the end of his story told her there was more that he hadn't said.

"What happened?" She almost didn't ask.

"He killed a boy. Broke his neck by stepping on the kid's back when he was trying to do push-ups." Sturgis crossed his arms over his chest. "He liked it the same way a normal person likes ice cream."

Just the idea of causing that kind of pain for another person made Ava nauseated again, but she was going to have to deal with it if they were going to find the person responsible for everything that had happened.

She wanted a couple of painkillers and about twenty-four hours of sleep, but wasn't going to get either. She'd watched River as he patched her up. He'd favored his left arm and shoulder.

"Your turn," she said to him as she put her hand down to help push herself off the seat.

He looked at her for a moment, then nodded and sat down. He pulled off his body armor and clothing down to his pants.

She examined the bandage. "Did Sturgis do this for you?"

"Did it myself. Been kinda busy ever since."

She pulled out a suture kit, put on a pair of gloves, and sewed up the wound under his arm. As much as that bullet hole bothered her, the three large mottled bruises decorating his chest made her stomach clench. Her fingers glided over them, and she caught her breath as his chest expanded to follow her hand as she pulled it away.

Giving him a repressive look, she pressed a little harder, checking his ribs. "Deep bruising, but no breaks." Her voice was quiet as she studied his chest. Her gaze lifted to meet his. "How are you? How are you really?"

The expression in his eyes was determined. "We're going to stop this. We're going to get him." It was a vow. She could hear it in his voice.

"If he doesn't get us first."

"Not going to happen."

She found her shoulders wilting under the stare of the college students. "We're pretty beat up."

"Wars aren't won with might," he said, leaning forward and lowering his voice. "They're won with intelligence, perseverance, and conviction."

He was right. Giving up was not an option, but the risks only seemed to be getting larger and larger. She took his hand and pulled him to his feet.

River helped by putting a hand around her waist and propping her up against him. "Ava?"

"Let's talk outside," she said softly, including Mr. Sturgis in her request.

River helped her limp out of the bus and another ten feet away. "I think this is good."

She nodded and looked at both men. "We need to figure out who the person responsible for this is. So, how do we do that?"

River gave her a half of a smile. "We go fishing." He looked at Sturgis. "I could use some bait."

"You mean, besides these fine young men here?" he asked, thrusting his chin at the bus.

"Yeah. I'm thinking the bait is going to need to be very special if it's going to work. Something the architect isn't going to see coming." River winked. "The last thing anyone is going to predict is you, DS."

"Stop with the compliments, Snowflake. You're making me blush."

"What can I do?" Ava asked. "You're not going to keep me out of this. I want to help."

"You," River said tilting his head to one side, "are going to be our backup, in case not everything goes the way we want it."

"Another one of your *plan for the worst, hope for the best* situations?"

"Absolutely. That's what makes the Special Forces special. Imagining all the ways a plan can go wrong, then making sure there's a plan for that, too."

Sturgis opened his mouth, then closed it again. "Nope, not going to get into trouble with your girl, Snowflake."

"Your politeness is refreshing," she told him.

"Not being polite, cautious. Any woman who can survive being blown up four times and keep up with Snowflake here, is not someone I want to cross."

"Wait until you see her with in a hazmat suit," River said, with a laugh. "She'll scare the shit out of you."

"So, what do we need to get this plan in motion?" Sturgis asked.

River's chuckle was full of bad news for someone. "A cell phone."

Chapter Twenty-Eight

1:17 p.m.

There were only so many people in a position to put all this terrorist shit into motion. If Agent Geer weren't already dead, he'd be at the top of River's list.

It was the timing of the fucking phone calls. The person pulling everyone's strings called only when success was in jeopardy. It was someone who had access to what the CDC was doing, as well as what Homeland Security was doing. A very small number of people were in a position to have that information.

It was very likely that he and Ava knew this person.

Geer, with his stubborn refusal to cooperate and his dogged determination to keep Ethan Harris out of trouble, nagged at River. But he couldn't see how the dead agent connected with the bacteria that was killing people. The guy hadn't considered the bug a huge threat. There had been *no* respect in the man for Ava or anyone else with the CDC. Unfortunately, he was dead.

If he was going to go fishing, he needed to bring Dr. Rodrigues into it. He pulled out the cell phone and made the call.

"River?" Dr. Rodrigues answered.

"Yes, ma'am."

"I was worried. There are reports of a large explosion at the university, and I was afraid you might have been involved in it somehow."

He winced. "I was."

"What? *Again?*"

"It's a long story, ma'am, and I don't think we have time for it right now."

"Make time."

River spent several minutes explaining the situation and what he wanted to do. In the end, Rodrigues grudgingly gave her blessing, and ordered him to communicate his plan to Agent Dozer.

Dozer was even less excited.

"That's a hell of a leap," Dozer said. "There's no one in a position of authority in this mess who could be in charge of a terrorist cell. No one has been in contact with militants in the Middle East. We did deep background checks on everyone."

"The leader isn't going to fall into the typical terrorist cell leader category," River explained. "I think this is a home-grown terrorist. Someone born and bred right here in Texas. Someone who's taking advantage of the world political climate and the availability of cannon fodder to create mayhem and kill people."

"What? Like a serial killer?"

"Yes, that. I think we've got a science-nerd psychopath who has the perfect backdrop for killing a lot of people and blaming it on some nameless terror group."

"Shit."

"This guy is having *way* too much fun, but he might not know that Ava...Dr. Lloyd was being held by his recruits. She heard enough to figure out none of them are in charge."

"Homegrown," Dozer muttered. "It could be anyone."

"There aren't too many people in the right position to have orchestrated all this. Your guy, Geer, would have been on the top of my list if he weren't already dead."

"Idiot," Dozer said in an almost pleasant tone. "It's a good thing he got himself killed. So, who's next on your list of contenders?"

"No one really stands out. Maybe Toland?"

"No, not him. He's too new. Could it be someone within the CDC?"

Henry Lee surfaced in River's mind before he discounted the man. He was a grumpy son of a bitch, but not a guy who killed for fun. If Lee did come across someone masterminding something like this, he'd probably take the killer down on his own. None of the other people he'd met had appeared to have the skills or personality to accomplish the horrendous destruction that had occurred so far.

"No one I've met. It could be someone in local law enforcement. Inside the bomb squad could be a possibility, or even a higher-ranking officer from Fort Bliss."

"Yeah, it looks like we need to go ahead with your idea. Are you sure you and Dr. Lloyd are up for this?"

"I'm good, and if I try to keep her out, she'll kick up a fuss. She's also the one with direct knowledge of what was said in the chem lab before it blew up. Our trap won't work without her."

"Fine. I'll see about having a few additional people on the lookout during the meeting. I just hope to hell our psychopath hasn't planted any more bombs."

River hung up and looked at the drill sergeant. "Got a good place to hide these guys and yourself?"

"Sure. The best place."

They went back to the bus, River holding Ava close as the

two of them limped on board.

"I don't know about you," she said with a sigh, "but after this, I'm asking for a raise and a better health care plan."

"Let me know how that goes. I might do the same."

Broken Arm sniffed. "Could someone please look at my arm now?"

"You sit," River told Ava. "Let me see what he's got."

She opened her mouth as if she were going to argue with him, but seemed to think better of it, closing her mouth and nodding instead. The DS started the engine, which sounded like it was going to wheeze its last any second, and drove away from both university and hospital.

River gave the kid a once-over. Aside from the arm, he had a few cuts on his exposed skin, but not as bad as Ava had received. His arm did look odd, but not necessarily broken. To find out, he was going to have to cut the kid loose. He pulled a knife out of a sheath strapped to his leg, not as long as a Bowie knife, but enough to intimidate this college idiot, then cut the para cord he'd used to tie the kid to the seat. He waited, prepared for the kid to attack him, try to take his knife, but the kid just cradled his arm and moaned.

River re-sheathed the blade and secured the loop over the hilt so it couldn't be yanked out. He gestured with both hands. "Let me see it."

Broken Arm sat up, hunched over his arm, and scooted closer.

"It's not broken, kid," River told him. "It's dislocated. I can fix it."

"I can't move it," he complained. "Are you sure? You're not a doctor, are you?"

"Nope, just a lowly combat medic." River crooked a finger at the kid. "Now, get over here."

He didn't move. "I don't think you should touch me. I'll wait until I can see a doctor."

"Listen asshole, 'cause I'm only going to say this once." River leaned down so he could growl into the kid's face and speak quietly enough that Ava wouldn't hear him. "You're a cock-sucking terrorist. You'll be lucky to survive your first day in prison. There aren't any doctors to take care of you now, because they're all busy trying to save the people dying of your fancy bacteria. You either get your arm fixed by me, or you don't get it fixed at all. Got it?"

The kid swallowed. "Yeah." He shifted until he was sitting on the edge of the seat in front of River. River grabbed the kid's arm with the elbow bent, lifted it so it was perpendicular to the ground, then jerked it back into the joint.

The kid screamed once, a short sound, then blinked a couple of times. "Is it over?"

"Move your arm, dickwad."

The kid did and grinned at River. "Wow, thanks."

"Don't ever thank me," River snarled him. "For anything."

He took the paracord and tied the kid up again, then strode to the front of the bus where Ava was sitting, alternating between watching him with the kid and watching the road.

"Nicely done," she said to him when he sat down next to her.

"He's lucky I didn't break his neck."

She rested her head against the back of the seat and gave him a strange sort of sad smile. "You know what I'd like to do right now?"

He grunted and wagged his index finger. "That is a trick question."

She laughed. "Yeah, I guess it is."

He liked seeing the smile on her face. He liked seeing her face, period. "Tell me, Mouse, what would you like to do right now?"

She waved him closer, and he leaned toward her. She did it again, then put a hand on his shoulder and pulled herself up so she could whisper in his ear, "I'd like to take that respirator off you and kiss you, silly."

She let go of him and resumed her previous position on the seat. He sat perfectly still. It took just about everything in him to not rip the mask off and grant her wish.

"I'm sorry," she said, with as close to soundless as a voice could get. "I didn't mean to make you feel uncomfortable."

He looked at her and realized she thought he was embarrassed or some shit like that.

"I'm uncomfortable," he murmured. "Because I've had a damned hard-on since I bandaged you up." Her pupils widened, and her mouth dropped open. "When this is over, you can kiss any part of me you want for as long as you like, just as long as I can return the favor."

"Oh," she breathed out. When her tongue licked over her lips, he had to chain his hands to his sides to keep from grabbing her.

Though a blush heated her cheeks, tears filled her eyes until they spilled over and tracked down her face. "Chances are, that's just a dream."

It just about killed him to see her so sad. "Hey." He couldn't keep the growl out of his voice. "No Negative Nancys allowed on this trip."

"I've got a headache, River. A fever can't be far behind."

"That happy bastard Henry is going to come up with some kind of magic potion that will kick this bug's ass."

"If that were possible, we'd know."

"We've been so busy blowing shit up, we might not have been told."

She slanted a disbelieving glance at him. "You just spoke with our boss. I think she would have mentioned any magic potions, if they'd been available."

He ran his hands through his hair. "Could you work with me, Mouse? We've got a mass murderer to catch, and I need you ready and able to help reel in the son-of-a-bitch."

"Ah, I see what you're doing. Trying to put me in a good mood."

"Jesus fuck, woman, you think I'd tell you how much I want you just to put you in a good mood?" He leaned down, grabbing the top of the seat on either side of her head. "Do I look like a motivational speaker?"

She studied him, her gaze flicking across his face and uniform. Covered in dirt, debris, and blood, he looked like a walking nightmare. "You look like a soldier on a mission."

"That's true, but not all of it." He whispered, "I've got another mission. A personal one. *You*."

Her breath hitched. "You don't play fair."

"Damned straight, and…"— he shook his head slowly, keeping his gaze on hers—"I don't intend to start now."

She dropped her gaze, then looked at him from beneath her lashes. "So, what do you want me to do, exactly?"

He let both his eyebrows rise, and she rolled her eyes. "I mean about catching the bad guy."

"Two things. First, don't mention the drill sergeant."

The DS grunted, but didn't say anything as he drove.

"I want everyone to think I drew the terrorists out and captured them one by one."

"Okay."

"Second, no matter what you say, be certain. Confident. I suspect there are going to be people who'll try to undermine your account of events or marginalize your opinions."

"That, I'm used to. I've worked in many countries where a woman's opinion isn't usually worth much. I've had to reinforce my status and position many times."

"What do you want me to do, Snowflake?" DS asked. "Besides keep these boys out of the way and alive?"

"What do you mean, keep us alive?" Broken Arm asked from the back of the bus. "The cops wouldn't…shoot us, would they?"

River turned and looked at them. "Someone has been pulling your strings all along. Someone used you like ammunition. You weren't supposed to survive the bomb that just exploded, and I think when that someone discovers you four aren't dead, they're going to panic. Try to kill you. Make a mistake." He gave them a grim smile. "The drill sergeant is going to keep you out of harm's way, so I suggest you cooperate."

He turned to talk to the DS. "Be ready for anything."

Chapter Twenty-Nine

2:00 p.m.

"I can't believe we're driving this car wreck to the hospital," Ava said, her entire body one big ache. Her head and neck hurt worse than everything else, but she didn't know if the pain was due to physical bruising or as a result of being infected. They'd dropped Mr. Sturgis and the merry band of terrorists off at a transit authority garage, to wait for River's call.

"Think of the statement this ride will make," River said in a tone that was almost insufferably upbeat. His uniform, torn and dirty, made him look like a walking nightmare.

The ludicrousness of their situation made her laugh. "That we need medical attention?"

"Hah hah." He tossed a wink over his shoulder at her. "That we're *badass*."

Men are so weird. "We'll be lucky if Dr. Rodrigues doesn't fire us both before we open our mouths."

"What did I say about negativity?"

"I'm not being negative, I'm being realistic."

His response, "Bullshit," came out sounding lighthearted, except for a deep, dark thread of anger. She took him in—tense shoulders, clenched fists, and eyes as hard and flat as stone—and realized anger was too tame a description. He was filled with rage.

Ahead were numerous police and emergency lights. Enough that the road wouldn't be passable.

"Hmm, roadblock ahead? Might not be able to make that badass impression."

"You're harshing my mellow, Mouse." The threat implicit in his tone made her reckless. She wasn't going to allow fury to poison him.

"That's too bad," she whispered in his ear. "I was looking forward to doing more than that to your mellow."

"You shouldn't tease a predator," he growled, the sound sending a pleasurable shiver up her spine. "It might get you eaten for lunch."

She had never been this forthright, this brave with her sexuality in her life. Despite the pain she was in and the possibility she might die of meningitis, she was having the most fun. "I certainly hope so."

River growled again.

Police weren't the only people waiting for them. A number of news vans and reporters were parked haphazardly along the street leading to the hospital. As their worse for wear bus approached, the reporters ran toward them.

"That's what I'm talking about," River said. "This is perfect." He brought the bus to a stop about twenty feet from the barricade of police cars. The reporters and camera men hurried over to the door, shouting questions at them even though he hadn't opened it.

"Do we let them in?" she asked.

"I think I'll wait until Dozer comes to get us."

"You think it'll be him or one of his agents?"

"It'll be him. He's going to want to know what the fuck we're doing."

"He's not the only one," she muttered under her breath.

"Hey, have a little confidence in me. This isn't my first rodeo."

"You mean you've been blown up four times, shot, stolen a transit bus, and robbed a pharmacy in less than twenty-four hours before?"

"Geez, when you put it like that, I sound like an escapee from a mental asylum."

One of the reporters banged on the bus door. "Exact change only," River shouted at him.

Ava rolled her eyes. "That isn't going to help."

He shrugged. "But fun. Here comes Dozer."

The Homeland agent was accompanied by a couple of uniformed police officers and several armed national guardsmen who pushed the reporters and cameramen away from the bus. Once the squawking horde had been cleared away, River opened the door.

Dozer strode up the two stairs, then stopped. Stared. Whistled. "What the hell happened to you two?"

Ava and River exchanged glances. "Didn't Dr. Rodrigues mention that we'd been blown up?" she asked him.

Both of Dozer's eyebrows rose. "Which time?"

A police officer stepped onto the bus behind Dozer. "Are they okay?"

"Hello, Officer Palmer," Ava said, giving the man a tired smile. "We're not okay, but we're alive."

He stared at her. "You're not wearing a mask."

"No, mine was…" Ripped off her face, removed by force? There was no short way to describe what had happened. "Destroyed."

"This last explosion was pretty significant," River said, after clearing his throat and giving Dozer a raised eyebrow.

"Our number-one priority right now is getting Ava some medical attention."

She glared at River. "I'm not the only one."

Dozer's lips twitched. "Yeah, you both need help. Come on."

Ava leaned toward River and whispered, "Does he mean help for our injuries or help for our mental problems?"

"Probably both," River whispered back.

"Fantastic," she muttered as she got to her feet. "Our credibility is obviously in the toilet."

"It could be worse," River said in a too cheerful voice.

"Really," she asked. "How?"

He stopped, stared at nothing for a moment. Finally, he said, "We could be dead."

Dozer and Palmer led them off the bus. As soon as they were on the pavement, the soldiers formed up around them, sometimes having to shove the reporters away as they walked toward the hospital.

"Where did you get the bus?" Palmer asked.

"We, uh," River seemed to be searching for an answer. "Borrowed it."

"You *stole* a transit bus?"

River gave Palmer a wince. "Can I plead the fifth?"

Dozer chuckled. "This is going to be an entertaining report."

"If you mean shocking, amazing, and stunning that either one of them is still alive?" the police officer asked in a tone that was all of those things. "Yeah, I agree with you."

Ava glanced at River and found him staring at her. He winked.

She rolled her eyes and shook her head. If the cell leader was someone peripherally involved in the investigation and observing them, River's attitude was going to be highly irritating.

He was going to get her dead yet.

Soldiers who thought they had nothing to lose were dangerous partners to have. The thought didn't bother her as much as it would have yesterday, but she was too tired and in too much pain to consider why.

The walk to the hospital was certainly entertaining. The number of uniformed police and EMS personnel equaled the number of civilians. Those civilians were being divided into two groups. One, who appeared to be the obviously sick, and two, who seemed to be everyone else.

A lot of people were taking video with their phones. This disaster was probably all over the internet, which meant no one was in control of the information being put on social media.

That was a problem. The bad guy, whoever he was, could be watching the situation from a distance just by monitoring his laptop.

Dozer led them to a deserted staff entrance and inside. Silence muffled all sound like someone had pulled a funeral shroud over the building. They followed him to a stairwell and up a flight. When he opened the door, noise slapped her across the face. The change in sensory information disoriented her, and she listed to one side. The only thing keeping her on her feet was River's grip on her arm.

They ended up in one of the patient conference rooms off the ER. All the furniture had been removed except for several chairs and a table. Dr. Rodrigues sat behind the table talking with a man who was reviewing something on a tablet with her. A half dozen other people, some in uniform—police, Army, and CDC. A couple wore suits and had the air about them that Dozer had.

Their boss glanced up, saw them, and her eyes went wide. "Get me a trauma doctor," she ordered as she got to her feet. "Now."

Everyone stopped talking and turned to look at them.

"I'll get one," Palmer offered, disappearing from the doorway.

"It's really not as bad as it looks," Ava tried to explain.

"No," River corrected. "It *is* as bad as it looks." He hooked his thumb in her direction. "She needs stitches for that cut on her neck."

Tattletale. "You need your head examined," she murmured.

"You're the one with the concussion," he said, then glanced at her face. "Oh, you meant that as an insult." He turned a smile on the rest of the room. "Never mind."

"Dr. Lloyd," her boss said in a no-nonsense tone. "Sit down." She looked at River. "Sergeant, sit next to her. You both need to be assessed by the trauma doc when he gets here."

"We have a rather long report, ma'am," River said, suddenly behaving like the professional soldier he was. The jerk.

"You can give it while being treated." Rodrigues signaled someone at the door to come in. "A couple more people who need to hear your report are still on their way." She pointed at Ava. "Her first."

A physician wearing a full hazmat suit and carrying a large tray of medical supplies approached her. He put the tray down and studied her neck.

"What happened?"

She explained briefly about the explosion and bus. He peeled the bandage off that River had put on it and nodded when he saw the butterfly bandages. It oozed blood.

"It needs stitches."

"Yeah, I figured."

He injected a local anesthetic around the site, cleaned it with several swabs, and sewed it closed. By the time he put a new bandage over it, Dr. Rodrigues was greeting two more people who had come into the room. He cleaned and re-bandaged several other cuts on her shoulder, back, and arm.

The trauma doc checked both her pupils and pronounced her concussion free, but cautioned her against any more injuries.

He gave River a quick once-over, cleaned and bandaged a few of his cuts, then pronounced him good enough and left the room.

"Excellent," Dr. Rodrigues said. "Officer Palmer, come in and shut the door. Don't let anyone in unless you've checked with me first."

It took River several minutes to give his portion of the report, mostly because he had to answer several questions along the way. Finally, he got to the point where Ava had to take over. The news about the big bomb from their last explosion did not go over well.

"Oh my God," her boss whispered.

"That was when the shouting match started." She looked at River. "Did you plan what to say in advance?"

"No, I just went with the flow." River shook his head. "This Sam wasn't much of a leader. Too busy flapping his gums."

"Wait. I thought the terrorists left you behind?" one of the suits asked.

"Oh, they did, but I called Dozer here, who got me a vehicle, then helped me track Dr. Lloyd's cell phone back to the university. I was maybe twenty minutes behind them." River grinned. "That's when the fun started."

Chapter Thirty

2:28 p.m.

River had to work at not reacting when Ava rolled her eyes at him. Respirator or not, his expression would give his amusement away. So far, the report she'd given was damn near perfect. Delivered with the correct amount of disdain and disrespect to make any leader of a cause want to do violence.

"Once River got me out," she said, "we both knew it wouldn't be long before Sam set off that bomb, so we raced out of there, got the bus started, and were leaving the area when the bomb went off."

She touched her neck. "I was standing at the time and got hit by flying debris."

"That's how we know Sam was only middle-management in the cell."

"It could have been anyone calling," Dozer observed.

"No, whoever it was, their ringtone was set to the Darth Vader theme song. The same ringtone used to tell Roger

Squires it was time to blow up his bomb at the coffee shop. There's still one guy out there, one guy who's responsible for all this shit."

"You can't know that," the suit protested.

"You think there's more than one?" River asked. "I suppose it's possible. Someone murdered your client." He gave the man a slanted look. "Or is it your client's son? Who are you representing?"

The lawyer took a moment to answer. "Senator Harris."

"I'm sure Senator Harris is very concerned about apprehending the person responsible for his son's death," Dr. Rodrigues said in a soothing tone. "I will update him as soon as I know something more." She gestured for the lawyer to leave.

"But…" he sputtered.

"The remainder of this meeting is for law enforcement only," Dozer told him as he signaled Palmer.

The police officer took the lawyer by the arm and walked the guy out.

Once Palmer was back and the door was closed, Dozer gave River a glare. "Okay, what did you leave out?"

He grinned at the agent. "We've got four surviving terrorists to question, and at least one of them swears he knows how to get a hold of their mysterious leader."

"How?"

"He wants a deal before he'll say anything. Complete immunity and a new identity."

"A deal?" Dozer sneered. "We don't give terrorists deals."

"He says when you find out who it is, you'll kiss his feet." River flashed a palm at the agent. "His words, not mine."

"How can we trust this traitor?" Palmer asked, his fists clenched so tight the knuckles were white. "He could be fabricating an accomplice just to get himself off."

"He could be." River could admit that much. He wasn't

going to belittle Palmer's question. It was a valid concern. "He says he has proof, some kind of insurance."

Dozer crossed his arms over his chest. "Kiss his feet, huh?"

"I need this situation under control," Dr. Rodrigues said. "Bring all of them in."

"Yes, ma'am."

"Where are these terrorists?" one of the FBI agents asked.

"I stashed them in a safe place until I could find out what she wanted to do with them." He angled a thumb at Rodrigues.

"Where are they?" FBI asked. "I'll send a team to retrieve them."

River looked at Dozer. "I still don't think bringing them here is a good idea."

"What about city lock-up?" Palmer asked. "With most officers helping with the emergency, there aren't that many people in the building."

"Clear it with your captain," Rodrigues ordered.

"Yes, ma'am." He left, closing the door behind him.

"So, where are they?" Dozer asked.

"Actually, they're with a friend."

Dozer stared at him. "You left them with…our mutual friend?"

"Yeah."

"Makes for a pretty shitty chain of custody," one of the FBI agents said.

"As soon as Officer Palmer gets back with confirmation that the city lockup is a go, make the arrangements to get those men into official custody as soon as possible."

Someone banged on the door.

One of the FBI agents opened it and said something to the person outside.

"Get the fuck out of my way." The man's voice was a tired growl. "And if you flash that gun at me again, I'm going to shove it up your ass."

"Henry," Rodrigues said, her tone one of strained patience. "Please stop threatening the FBI."

"I will if they will."

The agent glanced at Rodrigues, then stepped aside and let Henry Lee in.

"Please," Rodrigues said in a tired voice. "Give me some good news."

"I figured it out."

For a couple of seconds, no one moved.

"You...found a treatment?" Rodrigues asked.

"I found an antibiotic that works. Of course, I had to Sherlock it first, but once I figured that out, I knew what to use to eradicate that shit."

"Be specific."

"A beta-lactamase inhibitor."

"I thought those worked with Methicillin-resistant Staphylococcus *aureus*? This is a Neisseria."

"If they used MRSA to make the Neisseria resistant, why not use what makes MRSA sensitive?"

"Isn't that sort of combination experimental?" Ava asked.

Henry shrugged. "Nothing else has worked."

Dr. Rodrigues sighed. "I foresee a long and loud conversation with the FDA. Perhaps I can convince them to allow it, due to the speed and lethality of the disease and its ease of transmission."

"Is this beta-lactamase inhibitor a new antibiotic?" River asked. "I've never heard of it."

"No, it helps the antibiotic get through the bacteria's cell wall. It's how the little buggers keep out the antibiotics they used to be susceptible to."

"The terrorists tore off my respirator. I think they were all sick with the Neisseria. It's likely that I'm infected." Ava glanced at River. "It's possible you are, too."

"I'm calling the FDA now." Rodrigues turned to Henry.

"Do you know what amount of beta-lactamase inhibitor we need to treat this outbreak?"

"A fuck ton."

"I need numbers, Henry. Figure it out. The FDA isn't going to accept *boatload* as an amount." She stopped before she could make it out the door and glared at Ava and River. "You two, stay here until there's an update. I'll have food sent for you."

Most of the staff left, though some updated the infected and deceased numbers on the wall. All the totals went up.

Ava lay back on the gurney set against the wall. "I think I could sleep for a week."

"Rest is good. Sleep, not so much."

It looked like she had to really work to open her eyes. "Why not sleep?"

"Because we're not out of hot water yet."

He didn't say anything more, and she didn't ask, but she did stay awake as people came and went. Dr. Rodrigues had turned it into a mini-communications center, so foot traffic was high.

While they waited, a nurse came and hooked Ava up to an IV.

About ten minutes later, Dozer strode into the room. "Okay, Palmer just got the sheriff onboard with us using the city lockup to house and interrogate our four young terrorists." He looked at River. "You want in on this?"

"You have to ask?"

"River?"

He could hear the worry in Ava's voice. "I'll be careful."

"How are you feeling? Any symptoms?" she asked.

"Nope. No headache or fever."

But the frown was still on her face. "Listen," he said, leaning closer and lowering his voice. "I'll be surrounded by law enforcement, in a police building. I'll be *fine*."

One corner of her mouth tilted upward. "No more explosions." It was an order.

"Yes, ma'am." He gave her a salute. "Work on getting better."

"I will."

He looked at Dozer. "Who's coming with us?"

"A couple of my agents from Homeland, Palmer, two people from the FBI, and an investigator from the military police."

"Let's get to it."

Dozer had a vehicle waiting with the other two Homeland agents. Even though it was a large SUV, the vehicle felt small. The FBI agents went with Palmer, who was leading the way. He'd joked that he should get a raise for having to babysit them all.

River agreed.

"Us, Homeland and FBI agents, a cop and an MP is a lot of testosterone in one room," River said. "We'll be lucky if our squealing terrorist doesn't piss his pants."

Dozer grunted. "We're going to be very polite, aren't we guys?"

The other two agents replied, "Yes, sir." In unison.

"What did you do to these guys, Dozer, feed them some of your special Kool-Aid?"

Chisholm glanced at River briefly. "Not funny, Sergeant."

"Sure it is. It has to be, or this kind of shit will kill you from the inside out. Humor is one of the best coping strategies for dealing with stress that there is."

They all looked at him.

"Seriously, it's right up there with playing with kittens and puppies."

"Is he always like this?" Korsman, a Homeland Security agent who'd been with Toland, asked.

"Like what?" Dozer asked.

"Irritating."

"Unfortunately, yes, but he's also right. Every soldier I've ever met, serving or veteran, has a dark sense of humor. It's practically trained into them."

Palmer's vehicle entered a parking garage, calling out the door code to Dozer so he could get their vehicle in as well. They parked next to the officer and gathered outside the two vehicles for a quick huddle.

Palmer used a key card to open the staff entrance to the building, then gave them a quick tour, ending up in the holding area or county jail.

"We're wasting time," FBI Agent 1 said. "Who's staying here, and who's going to get those damned terrorists?"

"I don't understand why some of us didn't pick them up before we all arrived here? That would have saved a lot of time," FBI Agent 2 said.

"Calm down," River said. "They'll be here in a few minutes."

Everyone stared at him for a moment.

"What the fuck is going on, Sergeant?" FBI Agent 1 asked, sounding royally pissed off. "You jerking us around?"

"I thought you were in a hurry," River replied. "Rodrigues managed to find us some secure transport." He held up his personal cell phone. "I just found out. They'll be here in about five minutes, so you should be happy, not trying to rip me a new one."

"Five minutes doesn't give us much time to get ready," Korsman said.

"We're questioning kids who probably aren't old enough to drink yet," River pointed out. "I'm not thinking we need much prep time."

Chapter Thirty-One

3:10 p.m.

Something cold slithered down Ava's arm toward her shoulder. She opened her eyes…when had she closed them?

Who put the IV in her arm? As her gaze followed the tubing up to a bag of saline solution and two much smaller bags, someone said, "Go back to sleep."

"Henry," Ava frowned and lifted her chilly arm. "What…?"

"Ampicillin." He touched one of the small IV bags. "Beta-lactamase inhibitor." He pointed at the other small bag.

She looked at her watch. "I only slept for thirty minutes. Dr. Rodrigues must have scared the crap out of the FDA to get permission to use an inhibitor so fast."

He grunted, but didn't look at her as he fiddled with the IV bags and made notes in the small notebook he always kept in his pocket. He closed the notebook, tucked it away, then turned and headed for the door, all without making eye contact. "I'll be back in a few minutes."

"Henry?"

He stopped, but didn't turn around. "What?"

"Dr. Rodrigues did get permission, right?"

He stood motionless for exactly two seconds, then left the room without answering.

Which was another kind of answer.

His departure must have been a signal to those who'd been waiting outside, because several people came inside to update the whiteboard with new numbers for both the sick and dead.

Talking on a cell phone, Dr. Rodrigues entered to sort through some of the papers on the table. She glanced at Ava, then mouthed, "FDA."

Oh no. Dr. Rodrigues didn't even know about the inhibitor being transfused into her. Was this the favor River had asked of Henry?

Idiots.

She had to fight the urge to cry, scream, and pummel someone. But, if she kicked up a fuss, others might notice there were more IV bags hanging above her head than there should have been.

Her boss ended her call and smiled at Ava. "The FDA is willing to consider the extreme situation. We should have an answer in a couple of hours." Dr. Rodrigues's cell phone rang again. "I have to take this," she said as she turned away.

Searing hot anger cleared away any lingering drowsiness. Ava was going to strangle River when she saw him. Well, maybe not actually strangle. Perhaps yell at him for a bit and step on his feet a couple of times. Her hands shook with the need to do something, anything, that might take the edge off her anger, fear, and frustration with a man who, despite being brilliant and more than a little dangerous, didn't know how to *listen*.

Why wait?

She dug around in her belted tool kit for her cell phone and texted River. *You are an idiot, and Henry is an idiot for listening to you.*

His response only took a few seconds. *I'd rather be an idiot than see you dead.*

Her thumbs flew across her screen. *Henry could lose his job. His career.*

No, he won't. Exigent circumstances.

If she wasn't careful, she was going to crack her phone's screen with one of her thumbs. *You ass. This isn't some remote battlefield in another country. This is the USA. You don't get to interpret the rules any way you want. We have LAWS!*

His reply came much faster than she expected. What he said made her insides go cold. *We're in a state of emergency. The rules have changed.*

The rules have changed. Those four words tumbled around in her head.

Was he right? Had the rules changed?

How had the rules changed?

"What special powers does a state of emergency give decision makers?" she asked out loud.

The FEMA director answered her. "The right to commandeer personal property, if deemed necessary. The right to detain people, if deemed a danger without charges for a limited amount of time. The right to call in additional help in the form of the National Guard, military, medical, or other entities that are deemed useful."

"So, essentially, in a state of emergency, help is called in, and all of that can be done quickly without all the bureaucratic nonsense?"

"Yeah," he said with a nod. "That's about right."

She felt no joy in his confirmation of her understanding. *Terror* was a better word to describe the emotion that constricted her airway.

She tapped the screen on her phone, and wondered if she'd missed something.

They'd missed something.

The terrorist attacks had started with an outbreak and evolved into suicide bombings and planned explosions in several high-value targets.

But, their last bomb only succeeded in blowing up their own people. They didn't stream it live, nor did they make any last demands, making it meaningless.

It didn't make sense.

Unless, something had changed. She'd been in the chemistry lab with the last of the terrorists. River and Mr. Sturgis had harassed and captured four of the students and wounded Sam, who'd told her…too much?

What had he said?

She was going to be famous. Blah, blah, blah. They knew what the government and every law-enforcement agency in the country was doing. Blah, blah, blah. They were going to change the world. Blah, blah, blah.

He'd named all those law-enforcement agencies. Even the CDC.

River believed there was someone inside the investigation who was the real cell leader. If that person blew up his own people so they couldn't talk, what wouldn't he do to stop River and the team of men with him from questioning the surviving terrorists?

Nothing.

Who was this person?

Someone close enough to the investigation to have reasonably up-to-date information, but not stand out. It wouldn't be any of the Homeland agents, who were obvious in their distaste in accepting her orders. That left the FBI, police, CDC, and military.

Not the CDC. If someone from the CDC was the leader,

they'd have chosen something much worse than Neisseria. The military hadn't gotten involved until after the bombing at their front gate, and the FBI agents had been working in tandem with Homeland—she never saw one without the other. That left the El Paso police. Their officers had been everywhere, involved in every level of the emergency, because this was their city and they knew it best.

Who was it?

Someone who'd been everywhere that damned ringtone had gone off. Starting with the coffee shop.

Her hands shook as she opened the camera app on her phone and looked through the pictures she'd taken of the crowd a couple minutes before the explosion. She'd been focused on the agitated member of the crowd who'd been particularly persistent in harassing River, but she hadn't looked at the police officers.

All she could see were their backs as they guarded the police line, until she got to the first picture she'd taken. In that photo, one of the officers had turned his head and was looking at River with an angry glare.

Officer *Palmer*.

No, he couldn't be…but he'd been with them at the campus dorm, at the microbiology lab, and he'd have been in a position to overhear Dozer or Dr. Rodrigues talking about River storming the chemistry lab.

Had anyone else been present at, or had knowledge of, all the bombing locations?

She flipped through the photos again, studying them to find another possibility, but none emerged. Her breathing became labored and choppy as an invisible band tightened around her lungs. Palmer was with River, Dozer, and their team now. They were in a building he knew as well as his own home. A building with any number of firearms, explosives, and other weapons inside it.

He wasn't going to let those four boys tell anyone anything.

He wasn't going to allow anyone to leave that building alive.

The room dimmed and her vision narrowed, until all she could see was Palmer's face on the screen of her phone. A buzzing ring got louder and louder in her ears.

No, there wasn't any time to pass out. She closed her eyes and focused on breathing, opening up her chest to take in more air.

She could be wrong, but what if she was right?

Ava texted River, a simple one-word message: *Palmer.* She attached the picture and hit send.

If she was right, River was in more danger now than ever. The building they were in was Palmer's second home.

River needed help, and it had to be the kind of help that wouldn't alert Palmer.

A few seconds later, she opened her eyes and said to the person closest to her, the FEMA director, "Can you get Dr. Rodrigues for me? I just remembered something important."

He looked at her, glanced at her hands clutching her cell phone so tight her knuckles were white, then studied her face. Whatever he saw there made him nod. "Will do."

He moved across the room to tap her boss on the shoulder. In the middle of a phone conversation, she tried to wave him away, but he pointed at Ava and said something into her boss's ear.

Dr. Rodrigues strode across the room, ending her call. She crouched next to Ava's cot. "What is it?"

"I think I know who the cell leader is." Before Dr. Rodrigues or the FEMA director could comment, she continued quickly with, "It has to be someone with access to information, someone aware of what River and I were doing. Someone able to remote detonate or start a remote detonator on all of the explosives within the correct time frames." She turned the phone around to show them the photo. "He's the only one who checks off all the boxes."

Ava watched Dr. Rodrigues's face pale. "If he's the cell leader, I don't think he's going to want anyone to survive it."

"Suicide vest?" Ava asked. "Roger Squires wore one."

"Very likely."

"How do we stop him?" Ava asked.

"We don't," her boss said. "We can't."

The FEMA director let out a short bark of a laugh. "That's why Sgt. River wanted to interrogate them in a *different*, controlled location. So, he could draw out the leader, but does he know who that is? Or will this guy"—he gestured at the phone—"blow himself and all of them up anyway?"

Oh, that was *helpful*.

Ava took hold of her frayed temper and managed to ask again in an even tone, "How do we stop him?"

Dr. Rodrigues gave her a tired, despondent look. "We have to warn River and Dozer, but Palmer has an ECC. What we say to them, Palmer is going to hear."

"I texted River, so he knows, but if all their personal phones start going off, Palmer is going to figure out that something is up."

Think, *think*.

"Mr. Sturgis," Ava said. "Palmer doesn't know anything about him. He's a retired drill sergeant. He helped River get me away from the student terrorists."

A deep furrow etched its way between the FEMA director's eyes. "You both failed to mention that."

If he was looking for an apology, he was going to be disappointed. "We didn't know the identity of the cell leader, so we left Mr. Sturgis out of our report."

"Dozer told me about him," Dr. Rodrigues said. "But I wasn't clear on how much help he was going to be."

"His voice should be a registered weapon," Ava said drily. "In just a few minutes, he wound up those college students so tight, they lost control of themselves and the situation."

Rodrigues looked at the FEMA director.

"Do it," he said.

Dr. Rodrigues nodded her agreement.

Ava typed a quick message to the retired drill sergeant. *The head bad guy is El Paso police officer Palmer. He's one of the men with River. River knows, but Palmer will be watching him. Can you pull off "feeble old man" long enough to grab him or something?*

Mr. Sturgis's reply was as cryptic as River's had been. *Or something.*

For a moment, her stomach went weightless, and nausea threatened to hijack her body. There were so many ways this could go wrong.

She sucked in a breath through her mouth, staving off the urge to vomit. "Done." She looked up at her boss and the FEMA director. "Now what?"

"*We* get back to work and pray the good guys are successful," the FEMA director said.

What about her? "But—"

"Ava." Dr. Rodrigues cut her off with a smile Ava recognized as the one she wore when explaining things to civilians. "You've done all you can. Your job now is to rest and wait for a reply." She smiled and patted Ava on the shoulder. "I think you've been blown up enough today, don't you?"

Ava wanted to argue, to insist that she be involved in the rescue of River and their people from a deranged maniac, but she also recognized the expression on her boss's face.

Permission would not be granted.

She made her body relax and sagged back onto the cot. "Yes, ma'am."

That earned her another pat. "As soon as you get a reply,

let us know."

Ava nodded and managed to smile. It was a weak effort, but enough that her boss and the FEMA director were satisfied enough to return to other concerns.

The room ebbed and flowed with people in hazmat suits, respirators, hospital scrubs, military uniforms, and three-piece suits. They came and went like a tide, sweeping in information and questions and retreating with far too few answers.

The phone in her hand buzzed. *Thanks.*

She stared at the screen. Thanks. That's *it*?

She typed a reply. *What are you going to do?*

Take care of the problem.

Fingers shaking with frustration, she typed: *HOW?*

The Army way.

Well, she wanted an answer. Unfortunately, it didn't tell her anything.

Out of all the people available to her right now, Henry was the only one who might reasonably know what constituted the *Army way*.

She texted Henry, copying her conversation with River and sending it to him. She ended her text with: *What does Army way mean?*

Henry responded almost immediately. *I'll be right over.*

Ava glanced up. The antibiotic and its helper were both finished infusing. She didn't feel appreciably better, but she also didn't feel any worse.

A hazmat-suited Henry walked in, looked at her, looked at Dr. Rodrigues, and said, "Do you mind if I steal her? She'll get more rest in the tent by my lab."

"Yes," their boss answered. "We could use the space." She smiled apologetically at Ava. "Sorry."

"It's fine," Ava replied, getting off the cot. "I'm feeling very superfluous here."

Henry grabbed her IV bags and her belt tool kit and

practically galloped out of the room.

"Slow down, before you pull my IV out."

Henry winced and reduced his giant strides to something she could keep up with.

They dodged people and gurneys and managed to emerge outside without incident. He didn't slow down, however, until they reached the decontamination area.

He made her put on a respirator, gloves, and safety glasses, then ushered her inside his tiny lab.

There were two rolling stools in the cramped space. He pushed her onto one and took the other.

"So," he said as he crossed his arms over his chest. "What the fuck?"

"Yeah, that's about where I'm at, too." She wasn't going to cry. She *wasn't*. "Palmer is the cell leader."

"Palmer is the fox? *Palmer*?"

She pulled out her phone and showed him the picture of Palmer she'd taken prior to the coffee shop explosion. "What does the *Army way* mean?"

"Basically, whatever force is necessary to achieve the mission goals."

"Guns, grenades, guts, and gore. Is that what you mean?"

"Pretty much."

"But, he's probably wearing a suicide vest. Shooting him could set it off; then they're all dead."

"They can't shoot him until they know he's a genuine threat. If they shoot him before making sure he really *is* the bad guy, it's called murder."

"Even though we're in a state of emergency?"

"Yeah."

"How do we prove he's the bad guy without him blowing himself up?"

"What's the connection between Palmer and that Sam dude you thought was the leader at first?"

"I don't know. I don't even know if anyone has done a check on Sam's background."

"Send me that picture."

Ava did as ordered.

Henry sent what seemed like a long text message to someone. "I've asked an old friend to look into Palmer's background. Hopefully, he'll get back to me in time."

"But, River needs help now," she insisted.

"He knew the moment he left the hospital that he was on his own with whoever was with him."

She wanted to cry. "But—"

Henry put his hand on her shoulder. "I think you're forgetting something. He's a Special Forces soldier. He knows how to hide in plain sight better than anyone else there."

Chapter Thirty-Two

3:31 p.m.

We're fucked.

River glanced at his cell phone again, at the lone word on the screen again, and admitted to himself that he hadn't seen this coming.

Palmer.

That's the entire message Ava sent him, that and the photo, but it was enough. The expression on Palmer's face, the disdain and contempt, convinced him.

He should have noticed it earlier, but he'd been too focused on the shit disturber in the crowd.

Palmer, an officer of the law, was the cell leader, the man responsible for all the death and destruction in the last twenty-four hours. The man responsible for blowing Ava and him up four times. A man who appeared to be after an all-time record for Americans killed on American soil in a domestic terrorist attack.

He was probably wearing a suicide vest. His torso did

look a little too thick for regular body armor.

Somehow, River had to find a way to prove the bastard was the man they were looking for without setting off the explosives he was wearing. Preferably before the asshole set them off himself. Would he wait to do it until he saw the four surviving members of his cell? Or at the first hint of someone new coming their way?

Why do any of it?

Searching for some explanation, River studied Palmer's face and body and realized the other man had been showing it all along.

His eagerness to help, to go into possible danger, to be on scene when shit went down.

It made sense in a sick, twisted sort of way. He got his jollies by setting off the bombs and bugs and laughing at everyone else trying to unravel his plan.

Asshole.

This wasn't Afghanistan. River couldn't just shoot him now. There had to be some proof that he actually was the terrorist Ava thought he was. She could be wrong.

Not bloody likely.

Still, he was going to have to get the man to show his true colors before he could accuse him of being a terrorist.

Palmer reached into a pocket and pulled out a cell phone.

River watched him at an angle, keeping the cop in his peripheral vision while seeming to examine their surroundings in detail.

"There's a city worker requesting entry," Palmer reported. "What should I tell the guys in the communication room? Is this the person you're expecting?"

"Probably," River replied, taking a moment to make it look as if he were thinking it over. "Yeah, it's got to be him. No one else would be driving around during quarantine."

"Who is this person?" Palmer asked, as he texted a reply.

"Oh, he's an old friend. He retired from his Army desk job a few years back, but got bored so he went to work as a transit driver for the city of El Paso."

"That's what I have to look forward to in my retirement?" Agent Korsman asked. "Driving a bus?"

"Would you rather greet people at your nearest department store?" Dozer asked. "Or does mall security sound more your speed? I'd be happy to write you a recommendation letter."

There was movement down the hall. Then someone said in a rough, irritated voice, "Come on, you fuckwits, I don't want to be late for my evening bowel movement."

The first of the four surviving terrorists appeared, his hands tied behind his back with paracord, followed by the next three, all tied together so that if one ran, he'd drag his buddies with him.

"Still inspiring young men to do their best?" River asked the grizzled old man.

He snorted. "I'd need to have them for three months, twenty-four seven to get them to barely adequate."

River watched Palmer's face as the four came into view, but saw no recognition. Nor did he see any on the boys' faces when they looked at the various law-enforcement professionals in front of them.

Could Ava be wrong?

His cell phone buzzed. He pulled it out. The message was from Ava.

Henry called in a favor. Did a background check on Palmer and illegally accessed his medical file. He's Sam's older half-brother.

Fuck. He set his own brother up to die?

Palmer's mother killed herself when she found out her husband had an affair with another woman and had another child, too. Palmer was about five years old when it happened.

She was found hanging in her bedroom. The kid was sitting on the floor talking to her corpse when EMS arrived. He had some trouble as a young teen—started a couple of fires, but a stint in juvenile detention seemed to end it.

Nah, it hadn't ended it. Juvie just taught him how to compartmentalize it.

Shit. Other than causing more chaos, this asshole had nothing to live for.

Another text came in.

Do not get blown up!

Problem was, he couldn't guarantee it. He put his phone away without answering. His focus now was talking this maniac down, or as a last resort, taking him out.

He really didn't want to kill him. A dead man couldn't stand trial, couldn't pay for his crimes. Palmer *needed* to pay for his.

Keeping Palmer in the corner of his eye, River walked over to Dozer. "I think you and your guys have earned the right to ask your questions first," River said. "I suspect we're looking for the same information."

"Appreciated." The big agent glanced at Palmer. "Can we get four chairs for our young friends here from somewhere? I think we need to have a very eye-opening conversation."

"No problem." Palmer's tone sounded curious, invested.

Good.

Palmer and the two FBI agents got the chairs. Dozer arranged them in a line and plunked each kid down in a chair with more force than was probably necessary.

Dozer stood in front of them and just stared. He didn't say anything. Didn't move, just met the gaze of each kid until they dropped theirs.

Finally, he asked one word: "Why?"

The four blinked at him.

"Why, what?" Whiner asked.

"You've detonated explosions all over the city and the Army base and caused the outbreak of a dangerous pathogen that's killed hundreds of people." He paused to stare at each of them. "*Why*?"

"Our government—"

"That's a bullshit answer," Dozer barked at him. "Politics didn't provide you with the motivation to participate in mass murder." He paced in front of them, walking so close to them that he almost stepped on their feet. "Murder. Of children, women, grandmothers, your own goddamned relatives."

He continued to pace. "How could any of you believe there wouldn't be any consequences?"

Dislocated Arm spat on the floor. "We're fighting a revolution. Risks have to be taken to ensure success."

River winced. He'd said almost those exact words to Ava for the exact same reason. The goal was all important. Nothing got in the way of the goal. Nothing.

What an ass he'd been.

Dozer gave all four idiots a shark's smile. "Another bullshit answer."

River glanced over at Palmer. Now that he knew what to look for, the cop watched Dozer with an intensity River had misinterpreted as dedication and determination. Now he could see the excitement in Palmer's body language—the tense muscles and the shifting of his weight from foot to foot. And yet, his expression was eerily calm.

Was this guy a psychopath? Or was he as disenfranchised as the students he'd recruited? If he was the former, he wouldn't care about anyone but himself, and would hurt anyone in his way. If he was the latter, he'd feel guilty, but also determined to finish what he started.

He might be able to negotiate with someone who had a guilty conscience. A psychopath, probably not.

River slowly walked over to Palmer and leaned over to

say softly, "I said the same thing about risk yesterday."

He glanced at River. The curiosity on his face was out of place. Everyone else looked ready to kill all four terrorist wannabes. "Yeah?"

"Yeah. Dozer is right. It's a bullshit answer."

Palmer smiled, then tried to hide it with wide eyes. "Um, it has to be the answer sometimes, or I wouldn't have a job."

"How do you see your job?" River asked. "Do you protect the people, or the status quo?"

"I enforce the law." He said it as if it was a mantra, but it was too practiced, too rote. "Everyone is subject to the law, no matter who they are." He thrust his chin at the four students. "They'll pay for their crimes." He smiled, and it was on the evil side of happy. "I hope they get the death penalty."

"I don't know," River said. "I think prison for the rest of their lives would be worse."

Palmer sneered. "I've seen too many kids who think they're entitled to everything. They don't care about the law. All they care about is getting what they want. The only way to put a stop to it is to scare the rest into acting like adults." He looked at River. "You know what I mean, you're a soldier. You've seen their kind of stupid before."

"Stupid, yes. But these ones were influenced by someone else." River said. "Convinced that they could do what they wanted and get away with it." He regarded Palmer with steady eyes. "That's the guy I want to see pay for his crimes."

Palmer stared at him, his brows crowding his eyes. "The guilty deserve to die. They could have said no, or called the police, but they didn't. They got caught." There was the dedication, the commitment that should have been in the man's voice before.

"Not our call to make. I'll kill if I have to, but I don't look for it and take no satisfaction from it."

"You don't take pride in doing your job well?"

"I take great pride in doing my job well, but I believe my job is quite different than what you think it is." River shrugged. "A common misconception."

"You're a soldier. You go into other countries to kill or kidnap or rescue—whatever your commander tells you to do."

"Don't believe the all shit you hear in the news. We don't go on missions like that very often. Mostly, Special Forces are involved in supportive roles with foreign militaries. Training, for the most part."

"Training." Palmer snorted, as if it were a dirty word. "Do you ever wonder why you're sent all over the world to train some other nation's people or hunt down the CIA's most wanted, when you could be using those skills right here at home?" He casually pulled out his sidearm, a Berretta, and checked the magazine.

"That's what guys like you are for," River said, watching the other man's hands. A man who didn't holster his weapon, but rather held it in his right hand with a strong grip. "You're the leaders here."

What the fuck was he up to?

Palmer turned to face River. "I respect you. You don't back down from a fight, and you're willing to do what it takes to get your job done."

"Is that why you volunteered to help?"

"You were doing something useful, not running around trying to put out fires by pissing on them."

"I was also getting blown up."

Palmer grinned. "But not dead." In his right hand was his weapon, in his left was a cell phone. Time to rattle this rat's cage.

"Why the Darth Vader ringtone?" River asked.

Palmer didn't hesitate to answer. "Vader represents order where those idiots"—he pointed his gun at the four college students—"represent the selfish ignorance our entire society has succumbed to."

"Holy fuck," Whiner said, staring at Palmer as if he'd seen the devil himself.

Palmer laughed, a dry, flat sound, pointed his gun at the kid, and pretended to shoot.

Around them, the other agents also pulled their guns, some pointed at the student terrorists, a couple pointed at Palmer.

Whiner ducked, and Palmer laughed at the expression of terror on the kid's face.

"We're like the Roman Empire right before it fell. Bloated, wasteful, and full of our own superiority. To ensure we remain great, we need to trim the fat, useless, uneducated masses and the entitled elite until we're young and vigorous again."

"Aren't you getting ahead of yourself?" River asked. "I don't see an army backing you up." He gestured at the kids. "They're all you have left, and like you said, they're not much."

"Sam was supposed to have survived, not them." For a moment, Palmer almost looked sad, but it was gone the next second, his expression appearing now only mildly annoyed.

"*You* sent him the signal to detonate the bomb," River said. "*You* killed your own brother."

"He didn't stick to the plan, and it was a great plan."

"Now you sound like some second-rate movie villain." There was movement behind Palmer, but River ignored it and stayed focused on the crazy man's face.

"Second-rate?" Palmer demanded. He held up the cell phone in his hand. "The hell I'm about to bring down on you isn't second-rate anything." He grinned, and there was a sudden jerk of movement behind him. He grunted, his eyes rolled back into his head, and he collapsed at River's feet.

The DS stood there, his crowbar in his hands, and

shrugged. "I got tired of listening to the bullshit."

If he didn't think the DS would slug him, River would have kissed the old man.

Dozer was there, patting Palmer down, checking his body armor. "Yeah, he's wired, all right. Enough explosives here to kill all of us."

"We need the bomb squad. Again," River said.

Dozer, who was already talking on his ECC device, requesting assistance, nodded. His two other agents were searching Palmer for other weapons. One of them picked up Palmer's cell phone.

He showed it to River. "What does this mean?"

On the screen of the phone was a text message, *11111*, sent to an unknown number. The bomb on Palmer's chest hadn't gone off, so…*fuck.*

River took the phone with care and showed it to Dozer. "I think we've got one more bomb to deal with."

"Where? Here?"

"He didn't need to have one planted here. *He's* the bomb for this place."

What high-value targets were left? Where had he had time to plant a bomb?

"The medical center. I think that's the most likely place for it. He was in a position to plant a bomb practically anywhere he wanted."

"It's crawling with people," Dozer growled. "If a bomb goes off there…" He didn't finish. He didn't have to. The result of an explosion there would be…unthinkable. "Has it already gone off?"

"In the coffee shop, the call came through about five or ten minutes before the bombs went off."

"That's not a lot of time." Dozer spoke into his ECC device while the FBI and Homeland agents all began making calls of their own.

River called Ava. He didn't wait for her to say hello, just barked into the phone, "We think there's a bomb about to go off at the hospital. Get out. Get out now."

"What?" She sucked in a breath.

"Maximum damage, Ava. The bomb has got to be somewhere in or around the hospital. He sent a text message somewhere. I think you've got less than ten minutes."

"That's…" She sounded breathless. "There's not enough time to evacuate."

"I know there's no time, but *you* need to get out."

"There's a travel ban…and I don't—"

Muffled sounds. Then a new voice. "This is Henry. We've got a bomb?"

"Yeah, on a short fuse," River said. "If you were the sociopath who'd orchestrated all this chaos, where would you plant a bomb?"

"Palmer showed up on my security camera a few times. Looking around my lab-in-a-box."

"Have you cleared the exterior for explosives?"

"Fuck." It sounded like he dropped the phone.

More background noise, then Ava saying, "I assume he's gone to look for the bomb." She sounded tired, so tired.

"Ava, *get out of there.*"

"I have a really bad headache." She paused to take a breath, then said softly, "Not much point in running."

"No. Don't you do that," he growled at her. "Don't you give up."

She didn't say anything, not for a couple of seconds. Then, in a tone so sad and lonely it hurt to hear it, she said, "I wish I could have been your mouse."

No, no, *no.* Fear sliced into his gut, filleting him, leaving every nerve ending he had exposed and screaming in the open air. "Ava, get out now!"

"Smack Palmer once for me." The phone went dead.

"*Fuck!*" It took everything he had not to smash the phone on the ground.

"Snowflake," the DS called. He threw something at River. Keys. "My second set of wheels is outside. Go."

"I'm coming with you," Dozer said to River. He pointed at the DS as they ran for the exit. "And you, I have a job offer for you."

"If I have to wear one of those ugly-looking suits," he shouted after them, "no thanks."

River hardly remembered the sprint through the building. He burst through the doors and beelined it to the transit bus parked in the roadway designated for emergency vehicles only.

"A bus?" Dozer asked.

"That's what he drives," River replied leaping up the stairs and into the driver's seat.

Dozer punched the front passenger seat. "We won't get there in time."

River flipped him the bird. "You haven't seen me drive." He shut the door, gunned the engine, and laid rubber on the cement.

Chapter Thirty-Three

4:05 p.m.

Henry sounded as if he were fighting a war with himself. He ran around the outside of his portable lab, checking everywhere for the bomb, swearing like nothing she'd ever heard before.

Why did he think the lab was the target?

"Get the fuck out of here, Ava."

If Palmer's goals were fear and killing people, wouldn't it make more sense for him to have left the bomb in someplace full of people, someplace those people felt safe?

Henry used to be a soldier. If the bomb was planted here and he couldn't find it, no one could.

Experience with Palmer's previous bombs told her it was going to explode in a few minutes. Also, he preferred high-value targets with lots of visibility. The lab was virtually invisible, but there was a building next door that would qualify as perfect.

Where would he have put a bomb inside the hospital?

Where would he get, as River said, the biggest bang for his buck?

Ava stood and walked toward the nearest entrance to the hospital. "Fine, I'm going, but I think I'm dead already."

She took the most direct route to the hospital, past the decontamination area, where she left her respirator, glasses, and gloves. They were just irritating her more than anything.

No one paid her any attention, at least not until she approached the guarded checkpoint. The guards frowned at her, but let her leave without a challenge.

Nope, the challenge would happen when she tried to get back in.

She was almost to the door when Henry yelled at her. "Ava?"

Now what was he yelling about? She ignored him and went inside.

The building was full of people. And noise. Yelling, crying, begging. Hospital staff were running in all directions, and security was attempting to subdue a man who looked like a typical suburban husband and father who was threatening to kill everyone in sight with a baseball bat.

Society sure had broken down in here in a hurry.

Ava walked past it all and entered the ER waiting room. Every chair was occupied, every piece of wall was used as a place to lean or a spot to rest a gurney carrying a patient. There was even a news crew, all wearing respirators, trying to interview a crying woman.

What could be more visible than this? Now, where would he have left the bomb?

She scanned the floor and under chairs and side tables. There were plenty of purses, messenger bags, and backpacks. In one corner, several bags were jammed under a side table being used as a chair by a man who would have looked right at home in the middle of a biker gang. Tattooed and dressed in jeans, a T-shirt, and leather vest, he looked as if he were hanging onto consciousness by the skin of his teeth.

Ava walked up to him. "Hi, are any of the bags under there yours?"

He frowned, blinked, then shook his head.

She got down on her knees and reached under the table to pull the first couple of bags out.

"Hey, that's mine," a lady sitting in the chair to Ava's left protested.

"Sorry." Ava handed the woman her bag.

No one claimed the other bag, which was a large, carpet-bag style purse. She couldn't see Palmer using it. It didn't make the right statement.

There was a black backpack shoved up against the wall. To reach it, she was going to have to crawl under the table.

She gave the biker an apologetic smile and said, "Don't take this personally." Then she scooted between his legs and under the table to snag the bag.

"Anyone own this?" she called out.

"You shopping for a new bag?" the biker asked, his voice slurred.

"No," Ava answered as she unzipped the main compartment and peeked inside. "I'm looking for a bomb."

"Lady," he muttered. "You've lost your mind."

The bag was full of wires and wrapped bundles. "Found it." She flashed the guy a smile and hurried out of the hospital the way she got in. It seemed to take forever, as if she were swimming through honey.

Henry nearly ran over her.

She held up the pack as soon as she saw him and said again, "Found it." She handed it to him. "Now what?"

He didn't answer, just spun around and half ran, half limped away.

"You're welcome," she shouted after him. Huh, that

probably wasn't an appropriate thing to say.

Okay, that bomb was just explosives, but was it the only one? There never seemed to be just one. What if the explosive device was a decoy for a larger biological weapon? An outbreak could spread to kill or injure more people without regard for borders than any IED created. Palmer had had unrestricted access to this hospital and the CDC's equipment. He could have easily left more than one bomb lying about.

Ava walked back into the bull pen of the ER, letting her gaze search for another possible bomb, one with more than explosives.

"Dr. Lloyd."

Ava followed the sound of her name to her boss, who was waving at her. Next to her stood a tall soldier wearing a respirator and a rifle that looked like River's favorite weapon. Ava approached them, still allowing her gaze to wander the room.

"Ava, this is a friend of Sergeant River's, Sergeant Smoke."

The man nodded. "Just Smoke."

Rodrigues's phone beeped, and she stepped away from them.

Ava and Smoke stared at each other. The frown on his face told her he had a question, but he didn't say anything. Finally, she asked, "What to help me find a bomb?"

He continued to stare at her, but after several seconds he finally nodded once. He probably thought she was nuts. Not much she could do about that. She carried on, looking for a backpack with no owner.

"Description?" he asked as he stalked behind her.

That was a good question.

"I've seen two kinds," she said as she got down on her hands and knees to look under the chairs behind the bull-pen counter. "Grenades out in the open, or backpacks created by malcontented students. We're looking for one that contains weaponized bacteria. The bomb's goal isn't to kill people, it's to infect them."

"Assholes."

"Yep."

Something beeped. Smoke pulled a cell phone out of a pocket and barked, "Smoke."

His gaze jerked to meet hers and stayed there. His eyes narrowed.

"That's River, isn't it?"

"I'll make sure she's secure," he said into the phone, then ended the call.

Ava rolled her eyes and walked over to a chair that held several sweaters and purses. At the bottom was a brown messenger bag with an El Paso police emblem sewn onto it.

Ava opened the bag. Wires, taped bundles, and a clock ticking down.

Twenty.

Nineteen.

Eighteen.

Well, didn't this suck. Seconds, she only had seconds to do something with the bag. She'd never make it outside.

Limited options.

She picked up the bag and walked to the washroom at the back of the space. Before she opened the door, she made eye contact with Smoke, raised the bag with one hand, and pointed at it with her other hand. Then she opened the door, set the bag on the floor, and closed the door.

Smoke was running toward her.

Not fast enough.

She only got two steps away before the bathroom blew up.

• • •

River managed to make it around the corner without losing control of the bus, but it was probably a good thing there wasn't any other traffic on the road.

"I don't like saying this, but," Dozer said in a tone that could only be described unnaturally calm, "we aren't going to get there in time."

River didn't reply. He knew they weren't going to get there before the bomb went off, but that didn't change his determination to try.

As they approached the hospital, the flashing lights of police vehicles reminded him traffic was at a standstill within two or three blocks of the place.

"Fuck it," he muttered, as he braked and parked the bus along the far edge of the cemetery that bordered the west side of the hospital's property.

"What are we doing?" Dozer asked as River bolted out the door and vaulted the fence.

"Running," River yelled over his shoulder. "Try to keep up." He kicked his stride into high gear, jumping over gravestones, crosses, and memorials as if he were an Olympic hurdler.

Ahead of him, someone was running, heading toward the street to River's right. It was clogged with cars and trucks, but the runner slid over engine hoods as if he were a good ol' boy with the cops on his tail. No one was following him, so why was he in such a hurry?

The runner stopped between two cars and disappeared. A loud, metallic *clunk* drew River's attention. In order for him to hear it at this distance, it had to be significant. River slowed.

New threat?

Another metallic *clunk*, and then the runner came bounding over a car and the cemetery fence into the graveyard.

The guy was wearing a hazmat suit.

Henry Lee.

"Hit the dirt!"

One did not ignore an order like that from a man who was as much a soldier as River.

He didn't quite make it before the ground rocked beneath him, hard enough to put him on his face. The boom wasn't far behind. The manhole cover rocketed into the air and caved a crater in an empty car's roof.

River managed to get to his feet. "Henry? Was that the bomb?"

Lee was lying on his back, not trying to get up yet. "Yeah." He sounded irritated and more than a little pissed off.

"Where'd you find it?"

"I didn't," Lee said as he rolled to his feet. "Ava did."

What. The. Fuck. "How did that happen?"

"I don't know. I was running around the lab, looking for it. She just walked away, went into the hospital. I didn't think much of it. Then it occurred to me that she'd been acting a little off."

"Off?" River asked. "Where is she now?"

"Staff entrance is where I ran into her. She had the damn bomb in her hands."

River started toward the medical center at a fast walk, but as soon as he got out of the cemetery, he broke into a jog, then a run. Just before he reached the door, the whole building vibrated as if King Kong had landed a punch on it with a heavy fist.

A second bomb? That fit with Palmer's MO. Not once had he used just one. He opened the door so hard and fast it banged against the exterior. The power flickered inside the building, but River ignored it and rushed into air hazed with…dust?

Where would she be? ER? Going there first solved the secondary question of what happened.

The ER bull pen had been turned into a slaughterhouse. A ragged hole in a wall gaped open at the back of room, water spraying out of it like a fountain on speed. Dust and debris coated everything. People were strewn about the floor like drunk frat boys after a three-day party. The only difference was the blood smeared indiscriminately over every surface.

Fuck.

Some of the bodies moved, moaned, and tried to get up. One of them wore an Army uniform.

"Smoke?" River strode over to his friend. "Where's Ava?"

Smoke glanced around, then pointed at a door that had been ripped off its hinges and now lay haphazardly. "Under that."

River strode over and lifted the door off her. She lay crumpled and unmoving. He checked her pulse. Strong and regular. He did a quick check with his hands to see if she had any injuries. Nothing obvious.

Lee caught up to him. "She okay?"

"She's out cold and putting out heat like a furnace in January."

"This place isn't secure," Lee said, looking around. "Bring her to my lab. She can rest on that cot set up outside in the tent."

River picked her up very carefully, then looked for Dozer. The Homeland agent was bent over another figure on the floor. Dr. Rodrigues.

"Rodrigues?" River called out.

"She's conscious," Dozer answered. "Ava?"

River shook his head. "Lee has a cot out by his lab."

"Yeah," Dozer replied to River's unasked question. "That's probably the best place for her right now. Come back once you've got her tucked in. I'm going to need every pair of hands I can get."

River looked at Smoke.

"Go," the other man said. "I'll help here."

River didn't waste time replying. He just moved as quickly as he dared, with Ava in his arms.

He laid her down and waited for Lee to come back with…hopefully something that would combat this damned infection.

Lee returned with a bag of saline and two smaller bags of fluids. He hung all three up on the IV pole on the other side of the cot, then picked up Ava's hand. On the back was an IV needle capped and waiting for the business end of a line.

"I already gave her a dose of antibiotic and a second drug I think will make the bacteria sensitive to that antibiotic, but this…" He paused, looking at her. "Isn't a good sign." He connected the bags to the tubing and started the drip.

"You *think*?" River asked.

Lee winced. "It's only been used in a couple of studies."

"And you gave it to her?" River couldn't believe it. The medication dripping into Ava's vein was fucking *experimental*.

"It was that or nothing." Henry threw his hands up in the air, showing for the first time how frustrated he was. "Five hundred plus people have died of this infection so far."

"Will it work?"

"I don't know." Lee's voice was bleak.

That sucked ass.

"Will it make things worse?"

"No. The worst it could do is nothing."

He really didn't give a shit about whether or not the treatment was fifty years or five minutes old. As long as there was a *possibility* of it working.

Fuck. He'd done this to her. He'd played a game of strategy and tactics with a lunatic, but had forgotten the most important and immutable rule of war.

People died.

He'd gambled with her life. Even if she survived, she'd

never forgive him. He'd never forgive himself.

Fucking selfish bastard.

Sweat beaded on Ava's forehead to trickle across flushed skin and past swollen eyes. Fear crawled up his spine on spider legs, threatening to take control and paralyze him. He couldn't move, could only watch as men ran over the sand, shouting and shooting, the pain in his head blurring his vision until all he could see were watery shadows.

No, *no*, he wasn't paralyzed. Wasn't in the Middle East. Wasn't bleeding on the sand.

River closed his eyes and focused on the sounds around him. All the conversation he could hear was in English. The sirens of police and EMS vehicles was uniquely American. He opened his eyes to see Lee taking Ava's temperature.

"Where did she find the bomb?" River asked, forcing words out of his desert-dry mouth.

"I don't know that, either." Fuck, Lee looked ready to rip his hair out. "When I realized she was gone and I hadn't found the bomb, I decided to follow her. She was coming out of the building, and when she saw me, announced she had it like she'd found her keys or something."

"What about the second one?"

"Didn't know a thing about that one."

River sat down on the edge of the cot. He should probably be helping Rodrigues, but he needed to sit, to listen to her breathe, and convince himself that she was going to be okay.

Dozer walked up to the tent. "Is she…?"

"Unconscious," Lee replied.

The agent nodded, but didn't say anything, his gaze sharp on River and Ava.

River met the other man's assessing gaze. "Thanks, by the way. You helped save a boatload of people."

The other man snorted. "Boatload? I thought you were Army."

"Yeah." He ran a hand over his short hair. "Speaking of Army." River gestured at Lee. "Henry Lee Sergeant, Special Forces, retired, this is Homeland Agent Dozer."

The two men shook hands.

"Retired?" the other man asked, giving Lee a once-over.

River had to admit, the guy hadn't let himself go. He looked in top shape and had sprinted like a man who could have done it for miles.

Lee rapped a knuckle against his left pant leg. The sound of metal made Dozer's eyebrows go up.

"IED convinced me a change in occupation would be a good idea." He shrugged and turned his attention to the IV, continuing absently, "Though, I have to admit, I miss the adrenaline rush."

"How long until we know?" River asked as he watched Ava's face, unwilling to consider the possibility she might not wake up.

"I don't know. Hours, maybe."

River inspected his uniform. He looked as if he'd been wrestling with a porcupine and lost. "I guess I should talk to Dr. Rodrigues." He glanced at Dozer. "What about you? You want to go back to the police station?"

"There's a travel ban in effect," Dozer countered. "Now that we've stopped the terrorists, we should probably follow the rules, don't you think?"

"Yeah, probably."

"Look, son," the agent said, crouching next to River. "I'll stay and watch over Dr. Lloyd while you talk to your boss. How about we do that?" He thrust his chin at Lee. "Mr. Lee can assist as needed."

Henry looked momentarily surprised, then came to attention and barked, "Aye, aye, sir."

Dozer rolled his eyes. "I can do without the flirting."

River shook his head and got to his feet. "Okay, I'm going

before you two pick out the china." As a joke, it was a weak effort.

He didn't move for a couple of seconds, then gave both men a nod and left.

Behind him, he heard Dozer ask Lee, "What are her chances?"

River walked faster and managed not to hear the answer.

He found Dr. Rodrigues in the same room he'd left her in, a room with walls now decorated by whiteboards. One detailed the University Medical Center's infected and casualty numbers while another provided the stats of other hospitals from around the city. Another board had been turned into an evolving timeline of both the infection and the explosive terrorist attacks. He stared at the boards and compared it to his mental timeline of events. Could Palmer have any other accomplices?

Dr. Rodrigues joined him. "There was an explosion outside as well?"

"Yeah. Ava found a bomb in here somewhere and gave it to Henry Lee. He managed to throw it into the sewer system in the street outside the hospital," he told her. "How many did we lose here?"

"None."

At his frown, she said, "I don't think the bomb was meant to kill anyone outright."

"What do you mean?"

"It didn't cause a lot of damage, and we found something in the debris that tells me this bomb's real goal was to spread the infection."

"Did it?"

She gave him a sad smile. "If Ava hadn't moved it, it would have exploded in the middle of the bull pen. It might have killed people, but it would have certainly infected many, many more."

"How?"

"Neisseria can produce spores. They were inside glass pressure tubes, so when the tubes shattered…" Her hands pantomimed an explosion.

"The bathroom kept it contained."

"Yes."

Okay, so, she did good. Was her heroism going to kill her? "I took her back to the cot Henry set up for her." River had to clear his throat. "She's not doing very well. High fever."

"I'm sorry."

If he thought about Ava, he wasn't going to be able to do anything useful. "I left things at the police station a bit unresolved."

"Don't worry. A Mr. Ken Sturgis contacted me. He's put the four college boys into the lockup at the station, left one FBI and one Homeland Security agent behind to make sure no one gets in there to kill them, and is now on his way back here. He says you have his bus."

No one gets in to kill them? "Have threats been made?"

"Somehow, the information on the four was leaked to the media. We'll be lucky if a lynch mob doesn't storm the police station and hang all four of them."

"Leaked, huh?"

"A lot of people are very angry." Rodrigues's eyes looked grim, and she looked him over. "You're off duty until I say otherwise."

"Mind if I hang out over by Henry's lab? I'd like to be there when Ava wakes up." He saw the objection on her face. "I promise to sleep."

Rodrigues closed her mouth and studied him for a moment. "We don't know if the combination of drugs Henry is giving her is going to work. The FDA still hasn't made a decision about allowing us to use the combination to treat people. Success in the lab and success in the real world don't always equate."

River left the room and went back to the tent outside Henry's lab. He stood over Ava's cot and watched her breathe for a long time. Sweat had darkened the roots of her hair, and a shiver rolled through her. And kept rolling.

Seizure.

"Shit." River turned her onto her side so if she vomited, she wouldn't aspirate it.

Henry appeared next to him and stuck a digital thermometer in her ear. 105 °F.

A fever that high was enough to freeze his insides solid. "A febrile seizure? I thought that only happened to little kids."

Henry darted a glance at her. "She's got meningitis. That changes the rules."

"Could this result in brain damage?" He should know this, but he was too tired, too worried, and too...*everything*... to think straight.

"It doesn't usually cause any damage in kids," Henry said. "But, she's not a kid."

Ava's body finally stopped shaking.

"We're in a wait-and-see holding pattern," Henry told him. "We have to give the antibiotic and its friend some time to do their work."

"*If* they work."

Henry didn't respond. What would be the point? They both knew it was a shot in the dark.

"Okay." River nodded. "Rodrigues told me to rest. Got another cot or something I can sleep on right here?"

"I found a camping mat. Just give me a second." Henry left the tent. He came back with a roll and handed it to River.

"You wake me if anything changes," River ordered.

"I will."

River unrolled the mat on the ground next to the cot, lay down, and closed his eyes.

If Ava didn't wake up, he wasn't sure what he'd do with himself.

She was amazing. Smart, funny, and so fucking cute. He couldn't wait to see her naked, wanted to touch her, stroke her, and taste her all over. The taste of her he'd had only a few hours ago was enough to make him ravenous for her. He wanted all of her.

She got him. Every sarcastic, geeky comment and joke.

Twice, Henry came over to check on Ava. The second time, he hung new bags of fluid on her IV pole. River stared at them, invisible fingers wrapping around his throat and closing it tight.

This was his fault. All of it. He'd gotten her blown up four times, kidnapped by terrorists, and infected with this killer bacteria. He'd treated her like another soldier, but she was a fucking doctor. Trained to investigate disease, not assholes with guns, bombs, and a cavalier disregard for life.

He wanted her. All of her, but he sure as hell didn't deserve her.

Dizziness crowded his vision, but his lungs wouldn't work, those ghostly fingers strangling him.

He pushed to his feet, sat on the edge of the cot, and took Ava's right wrist in his hand. Her pulse was strong and steady. He closed his eyes, focusing on the rhythmic throb under his fingers. She was alive.

The pressure on his neck lessened enough to allow him to suck in a breath.

Footsteps approached. Dozer. River didn't move, didn't release Ava's wrist. The song of her pulse brought him a comfort he wasn't ready to give up yet.

Dozer entered the tent, then crouched on the ground a couple of feet away from River and the cot.

"We searched Palmer's apartment," he said, then sighed. "This guy's been planning something big for years."

Years?

River shook his head. "Asshole."

Dozer grunted. "Yeah. It didn't become a terrorist-style attack until a year ago. That's when he recruited all those college kids, including his brother. Before then, he was on his own." Dozer paused to sit on the ground. "Typical serial killer stuff. He had a couple of huge bulletin boards full of antiestablishment bullshit and a list of people he wanted to murder up close and personal. There's a ton of explosives in his place, which we are now removing very carefully."

"What about this outbreak?" River asked. "What info did he have on that?"

"Surprisingly little. There were instructions on how to spread the bacteria around, but no actual information on the bacteria itself. It was like he ordered it ready to go off the internet, and it came with an instruction booklet."

"What the fuck?" River tried to merge the two goals in his head. "So, he's been building up to a mass-shooting scenario for years, but adds bioterrorism to the plan only in the last year? Was there any evidence of why he decided to play cult leader and recruit other people and form a terrorist cell?"

"Not that we've found, but it's going to take some time to go through everything. There's enough material in his apartment to keep a half-dozen behavioral analysts busy for a long time."

"So, did he come up with the bug on his own, or did he have outside help with that part?"

"That's a question a lot of us want answered." Dozer glanced at Ava. "How is she?"

"Still unconscious." He cleared his throat of the sudden lump stopping him from speaking. "Is the quarantine doing any good?"

"Hard to say. The number of new cases arriving at the medical center has dropped, but the death toll is still climbing." He stood and waved his hand toward the IV pole and the bags of fluid hanging there. "If this doesn't work, we could lose thousands."

"Right now," River said, his voice sounding rough even to himself, "I only care about one."

Dozer looked at Ava's wrist locked in River's grip. "I hope she makes it."

River's first response was to tell the other man to fuck off, but he managed to keep his mouth shut. She was going to be fine. No other outcome was acceptable.

"You get any sleep?" Dozer asked.

"Some."

"Good. I could use your help. We're short of intelligent people who don't panic easily."

"Flattery will get you nowhere with me."

"How about a direct order?"

River stared at Ava's pale face and didn't answer.

"You'll drive yourself crazy if you sit here and mope."

River grunted out a noncommittal sound.

"You might as well keep busy until she wakes. You can get all mopey dopey then."

He didn't want to leave her, but Dozer was right. If he didn't keep busy, he'd go mad. "All right, let's go."

He got up and followed the other man out of the tent, away from the one person he never wanted to let go.

Chapter Thirty-Four

9:16 p.m.

Ava could hear voices, male, talking somewhere close, but quietly. Her skin felt clammy and sticky, and when a breeze swept over her, she shivered.

The voices went quiet, and she sank down into a dark place, floated there, but something caressed her skin. The touch brought her out of the darkness and closer to the light. It left again, and she let sleep take her.

It was the scent of decomposing flesh that woke her next. It roiled her stomach until she feared she'd vomit. Breathing through her mouth, she opened her eyes. White, everything was white. No, this was a tent, and she lay on the cot Henry had set up outside his lab. She turned her head, but the front of the tent had been closed, obscuring her view. The smell lingered. Had the CDC been forced to store the dead outside? How many dead bodies did there have to be for them to stack them outside somewhere? She couldn't hear anything that might indicate the public in a panic. The only EMS sirens seemed to be coming from far away.

She let herself fall into a light sleep.

A slight tug on her arm woke her. Henry was hanging new IV bags.

"Hey," she said, though it came out more of a croak.

"Hey." He studied her face. "You look better."

She raised a brow. "Right."

"You didn't see yourself about eight hours ago."

She snorted.

"High fever, sweats, and a seizure. We couldn't wake you."

"We?"

"River and I."

A quick look around confirmed the obvious—River wasn't anywhere in sight.

"He wouldn't leave."

"Who wouldn't leave?"

"River. He slept on the mat next to your cot for a few hours, then he sat with your wrist in his hand so he could feel your pulse." Henry said it as if it was a strange thing to do.

"What's unusual about that?"

"He sat there for an hour."

He *what*? Ava found it hard to breathe. As much as she admired River for his intelligence, dedication, and creativity, and despite how attracted to him she was, he also scared her. Because, if she let him in, if she allowed herself to fall in love with him and he died or he left her, she'd break.

She wasn't strong enough to go through what she went through with Adam again.

"You look like a spooked horse," Henry said. He studied her for a moment. "Are you going to run?"

When she didn't answer, he asked, "You want to keep him in the friend zone?"

She shook her head. "That's not it. I...don't know if I can trust..."

"Him?" Henry asked. "He'd die for you."

She raised her gaze to meet Henry's and whispered, "That's what I'm afraid of."

• • •

River spent the next ten hours keeping the crowd of sick people and their family members from rioting outside the emergency entrance to the medical center. He was given a few hours off to rest, so he went back to Henry's lab and the tent next to it. Ava was asleep, more of the antibiotic and its buddy dripping into her veins. He slept for four hours, got up, ate, and went back to crowd control.

Dr. Rodrigues announced the FDA had approved the use of two medications to treat the outbreak, but only in a test group of twenty. She asked for volunteers spanning a variety of ages, as well as men and women.

That request almost caused the riot his boss was so afraid of.

When he went off duty next, Ava was gone from the tent. Henry told him she'd been sent to Atlanta to recover at a CDC facility. She'd regained consciousness and was still very sick, but they wanted to see how the antibiotic and the inhibitor worked for themselves.

River pulled out his phone to text her and discovered she'd beat him to it, having sent a text to tell him getting ahold of her would be difficult for the next few days. She was in an isolation room, and cell phones weren't allowed.

He was about to text her back, catch her up on everything, but stopped himself. Maybe this was the best way to protect her. Stay away from her, keep her out of his violent world. Keep her safe.

He had himself three-quarters of the way convinced of that when Dr. Rodrigues put her job offer to him in writing.

Well, fuck. Two days ago, he'd have taken it without hesitation. Now, though… So, he delayed giving her an answer.

Three days later, he sat in a camp chair outside Henry's portable lab, sucking down a bottle of water. It was late, and he'd probably be back at it in only a few hours, but he wanted some time to think.

Henry came out to sit next to him in a matching chair. "I hear you got an offer from Rodrigues."

"Yep."

Henry turned to look at him. "What's the holdup?"

River shrugged.

Henry's gaze sharpened. "Ava?"

Nosy bastard.

Henry never let up on the stare. "She not good enough for you?"

River gave the veteran soldier a glare. "Fuck you."

Henry just grinned an *I'm about to start shit* smile. "So, the problem is with you."

"Yeah, it's with me." River dropped his head back to stare up at the night sky. "I got messed up during my last deployment."

"Said every soldier ever," Henry muttered. "So, what are you going to do about it?"

"Fuck if I know."

The silence after that was a long one.

Finally, Henry asked, "Are you a danger to yourself or others?"

"You sound like a shrink."

"Answer the damn question."

"No, I…I don't think so." He blew out a breath. "I have flashbacks. Sometimes they're just memories, sometimes it's worse than a memory. It puts me back there entirely, bleeding on the sand, waiting for the next kick that will cave in my head."

They both stared up at the sky for a minute.

"Shit happens to all of us," Henry said. "Your job now is to figure out how to cope with it."

"Easier said than done."

"Truth. What are your triggers?

"Heat," he replied immediately. "Scent and sound. Pain a couple of times."

"What do you do?"

"Nothing…so far."

"Okay. That's a good sign."

"What if I…"

"You call up a battle brother and talk it out."

River looked at the other man. "I'd ask you for your number, but you might get the wrong idea."

Henry chuckled. "Humor is good. If you can make yourself laugh, you're halfway there."

Another long silence.

"How bad do you want her?" Henry asked quietly. "Is she worth the fight?"

"No question, but—"

"No buts. If she's worth it, then so are you. Pull on your big-boy panties and get to work, asshole."

River took a swig of water before saying, "It's not as easy as all that."

Henry snorted. "It never is. I've been floating downstream on shit creek since I lost my leg."

River gestured at Henry's lab. "You look like you've got your head on straight. A job that keeps your brain engaged, people who give a shit."

"You'd think that, wouldn't you." Henry got up and tapped his thigh. "I lost something a whole lot more important than my leg ten years ago." He turned and went into the tent. The cot creaked, indicating the man had lain down. Probably wouldn't get anymore sleep than River would.

He looked up at the night sky, wanting his mouse with a ferocity that twisted his gut.

She was worth it. He was the damaged one.

• • •

Ava walked into her small apartment, closing and locking the door behind her.

Her whole body ached. Spending almost a week in an isolation room so people could poke, prod, and monitor her had been equal parts boring and frustrating. At one point, she gave serious consideration to ripping one of the CDC doctor's heads off. He'd talked to her as if she were five and dismissed all her observations regarding the course of her Neisseria infection. Since she was the patient, she wasn't objective enough to contribute to her own case.

Asshat.

If River had been around…but he wasn't.

He hadn't texted her. Not once.

Not quite believing it, she texted Henry while she rode in the taxi on her way home and asked if River was still working with the CDC. He'd replied, saying no. He'd left two days before, recalled by the Army.

He'd left no message.

A message of its own. One that hurt worse than any of the injuries and illness she'd suffered through.

She'd gotten past her fears, and she'd thought he'd done the same. As much as it hurt, she couldn't help him if he wouldn't let her. Tears rolled down her face at the thought of not being with him. She wanted him with a fierce desire that drowned out the lingering ache in her muscles without effort. That desire, to share everything—her job, family and future—with him had allowed her to see what she had to let go of. Control. And what she had to gain. Trust. That he would catch her if she fell.

Instead, he'd walked away.

It left her empty. Of everything.

No, she was just tired. It had been days since she'd slept more than two or three hours at a time. Dr. Rodrigues had told her not to show her face anywhere for at least five days. That much sleep sounded good.

Ava turned her phone off. Took a hot shower and collapsed into bed.

• • •

Someone was pounding on River's head.

He exploded out of bed, ready to tackle whoever was hitting him, but no one was there. He was in his hotel room, alone.

Alone.

He fucking hated it. Waking or sleeping, something was missing. Someone. Ava.

She'd recovered okay, he knew that much, had been glad Henry Lee took the time to text him a message saying she was back to work, but *she* hadn't told him.

It was his own damn fault. He hadn't responded to her text explaining what was happening to her, held up in an isolation ward with no way to talk to anyone. He hadn't said a word to her, not even good-bye. Message clear, he was done and didn't want more, and she'd done exactly as he'd hoped. Gone back to her life, safe and sound.

It was a fucking *lie*.

He wanted more. Fuck, he wanted *all* of her, but she'd never be safe with him around. There was too much shit in his head, and violence followed him like a shadow, never far, never quite going away.

So, he'd stayed quiet, convinced it was for her own good.

Now, instead of memories of sand and blood haunting him, it was the feel of her skin, the scent of her hair, and the passion in her gaze that kept ambushing him. She'd challenged him in every way, made him think, made him look at the world and see things he hadn't noticed before. With her, everything was *more*. Without her, the world was a pale imitation of itself.

Cowardly ass.

He'd gone back to base after the emergency was over in El Paso, took a look at the classroom he'd been teaching in, and promptly took the open offer of a discharge.

Working with Ava, protecting her, using his brain and skills had given him something he'd lacked. Focus and purpose.

Love.

He wanted her with everything he had in him, but had he gone after her? No, because he didn't know how to go about apologizing. A simple *I'm sorry* wasn't going to cut it.

What if she tossed him to the curb?

Fucking coward.

Man up and crawl, if that's what it took.

He would. He'd go and get down on one knee, but first, he needed to murder the asshole trying to break into his hotel room.

The pounding had resumed, but had risen a couple of points on the Richter scale.

Fuck. He made himself relax and walk over to look through the peephole.

Why the fuck was Henry Lee bothering him?

Last he heard, Lee was still in El Paso. River unlocked the door and opened it.

"You're a sound sleeper," Lee said in a sour tone. "I've been attacking your door for the last ten minutes." He swept past River and into the room.

He closed the door and watched Lee pace around the small space. "What are you doing here?"

"Looking for you. Don't you ever check your phone?"

Why would he, when he knew what he wasn't going to find? Messages from Ava. "My time is my own now, asshole."

"I heard you got your discharge." Henry crossed his arms over his chest and sneered as he asked, "How's life as a civilian working for you?"

"Go fuck yourself."

"Got too much too do."

"How nice for you." River didn't want to hear the lecture he was certain was coming. "Get out."

"Can't. I need a wingman."

"We were Army, not Air Force, or did you forget that?"

"Ava's in trouble."

Gravity stopped working. "What?"

"We got called in to a warehouse in El Paso the police thought might have been the dirty lab we've been looking for. You know, where that bacteria was weaponized? Only it wasn't a microbiological lab."

"Don't tell me…"

"Yep, a drug lab. Big one. Before they knew it, Ava and the decontamination team were being held hostage by some drug cartel. The cops are shitting bricks, Homeland thinks there's a terrorist angle involved, and the DEA is willing to do damn near anything to get their hands on any of the cartel alive."

All that testosterone would not sit well with his mouse. "We need to get her out of there, before she does something to get herself killed."

"She won't do that."

"Oh yeah, how would you know?"

"She's Dr. Ava caution-is-my-middle-name Lloyd."

"She found two bombs, gave one to you, and moved the other with less than ten seconds on the clock. Does that sound cautious to you?"

Henry scowled at River. "You're a bad influence. I blame you."

"I blame me, too, but we'll have to wait for the flogging until after we rescue the hostages."

"You're going to have to sign this first," Henry told him, handing over an envelope.

River opened it. The CDC job offer. Like he had time to read it.

"Can I use my personal weapon?"

Henry grinned. "Of course. I made sure to include that part."

River signed it, then began pulling on clothing suitable for a firefight. Black jeans, gray T-shirt, and combat boots. "Got any body armor I could borrow? That I don't have with me."

"Yeah, I think I've got extra that should fit in my truck."

River grabbed his gun case. "Are we coming back?"

"Nope."

He took two minutes to gather the rest of his shit.

"Okay, let's go get my girl."

Chapter Thirty-Five

Ava leaned a little more of her weight over her hands. Bill had lost too much blood already. The bullet wound was an inch or two right of the lower end of his sternum. Not a good place to get shot. Not that there were any good places to get shot, but the amount of blood she was seeing indicated internal hemorrhaging, possibly a lacerated liver.

If he didn't get advanced medical care within the next ten or fifteen minutes, he was going to bleed to death.

She'd been in this situation before, and it hadn't turned out well.

One of the men who'd stormed the warehouse walked closer, watched her. "Why do you waste your time?" the man asked. He wore a bandana over his mouth and nose, so all she could see of his face were dark eyes and bushy eyebrows. "He's dead already."

"He's my friend," she answered, then shut her mouth before she could say anything that might get herself shot.

Bill had tried to explain that they weren't police, that they were CDC, but all that got him was a bullet to the chest.

Bastards.

Anger rolled her gut, lent her arms strength, and cleared her mind of fear. She'd survived Ebola and terrorists wielding explosives and bioweapons. These drug-dealing wackos were barely worth her notice.

Glass shattered from multiple windows as canisters spraying out some sort of gas landed on the concrete floor. Tear gas.

The dozen or so men who claimed to own this sleazy drug factory shouted to each other in Spanish and began firing wildly at the windows and doors.

People, drug runners, and CDC personnel all over the large space began to cough, and Ava tucked her face into her sleeve to try to escape the worst effects. Her eyes burned and watered, then the burn slithered into her nose and down her throat. Gasping for breath only made it worse, exacerbating her cough enough to make her hands slip off Bill's chest. She put her hands over his wound again, careful not to let her continued coughing dislodge her again.

More gunfire, now interspersed with screaming, had her peering toward the area closer to the windows and main door. Tear gas swirled as bodies moved, running and fighting. A bullet ricocheted off the cement floor on a few feet away from Bill's head. She'd be lucky if she didn't get shot by accident.

The drug runner who'd spoken to her right before this catastrophe of a rescue ran toward her, gun pointed at her. She didn't move.

He stopped and shouted something in Spanish again.

He jerked as blood bloomed on his chest. He was still looking at her, but his gaze was empty now. Lifeless. His arm dropped, and he went down.

Behind him, two men ran toward her, both wore gas masks, but she knew who they were despite their obscured faces.

"Get an ambulance," she shouted at Henry Lee. "Bill's been shot, and he's lost a lot of blood."

Henry nodded and ran back through the gas.

She looked at River. What was he doing here? His lack of communication had made it clear that he wasn't interested in a relationship.

He shook his head. "People tend to get shot a lot around you."

"Not as often as they get blown up," she corrected with a fake smile. Another coughing fit kept her too busy to trade verbal barbs with him.

Something touched the top of her head, and she reared back, only to discover that River had removed his gas mask and was trying to put it on her.

"What are you doing?" she yelled as she jerked her head around, dodging his hands. "Get that thing away from me."

"You need this."

"I don't have a gun to shoot people with," she hissed, despite how badly she wanted to cough.

He glared at her, his eyes watering as badly as hers, but he put the mask back on.

A flurry of movement from the direction of the door had River turning, his weapon up, but he lowered it almost as quickly. Paramedics with a stretcher stopped next to Bill, and they began pummeling her with questions. She gave them all the answers she had, as well as her suspicion that Bill had an internal bleed of some kind before they had him packed on the stretcher and were racing him out.

"Come on," River said to her. "The police want everyone out of here yesterday."

"Why?" Ava got up slowly, her knees stiff from kneeling on the floor for so long.

"Apparently, some of these chemicals are highly flammable. They're afraid there could be an explosion."

Ava rolled her eyes. Of course they were.

River grabbed hold of her arm and pulled her through the warehouse and out the door. She didn't start resisting until they were outside and away from the majority of the commotion.

"I'm perfectly capable of walking on my own." She twisted her arm in his grip.

He hung onto her for another second or two, then let go to rip off his mask. "You're welcome."

Her jaw dropped. He thought she should be suitably *grateful* for his rescue? "Thank you," she said with enough sugar in her voice to hopefully rot his teeth. She turned on her heel and walked away.

"You look…better," he called after her.

She spun around. "How nice of you to check up on me after all this time." She resumed her course, heading for the first CDC vehicle she could find and a cell phone so she could report in. Her nose and eyes were still very irritated. That's why she was sniffling and crying. It had nothing to do with the man who'd just shown her how much he didn't care.

Behind her, River muttered, *"Fuck."* Footsteps followed her. "Ava, wait."

She stopped, wiped her face, then spun around and put her hands on her hips. "What?"

He jerked to a halt several feet away, his posture wary. "I'm sorry."

He was *sorry*? "For what, exactly?"

"I'm an asshole."

She knew that already, so she just stared at him.

"I'm also an idiot."

She knew that, too.

A group of police walked past them with more people in marked uniforms from the CDC, DEA, and FBI coming right behind.

River got a glimpse of the numbers and shifted closer to her. "I need to talk to you, about a bunch of stuff. Can I come by your apartment after I've finished all the paperwork on this situation?"

She should say no, tell him not to bother, but she was also curious, and…she missed talking to him. Missed having him around.

"Fine, but if you don't show up, I'm never speaking to you again."

"I'll be there."

"Do you even know my address?"

"Yeah, Henry gave it to me." He flashed her a grin, then disappeared into the mob of law-enforcement people all around.

Now that he was gone, all her anger drained out of her, leaving her exhausted physically and emotionally. Bill had been alive when the paramedics left with him, but the memory of that student terrorist, pale from blood loss, wouldn't leave her mind.

She got into the CDC van she arrived in, fished her cell phone out of the locked glove box, and called Dr. Rodrigues.

• • •

River arrived at Ava's apartment a few hours later and managed to get inside, thanks to a lady on her way out. He knocked on Ava's door, and it took a minute before he heard footsteps. A moment later, the door opened.

She looked so sad, and he feared the worst. "Bill, did he…?"

She backed up, silently inviting him in. "No, he's alive. In surgery still. The bullet nicked his liver."

River closed the door behind himself. "Good, that's good news," he said, looking her over. "Is that why you look so tired?" She did, with bags under her eyes and pale face.

"I don't know." She retreated further into a comfortable living room and took a seat on a one end of a couch. "All I can think about is that stupid kid who died at the café." She rubbed her face with both hands. "Work has been busy, too. We've been trying to unravel that strain of Neisseria, but whoever mucked around with it did it in a way that doesn't seem to make sense."

She was trying to keep the conversation on work. Nope.

He sat down next to her, giving her a foot or two of space. "I retired from the Army."

She blinked at him. "You...what?"

"I work for the CDC now."

"But, you...why? I thought you loved what you did in the Army."

"I did, but it was time for a change. *I've* changed. Active duty in the Special Forces is tough on a body. Mine has been telling me it was time to get out for a while. Plus, I want to be able to spend time with my girl. See her every day. No long deployments, no trying to shorten the distance between us with phone sex."

That made her choke. "Phone sex? That would require you to actually *talk* to m...this girl."

He winced. "I had to get my shit figured out first. For a while, I thought I was no good for her."

"No good?" She pressed her lips together, then punched him. "What does that mean?"

"I live a dangerous life. At least, I used to. My new life might still have some scary moments, but I'm hoping we can work around it."

Her mouth hung open for several seconds. "You're really not in the Army anymore?"

"Nope. Now, it's just me and her," he said, inching toward her to cup her face in one hand. "Naked on a bed, in a room with a locking door."

Her jaw dropped open again, and she sputtered. "You…
me…" Her voice trailed off into a panicked pant. "I…"

"Easy," he said, rubbing the back of her neck. "I love you.
I figured that out in the first twelve hours after I met you, so if
you don't feel the same, you'd better tell me now."

A sob broke out of her. She buried her face in the hollow
of his shoulder and clutched him tightly.

He settled her in his arms and rocked her for a couple of
minutes, murmuring reassuring words in her ear.

When she quieted, he pulled back to look at her. "You
okay?"

She nodded, sniffed, and he handed her a tissue from the
box on the table next to the couch. "I had a fiancé," she told
him. "He was a soldier, like you. He died in Afghanistan a
year ago. Friendly fire incident."

"I remember."

"He took risks. More than he should have, I think, but no
one could stop him when his mind was set. He thought he was
untouchable. Invincible. Until he wasn't. I felt like he left me
every time he was deployed." She stared at him, fear etched
on her face right to the bone.

"I'm not a soldier anymore," he said, tilting her face up
so she met his gaze. "I'm not going anywhere, unless it's with
you."

"Promise?"

"Promise."

She slid one hand off his shoulder to play with one of the
buttons on his shirt and whispered, "I love you, too."

Chapter Thirty-Six

Ava couldn't maintain eye contact with River, not when the heat in his gaze was hot enough to burn her clothes off.

He kissed her nose, her cheek. Then, slowly, gently kissed her lips. It was a chaste kiss, but when he came back again, that kiss wasn't chaste at all. He licked her bottom lip and nipped it. When she opened her mouth to him, he took her mouth like a man who'd been forbidden to drink for days.

His taste went to her head faster than any hard liquor, and she climbed up him so she could straddle his hips.

He took her hips in his hands and said, "No."

The spear of hurt that word sank into her chest damn near killed her.

"I want you on a bed," he growled, standing with her still in his hands. Once on his feet, he snugged her hips up to his and urged her to wrap her legs around his waist. "Where is it?"

She managed to breathe again, though it was shaky, and pointed over her shoulder at the hallway behind her. "It's on the left."

"You thought I was refusing you?" he asked, his voice quiet.

She didn't answer, too embarrassed and scared he'd take offense.

"You," he said into her ear, his lips caressing the sensitive skin there, "always come first." He started walking. "That means you get the first several orgasms, in case you were wondering."

She laughed. She couldn't help it. *"Several?"*

"Many." He groaned into her ear. *"Lots."*

She giggled until he set her on the bed and fell on top of her.

His kiss was ravenous, his hands everywhere. He managed to pull her shirt off, then stopped to stare at her breasts. She'd worn a nice bra today, one decorated with lace and ribbon. He kissed the skin above the cups while his hands reached under her to undo the clasp.

He pulled the bra off and cupped her breasts with both hands, his thumbs stroking over her nipples. It sent a shot of pleasure through her, and she arched her back.

"River?"

He kept playing with her. "Hmm?"

"I need your mouth on me."

He glanced at her face, and whatever he saw there drove him over some invisible edge, because he groaned and fell on her like a beast.

She didn't remember pulling his clothes off or when the rest of hers were removed, but his skin was warm under her fingers. He sucked on one of her nipples while one of his hands teased her clit and the sensitive opening of her vagina.

"What do you like?" he asked as he kissed his way up her neck. "What will get you off?"

"I love—" Her breath hitched as he found a spot inside her that made her limbs shake. "That."

"What else?"

"Um…" She'd only been with Adam before him.

He stopped kissing her long enough to gaze at her with a slow grin. "I guess we get to go exploring."

"Yeah," she said, wiggling her hips. "Later?"

"Whatever you want." He kissed her, thrusting his tongue into her mouth, a prelude to what he was about to do with her body.

She palmed his cock and discovered it as big as she remembered. "Wow, you're…" Her voice trailed off.

"You're giving me a swelled head."

"I sure hope so."

His gave her neck one last suck and nip, then circled the entrance to her body with the head of his cock before pushing in. And in. And in.

Ava arched her back and rotated her hips as far as she could, which wasn't very far, because River had a good grip on her. "Oh my God."

He pulled out a little and pushed back in until he bottomed out. "Fuck, you're tight."

"It's been a long time," she panted, wiggling again. Need was a growing pulse in her blood, her body. *"Please."*

He groaned again, braced his forearms on either side of her head, and began to move. He increased his pace and the strength of his thrusts until she was nearly mindless with pleasure. It built and built, and then he changed the angle of his thrusts, and it sent her into the stratosphere.

She rode the high for a long time before coming down enough to realize that he'd just slowed things down for a little while. As soon as she met his eyes again, he gave her a grin and said, "I want to watch you do that again."

She climaxed twice more before he followed her into bliss and sank down onto her body, holding her close.

"Three orgasms," he said. "I'll do better next time."

That made her laugh out loud.

•••

River was making Ava and himself a bed picnic of peanut butter and jelly sandwiches when his phone buzzed.

Dozer.

He answered the call. "What's up?"

"We finally got into Palmer's computer," Dozer said without preamble. "The son of a bitch had help."

"What kind of help?"

"Help from someone whose computer was located in Kuwait. We're still piecing it together, but it looks like Palmer received instructions and something he refers to as a *gift* almost a year ago. There are one or two references to other people expecting other *gifts*."

"Well, that's fucking shitty news."

"Yeah, ain't it just." Dozer cleared his throat. "You and Ava doing okay?"

"We're absolutely awesome."

Dozer huffed a laugh. "Don't rub it in. Asshole."

River just laughed.

"Listen, you got any Army buddies who might be interested in joining the Outbreak Task Force? Rodrigues is nagging at me for more people, but Homeland doesn't have any to spare right now."

River thought back to his last overseas deployment and his friend Smoke, who rarely spoke, but was a man he'd have at his back any day. "Yeah, I might have a name or two."

"Fantastic. Let Rodrigues know so she'll stop bugging me. I'd like to get some sleep this year."

Bugging him? Not likely. River had seen how Dozer watched Dr. Rodrigues when he thought she wasn't looking. The guy was more than a little interested.

"Will do. Stay frosty."

Dozer's answer was a grunt and a dial tone.

"River?" Ava's sleepy voice found him.

"Be right there," he said. "On my way with PB and J."

Her laughter reeled him in as if she were a competitive angler and he was the catch of the day. "You say the sexiest things." She reclined on the bed, wearing nothing but a grin.

"You inspire me." It came out a growl. "To do illegal things to you with my tongue."

That had her laughing and snatching a sandwich from the plate he carried. "I can't wait."

He lay down next to her to eat his own sandwich. "Eat up. You're going to need it."

She laughed again.

"Are you busy next weekend?" he asked.

"Not that I know of."

"Cool. Want to go to Vegas and get married?"

She blinked. "For real?"

"Yeah." He rolled his eyes. "Rodrigues isn't going to give us a ton of time off."

The grin that spread across her face could have powered a city for a day. "Yes, please." Then she grabbed the sandwich out of his hands, tossed it aside, and tackled him, kissing him everywhere. "Yes, yes, yes!"

"I'm sorry," he asked as she tried to hold him down and kiss his entire torso. "That was a vague answer. Could you be specific?"

"Oh, you." She tickled him, then planted a big kiss right on his mouth. A kiss that grew heated fast. "I'm gonna specific you."

"God, I hope so," he replied, then rolled them both over so he was on top. "I love you, Mouse."

"Back at you, Mr. Smooth."

Acknowledgments

Writing a book is not a solitary process, and without good editing, it wouldn't happen at all. Thank you, Robin Haseltine, for being my creative partner.

About the Author

Julie Rowe's first career as a medical lab technologist in Canada took her to the Northwest Territories and northern Alberta, where she still resides. She loves to include medical details in her romance novels, but admits she'll never be able to write about all her medical experiences because "Fiction has to be believable."

Julie writes romantic suspense and romantic military thrillers. Her most recent titles include *Viable Threat*, the first book in the Outbreak Task Force series, and *Viral Justice*, book three of the Biological Response Team series. You can find her at www.julieroweauthor.com, on Twitter @ julieroweauthor, or on her Facebook page: www.facebook.com/JulieRoweAuthor.

Discover more Entangled Select Suspense titles...

The Boss
a novel by Melissa Schroeder

Mac never asks for help from anyone, but chased by the CIA, the Russian mob, and the FBI, she runs to the one man she knows can help—her former lover and partner, Vic. They'll need to get out alive before they can have a second chance at love.

Burn
a novel by Dawn Altieri

Chloe Addison is on the verge of a promising career in real estate development until an explosion destroys her first major project and casts suspicion on her. Her career is suddenly at risk—and possibly her life. Firefighter Ryan Monroe might be the perfect guy to rescue her, but their attraction could bring them both down in flames.

Seduced by Sin
an *Unlikely Hero* novel by Kris Rafferty

Caleb took the FBI's assignment because he wanted to end the tyranny of a man who'd hurt the people he loved. Odds of success were slim and the danger high, but he knew the risks. Francesca Hamilton didn't and was completely in the dark about her family's "business." And the more time he spends with her, the harder he falls for the gorgeous blonde. But to finally get retribution, he'll have to destroy her world...